TABLE OF CONTENTS

Salt and Stone

Anna Bowman

Salt and Stone
First Edition

ISBN Paperback : 979-8-9988316-9-0

Cover design by Melody Kepler
Interior design and formatting by Melody Kepler

Published by Kepler Production Studios
https://keplerpstudios.com

Editing: Anna Bowman

"Kepler Production Studios" and the KPS logo are trademarks of Kepler Production Studios, LLC.

TABLE OF CONTENTS

For Mel,
who saw the romance before I did, and helped me hunt down
rogue *hads* like a merciless word assassin.

This book wouldn't be what it is without your sharp eye
steady cheer-leading.
You're the best!

Prologue:

The fire crackled softly in the center of the clearing, its warm glow chasing shadows into the thick trees surrounding Rootspire Island. Seven children sat in a rough circle around the flames, their faces flickering with uncertainty and fear. The youngest, a boy with wide eyes and a trembling chin, pressed himself against the older boy next to him. The older boy wrapped an arm protectively around him, his shoulders squared and defiant, even as his own unease showed in the way his fingers tapped nervously on his knee.

"Do you think wolves will come and eat us?" the youngest whimpered, his voice barely audible above the pop and hiss of burning wood.

The older boy squeezed his shoulder. "If they do, they'll have to get through me first."

Nearby, a boy with tear-streaked cheeks buried his face in his hands, his sobs muffled but persistent. A girl, her tangled brown and copper curls catching the firelight, scooted closer to him, offering a piece of moss she'd plucked from the ground. "It's soft," she whispered hesitantly. "It's good for scrapes and crying too, maybe." The crying boy lifted his head slightly, accepting the moss with trembling fingers.

"My sister used to give me leaves when I cried," he murmured, running his thumb over the moss's velvet surface.

The others sat in varying states of confusion. A pale boy perched on the edge of a log, his sharp features twitching as he scanned the trees. "There's something out there," he hissed, making the others stiffen. "I keep seeing shadows move."

Across from him, a dark-skinned girl with long braids glared at the fire, her hands clenched into fists on her lap.

"There's always something out there," she snapped, but her voice wavered. "Doesn't mean it's coming for us."

One boy sat hunched forward, poking at the dirt with a stick, while another reclined stiffly, as if trying to seem unbothered but failing. The stick-wielding boy traced patterns in the soil, then quickly scuffed them out.

Wind shifted, carrying the scent of damp earth and smoke as a figure emerged from the shadows. The children fell silent, drawing closer together as an old woman approached. Her face was a map of deep lines and ancient secrets, eyes the color of storm clouds set deep beneath silver brows. A shawl of intricate patterns draped around her thin shoulders, and her white hair was woven with colored threads and tiny bells that chimed softly with each step. She stooped as she walked, but her movements were deliberate, like a dancer remembering steps from long ago.

As the woman entered the circle, the youngest boy gripped his protector's arm tightly. Her long cloak swept the ground behind her, shadows seeming to dance in its wake. Without a word, she knelt by the fire, her bony hands working quickly to open the pouch at her side and toss a handful of powder into the flames.

The fire hissed and roared, exploding into brilliant hues of green and blue. Gasps rippled through the children as the flames twisted and writhed, shapes forming within the blaze. The girl with copper curls scrambled backward, bumping into the crying boy, who had frozen mid-sniffle.

"Long ago…" the woman began, her voice rich and weathered, filling the silence like the first drop of rain on dry soil. She reached into her pouch again, tossing another pinch of something into the fire. The flames leapt higher, taking the shape of a sprawling tree with branches that seemed to stretch beyond the heavens.

"Is it real magic?" the youngest boy whispered to his protector, who could only shake his head in wonder.

"…there was a world untouched by chaos, guarded by seven Oathbound, each chosen by the Earth herself."

The children leaned closer, entranced despite their fear. The dark-skinned girl's fists slowly unclenched as the flames shifted to show figures standing beneath the great tree. Their forms flickered and shimmered, their faces hidden but their postures resolute. The storyteller's voice wove around them like a spell.

Prologue

"They were taken from their homes, stripped of what they knew, and shaped into protectors. Bound not by choice, but by destiny, they were the keepers of the balance. The shield against the storm."

The pale boy's constant scanning of the woods had ceased, his eyes now fixed on the dancing figures.

"But to be Oathbound," the storyteller continued, her voice dropping to a near whisper, "is to sacrifice everything. Your past, your future… even your name."

Flames shifted again, swirling into the image of a fierce battle—clashing swords, roaring winds, waves crashing against cliffs. The brown-haired girl hugged her knees to her chest, eyes watching intently. The old woman's voice rose with the scene, her hands weaving patterns in the air that seemed to make the fire dance. "It is the Oathbound alone who stand between the realms and chaos. It is their burden to bear, their gift to the world."

The final burst of flames died down, and the figures within it disappeared, leaving only the familiar orange glow of flickering embers. The storyteller stood slowly, brushing ash from her gnarled hands, the tiny bells in her hair singing softly with the movement.

"Rest now," she said, her voice softer. "For tomorrow, the earth begins to shape you."

The children sat in silence as the woman disappeared into the night, the patterns of her shawl seeming to shift and change until she melted into the darkness. Though the fire continued to crackle, its warmth now felt oppressive, burdened by the gravity of what they'd just witnessed. The older boy glanced at the younger one and gave his shoulder a reassuring squeeze. The girl with the moss quietly placed another piece in the crying boy's hand.

PAIN CAME FIRST. Fire in his veins, a blade of lightning through his chest—Storm's final gift before retreating. Victor shuddered as his body fought the pull of death, each heartbeat a battle, each breath agony. He shouldn't be alive. He didn't want to be.

The waters of Rootspire lapped at his wounds, their crystalline depths now tainted with blood—his blood, and that of the others. The Oathbound. His family. His brother.

"Why…?" The word crawled from Victor's throat, rough as shattered glass. His trembling fingers clutched at the muddy shore as he tried to drag himself free of the healing waters. He needed to die. Deserved to die.

"Be still, Victor." The voice washed over him, gentle yet unyielding. A figure knelt beside him, pale hands hovering over his wounds.

Linden

Her silver hair drifted around her like mist, and her storm-gray eyes held galaxies of sorrow. Light emanated from her fingertips, seeping into his torn flesh, stitching back together what Storm had broken.

"Let me die," Victor pleaded, his gaze searching the shore where still forms lay motionless in the shallows. Six bodies—their faces peaceful in death, as if merely sleeping.

His brother lay where Victor left him, half-submerged in the waters they'd called home for so long, arms outstretched as if reaching for something—or someone—even in death.

Her.

Victor's chest heaved with a sob. "I killed him," he whispered, the confession tearing from his soul. "My brother." Memories flooded back—the spy's whispers, promises of power, of respect, of *her*. The stone's power calling to him. An unforgivable choice.

Orson's face below the water. The struggle. The moment he went still.

"I know." Linden's voice carried no judgment, only a weight as ancient as the massive oak that towered above them, its roots plunging into the depths where Orson had drawn his last breath. "The Betrayer's role was always written. I had hoped…after watching over them for all these years…" She shook her head, her hands never ceasing their work. "Storm manipulated you, but the choice was still yours." The sadness in her voice was worse than any condemnation.

"Let me join them!" Victor's voice broke. "Let me pay for what I've done!"

Healing light flickered as Linden drew a slow breath. "Death would be a mercy, Victor." Her eyes reflected centuries of knowledge. "And mercy is not what you've earned."

While the pain in his chest faded, a more acute, deeper torment replaced it—a visceral agony that touched something fundamental within him. Victor screamed as Linden pressed her palm over his heart, her touch burning like ice. Beneath her fingers, his skin began to change, ancient symbols etching themselves into his flesh in patterns of raised scar tissue.

"What are you doing to me?" he gasped, trying to pull away.

"Binding you to your oath," Linden said, her voice steady, though her hands trembled with exertion. "The others will be born again. They will live new lives, free from the burden of remembering—until it is time."

The full meaning of her words crashed over him. "And I…?"

"You will remember." Her eyes held both compassion and resolve. "You will carry the weight of what you've done through the centuries. You will watch over them in each new life, protect them as you failed to do in this one."

"How long?" Victor rasped, afraid of the answer.

Linden's gaze drifted to the horizon. "Until the seven are united once more. Until the balance is restored." She released him, her own strength clearly waning. The transformation had taken its toll on her as well; silver streaks now ran through his dark hair, mirroring her own.

Victor pushed himself to his knees, his wounds healed but a new emptiness yawning inside him. "And Storm? He has the stone—"

"He has a fragment," Linden corrected, her voice fading. "And it will poison him as surely as your betrayal poisoned you. The true power was never in the stone, Victor. It was in the oath itself."

She rose unsteadily, her form already growing translucent as she moved toward the massive Mercy Oak. "I have given the last of my strength to set this right. Now the path is yours to walk."

"Linden, wait!" Victor staggered after her. "I can't—I don't know how to—"

She paused, turning back one last time. Her smile held the weight of eons. "You will learn." Her fingertips, now barely corporeal, brushed his cheek. "And when the time comes, you will know what to do."

"Please," he begged, though he wasn't sure what he was asking for. Forgiveness? Understanding? An end to the loneliness already settling into his bones?

But Linden was already merging with the Mercy Oak, her form dissipating like morning mist. "Find them, protect them, guide them," her voice echoed, growing fainter with each word. "And perhaps, when they remember, you will find redemption."

Then she was gone.

Victor stood alone on the shore, the weight of centuries settling onto his shoulders. Around him, their bodies — his friends, his family—lay still and silent, their powers already seeking new vessels in which to grow.

He moved first to Orson, gathering his brother's cold form in his arms. Water streamed from his lifeless body as Victor carried him to higher ground. He retrieved the others next, one by one, each heavier than the last.

As the sun set over the island, Victor built a pyre. The flames caught quickly, dancing over the seven bodies with almost reverent care. He watched until only ashes remained, until stars pierced the darkness above.

"I will find you," he promised the night. "In whatever lives you lead, whoever you become. I will be there." His hand pressed against the mark on his chest, the reminder of his betrayal that would never fade. "And I will make this right. No matter how long it takes."

The Mercy Oak's branches swayed overhead, witness to his vow, as Victor turned away from the pyre and took his first step into the endless years that stretched before him.

Chapter 1

Memori

Stone Gate Village clung to the rocky edge of the lake, where the remnants of the ancient dam jutted from the water like broken teeth. The cliffs loomed high above, casting long shadows over the settlement as the wind funneled through the ravine, carrying the scent of damp stone and pine. A narrow rope bridge, frayed but sturdy, swayed above the mist-choked valley, the only connection between the village and the Kraken Inn. Once a stranded pirate ship, it was now an aging relic re-purposed for weary travelers and drifters.

The village itself was a scatter of weathered stone cottages and timber buildings, their roofs thick with moss and windows aglow with the soft flicker of lantern light. Merchants lined the winding main path, hawking everything from dried venison and carved bone trinkets to old navigational tools—remnants of the lake's long-forgotten past. Along the main path, carved wooden posts stood at crossroads, each depicting a figure from old tales—the Guardians. Their faces had softened with time and rain, but children still traced their fingers over the weathered etchings, whispering names passed down in lullabies.

Despite its quiet appearance, Stone Gate had a restless undercurrent. The dam groaned under the weight of time, its stonework slick with moisture. Some swore they could hear water whispering through unseen cracks, a reminder that nothing—no village, no ship, no history—was ever truly safe from the forces that shaped the land.

Memori understood that precarious balance all too well. As she wove through the morning market, her satchel of herbs held close, she kept to the shadows of the weathered buildings. The scent of dried pine and rosemary mingled with the damp air—familiar comforts that did little to ease her wariness of what the day might bring.

The Vanguard, General Storm's elite cadre of cutthroats, was reason enough for caution. Clad in stark black and silver uniforms, they moved like living nightmares, a scourge sent to root out every unauthorized healer. They hunted those who dared defy their authority, cutting them down without mercy, or conscripting the unwilling, and stripping away all that was precious in a desperate bid to survive. Each step they took left a trail of broken lives and smoldering ruin—a visceral reminder that in this world, cruelty reigned supreme.

And so, when she heard the hoof-beats thundering–cutting through the morning quiet–the dust rising from the road like a brown haze–Memori froze in place. Here, in the open light of the village, she felt exposed—vulnerable to the predatory gaze of the Vanguard. As if summoned by her deepest fears, a chorus of screams erupted from the crowded market. Agonized pleading—raw and desperate—ripped through the din. Instinct took over. Without a second thought, Memori dove into a thicket by the main road. Brambles and thorns tore at her arms and legs, but she remained frozen, her breath shallow and her body pressed tightly into the cold undergrowth.

Through the dense leaves, she peered out cautiously. In a small clearing illuminated by the weak morning light, she saw a scene that shattered her composure: a young woman, no older than eighteen and unfamiliar to her, trembled uncontrollably as she sat slumped on the ground. Next to her, in the lap of one of the Vanguard soldiers, was a small boy— barely two years old—whose wide, terrified eyes mirrored the anguish in her heart.

Memori's stomach twisted with unspeakable grief. She knew too well the ruthless pattern: when the Vanguard forced themselves upon women, a child was often the cruel byproduct. And with every such act, the possibility loomed that these monsters would kill the child, kill the woman–or whatever pleased them. The sight before her was a living nightmare. One that hit so close to home she had to clamp her hand over her mouth to keep herself from screaming.

Memori crouched deeper into the brush, her mind reeling with the weight of memories and the terror of what might be coming next. Every rustle of leaves, every echo of approaching footsteps, heightened her dread, as she prayed silently that this hideaway would shield her from the relentless cruelty of the Union's forces. The look on the soldier's face was of utter disregard as he picked up the boy, mounted his horse and rode away, leaving the girl sobbing in the street.

After the screams had died down and the streets fell into an uneasy silence, Memori bolted. Her heart pounded as she raced back to the Inn, her feet pounding on creaking planks as she sprinted across the rope bridge. It swayed and groaned under her weight, each step a desperate bid to outrun the nightmare behind her. She passed the kitchens, where the clatter of late-night preparation still echoed off weathered walls, and the rest of the ship faded into a blur of shadow and sound.

Her lungs burned with every gasping breath, and anxiety weighed on her chest like a leaden ball. Finally, she reached her quarters and flung open the door, slamming it shut behind her. Leaning against it, she clutched the doorframe and tried to steady herself, her heart racing and her mind a chaotic jumble of fear and sorrow.

In the soft half-light of the room, a small child sat on the edge of the bed, absorbed in a worn book. The child's delicate fingers paused on a page depicting a noble guardian—a figure of valor and hope that the little one adored. As Memori's heavy breathing filled the silence, the child's eyes brightened, and a wide smile spread across her face.

"Memma!" the child exclaimed, leaping down from the bed and rushing forward to envelop her in a warm, eager hug. Relief flooded over Memori in finding the girl safe.

In that moment, as the child's arms wrapped around her, the harshness of the outside world softened, and for a few precious seconds, Memori allowed herself to be carried by the innocent comfort of that embrace.

Chapter 2

Dollan

Black and white uniforms materialized from the smoke like wraiths, their polished buttons catching the firelight as Elmswell burned. The flames turned the peaceful fishing village into a nightmare of shadows and screams, reflecting off the river's surface in terrible mockery of the sunset.

Commander Kol held a young woman by her hair, her feet barely touching the ground as she sobbed. "The pirate, girl. The one who calls himself Dollan." His voice carried the casual cruelty of a man who enjoyed making others bend to his will. "Where does he hide?"

Her silence earned her a savage shake. Around them, the Vanguard methodically destroyed what generations of villagers had built. They smashed windows, kicked in doors, dragged people from their homes with mechanical efficiency. Their uniforms, pristine despite the destruction they wreaked, made them look more like demons than men.

From his hiding place in Widow Tolson's abandoned root cellar, James Dollan's joints creaked in protest as he shifted position. The Tidestone pressed against his heel where he'd hollowed out his boot sole, its weight a constant reminder of his responsibility. Forty years at sea had taught him patience, taught him when to wait and when to strike. But the sounds filtering down through the floorboards tested every lesson he'd learned.

A woman's scream cut through the chaos, followed by rough laughter. The sound of fabric tearing, of a struggle. "Damn these old bones," Dollan muttered, checking the pistol he'd kept oiled and ready for just such a day. The weapon felt right in his hand, familiar as an old friend. Above him, the floorboards creaked with heavy boots.

He didn't hesitate. The cellar door exploded outward as he emerged, sending a Vanguard soldier sprawling. The man's companion had a woman pinned against a wall. Dollan's pistol cracked like thunder in the confined space, and the soldier dropped.

"If a pirate's what you're lookin' for," he called out, his voice carrying across the burning street to where Kol stood, "you found one." His bones might ache, his hair might have gone white as sea foam, but James Dollan's aim hadn't faltered with age. The second soldier's hand had barely touched his weapon before Dollan's next shot took him in the shoulder.

As Kol's stony gaze found Dollan, the woman fled. The commander released his victim, letting her crumple to the ground as he drew his sword. A smile played across his lips. "The famous Captain Dollan," Kol said, advancing with measured steps. "Reduced to defending peasants in a backwater village. How far you've fallen."

Dollan's empty pistol clattered to the cobblestones. His hand moved to the cutlass at his hip, though they both knew he'd never reach it in time. "Better a fallen captain with honor than a uniformed butcher without it."

"The Wraith of Avalon," Kol mused, circling closer. "That's what they called you, wasn't it? Before you washed up in this mud heap of a village."

Dollan felt the stone pulse against his heel, a reminder of promises he'd made–his old shipmate had a way of persuasion. Now it was time to keep his word.

"Heard you lost your taste for piracy," Kol continued, boots crunching on broken glass. "Gone soft in your old age, Wraith?"

Dollan's laugh was as rough as storm-weathered timber. "Soft?" He nodded toward the soldier he'd shot, who lay groaning in the dirt. "Ask your man there how soft I've gotten."

Flames crept closer, consuming the life he'd built here plank by plank. Twenty years in Elmswell, watching, waiting. The villagers had taken him in without question. He'd kept to himself, and they'd done the same. Filling his nets with fish, watching the boy grow. Waiting for the right time.

"You're a relic," Kol spat, his sword catching firelight. "A legend past his time. The Union is the future. Order. Control." His eyes gleamed with fanatical certainty. "Tell me where you've hidden it, old man, and I'll make your death quick."

The stone seemed to grow warmer, as if responding to the threat. Or perhaps it sensed what was coming–the tide of change Vic promised. The boy—now a man—would cross his path soon enough, drawn by the power he didn't yet understand or know existed. Dollan's task was nearly completed, and he could rest in the peace of his honor kept.

"You want to know what I've hidden?" Dollan's hand moved to his belt, where a small flask hung. The liquid inside caught the firelight like liquid gold. "Come closer, Commander. I'll show you a trick I learned on the southern seas."

Kol's laugh was bitter as he advanced. "More parlor tricks from the Wraith of Avalon? Your reputation grows more disappointing by the moment."

Dollan uncorked the flask with his teeth, the sharp smell of spirits filling the air. "Disappointing, you say?" With a fluid motion belying his age, he flung the contents toward the nearest torch. The alcohol caught fire instantly, creating a wall of flames between him and Kol's men.

"Secure him!" Kol's order cut through the roar of fire. His soldiers circled wide, trying to flank the old pirate.

Dollan backed toward the river, his boots finding familiar patterns in the cobblestones. He'd walked this path a thousand times, knew every loose stone, every dip and rise. The stone pressed against his heel with each step, a constant reminder of what was at stake.

The first soldier rushed him from the left. Dollan pivoted, his elbow catching the man's throat. The second came from behind, blade whistling through the air. Pain bloomed across Dollan's shoulder as the sword found its mark, but he used the momentum to spin, driving his knee into the soldier's gut.

Then Kol was there. His sword opened a line of fire across Dollan's ribs. The old pirate staggered, one hand pressed to the wound as warm blood seeped between his fingers.

"It's over, Old Man," Kol said, bringing his sword pommel down hard.

The world exploded in white light as steel met skull. Dollan fell, the cobblestones rising to meet him. Through dimming vision, he saw Kol's boots approach, heard orders being barked. Rough hands seized his arms, dragging him toward the Vanguard wagons.

"The stone" Kol's voice seemed to come from very far away. "The General will have it–or your head."

Darkness crept in at the edges of his vision, consciousness slipped away like sand through a sieve, and Dollan surrendered to the dark, content in knowing he'd kept his word.

Chapter 3

Memori

Medicine is equally important for all.

Memori thumbed through the gold-lined pages of the Healer's Codex as dawn broke over the horizon, pouring purple light through the ship's porthole. The curved window, set into the weathered hull of what had once been officers' quarters, offered a clear view across the valley to where Stonegate Village sprawled below the cliffs. Fog clung to the swinging bridge that connected their clifftop refuge to the mainland, making it look like the rickety boards floated on air.

Each formula and diagram etched into the ancient text felt like a lifeline—one she could never share openly. Outside her room, the Kraken Inn stirred with the murmur of early risers, their footsteps echoing against wooden planks that had endured countless storms before being stranded here, turned from seafaring vessel to an unlikely inn. But here in the quiet of her converted cabin, the only sound was the rustling of pages and Elowen's soft snores.

The wind carried the scent of spring flowers through the open porthole, but it didn't soothe the knot in Memori's chest. From her perch in this unusual home—a ship frozen in time atop a twisted cliff, she could see the Blacksmoke Union flags waving in the breeze above Stonegate's walls. Even here, in this refuge of old legends and stranger truths, their shadow reached.

"We do not answer to kings or tyrants; we answer only to the soul of the earth, which grants us our wisdom and medicine."

Those were not words written in the Codex, but they were burned in her mind from that tragic day long ago. Memori felt a wave of grief crash over her as her hands clenched the aging book so hard the pages crinkled. Here she was, the child of a healer, hiding her knowledge. Keeping her gifts under lock and key. And why? Because of kings and tyrants.

A furious tear rolled down her cheek, splashing on the page like an exclamation point. Keeping her mother's gift hidden was as necessary as it was dangerous. The Blacksmoke Union demanded total control over medicine, branding unlicensed healers as criminals. If they ever discovered the *Codex* in her possession… Memori forced herself to stop imagining the consequences.

"Momma?" A sleepy voice broke the silence.

Memori glanced over her shoulder to see Elowen rubbing her eyes, her curls a chaotic halo around her face. The girl's small cot was wedged into an alcove that had once held navigation charts, now draped with the colorful quilts that helped transform their cabin from a drab ship's quarters to something like home.

"It's Meh-ma, Elowen," she corrected gently, her tone warm but firm. Through the porthole, she could hear the early morning clatter of the kitchen staff three cabins down, preparing for the inn's breakfast rush. The sound carried differently through the ship's curved halls than it had through her childhood home in the village.

"Meh-ma," the girl repeated, giggling. "I'm hungry."

"Of course you are." Memori smiled, crossing the salt-worn floorboards to plant a kiss on her forehead. "Get dressed, and I'll see if Jace has something ready in the galley."

Elowen hopped out of bed, her bare feet pattering against planks that still held the faint, sweet scent of ancient timber. She rummaged through a sea chest that now served as their clothes trunk, the brass fittings dulled with age but still bearing traces of elaborate scrollwork.

Memori watched her with a bittersweet mixture of love and fear. To the world, Elowen was her sister. No one questioned the extended age gap, or an older sister looking after her younger sibling in the strange maze of the Kraken's converted halls. It was the perfect story to keep Elowen safe.

She carefully tucked the Codex into its hiding place beneath a loose floorboard–sliding it into the hollow space alongside a small pouch of herbs. The gap between the ship's inner and outer hull had proved useful for more than just keeping the vessel afloat.

"You can't leave anything out, Memma," Elowen said in a singsong voice, mimicking one of Memori's frequent warnings as she peered down at the hidden compartment.

Memori smiled as she closed the board with a soft click, the sound nearly lost beneath the constant creaking of the ship's timbers settling on their clifftop perch. "That's right. Nothing left out." To Elowen, it was all a fun game—secrets only they shared.

A knock on their cabin door shattered the calm, the sound echoing oddly against the curved walls in a way that still caught visitors off guard, even after the Kraken's decade of service as an inn.

"Customer for you, Memori." Jace's voice carried through the weathered oak, probably leaning against the doorframe as he always did. The kitchen master had learned to navigate the ship's tilted passages like he'd been born to them, unlike the steady stream of guests who still stumbled on the subtle pitch of floors that had never quite settled after the vessel found its unlikely perch.

"In a minute, Jace," she called, motioning for Elowen to finish brushing her hair. Through the porthole, she could see the inn's morning crowd already gathering on the gangplank-turned-entrance bridge, merchants and travelers drawn by both Jace's famous breakfast spreads and the novelty of dining aboard a legendary vessel.

"He says it's urg—"

"I said in a minute!" Memori snapped. Jace mumbled something before the sound of his retreating footsteps confirmed he'd sodded off—as he should. The sound grew fainter as he descended the companionway to the converted dining hall, where gleaming wooden tables had replaced gun deck stations, and elaborate lanterns hung where cannon shot was once stored.

Imagine bothering someone at this hour with a headache or a need for clarity. The villagers came to her for endless frivolous ailments she marketed as "magic tea" to avoid suspicion. Her small shop in the aft hold might have once stored a pirate's plunder, but now it held only herbs and hopes that she wouldn't draw the wrong kind of attention. Guardians forbid she actually save someone's life without the Union's approval.

As Elowen darted toward the door, she bumped into the small writing desk wedged beneath the porthole—salvaged from the captain's quarters, Jace had claimed, though Memori had her doubts about half his tales of the ship's history. The collision sent a stray ink pot clattering to the floor. Memori flinched, rushing over to steady the desk. In her haste, her foot caught the corner of the Codex where it poked out slightly from the loose board.

The impact caused the aged book to topple free, its binding splitting slightly along one edge. Biting back a swear, Memori hurriedly put the book back in its hiding place and guided Elowen to the door.

Overhead, the rigging swayed with the morning breeze, adding a faint, mournful whine to the deep creaks and cracks of the hull adjusting to the day. Memori kept her head down, pulling Elowen behind a stack of supply crates as a cluster of Vanguard soldiers stumbled past, their laughter coarse and suffocating.

Elowen pressed close to Memori's side. "It's loud this morning," she said, her voice barely louder than the rhythmic groan of the ship. Another group of soldiers clattered down the companionway, and Memori tugged Elowen into the shadow of an old gun port.

"It's just the Kraken waking up," Memori said, her tone calm but her smile faint as she waited for the men to pass. She glanced at the beams overhead, weathered but sturdy.

They wound their way through the lower deck, Memori careful to keep them behind pillars and in shadows whenever boots sounded above. The path to the galley was longer this way, but safer. As they reached the kitchen door, the hinges gave a drawn-out creak that sounded almost like a sigh. Memori pushed it open to reveal the warm, bustling heart of the inn, where Jace had transformed the ship's original galley into something that drew visitors from across the realm.

The air was thick with the comforting aroma of fresh bread and spiced tea. Jace greeted them with a wave, and a steaming loaf of bread fresh from the ovens that replaced the ship's original copper cauldrons. "Breakfast for you two?"

"Yes, please," Memori said, grateful for his easy demeanor. She guided Elowen toward the back corner, where stacked barrels created a natural hideaway. The kitchen staff learned quickly not to question why she preferred the shadows to the cheerful tables in the converted mess hall beyond.

Elowen reached for a piece of bread just as heavy boots sounded on the deck above. A group of soldiers were descending the nearby stairs to the galley, their voices carrying through the wooden beams. Memori's stomach clenched, her grip tightening on Elowen's hand. One of them glanced their way as he entered, but the man eventually turned back to his drink.

Elowen tugged at her hand, oblivious to her mother's tension. "Can we go see the flowers later, Memma?" She was looking toward the stern windows where spring blooms from the clifftop garden spilled over the ship's rail.

"Maybe," Memori murmured, her gaze darting toward the door as more patrons filtered in for their breakfast. "Right now, Memma has to get to work. Stay with Jace, and I'll be back to get you soon."

She looked at Jace with a silent plea. He rolled his eyes but gave a resigned nod, already moving to position himself between Elowen and the main room's view.

Memori slipped through the rear door, taking the narrow service passage that led to her shop. The Root & Blossom occupied the main hold at the far aft of the ship, where dim light filtered through the circular gun ports, casting shifting patterns on bundles of dried herbs hanging from the low ceiling.

The air was thick with the earthy scent of rosemary, chamomile, and thyme, mingled with a faint trace of salt from past voyages. Behind her worn counter—salvaged from the ship's original chart table—was a modest kitchen where she brewed her "magic teas." Every time she worked here, the familiar smells and motions brought memories she wished she could suppress. Things her mother taught her in their old home in the village. Before everything changed. Memori set her jaw, brushing away the thought as she saw the stranger waiting for her.

She stepped inside her shop, the creak of the wooden floor echoing in the confined space. Regular customers from the village typically slouched in chairs salvaged from the officer's mess, or shuffled about examining her carefully labeled jars, but this man stood stiffly at her counter. He leaned heavily on one arm, his coat hanging loosely, left hand pressed tightly to his side.

Morning light filtering through the gun ports cast strange shadows across his face, making his already pale features look almost ghostly against the dark timbers. His face was drawn, jaw tight as though holding back pain. The way he carried himself—the squared shoulders, the controlled posture—hinted at military training, but his dark hair was too long for a Vanguard soldier, falling past regulation length.

"Morning," Memori greeted, forcing a bright tone as she approached. She flicked on the lantern that hung from an old cargo hook, casting warm light across the shadowed room. The flame caught the brass fittings that still adorned the walls, remnants of the ship's more glamorous days. "What's ailing you today, sir? Headache? Nerves?" She reached for a glass mug, setting it on the counter with a deliberate clink. After a beat, she added with a half-smile, "…love-sickness?"

For a moment, the man's green eyes locked onto hers, sharp and assessing. She thought he might laugh, but his expression cracked just enough to offer a faint, wry smile before it twisted into a grimace. "Got anything for…shot by a Vanguard…damn near bled out?" he rasped.

Memori froze as he pulled back his coat, revealing a jagged tear in his shirt and the dark, wet stain spreading beneath it. Blood seeped sluggishly from a deep wound in his side, looking stark and violent against the weathered wood of her counter. The raw edges of the injury looked days old, and infection had already begun to set in.

"I..I..let me check and see what I have," she said quietly. A thousand instincts flared at once: compassion, suspicion, fear. A man with a wound like that, claiming to have tangled with the Vanguard? That kind of trouble would follow her if she wasn't careful. And what would happen to Elowen then?

Through the thin walls, she could hear the soldiers' laughter from above, a reminder of how close danger always was.

Her mother would have helped him without hesitation. Her chest constricted at the thought, and she forced herself to breathe. She wasn't her mother—she couldn't afford to be. Still, she drew a steadying breath, hand sliding towards a cutting knife on the counter.

Before her fingertips reached the handle, the man's face twisted in pain, his knees buckling. His hand shot out to catch himself on a support beam, but missed. Eyes rolling back in his head, he slumped forward onto the bar and slid the rest of the way to the floor. The impact sent vibrations through the old timbers, and Memori's heart stopped. Would the sound carry over the noise of the drunken men above?

Knife forgotten, Memori opened her mouth to call for help, but the words caught in her throat. For a second, she thought of running—the back passage to the cargo hold was still clear. But the blood pooling on her floor was a stain she couldn't erase, no matter how hard she tried. Just then, the patter of familiar footsteps in the service corridor made her pulse spike.

"Memma!" Elowen's voice carried through the thin partition, followed by the creak of the shop's rear door. The girl must have slipped away from Jace.

She stood in the doorway, her wide eyes taking in the scene. She was frozen, just as Memori had been a moment before. The girl's gaze flickered from the bleeding man to her mother, as if unsure whether to ask what had happened or to flee from the danger.

Memori's heart twisted. She forced herself to remain calm, not letting the fear rise in her chest. She couldn't afford to be seen as a healer, but she couldn't ignore the first principle of the Codex either.

"Memma?" Elowen whispered, her voice small but full of concern in the close confines of the shop. Memori squeezed her eyes shut for a moment, steadying her breathing. She wanted to pull Elowen away, to tell her everything was fine, but she knew better than to lie. Not with danger a breath away. Elowen ran forward, dropping to the ground and placing a small hand on the stranger's forehead before Memori could stop her. "Memma, he's hurt! You're going to help him right? Right, Memma?!"

Memori's heart pounded in her chest as she met her daughter's eyes. There was no more room for hesitation, no more time to fear the consequences. The question had already been asked, and in her daughter's innocent voice, it sounded like a plea—a plea Memori couldn't ignore.

"Yes, Baby. I'm going to help him."

Chapter 4

Memori

What kind of lumbering fool would get himself shot by the Vanguard and then come here, of all places? Memori's heart pounded in her chest, her breath coming quick and shallow as she stared at the stranger sprawled across her shop floor. The pool of blood beneath him was spreading, seeping into the aged wood grain. A sharp curse slipped from her lips, and she forced herself to move.

She crouched beside him, her fingers trembling as she grabbed the thick collar of his coat. The fabric was rough and damp with blood, making her stomach churn, but she yanked hard–man's limp body sliding a few inches with a dull scrape across the floor. The sound seemed too loud in the close confines of the converted hold.

"Memma, I can help!" Elowen's small voice broke through the haze of panic.

"No, stay back—" Memori began, but Elowen darted forward, her tiny hands clutching at the man's sleeve. She moved with the confidence of someone who knew every beam and corner of this shop, who had played beneath these low-hanging herbs since she could walk.

"I'm strong too!" the girl insisted, her curls bouncing as she tugged with all her might. The sight wrenched at Memori's heart. Above them, boots crossed the main deck, and Memori held her breath until they passed.

"Alright, alright," she relented, her voice tight as she shifted to brace the man's shoulders. "Hold on to his feet, Elowen. Just like that. Be careful—don't touch the blood." She guided them toward the narrow door that led to her private workroom, where the ship's curved hull created a space too awkward for normal storage—perfect for secrets.

Elowen nodded, her face scrunched in determination as she grasped the man's boots. Together, they heaved, dragging him inch by agonizing inch across the creaking floorboards. Every groan of timber felt like a shout to Memori's ears. Her arms ached, her legs burning from the effort, but she didn't dare stop. Not with soldiers in the galley, their laughter carrying through the thin walls that had once kept cannon fire at bay.

The stranger's head lolled to one side, his labored breathing barely audible over the pounding of her pulse and the constant settling of the ship around them. Each groan of the floorboards felt like a shout, every second a chance for someone to come bursting through either door to find them.

When they reached the edge of her workroom, Memori's back hit the rough wood of the hull, and she paused, sweat dampening her brow. Elowen let go of the boots and stood beside her, panting but proud. The morning light filtering through the small port window caught the dust they'd disturbed, making it dance like golden snow.

"See? I helped!" the girl declared, beaming up at her mother.

Memori managed a strained smile, brushing a stray curl from Elowen's face. "Yes, you did. Now I need you to fetch some water from the barrel by the stern window. Quickly, Elowen!" The barrel was closer than the galley pump, and more importantly, wouldn't take Elowen past the morning crowd of soldiers.

Elowen nodded, her small feet pattering across the floorboards as she ran to fill the jug. Memori turned back to the man, her fingers already reaching for the knife strapped to her belt. The familiar weight of it reminded her of countless harvesting trips, back when gathering herbs hadn't meant risking execution.

"We don't have much time," she murmured, more to herself than anyone else. Through the thin walls, she could hear the morning crowd growing. Her fingers trembled as she pulled the man's coat open, cursing him under her breath. As if she didn't have enough trouble with the Vanguard already. Elowen stood beside her, wide-eyed but silent, clutching the jug of water like a lifeline.

"Scissors. Quickly, Elowen," Memori instructed, keeping her voice steady despite the chaos inside her head.

The girl reached for the drawer where they kept their tools hidden behind rolls of bandages. She passed over the scissors, and Memori cut through the man's blood-soaked shirt, her jaw tightening as she exposed the deep wound. The sharp, metallic scent of blood filled the air, mixing with the herbs hanging overhead.

"Memma…will he die?" Elowen whispered, her voice trembling.

"Not if I can help it," Memori replied, sparing her daughter a quick glance. "Pour some water into that bowl—carefully."

Elowen obeyed, her small hands steady despite the fear etched on her face. Memori grabbed a jar of powdered herbs from its hiding spot and doused a liberal amount onto the wound.

The reaction was immediate. The man's eyes flew open, and he let out a guttural yell, his hand shooting up toward Memori's throat. She scrambled back, hitting the hull with a sharp thud that seemed to echo through the whole ship.

"Memma!" Elowen cried, rushing to her side.

"Stay back!" Memori snapped, her heart hammering in her chest as she held the stranger's furious gaze. Heavy footsteps paused in the corridor outside, and for one terrifying moment, she thought it was all over.

The man's breathing was ragged, his chest rising and falling like a stormy sea. He looked down at the wound, then back at Memori, his expression softening as realization dawned. His hand dropped, and his head fell back onto the floor with a weak groan as the footsteps moved on.

"S…sorry," he stammered, his voice barely above a whisper.

Memori sat up, rubbing the back of her head. "You should be!" she shot back, her voice shaking with anger. Elowen hovered beside her, clutching her arm as if to anchor her.

Memori pushed herself forward again, grabbing the powder and pouring another helping onto the wound. The man's face contorted with pain, but he didn't lash out this time. She pressed a folded piece of cotton against the injury, her hands firm but quick.

"I'm not licensed, you know? I could be killed for this," she muttered under her breath, more to herself than to him.

"Memma, what's 'licensed'?" Elowen asked, her voice small but curious.

Memori froze for half a second before shaking her head. "It doesn't matter, Baby. Just…stay close and hand me what I need."

Her daughter nodded solemnly, her little hands reaching for the clean strips of linen. Elowen passed them over one by one, her eyes flicking between her mother's tense face and the stranger's pale features.

Time blurred as Memori worked, her hatred of the Vanguard temporarily overtaking her fear. She didn't even notice the blood smeared across her apron and hands until the sound of boots on the companionway made her freeze.

Her breath caught. She shot to her feet, looking at the dark streaks of blood leading from the shop to the workroom. Elowen tugged at her apron, her voice barely a whisper. "Memma, what do we do?" The boisterous singing of a vulgar song cut through the air like a blade, sharp and unwelcome. Her breath caught as she froze, panic rushing in.

Kol.

Memori's gaze darted to her hands—blood-streaked and trembling—and then to the stained apron tied at her waist. She grabbed a nearby cloth and hurriedly wiped her hands, smearing more than removing the blood. The apron was worse, dark streaks soaking through the fabric. She tugged it loose with shaking fingers and shoved it behind a barrel just as Kol's boots sounded against the floorboards above. "Hide!" she whispered. Elowen nodded, scurrying quietly into the cabinet beneath the workbench, a space they'd cleared long ago for exactly this purpose.

"There you are!"

The voice sent a chill down her spine, even before she turned to face him. Commander Conrad Kol of the Vanguard—the spoiled, arrogant son of a powerful Union leader—stood in the doorway, his tone mocking, his smile as insincere as always.

Memori felt bile rise in her throat. She forced herself to keep her expression neutral, though her hands clenched into fists at her sides.

"What are you doing here?" she asked, trying to keep the hatred from her voice as her heart pounded.

Conrad's gaze flicked over her, but his smirk didn't waver. "That's a rude greeting. Show me how happy you are to see me." He opened his arms, gaze flicking to where Elowen hid and back to Memori, his grin widening cruelly.

Memori's stomach twisted. She walked into his embrace, planting a hesitant kiss on his expectant lips. He pulled her into him, hands sliding down her back, hungrily deepening his kiss. Memori fought back nausea, feeling like she was drowning the whole time–each second he touched her like a minute under water.

The thought of her daughter so near this man filled her with harrowing disgust and fear. If Conrad ever decided she wasn't fit to care for Elowen—or if she displeased him—he would take her. Or worse…

Memori swallowed hard, shoving the thought away before it could fully form. Her mind shifted to darker paths in moments like these, ways to escape entirely. The venomthorn jar in her cupboard. The tiny vial of grimshade extract hidden beneath the floorboard. Just a pinch, a drop in her tea, and she'd drift away for good.

It would be so easy…

But then she would see Elowen's face in her mind, hear her laugh echo in the shop's quiet, and the thought would dissolve like ash in water.

Kol released her, his fingers sliding suggestively down her collar. "The ship's been cleared," he said, "I had everyone evacuated. Hunting a traitor, you see." His smile was hollow. "Though I must say, finding you down here alone is… an unexpected pleasure."

Memori shifted her weight, trying to draw his attention away from that side of the room. "Shouldn't you be leading the search?" she asked, forcing her voice to stay steady. "Your men will look for you."

"My men know their duties." He reached out to touch her face, and she forced herself to remain still, though every fiber of her being screamed to pull away. His fingers were cold against her skin, and the cloying scent of cherry tobacco washed over her as he leaned closer. Something predatory flickered in his eyes. "Besides, I thought we might have a moment to… reminisce. Like last time I was in town. The usual spot." His fingers coiled around her throat and he moved to kiss her again.

Memori knew the cost of refusal—had seen too many children torn from their mothers' arms by his men. The thought of Elowen suffering that fate…

"I should clean up first," she said quickly, taking a step back. "A customer spilled something earlier. I need to change–"

"Why?" Kol looked her up and down, eyes narrowing. "It's not like you have anything better to change into." He stepped closer, and she could see the familiar gleam in his eyes—the look that had haunted her dreams for five years. His arm snaked around her waist. Memori resisted for a heartbeat and Kol's grip on her tightened.

"None of that." There was a chilling hardness to his tone, and Memori gave in, hating herself for it. His fingers curled around the nape of her neck, the other hand reaching for the top button of her dress. "That's more like it."

She wanted to scream—to wipe that stupid self-obsessed look off his face—to run far from Stonegate–from the entire realm–and never return. The harshest rejections were on the tip of her tongue, but she couldn't find the courage to speak them. As he leaned in closer, his hot breath on her neck, his attention suddenly shifted to something on the floor.

Kol stilled. His hand fell from her dress as his shrewd blue eyes narrowed. His gaze tracked from the stain to the droplets that had fallen from her hem onto the floor. He dragged the toe of his boot through the dampness, examining what came away.

Memori felt her heart skip a beat, watching him discover what she'd desperately tried to hide.

His head cocked to the side. "This is fresh blood." He crouched down and dusted at the floor with his hand."Memori…what are you hiding from me?" His glance at her turned sharp.

"Conrad, wait—" Memori grabbed at his arm, but Kol slung her off, sending her crashing into a nearby table. Tears stung her eyes as she caught herself from falling.

"Don't you touch Memma!" Elowen screamed, rushing from her hiding spot and right into him, tiny fists raised.

With a half-interested look, Kol shoved the girl aside, and she fell against the wall, crying in rage for him to leave Memori alone. Ignoring them both, he strode into the workroom. This was it, Memori realized. He would kill the stranger, then Elowen, and, as a matter of cruelty, save her for last.

Memori's world narrowed to a single thought—protecting Elowen—when Kol suddenly flew backward out of the workroom. He hit the floor like a rag doll; the impact shocked her out of her despair. Blood seeped from a fresh cut on his head, and for the first time since she'd known him, she saw genuine fear in his eyes.

"Fuckin' throw a little girl around, will ya?" The stranger's voice was barely more than a rasp, but the fury in it made even Memori flinch. He stood in the doorway, one hand pressed against his wound, the other braced against the frame, but his eyes burned with a rage that transformed him from wounded fugitive to avenging fury. "Not much of a match without ten men to do the fighting for you."

Blood dripped through Kol's fingers as he wadded a handkerchief and pressed it against his head. "You'll hang for this, Irons." His glare flicked to Memori, and she saw the promise in his eyes—the same look he'd worn when he'd ordered Mae's execution. And later when he'd told her exactly how long he'd made the healer suffer. "And as for you"

The walls seemed to close in on Memori as her pulse pounded in her throat. She knew what waited in the Union's cells, had heard the screams of those who'd defied them. But worse was the knowledge that Elowen would be left alone with him.

Irons scoffed, drawing Kol's attention from Memori. "Hanging me twice, then?"

"If only I could." Kol's gaze shifted angrily back to his would-be prisoner. "Deserter scum."

Irons moved with a speed that belied his injuries, though each motion left fresh blood seeping through his bandages. He yanked the commander to his feet, head butted him, kneed him in the stomach, and hurled him across the room. The effort nearly dropped him—Memori could see his legs shaking, the grey pallor of his skin—but his eyes never left Kol as the commander scrambled to his feet and ran.

"Cowardly shit!" Irons muttered, gripping the nearest table to keep himself from falling. Above them, alarm bells rang, and the thunder of boots on the deck told them Kol's men were coming. "Sorry about this." He glanced at Memori, pain etching deep lines around his eyes. "But it'd be best if you follow me now."

It felt like things were moving in slow motion. Irons had ahold of her hand. She wanted to pull away, but couldn't. "This way," he said, leading her toward the stern of the ship. She caught Elowen's hand as they passed, pulling her daughter close.

They'd nearly reached the main mast when Irons dropped to his knees, his breath coming in sharp gasps. He ran his fingers along the planking and pried one loose. Every moment he spent searching felt like an eternity with the thundering of boots nearing every second.

"Hurry," he said urgently, taking Memori's hand and lowering her into the dark, cramped crawl space. "After you, Little Lady," he hid the pain behind a smile as he lowered Elowen into Memori's arms. Fresh blood soaked his bandages as he followed in after and slid the plank back in place.

"What are we doing?" Elowen whispered, her small body trembling against Memori's.

"Shhh Baby!" Memori urgently held a hand over the girl's mouth, her heart thundering so loud she was certain the soldiers would hear it.

"Playing cat and mouse," Irons whispered, trying to sound playful despite his labored breathing. "Mustn't let the cat find us." Memori felt Elowen relax in her arms at the thought of it being a game. Only a few moments later, they could hear footsteps running overhead, dust sifting down through the cracks between the planks.

Memori held her breath until they passed, certain they would be found. The search party circled back, and she thought her heart would jump out of her chest. But they kept going. The stranger let out a heavy breath, slumping over momentarily. Even in the dim light filtering through the planks, she could see how much paler he'd become. "Who the hell are you?" Memori snapped, wishing she could see his face to better tell him off.

"Orson Irons." He started moving again, more dragging himself than crawling down the tunnel as he talked. "Deserter of the 5th Platoon Vanguard. I would say at your service, but…I'm not sure how much longer I can keep that promise."

"Kol's going to kill me," Memori said in a hoarse whisper, urging Elowen to crawl ahead of her. The words felt hollow compared to what she knew he'd really do to them.

"Probably better than living with him." Even in a whisper, Orson managed to sound venomous. "What could you possibly have seen in that pale-faced troll, anyway?" He spared a glance over his shoulder, frowning at Elowen.

Angry tears came to Memori's eyes and her voice accidentally cracked when she spoke. "I saw nothing in him. Nobody tells the Vanguard no—but you wouldn't know anything about that, would you?"

Orson stopped moving and winced, clutching his side where the blood seeped between his fingers. His voice was softer this time, almost broken. "I'm sorry… Memori… may I call you that?"

The way he looked at her—eyes shadowed with guilt—made her chest tighten against her will. She didn't want his sympathy. He was the one bleeding to death, not her.

"I shouldn't have said it," he continued, his breath hitching. "I—I don't have the right." His knees wavered, and for a moment, she thought he might collapse right there.

Memori rolled her eyes. "May as well. Since we're about to hang together."

Orson gave a weak-sounding chuckle. "They still have to catch us."

"They'll never find us!" Elowen chimed in excitedly. "I'm Elowen! My Memma helped you—so did I!"

"She's my sister," Memori cut in quickly.

Orson pressed a hand to his side, pausing as his breath hitched. "Thank you…Elowen." He sucked in a steeling breath of air, then continued down the passage.

As they navigated the ship's dimly lit interior, the sensation of being within a living relic was almost suffocating. The walls groaned softly, as though the vessel itself whispered the weight of countless secrets. To Memori, it felt less like stepping into a legend and more like being swallowed by something ancient and relentless. Legends were for people who didn't have to worry about survival.

Every creak above made her imagine Kol finding them, seeing Elowen's face in better light, noticing the eyes that matched his own. One look was all it would take to destroy everything. Memori found Elowen's ankle as they crawled, reassuring herself she could pull her daughter to safety in an instant if needed. She bit back a curse as splinters bit into her hand. Each sting reminded her of what truly mattered—not fables or glory, but escape. Freedom. A life where the Union's shadow could no longer reach her and Elowen. Where the memory of Conrad Kol would erode, like rock worn smooth by the relentless patience of the ocean.

Ahead of her, Orson fumbled. His shoulder clipped the wall as he caught himself, a wet cough wracking his body that had nothing to do with his recent wound. "Orson?" Her tone was sharp, but there was a flicker of concern.

"I'm fine," he muttered, though his words carried little conviction. The match he struck illuminated faint red markings on the plank, his hands trembling as he held the flame.

"How long can that last?" Memori asked.

"Long enough." His eyes seemed dimmer now, like a candle burning at both ends. "I know something they don't." He pressed his palm against the marked plank, and the wall creaked open to reveal a narrow passage and ladder.

"You're slowing down," Memori said, slipping an arm under his to support him.

"Just wish I had more…" he murmured, his gaze lingering on Elowen with a wistful smile. "Time's not exactly on my side."

"I can help!" Elowen gripped his other arm with surprising strength. "Memma, is he gonna be okay?"

Orson blinked hard and looked away, but not before Memori caught the look in his eyes—the same one she'd seen in her mother's face, in the mirror—of someone measuring their remaining days in heartbeats.

"Get Elowen up first," Orson said, leaning heavily against the wall. A commotion overhead sent tremors through the timbers, releasing dust that drifted down through narrow spaces.

"No." Memori frowned, watching him struggle to stay upright. "She stays with me." Her tone was sharper than she meant it to be—too many years of keeping Elowen close, of trusting no one else with her safety.

Orson met her gaze steadily, something too knowing in his eyes. "Trust me. The landing up there has more room, and she's small enough to slip through easily. Then you can both help pull me up." He paused, another cough shaking his frame. "Unless you'd rather I pass out halfway up and fall on you both." A shout echoed through the passages behind them, followed by the crack of wood splintering. They were getting closer.

Memori hesitated, then nodded curtly. "Elowen, up you go. Quick now."

Elowen scrambled up the ladder with surprising agility, disappearing through the hatch above. "I'm up!" she whispered down to them.

"Well done, El," Orson called softly.

"Her name's not El," Memori snapped, the familiar fear tightening her chest. Even a nickname was too much familiarity, too much attention.

Something flickered in Orson's eyes—understanding, maybe pity. He must have seen enough of Kol's "arrangements" in his time with the Vanguard. "My mistake," he mumbled. Then, louder, "You next."

But Memori was already moving to brace him. "Shut up and climb," she muttered. "I'm tired of arguing with a dying man."

A weak chuckle escaped him, ending in another wet cough. "What gave it away? We've only just met."

"Be quiet," Memori hissed, her hand steadying his shoulder as he swayed. Each rattling breath he took bounced off the damp wooden walls, making her pulse skip. The sound might as well have been cannon fire announcing their location. She could feel the heat of fever through his coat, spreading beneath her fingers like a warning.

The climb was agonizing to watch. Every few rungs, Orson's strength would falter, and Memori would have to steady him from behind, her fingers digging into his coat. His breathing grew more labored, each exhale carrying a wet rattle that scared her more than the wound in his side. This was something deeper, something no bandage could fix. The sour tang of sickness mixed with copper-scented blood, a combination she remembered too well from her mother's final days.

More shouts echoed below, closer now. Memori felt caught between the urge to hurry him and the fear he'd fall if pushed too hard. The same fear that had haunted her as she'd watched her mother fade—this helpless knowledge that moving too fast or too slow could steal whatever precious time remained.

"Where exactly are we heading?" she asked, trying to distract him from the effort, trying to ignore how his labored breathing matched the rhythm of her own rising panic. She didn't want to care. Caring about dying people only led to more scars, more memories to bury.

You'll see," he managed between breaths.

Memori pushed him forward through the open hatch, her hands at his back as he crawled through on trembling arms. She followed close behind, scrambling up the ladder as he dragged himself the final distance. When they emerged at the top, she hauled him through with a grunt, her arms shaking from the effort. His fever burned against her skin where she gripped him, each of his labored breaths shuddering through his frame.

Elowen was already waiting there, her small face scrunched with worry as she tugged on his sleeve and pressed a folded piece of cloth against his arm. The gesture was so like her mother's teachings that Memori had to look away.

"They'll hear your cough," Elowen whispered. She squeezed Orson's hand when she told him, and something in Memori's chest twisted at the gesture. Her daughter had always been too quick to care, too ready to trust—just like she had been, once.

"I know, little one." His fingers tightened around Elowen's momentarily before he braced himself with a heavy swallow. The tenderness in his voice caught Memori off guard, making him suddenly, terrifyingly human. Not just another soldier, not just another threat to avoid. Somewhere between the shop and this moment, he'd become someone whose death would matter. Orson blinked down at her, a weak smile tugging at his lips as his hand closed around the cloth she offered him.. Sweat beaded on his forehead, but his eyes softened at Elowen's concern. "Thanks, El."

"Her name's not El," Memori frowned, the familiar fear rising. But her sharp words died in her throat as she looked around and froze. The room was unlike any she'd seen in the inn before. Dust-covered barrels and wooden crates filled the corners, their surfaces thick with neglect. The air felt different here—heavy with secrets and stale time. Two cannons, dark with age but menacing in their presence, stood ready at the hull like sleeping giants. They faced latched doors barely wide enough for their barrels, salt-crusted hinges telling tales of long-forgotten battles. The wood here felt older, untouched by the inn's renovations, as if they'd stepped through time into the ship's true heart.

"It's not just a rumor," she murmured, her voice caught somewhere between awe and disbelief. Her fingers traced the weathered grain of a nearby crate, coming away with the grit of decades. "This is an actual ship."

"Not just any ship." Orson pushed himself onto one elbow, his breath coming in shallow gasps. Despite his pallor, a faint smirk tugged at his lips, and for a moment, she glimpsed the soldier he must have been before illness carved him hollow. "It's the Crimson Ghost."

Chapter 5

Memori

Orson looked suddenly paler, and he fell forward, crashing roughly to the floor with a sickening thud. Beads of sweat dotted his forehead, catching the dim light as they traced down his face. His breath was shallow, labored, and his eyes were wild as he struggled to push himself up. Elowen's eyes widened as she rushed to help.

"No, go hide," Memori snapped, the sharpness in her voice making Elowen freeze mid-step. Her hands tightened into fists at her sides, retreating to her hiding spot behind the crates. This was a familiar routine for the both of them— Memori's fierce protection. Elowen's careful compliance. Still, her worried eyes lingered on Orson's pale face, fingers twisting in her skirt as she watched him struggle for breath. "Are you alright?" Memori asked Orson, surprised at the wave of concern that rose unbidden in her chest. She moved to his side, her hand brushing his arm as she helped him rock back on his heels. Her fingers tightened when she felt the tremor in his muscles, his strength waning under the weight of the injury.

"Probably not." His eyes met hers, his smile strained but somehow familiar. "Thanks for trying, though. You should probably find somewhere to hide, truth be told. Get as far away…" He sucked in a sharp breath, a wince twisting his features. For a moment, his body went rigid before he finished, voice low. "…from me—as possible. Keep your…sister safe."

The lie twisted in Memori's chest. Sister. The word they'd agreed upon, the story they told the world. She caught Elowen watching them, the girl's eyes too knowing, too old for her young face. Something in the way Orson's gaze lingered made Memori's chest tighten further. There was an unspoken question there, one that made her feel exposed.

"We need more bandages," Elowen said quietly, already tearing strips from her apron. Her movements were precise, practiced—Memori's heart ached at how quickly she'd learned to treat wounds. A skill that could get her killed. She rushed to Memori and pressed them into her hands before hurrying back to her hiding place.

"Just wrap it, if you must," Orson pleaded through clenched teeth. "Quickly."

"That's not how this works." Memori pulled her hand free, pressing the cloth against the bleeding wound. His body shuddered under her touch. "I need to clean it properly or it'll get more infected."

A bitter laugh rose from his throat, ending in another wet cough. "It won't matter, anyway."

"What is that supposed to mean?!" Memori's fingers stilled against his skin.

He shook his head, the movement slow and deliberate. "Never mind." His voice was hoarse, the words heavy with a weariness that made Memori's skin prickle.

"The wound needs cleaning," Elowen said firmly, peeking her head above the crate. The determined set of her jaw was pure Memori—the same expression she'd worn at that age.

Memori frowned, watching the way Orson's lips pressed together, like every word pained him. "Tell me what you're trying to do at least," she pleaded, "so I can help you."

Orson paused, gaze hardening, before he nodded curtly. "I need to move the cannons."

"The cannons?" Elowen whispered, her eyes widening as she looked between them.

Memori scowled, rolling a barrel against the door with a creaking groan. The sound of the wood scraping against stone reverberated through the room. "Why? The door's barely holding. They'll be inside before you can—"

"Trust me!" His voice was tight with pain, and sweat dripped down his face, mixing with the grime that covered his skin. His hands trembled as he adjusted the cannon's aim, his fingers slipping slightly on the metal.

"Memma" Elowen's voice was soft but steady as she moved to help with another barrel.

"No." Memori caught her arm, pulling her back. "Stay by the far wall."

She glared at Orson. "You're not exactly inspiring confidence."

Orson gave a weak chuckle, though the sound was jagged, like it hurt to laugh. His eyes flickered briefly toward Elowen before meeting Memori's gaze again. "Confidence doesn't stop a flood, Memori."

Her brow furrowed, the words pulling at her. "A flood?" He didn't answer, his eyes turning to the cannon, his movements methodical despite the strain. He reached into his coat and pulled out a small bundle of fuses. The smell of gunpowder and sulfur clung to the air as he unwrapped the bundle, the faint, bitter scent filling the space between them.

"You're going to blow the dam!" Memori's voice cracked with disbelief. She felt the cold press of fear creeping into her thoughts, imagining the water rushing through the streets where her daughter had played just yesterday. "How?"

Orson's gaze met hers, the intensity of his look cutting through the tension in the room. "I planted charges days ago." His eyes were dark with guilt, but the determination in them was unmistakable. "It's the only way."

Memori's chest tightened, a lump forming in her throat. "And what about the people downstream? The villagers?"

"We have to warn them," Elowen said, her small hand finding Memori's. The touch anchored her, as it always had since the first time she'd held her daughter's tiny fingers.

He hesitated, his voice dropping to a softer, almost regretful tone. "They'll have time to get to higher ground. Vanguard's already evacuated the ship."

The lack of confidence in his words sent a shiver down her spine. For a moment, the acrid scent of burning flesh filled her nostrils—a phantom memory of the night they burned Healer Mae. The night before they'd come to the Inn. She'd held Elowen close that night, both of them hidden in their hut, her daughter's face buried against her shoulder to muffle any sound. The villagers had drawn their curtains and pretended not to hear the screams. She could feel the weight of the decision on her shoulders now, knowing they wouldn't hesitate to turn them in as well. Let them burn or hang for healing people.

Sweat soaked through the back of Orson's coat as he pushed a crate against the door, his arms shaking with effort.

Elowen moved quickly between them, passing tools and supplies with quiet efficiency. What choice did they have? If Orson was caught, they would all share his fate.

"How do you know about this ship?" Memori muttered, more to herself than to him, trying to silence the protest rising in her mind.

"This ship," Orson grunted as he wedged a rickety chair under the door handle, "it's built from heartwood of the undying trees." His voice was low, almost a rasp, and something about the way he said it made the air feel heavy with untold secrets. "That's why Kol is after me. He ordered me to torture an old man to death for information about where to find it. I…may have been less than diplomatic when I declined the order."

Elowen's hand traced the worn planks beneath their feet, her expression thoughtful. "It feels… warm."

Memori wiped her hand on the crate beside her, her fingers feeling sticky with grime. The sharp, metallic smell of rust mingled with the sweat and blood in the air. She studied the wood where Elowen touched, noting how it seemed to pulse with a subtle warmth despite its age. "A ship that can't die—that's a stupid old legend."

"It's more than that," Orson said, giving her a grim smile as his eyes dimmed with the weight of the past. "They say it remembers. Every port, every hidden cove, every secret island it's ever visited. Like a compass pointing to all the world's mysteries at once." He paused, his expression darkening. "The old man thought that knowledge was worth dying over."

"Like the stories in my book," Elowen whispered, and Memori caught the familiar spark of wonder in her daughter's eyes—the same look she'd had as a baby, reaching for the stars through their attic window.

A lump rose in Memori's throat, but she swallowed it down, her chest tight. "I'm sorry."

Orson glanced toward the open cannon slot, his gaze distant. "Don't be. He died well…that's all we can really hope for." The smirk on Orson's face caused the sinking feeling in her stomach to take hold again; he wasn't talking about the old man this time.

The sharp crack of an axe splitting through the door echoed through the cramped hold. From where Memori stood between the two loaded cannons, she could see straight through the splintering wood to the torchlit corridor beyond. Her throat tightened at the sight of shadows moving behind the door—how many soldiers had Kol brought?

A cry cut through the air, making her heart stop. Elowen had stepped out from behind the towering coil of anchor chain where she'd been hiding, now standing exposed near the stern. The girl's face was pale in the flickering lantern light, her eyes fixed on the door as another axe blow sent splinters flying.

"Elowen, hide!" Memori barked, gesturing toward the pile of fishing nets stacked in the corner furthest from the door, behind the second cannon. The girl bolted without question. Memori watched until Elowen's slight frame disappeared into the shadows where the lantern light couldn't reach, before turning back to Orson.

He ignored the imminent danger, focusing instead on a box of matches he pulled from his coat with shaky fingers. Sweat beaded on his forehead as he leaned heavily against the port-side cannon. The weapon was aimed directly at the doorway. The faint scent of sulfur filled the air as he tossed the matchbox to Memori, who waited by the starboard cannon across the

"Here," he muttered, his voice hoarse with strain. "When I tell you to, set them off." He gestured toward the fuses trailing from both cannons before resting a hand briefly on her shoulder, his touch warm despite the cold that had settled in the windowless room. The gesture felt final somehow, making her stomach knot.

Memori opened the box with trembling hands, the scent of wood and sulfur overpowering the musty air. As she reached for a match, a booted foot crashed through the door. The impact made her jump, the box spilling open. Matches scattered across the worn planks between the cannon and the hull, tiny splinters of hope rolling away into shadows. Her hands shook as she stooped to gather them, painfully aware of Elowen's soft breathing from the corner.

Orson gritted his teeth, forcing himself to cross the short distance to the door despite the weakness threatening to overwhelm him. She could see the effort each step cost him, how his legs threatened to buckle. He yanked the chair from where it was wedged under the iron handle, his body trembling. The movement put him directly between the door and the cannons, blocking the soldiers' view of their true purpose.

Memori's eyes widened as understanding dawned. "What are you doing?" she mouthed, though she already knew. He meant to draw their attention—to keep their eyes on him instead of the cannons, instead of the corner where Elowen huddled in the shadows. Orson pressed a finger to his lips, a sly grin twisting his features despite the pain evident in his eyes. Then, in a swift motion, he raised the chair over his head.

Memori's heart pounded as she struck a match. It flared. And died, leaving only a brief flicker of light before it snuffed out in her hand. She cursed under her breath, panic surging through her. Her fingers found another match just as the remaining fragments of the door gave way and the Vanguard crashed in.

Orson met the first soldier with the full force of the chair, smashing it into the man's face with a sickening crack. The soldier flew backward, colliding with the ship's hull, his rifle clattering to the deck. Orson snatched it up, his movements sharp and precise as the others stormed in, their boots echoing against the wooden planks.

"That's far enough," he bellowed, his voice harsh as he cocked the rifle, aiming it directly at the nearest soldier. His stance was wide, commanding attention, keeping their focus away from the cannons' positions. The Vanguard froze, confusion flickering in their eyes as they turned to face their commander. Memori used their distraction to strike another match, shielding the flame with her body as she crouched by the first cannon's fuse. "Don't. Fucking. Move." Orson's voice was a growl, raw and commanding. His eyes narrowed, focus sharpening as his finger hovered over the trigger. The soldiers hesitated, glancing uncertainly at Kol, who had appeared in the doorway like a shadow made flesh.

"Kol, you abysmal piece of shit! Fancy seeing you here again," Orson's voice rang out, full of venom, drawing all eyes to him.

But Kol's attention had caught on something else. His gaze swept the hold, lingering first on Memori with a proprietary gleam that made her stomach turn. "My dear Memori," he purred. "I thought we had an understanding about your… position in Stonegate."

Then his eyes found movement in the shadows.

Three heartbeats.

Elowen had shifted in her hiding spot, just enough for the light to catch her face. Memori's blood ran cold as Kol's expression changed, something like recognition flickering across his features as he studied her daughter's eyes—his own eyes. She'd never told him, but he must have suspected. Now that he'd got a good look at her.

"Quite the little brat you've been harboring." His voice turned thoughtful, making it somehow worse. He took a step closer, gaze flicking between Memori and Elowen. "First, you defy me by helping this traitor, and now I find you've been keeping secrets." His smile grew cruel. "Those eyes of hers would fetch a pretty price in Driftmarch. Bit young, perhaps," He shrugged, the gesture casual but his meaning clear. "But there are those who don't particularly care about such things. And after this betrayal, my dear, you won't be in any position to stop me."

Two.

Memori's fingers trembled on the fuse, bile rising in her throat. Everything she'd feared, everything she'd hidden from, was crystallizing in Kol's cold smile.

The rifle in Orson's hands stopped shaking. Despite the fever-sweat running down his face, despite the tremor in his legs, his aim steadied. Something shifted in his stance—the soldier he must have been before illness carved him hollow emerging one last time. "You won't touch either of them."

One.

Orson moved with the last of his strength, swinging the rifle like a club. The crack of wood and metal against bone echoed through the hold as he caught Kol across the face. Blood sprayed in an arc that caught the lantern light, but the commander staggered back rather than falling, his hand already going to his sword.

"Take cover!" Orson shouted, his voice desperate now.

Memori dove for the pile of nets, her body instinctively curling around Elowen as she pulled her close. The fuses nearly spent, sparks reflecting in Kol's blood on the floor as he fled through the doorway. Her arms trembled as she pressed Elowen's face against her shoulder, shielding her from what was coming. She shut her eyes tight, feeling the fuses burn down through the thundering of her heart.

Chapter 6

Memori

The cannon's roar shook the ship, the concussion throwing them all to the floor. Through the ringing in her ears, Memori heard the secondary explosion—deeper, more devastating—as the blast triggered the charges Orson must have planted along Stonegate Dam's weakest points.

"Is Mr. Irons ok, Memma?" Elowen whispered against her ear as Memori caught hold of her.

"He'll be fine, baby," Memori squeezed the girl tightly, but her heart stuttered at the sight of him. The adrenaline that had kept him going was visibly draining away, his face ashen as he braced his rifle against his shoulder.

"What was that supposed to do?" Kol scoffed from behind his men. "Provide a distraction?"

Despite the tremor in his hands, despite the sweat beading on his forehead, Orson's smirk was triumphant as he forced himself to sit up. "I set the river free," he said, his voice hoarse but steady as he glared at the Commander. The distant rumble grew to a roar as the weakened dam gave way. "This entire valley will be flooded in minutes."

The Vanguard exchanged horrified glances, looking to Kol for direction as the sound of cracking stone echoed through the morning air. The water that had been contained for so long crashed through the breach, reclaiming its old path through the valley.

Kol was the first to turn and run. Orson's shaking finger squeezed the trigger, but his strength was failing—the shot went wide as the other Vanguard scattered.

Memori pulled Elowen with her to the cannon port, watching as the flood waters surged past. The tower that held the Crimson Ghost groaned and shifted like its formation was unnatural–not meant to last. Timbers protested as the rising water lifted the ship from its centuries-old perch, setting them on a course toward the Avalon Sea, toward freedom beyond Cibola's reach.

The rifle clattered to the deck as it slipped from Orson's nerveless fingers and he slumped to the floor. His face was grey now, the last of his strength deserting him, though that defiant half-smile still played at his lips. A lump rose in Memori's throat as she knelt beside him. "Orson?"

"Mm?" He couldn't seem to open his eyes. The wound on his side had reopened, blood seeping through his shirt.

"Don't die," she pleaded, trying to keep her voice steady. "I—I know nothing about sailing."

He managed a weak laugh that turned into a grimace.

"Meh-ma," Elowen whispered, her voice small. "What's happening?"

"It'll be ok, baby." Memori pulled the girl into her lap, but her eyes never left Orson's face.

"You alright, little one?" Orson's voice was barely more than a whisper, his gaze finding Elowen through the haze of pain.

She nodded hesitantly, her wide eyes fixed on the growing stain on his shirt. "You're bleeding," she said softly, small fingers clutching at Memori's sleeve.

"Not my first time," he tried to smile, but it came out as more of a grimace.

"Elowen," Memori's voice carried the sharp edge of fear, "grab that cloth—quickly!"

The little girl scrambled to obey, her hands shaking as she pressed the cloth against Orson's wound. "Don't die," she pleaded, tears spilling down her cheeks. "Memma needs you."

A weak laugh escaped him, cut short by a wince. His blood-stained fingers found Elowen's cheek. The gesture was gentle, protective. "You'll be alright."

Chapter 6

Memori's throat constricted as she watched him showing such tenderness to her daughter even as his life ebbed away. "Stay with me, Orson."

His gaze met hers, and in that moment, she saw everything he couldn't say—regret, hope, something deeper that made her heart stutter. His eyes shut. "Elowen," Memori whispered, fighting to keep her voice steady, "help me keep him awake."

The little girl gripped his hand in both of hers, her small fingers disappearing into his larger ones. "Don't go," she whispered, and Memori saw Orson's fingers tighten slightly in response.

"Memori" His eyes opened again, finding hers with effort. He raised his hand once more to her face, leaving traces of blood on her skin. "I'd ask you to marry me, but you're far too young to be a widow."

A sob caught in her throat, tangled with a desperate laugh as she wrapped her hands around his wrist. "You should try asking. Maybe I'd say yes." Orson smirked, his fingers curling as if trying to tighten around her hand, but unable to do so. His pulse fluttered beneath her fingers, too fast, too weak.

Her mind raced with terrible possibilities. What would she do if he died? The thought of consigning his body to the sea made bile rise in her throat. After everything he'd sacrificed for them…

With visible effort, Orson pulled his hand free. His fingers trembled as he reached into his coat, producing a small pendant of intricate design. In the dim light filtering through the cannon port, its craftsmanship seemed to catch and hold the glow, as if it carried its own inner light. "The Seawind" His voice was fading, each word a struggle. "It's a fishing trawler… they'll find you once the ship leaves Cibola." He pressed the pendant into her palm, his skin cold against hers. "Show this to them. They'll know it came from me." His hands enclosed around hers, the gesture almost like a prayer. "They'll sail the Ghost for you" His grip slackened. "Better than I ever could" His eyes rolled back as the last of his strength deserted him, his hand falling away from hers.

GENERAL STORM STOOD at the prow of his flagship, Dominion, staring across the rolling expanse of the Avalon Sea. The years had left little mark on his face, save for the web of scars that traced his jaw like silver threads - their origin the subject of whispered speculation among his subordinates. The faintest shimmer of dawn painted the water with streaks of molten silver, but the skies above told a darker story.

"Sir." The voice belonged to an unassuming man, his appearance carefully crafted to vanish into any crowd. No insignia adorned his tunic, no hint of his allegiance was visible. He stood at rigid attention, water dripping from the edges of his travel-worn cloak. "Stonegate Dam has been destroyed."

Storm didn't turn immediately. The shard embedded in his wrist pulsed once, a dull ache he'd carried so long it felt like an old friend. Finally, he turned, his cloak whipping around him in the rising wind. "Stonegate Dam," he echoed, his voice low and deliberate, each syllable weighted.

The spy continued. "There are rumors, sir. The flood waters - they say the ancient ship was freed from the cliffs. And Commander Kol of the 5th Vanguard, along with most of his men… they've vanished."

"Vanished," Storm repeated, mind already forming possibilities. "When?"

"The locals say they were last seen hunting a traitor."

A smile ghosted across Storm's face, devoid of warmth. "Kol sees a traitor on every corner." He turned, and the spy involuntarily stepped back, rightfully wary of Storm's mood.

"The man's an animal," Storm said, his tone almost appreciative. "But a useful one. The people fear him. The way he looks at their daughters, the way he makes examples of those who defy us." His hand unconsciously moved to his wrist, where the shard lay beneath his skin. The spy waited, silent. "I take it he was unsuccessful in completing his mission…"

Storm's boots thudded heavily against the polished deck as he moved to the ship's charts. "Deploy the Third Fleet. I want every ship with a Black Smoke flag in these waters by dawn." His scarred lips curved into something approaching a smile. "If there's truth to these rumors of an ancient ship, I mean to find it. And it's time the realms remembered why they fear the Union." Lightning flickered in the distance, and the faint rumble of thunder followed like a growl from the depths of the sea. Storm's expression hardened, the mask of civility falling away to reveal something terrible beneath.

"Oh, and one more thing," the commander's voice was deceptively soft. "When–if–you find Kol, bring him to me. I have use for him elsewhere."

The spy gave a curt nod, then melted back into the shadows, leaving Storm alone with his thoughts and the churning horizon. His hand drifted to the inner pocket of his coat, where a small leather pouch hung close to his heart. Inside, a single silver coin clinked against what appeared to be a piece of ancient wood, dark as old blood. Even now, the memory of certain gardens made his scars ache.

"Finally," he murmured, the word rolling off his tongue like a prayer, or a curse. His eyes gleamed with a dangerous light, a predator catching the scent of prey. "What will your move be this time, eh, Sloan?" The wind picked up again, colder this time, carrying with it the faintest echo of crashing waves and whispers from the depths. This wasn't about a dam or a missing commander. Something older was stirring, and Storm meant to be ready when it broke surface.

THE DECK OF the Seawind groaned under Victor Sloan's boots as he stood near the bow, his sharp gaze locked on the horizon where the sea kissed the sky. The wind, sharp and briny, suddenly shifted, carrying with it a scent that didn't belong. Around him, the crew tensed - they'd learned to read his moods like weather signs, knowing when storms gathered in his silence.

It was faint at first—a whisper of earth, damp moss, and ancient woodlands, overlaid with a fleeting sweetness like crushed wildflowers. Victor froze, his fingers tightening on the railing until the wood creaked. Dark clouds gathered overhead, though the morning had dawned clear. His sharp eyes scanned the empty waves, but there was nothing to see. Only the scent lingered, as vivid and impossible as a memory brought to life.

Wind tugged insistently at his coat, pulling him forward, urging him to act. Lightning flickered in the distance. Victor straightened, his voice cutting through the steady hum of the trawler's engine. "Jermany! Change course. Head for the Avalon Sea."

At the wheel, Jermany turned sharply at his command, her dark eyes flashing with a mixture of surprise and determination. Her long, braided hair shimmered with copper beads, swinging as she gripped the wheel. The waves seemed to calm beneath her touch, though the rest of the sea churned with growing unrest. Her movements were confident and deliberate as she directed the Seawind on a new course. "What is it, Captain?" she asked, her tone level but curious. She exchanged a knowing look with Sullivan at the helm - they'd seen this before, these moments when Victor seemed to hear calls only he could understand.

Before Victor could answer, Evander appeared at his shoulder, pale as moonlight against the ship's dark wood. The slim, wiry man seemed to hover, as though a strong gust might dissolve him into the air itself. Shadows gathered around him unnaturally, though none of the crew paid any attention. His narrow eyes scanned the horizon with suspicion, straining for any sign of the extraordinary.

"What do you see?" Evander's voice was barely more than a whisper, his words carrying only to Victor. Behind them, Peryn's hands unconsciously clenched and unclenched, the ferro-rings on his fingers catching what little light there was. Tiny sparks skittered across the steel inlays before he forced his hands still.

Victor didn't reply, his focus unyielding. The crew exchanged glances tinged with equal parts excitement and dread. They'd learned that Victor's hunts often led to danger, yet they followed without question. There was something in the air now - a charge that made their skin prickle with forgotten power. Each crewman moved with precision, like pieces of a puzzle falling into place - roles they'd played before, though none could say exactly when or where.

Victor stayed rooted to the bow, letting the shifting wind whip through his hair and that impossible scent fill his lungs. His lips curled into a grim, almost triumphant smile. The silver threading his hair caught the morning light, making him look ancient and young all at once. "Found you," he murmured, the words swallowed by the wind and the endless expanse of sea ahead. Thunder rolled in the distance, as if in answer to his voice.

Chapter 7

Memori

The weight of the pendant felt heavy in Memori's hand. "Can't you give it to them?" The words caught in her throat as she looked at Orson's still form. He didn't answer. Didn't stir. A wave of grief crashed through her, raw and overwhelming in its intensity. She hadn't expected this—this desperate, clawing fear at the thought of losing him. They barely knew each other, yet something about watching him slip away felt like watching a piece of herself dying too.

The vessel swayed with the turbulent current, the deck tilting and lifting as rushing waters cradled the newly freed ship. Orson's eyes remained shut, his breathing growing slower. Beside him, Elowen's small fingers wrapped around his hand, tears streaming down her face. "Mr. Orson?" she called, trembling.

The sight of her daughter crying shattered something in Memori's heart. She worked so hard to shield Elowen from the harsh realities of their world, to keep her safe from grief and loss. Yet here they were—trapped aboard a ship, watching a man who had saved them slip toward death. And for a terrifying moment, she was kneeling beside her mother's bed, gripping her hand as life bled away. The scent of medicine and damp linen filled her lungs, her mother's rasping breath echoing in her ears. She promised herself she would never feel that powerless again.

But here she was, breath stolen from her, frozen in place as if the past was back to claim her. And the worst part—the part she couldn't rationalize—was how much it hurt. Orson was practically a stranger. He had no claim on her heart. And yet grief swelled inside her, vast and merciless, drowning her in the same helplessness she had fought so hard to forget.

Memori Wren! Stop feeling sorry for yourself. Her mother's voice echoed in her mind, clear as day. The memory struck her like lightning—her mother's smile as she lay dying, refusing the very gift she now pressed into Memori's hands. *It is not for me, child. You will know the right time to use it– you're a healer.* Was this her mother nudging her from beyond the grave? Memori's fingers closed around the stone pendant as she watched Orson's chest rise and fall with increasing effort. She smoothed Elowen's curls, noting how her daughter clung to Orson's hand like she'd known him forever. "Baby, I need you to stay here with Orson." Memori hugged her daughter tight. "Will you do that for me?"

Elowen nodded, wiping tears with the back of her hand. "Yes, Mama."

"Good girl." Memori jumped to her feet and bolted for the door. Her mother was right. She wasn't helpless. She was a healer, and she'd be damned if she'd watch another person slip away when she had the power to stop it.

The interior of the Crimson Ghost had become a maze of shadow and chaos. Every step away from Elowen sent waves of panic through her chest. She'd never forgive herself if something happened while they were separated—if someone found her daughter alone, vulnerable. The thought of one of Kol's men still aboard the ship made her stomach turn.

Like the night they found Mae.

She'd been hiding in the cellar when they dragged the young healer out into the street. Mae couldn't have been more than sixteen. Memori had pressed her hands over her ears, trying to drown out the screams, telling herself there was nothing she could do. She'd stayed there, trembling in the dark, while Mae's tortured cries grew weaker and the crackling of flames grew louder. In the end, she'd been no better than the other villagers who'd barred their doors and shuttered their windows.

Never again.

The ship's tilting corridors forced Memori to career from wall to wall as she scrambled desperately toward her room, panic driving her forward despite the treacherous footing. Smashed bottles and spilled potions painted the floor—casualties of the ship's violent launch from its clifftop perch, and Kol's men searching for Orson no doubt. Each second away from Elowen felt like torture, but each moment of delay could be Orson's last.

Finally, she reached her quarters. The room she shared with Elowen was in disarray, but Memori knew exactly what she sought. Dropping to her knees, she pried up the loose floorboard where she kept her most precious possessions. There lay her mother's herbal codex, and beneath it, wrapped in plain brown paper and tied with butcher's twine, the last gift her mother had given her.

The memory washed over her as she clutched the package…

"Do you remember the story I told about the legend of the Specter's Mercy Tree?" Her mother's voice had been weak that day, but her eyes still sparkled with mystery.

"It's the rarest tree in the Seven Realms," Memori had answered, trying to hide her pain.

"The roots are said to tap into the well of eternal youth."

"Those are just stories, Ma." Memori had been too tired for fairy tales then, too wrapped in grief.

"Are they?" Her mother had produced the small packet from beneath her quilts, unwrapping it with trembling fingers to reveal a section of root unlike anything Memori had ever seen. It was white as ivory, twisted in intricate patterns that spoke of centuries absorbing ancient power. When Memori turned it over, delicate luminescent veins had pulsed with subtle radiance at her touch, as if recognizing a healer's presence.

"It's real!" she'd gasped.

Her mother had closed Memori's hands over the Mercy Oak root. "A gift. For you."

"But, Ma! Why can't we—"

"No, child." Her mother's head had shaken firmly before sinking back into her pillow. *"Not for me."*

Now, standing in her lurching quarters aboard the Crimson Ghost, Memori held that same root in her trembling hands. The veins still pulsed with that otherworldly light at her touch, as if it had been waiting all these years for this moment. For him.

"I hope I'm doing the right thing, Ma," she whispered, her heart racing with equal parts fear and determination. This gift—this treasure her mother had refused to use on herself—Memori would use it to save a man she barely knew. "I can't let him die. Not when I can stop it." She clutched the root to her chest and ran back through the swaying ship. The sooner she reached Orson, the sooner she could return to Elowen. She wouldn't let herself fail either of them—not like she'd failed Mae.

Chapter 8

Orson

Memori. What a beautiful name. Orson reached out to touch her, said something–he was unsure what. His side was throbbing with persistent, burning pain. Was he on fire? No. He was too cold for that–freezing, in fact. Damnation, he wanted to vomit! The sky was spinning. He probably didn't have much longer to live. If he was honest, he hadn't expected to make it this far.

Blinking his eyes back up, he said something else to the girl…his vision narrowing until she was the only thing there; bright, like an…angel! That was the word. God, she was beautiful! Hair like mahogany, eyes entrancing bronze. Something was wrong, though…tears streamed down her face. Deep inside him, anger flared. What absolute ass was responsible for making her cry? They would pay once he found them!

Light faded, and the girl was gone. Orson's anger faded with her and he wondered if she had ever been there at all.

IT STARTED MONTHS ago with the first attack. Luckily, no one was with him when the sudden onslaught of pain hit–crushing the air from his lungs and causing him to fall from his horse.

He was lucky to make it to the Vanguard healer–a stooped old man called Henry. Everyone knew these conventional healers weren't worth a damn, but there wasn't an unlicensed one in Cibola who would see a soldier. He didn't blame them. After the examples they made of those caught, he'd trust no one wearing a uniform either.

"I'm sorry, Guardsman Irons. There's nothing we can do." The well-meaning but useless physician gave him a sympathetic frown to go with the grim diagnosis, and a packet of white pills to help cope with the pain. Since then, there was a lingering sting on the left side of his chest–a constant reminder his days were numbered. Orson kept it to himself. That bastard commander would probably have him put down like a lame horse if he found out. And all that was just the first problem. The second, and more pressing, was the old man Conrad Kol was trying to extract information from in front of the Guardhouse. It was a fisherman by the name of James Dollan, who was from the same village Orson grew up in.

Clouds hung low, heavy with moisture, as the first droplets began their descent. Raindrops danced on the river's surface and wind jostled the trees. It would have been a calming scene were the view from the town he grew up in, rather than the Vanguard outpost.

It's funny how a terminal diagnosis changes one's outlook. Orson wondered after, would he have acted differently with a clean bill of health and the promise of likely old age? He hoped not.

"Hey!" Orson left the door of the barracks and into the rain. "Hey!" As they ignored him, he grabbed one of the Guardsman, spun him around and punched him in the jaw. "What the ever loving hells is wrong with you? He's a harmless old man!" He stopped Dollan from landing in the mud, becoming aware of the Commander's savage glare.

"Irons. What in God's name do you think you're doing?"

Orson used his shoulder to keep the old man from falling. "I've known him all my life, Commander–he's just a fisherman."

The two corporals looked worriedly at Kol for direction, poised to seize Orson. To their surprise, Kol had a different idea in mind. "Is that so?" He snapped his fingers at the Corporal to his left and motioned to his rifle. The man tossed it to Orson, who caught it with his free hand. "Make him talk, Irons." There was a cruel smile on his face as he raised his voice to carry above the pounding rain. "If he doesn't…make sure he never talks again." Kol looked like he meant to walk away–probably to dry himself by a fire — certain Orson wouldn't dare disobey orders. Just like he'd obeyed the conscription papers when they came to order him off to join the Union.

A spark of anger flared in Orson's chest, and he straightened. "I'll do no such thing, you maggot-tongued son of an aristocratic trollop!" He hurled the rifle at Kol and it struck him before either of the corporals could grab it. "A brainsick dog with a broken leg could give better orders than you!"

"Are you quite finished signing your death warrant, Guardsman?" Kol yelled, fuming, his cool-blue eyes flashing.

Orson paused, raindrops stinging his eyes as he glanced upward to think. "You're a piece of shit. Oh–and no woman would have you if they didn't fear the Union. Oh–and–" The blow across his head sent him sliding in the mud. "I hope I didn't forget anything," he muttered as he was dragged from the ground and hauled into the Guardhouse.

Moonlight streamed through the bars on the only window, allowing air into the building. Sprawled on the straw-covered floor of the cell, Orson touched his swollen lip, tasting blood and mud. Saying what had been on his mind for ages was worth the beating. But he hadn't expected to still be alive after all that. The seven gods had a cruel sense of humor.

"Orson," the old man rasped in the cell next to him. Orson rolled over onto his stomach, forced himself to his knees, and crawled to the bars that separated them.

The old man's eye was swollen shut, and his left leg twisted into an unnatural position, bone fragments jutting out. "By the Union," he breathed out in horror. They had done a number on the fisherman. "I'm sorry, Mr. Dollan," Orson whispered, wishing he could help.

"Orson, lad…" Dollan's voice was weak. He was holding his worn shoe in his quivering fingers; he thrust it through the bars at Orson with the last of his strength.

"What is it?" Orson picked up the ragged shoe. There was a tear in the lining and he worked it the rest of the way open. A strange stone pendant attached to a golden chain fell into his hand. When moonlight struck the rock, it swirled like waves of the sea.

"Listen carefully, boy…" Dollan spoke with great effort–every word holding weight. "I've a story to tell you."

MEMORI. HER NAME floated through his mind like a lifeline. Orson tried to reach for her, words tumbling from his lips though he couldn't make sense of them. The burning in his side had become an inferno, yet he was shivering, his bones aching with cold. His stomach lurched, and the sky—was there a sky?—spun above him like a child's top.

This was it, then. Death finally caught up with him. Though, he'd survived longer than any physician predicted. A bitter laugh tried to rise in his throat but emerged as a groan instead.

The memory shattered as consciousness dragged him back. Something bitter-sweet flooded his mouth, and he felt cool fingers against his brow. Memori again, but this time he knew she was real—her touch anchored him as liquid fire spread through his chest.

It felt like roots were growing through him, burning through every vein, every muscle. He thought he was fighting someone, his own screams distant and strange in his ears. Then something slammed into his chest, and he surged upward, gasping, his hands instinctively grasping slender wrists. Her face swam into focus, annoyed and determined and beautiful. "Stop fighting me, you idiot! I'm trying to help you."

"I–I'm sorry." His fingers loosened their grip as strength deserted him. He collapsed back onto what felt like a pile of blankets, trying to make sense of where he was. The armory. They were in the ship's armory. Reality tried to assert itself, but then he saw blue eyes watching him—Kol's eyes?—no, softer, framed by copper curls. "El?" he managed, but darkness was already pulling him under again.

A voice followed him down into the dark: "Her name isn't El."

Memori

MEMORI'S HANDS TREMBLED as she measured out the last precious grains of the powdered root. It wasn't enough—she knew it wasn't. The bitter tea might ease his passing, but that wasn't good enough. She couldn't watch another person die, not when she could still feel the phantom weight of her mother's cooling hand in hers. She pressed the cup to his lips, forcing him to drink. The liquid was bitter and sweet, stinging his tongue and warming his throat as he swallowed. When she placed her hands over his heart, trying to feel if the medicine was working, something shifted inside her—like a door opening in a room she hadn't known existed.

Warmth bloomed beneath her palms, different from ordinary body heat. It pulsed in time with his heartbeat, but more than that, she could feel his pain, his fear, his determination to live despite believing he was dying. The intensity of the connection terrified her. This wasn't supposed to happen. The Mercy Oak was just medicine, not… whatever this was.

She tried to pull away, but her hands wouldn't move. Or couldn't. Something was flowing from her into him, like water finding its way through parched earth, seeking every broken place inside him. His hands seized her wrists as his back arched off the floor, and suddenly she could feel everything—the weakness in his heart, the damage spreading through his body; the life flickering like a candle in the wind.

"Stop fighting me, you idiot!" The words tore from her throat, though she wasn't sure if she was talking to Orson or to herself, to this impossible thing happening between them. "I'm trying to help you."

His grip loosened, and he collapsed back onto the pile of blankets. Without conscious thought, her fingers began tracing patterns over his chest, following paths she somehow knew but didn't understand. The blue-black veins spreading across his skin faded beneath her touch, like ink washing away in rain. His flesh grew hot, burning against her palms as if tree roots of pure fire were spreading beneath his skin, mending what was broken.

Sweat beaded on his forehead as color returned to his face. She tried to tell herself it was just the Mercy Oak working, just as her mother had described. But her mother had never mentioned this—this bone-deep connection, this terrible intimacy of feeling someone else's life force entwine with her own.

For one terrifying moment, she couldn't tell where her heartbeat ended, and his began. She jerked her hands back, breaking the connection, but the echo of it lingered. His heart now beat strong, and she could still feel it, like a second rhythm beneath her skin.

She stared at her hands in the dim light, half-expecting them to look different. They appeared unchanged, but they felt altered, awakened to something she didn't dare name. Something that let her reach into someone and knit them back together—that was impossible.

Wasn't it?

"Memma?" The small voice made Memori start. Elowen stood at her side. "You're shaking," Elowen said, taking a tentative step forward. Her eyes moved to Orson's still form. "Did you make him better?"

Memori quickly wiped her hands on her skirts, as if she could erase the lingering sensation of that connection. "I… yes, love. He'll be alright now."

"You look scared." Elowen moved closer, her bare feet silent on the wooden planks. She reached for Memori's hand—the same hand that just channeled whatever that power had been—and Memori had to force herself not to pull away from her daughter's touch.

"I'm not scared," Memori lied, managing a smile. "Just tired." She squeezed Elowen's small fingers, grateful for their familiar warmth that helped ground her back in the normal world.

As she gathered Elowen close, her daughter's eyes still fixed on Orson's face, Memori couldn't help but notice how his breathing synchronized with hers, as if some part of her was still connected to him, still holding him safely in this world. "Memma?" Elowen leaned in, whispering in Memori's ear. "Can I give him a kiss to make him feel better?"

Memori smiled at the girl's sweet suggestion. "I think he would like that," she brushed Elowen's hair before releasing her hug. Elowen bent over, gently pressing her lips to Orson's forehead before standing back, looking satisfied. "There," she said, looking like she had completed an important task.

"I'm sure he'll feel much better now," Memori assured her, before guiding Elowen toward their makeshift bed. Better to focus on the solid reality of her daughter's needs than on the inconceivable things her hands seemed capable of doing. Better to be simply 'Memma' than whatever she just became.

Chapter 9

Orson

The first thing Orson noticed was the silence in his chest—the gnawing quiver in his pulse that haunted him for months was gone, replaced by a steady, strong heartbeat that felt almost foreign. Light flickered from a lantern in the corner, catching on copper strands in Memori's hair where she lay curled on a makeshift bed of linens, the child nestled against her like a small bird. The scene made his chest ache differently.

His stomach growled at the sight of a half-eaten potato on a plate near an empty teapot. How long had they watched over him? He threw off the blankets, pushing himself up on trembling arms. The movement made Memori's eyes snap open, alert despite obvious exhaustion.

"You're awake!" She extracted herself from Elowen's sleeping form, crawling toward him. "How do you feel?" Her hand pressed against his forehead. "I thought you were a dead man, for sure."

"So did I." His fingers found his chest, pressing where the pain should have been. Nothing. "Memori... what did you give me?" His mind reeled at a recovery that defied explanation.

She settled back, fatigue evident in every line of her body. "Specter Mercy Oak; a rare medicine. My mother left it to me." A yawn escaped as she gathered scattered dishes.

"Specter Mercy Oak!" He knew its worth—knew it was reserved for aristocrats who could buy their way past death. "And you used it on me?" Horror crept through him as lantern light caught the dark bruises circling her wrists. Bruises he'd put there, no doubt, fighting against her help like a wild animal. Guilt swelled in him. "Why? How could you waste such a precious thing on me?"

Her scowl should have withered him on the spot. "A healer's duty is to the nearest injured, no exceptions," she snapped, stacking dishes as if his guilt meant nothing to her. "Besides, I'm stuck on this ship, headed who-knows-where, with zero sailing skills—or had you forgotten?" The lopsided smirk playing on her lips made his heart skip a beat.

Orson sat there, staring absently at the floor, the weight of everything crashing down on him at once. He ran both hands through his hair, trying to stave off the terrible, gnawing remorse that ate at his core. This is all my fault. His groan echoed in the quiet armory. He'd dragged them into this mess—a healer and a child—and now they were fugitives because of him.

When Memori returned with a fresh cup of water, he tried to stand, swaying slightly. "Memori, listen–about everything…I didn't mean for this…"

"It's fine." Her cheeks flushed as she steadied him with one hand, placing the cup in his other. "I'm better off than I was, anyway."

The casual comment struck him like a blade between the ribs. Her voice carried no bitterness, no accusation—and that made it worse. Memories flooded back with savage clarity: whispered conversations in the barracks, the way the other Guardsmen would joke about the Commander's "moods" improving whenever he found a new girl to pursue. The way they'd all looked away, pretending not to notice. The way he'd looked away too, telling himself there was nothing he could do.

Water caught in his throat as realization hit, sending him into a coughing fit. Memori took the cup, offering a towel which he could barely bring himself to accept. Every kind gesture from her felt like another weight on his conscience. How many others had he failed with his silence? "You should be resting, not waiting on me."

Memori waved away his protest. "You'll be well soon enough. Oh–here." She held out the pendant, and when her fingertips grazed his palm, something electric shot through him. For a moment, he wanted nothing more than to catch her hand, to tell her everything would be alright. But he had no right to make such promises.

"I'll fetch us something to eat." As she left him alone again, he stared at the cerulean swirls in the stone, its patterns as turbulent as his thoughts. One problem solved—his miraculous recovery—but two more had taken its place.

Movement caught his eye as Elowen stirred in her sleep. Those eyes of hers—he'd seen them before, hadn't he? The same startling blue, but in a face hardened by cruelty rather than softened by childhood innocence. The possibility made his blood run cold.

Forcing himself to stand, he noticed his coat folded neatly on a barrel. Someone–Memori–had washed out the blood, each stain treated with careful attention. The bullet hole was mended with tiny, precise stitches, so fine they were almost invisible. She'd even reinforced the worn edges of the sleeves, as if the coat belonged to someone worth taking care of. Even his laundry—she'd thought of everything while he'd lain there useless like a bitter orange, while he'd been nothing but a burden. His stomach knotted with mounting self-reproach. Such kindness was more than he warranted.

His hands shook as he pulled on his boots, breath catching. The walls of the armory seemed to close in around him, heavy with the weight of debts he could never repay and secrets he wasn't ready to face. He had to see it—had to know this was real, that they'd actually escaped. That he hadn't dreamed it all while dying in some Union cell.

Stumbling out of the armory, he clung to the railing, each step a battle between weakness and determination. The corridor stretched endlessly before him, the ship's ancient timbers creaking a song of freedom he hardly dared believe.

First light spilled across the ocean's edge in colors of soft pink and apricot bleeding into warm golds. The sea mirrored the sky's canvas, each wave catching light like scattered gems.

"The Avalon Sea." Memori appeared beside him, the wind tugging strands of hair from her braid. "You shouldn't be up yet."

A silent laugh escaped him. "How many days has it been? Since we left Stonegate." His grip tightened on the wood as weakness trembled through his legs.

"Ten," she answered simply.

"And no sign of the Seawind?"

"None." She drew in the chilled morning air, eyes narrowing at the horizon. "I never imagined I'd see such a stunning sight."

The sunrise had turned her hair to living gold, like spring earth woven with morning light. "Stunning," he agreed, then caught himself, stepping away, tension coiling in his stomach. "There's something I have to tell you… about the trawler."

"What about it?" She stretched, stifling another yawn, and her sleeve slipped. The sight of those fading bruises on her wrists made him flinch. Maybe this could wait.

"You should rest first."

Her scowl was both fierce and endearing. "Would you just tell me what–"

She turned mid-sentence; her scream pierced the quiet dawn. Orson moved without thinking, years of training taking over. His arm went around her as she stumbled back against him, her fingers clutching at his sleeve. He shifted to put himself between her and whatever startled her, ignoring the protest of his weakened muscles. He'd failed to protect others before—he wouldn't fail again. Not her. Not the child sleeping below deck. His body moved to shield Memori before his mind fully registered the threat, even as some part of him recognized the absurdity of trying to protect someone when he barely had the strength to stand.

A boy seemed to materialize from the morning mist like a spirit from the sea itself. Water cascaded from his clothes, creating dark pools at his bare feet on the weathered deck. Black hair plastered to his face, and through the soaked bangs, dark eyes watched them with an unnerving steadiness no child should possess. The sight sent a chill down Orson's spine. "Hells, boy! Where did you come from?" The words escaped him before he could think better of them.

He felt Memori's grip on his sleeve loosen as her healer's instincts overcame her shock. She stepped forward, slipping from his protective grip, though he noticed her hands trembling slightly. "Are you alright? You must be freezing!"

"Nobody move!" The command cracked through the air like a whip.

Orson's heart lurched as he spun toward the voice, pulling Memori behind him once more. She pressed against his back, and he could feel her quick, shallow breaths. A figure emerged from the shadows, standing with easy balance, the wind tugging at his worn coat like dark wings. A silver earring glinted at his left ear, but Orson's eyes fixed on the curved short-swords that caught the dawn light with deadly promise. "Where's the captain?" The stranger's accent carried something ancient in it, something that didn't belong in these waters.

"The captain's dead." Orson felt Memori's fingers dig into his arm at his words, as if warning him to choose his next ones carefully.

"But he left me something to give you!" He raised his hands slowly, painfully aware of how exposed they were. Behind him, he heard Memori's sharp intake of breath. "It's in my coat pocket."

The man's dark gaze shifted past them to the dripping boy. One sharp nod was all it took. The boy moved like water itself, silent despite his sodden state. As he approached, Memori shifted closer to Orson, her presence warm against his back. Small fingers slipped into his pocket, withdrawing the golden chain. The pendant caught the sunrise, its cerulean swirls seeming to move in the light.

The armed man's stance shifted, subtle as a change in the wind. The short-swords disappeared into their sheaths, but his eyes remained sharp as drawn blades. "What name do you go by?"

Orson felt caught between threat and ceremony, though he couldn't have said why. "Irons," he answered carefully. "Orson Irons."

"Captain Irons." The man spoke the title like it was both gift and burden. "Victor Sloan, first mate of the Seawind, at your service."

"Viggo Sloan." The boy pressed the pendant back into Orson's startled hand. "At your service, Captain."

Orson took a step back, the taffrail pressing into his spine. The solid wood was the only thing keeping him upright as exhaustion crept back into his limbs. "Hang on—there's been an epic mistake."

"No mistake." Something like regret flickered across Victor's weathered features before vanishing behind that mask of stern authority. "The one who holds the tide stone is captain of the Ghost." He gestured to the sides of the ship, and as if summoned by his words, five more figures emerged from over the railings, landing on the deck. Three men and one woman, all carrying themselves with the same dangerous competence as their first mate. "And we are the crew sworn to the Ghost."

The crew formed a loose semicircle, arms folded, faces set in varying degrees of displeasure as they studied their supposed new captain. But when Victor spoke of the oath, they all nodded as one. "I'm a Union deserter!" Orson protested, feeling Memori press closer to his side as the crew closed in. His voice cracked with desperation. "An old fisherman gave it to me as he lay dying in a Vanguard cell."

"Did he tell you what it was?" The woman with intricate braids woven with glinting trinkets stepped forward, something almost hopeful in her tone.

The world seemed to compress around him, the deck tilting beneath his feet. A lie hovered on his tongue, but one look at the crew's faces told him deception would only make things worse. Memori was in enough danger already—he couldn't risk adding to it. The Ghost was a pirate ship, after all, and for all the romanticized stories and children's tales that tried to make light of them, pirates weren't to be fucked with. "Yes." The admission felt like surrender. His legs trembled beneath him, and he locked his knees to stay standing.

"Then the captain, you are." Victor's voice rose to carry across the deck as he turned to his crew. "To your stations— the captain need not waste anymore words on you—make ready to sail. Bring the Ghost up to standard!" They scattered like seabirds before a gale, one scaling the rigging like a spider, another taking the helm. Victor approached, and Orson shifted to keep Memori behind him, though his vision was starting to swim at the edges. "Now, Captain," Victor's voice dropped low, meant for Orson's ears alone, "care to tell me why you've been navigating in circles for the past three days?"

A cold rush swept through Orson's head, the world tilting dangerously. "Probably because I'm a soldier, and don't have the first sodding clue about sailing." The admission took the last of his strength. His knees buckled, and he felt Memori's arms trying to catch him as he slipped toward the deck. Victor's face swam above him, features twisted in what might have been exasperation. The last thing he felt was Memori's hands pressed against his chest, that strange warmth trying to hold him in the waking world, before darkness claimed him completely.

Chapter 10

Memori

Memori wrung her hands as she watched the broad-shouldered sailor lift Orson like he weighed nothing. The morning fog clung to the Ghost's rigging, wreathing the deck in shifting shadows. Her heart hammered against her ribs as a single thought consumed her: Elowen. What would these strangers do if they found her daughter?

She felt Victor's gaze before she saw it, heavy as a storm cloud. When she turned, she found him studying her, Orson still slung across his shoulders. Salt-stained leather creaked as he shifted his stance. "You're a healer."

Familiar fear clawed up her throat—the same terror she'd felt whenever anyone in Cibola had discovered her craft. Color drained from her face as she managed a weak, "Yes."

Victor's brow furrowed, irritation rippling just beneath his controlled expression. "You won't be harmed. We are not part of the Blacksmoke Union's idiotic laws." His voice shifted, becoming almost gentle. "Healers are honored among us. And from what I gather, the captain here still has need of your services."

Memori gave a short nod, swallowing her fear down. "Come with me." He made a swift motion with his free hand.

She followed him down below, each step along the narrow companionway increasing her dread. The Ghost's passages twisted like a maze, the old wood groaning with each roll of the waves. Every shadow might hide danger, every creak of timber a reminder that they were at these strangers' mercy. Through gaps in the planking, she glimpsed the water rushing past the hull, carrying them further from everything familiar.

When Victor shouldered open the captain's cabin door, relief flooded through her. There stood Viggo, holding Elowen's small hand in his as if he'd known exactly where to find her. "Memma!" Elowen launched herself into Memori's arms. Victor's expression didn't change at the child's presence, though something flickered in his eyes as he laid Orson on the bunk.

"Rest," he commanded. His gaze lingered on Orson's face a moment too long. "I'll have food sent shortly." He turned to leave, but paused in the doorway, his shoulders tense. For a moment, it seemed he might say something more. Instead, he shook his head and strode away, muttering about getting the ship in order.

The boy followed at Victor's heels, pulling the door closed with a gentle click. In the sudden quiet, Memori sank into the chair beside Orson's bunk, her legs trembling with relief. The cabin swayed gently with the ship's motion, lantern light catching on brass fittings and casting dancing shadows across the charts on the walls.

"Are we going to be ok, Momma?" Elowen whispered, her small mouth curved with worry.

Memori didn't correct the slip. Instead, she pulled her daughter close, smoothing those wild curls, and tried to sound confident. "Of course, Baby. The Guardians called these sailors from the depths of the waters." She made her voice dramatic, weaving together Elowen's favorite bedtime stories. "They're here to sail us to safety."

"Really?" Elowen's eyes narrowed with suspicion. "But those are just stories."

"Really." Memori settled Elowen in the chair, though her own stomach churned with uncertainty. "No more questions for now, alright?"

The door hinges creaked, making them both start. But it was only Viggo again, returning with a tray laden with food— a jug of water, bowls of tinned stew, and slices of bread that had seen better days. His dark eyes watched them with that unnerving steadiness as he set the tray on the bedside table. Without a word, he slipped away like a shadow.

Memori's hands shook as she poured water from the jug. Elowen happily tore into a piece of bread, but Memori couldn't bring herself to eat. The gentle lap of waves against the hull only reminded her how far they were from shore, from any hope of escape, if these sailors proved as dangerous as the ones Union soldiers.

"Memori?" Orson's voice was rough with sleep as he stirred.

She nearly dropped the water jug in her haste to reach him. "Here, drink this."

He struggled to sit up, taking the water with unsteady hands. As he lifted his arm to run fingers through his hair, he stopped short—the pendant wound around his hand, its cerulean swirls catching the lantern light.

"Shit," he muttered, as if his hopes of dreaming this whole thing had just shattered.

Her headache pounded harder as she stared at the stone. "Did you know this would happen?" She gestured at their opulent prison. "When you gave me that stone?"

"No."

"Really?" Heat flashed through her. "Because you gave that damned thing to me when you thought you were dying! What was I supposed to do with it?"

"I swear I only knew they wouldn't harm you if you had it." Orson's frustrated groan turned into a wince. "The fisherman who gave it to me—Dollan—he left out some important details, it would seem."

"The man Kol wanted you to kill?" She cringed at saying the commander's name.

"Yes." Orson's voice grew hoarse. "He was from my village. Odd old man kept to himself. Never unfriendly, though." His brow furrowed as his hand slid forward on the blanket. For a moment, she thought he meant to take hers.

A shadow darkened the doorway, and Orson's hand stilled. Viggo had returned, but this time he wasn't alone. The man who filled the doorframe seemed to make the cabin shrink around them. He stood well over six feet, his muscled frame wrapped in a weathered leather jacket. A beard reached to his chest, meticulously braided with beads and tarnished charms that caught the light.

"Finnian Sea Wolf Sullivan, at your service." His voice boomed in the confined space as he swept off his tricorn hat, offering Orson a mock bow. "Captain." The title dripped with careful irony. Even the smirk playing across his sun-weathered face suggested he answered to only one man aboard this ship—and it wasn't Orson.

His boots struck the planks like thunder as he stepped inside. "Ms. Memori," he inclined his head with exaggerated courtesy. "My young friend here 'll take you to see our First Mate. He needs to speak with you."

Fear seized her chest. Beside her, Orson threw off his blanket. "The hell he will!" He tried to stand, swaying dangerously. "She'll not go anywhere she doesn't want to, Seadog Sully, or whatever the hell your name is!"

Sullivan's laugh rolled through the cabin. He pulled back his jacket, revealing the pistol and cutlass at his belt. "Behave yourself, Captain. I have my orders, and all I really have to do is sit on you and there's nothing you can do about it."

Orson's glare could have set the sea itself ablaze, but he still needed one hand on the bed to keep himself upright. Memori jumped up, pressing her palm against his chest. "I'll go." She forced calm into her voice despite her racing heart.

His eyes locked with hers as he caught her hand, and though his fingers trembled with weakness, she read the fury in his grip. "You don't have to."

"I'll be fine." Heat crept up her neck at the intensity of his gaze. His fingers tightened briefly before reluctantly releasing her. "Elowen, stay with Orson, okay? I'll be back soon." She prayed her daughter couldn't hear the fear beneath her words.

Elowen nodded, shifting closer to Orson. Despite his condition, seeing his arm settle protectively around the girl's shoulders sent a wave of relief through Memori.

"Viggo," Orson's voice cut through the tension. "If any harm comes to her, you tell your sea-crazy, merman of a leader his head is mine!"

The boy nodded, as if receiving a simple message about the weather. But Memori caught how Sullivan's face darkened at the mention of the first mate, his massive arms crossing tight against his chest. "Off you go, lad." His voice grew gruff with something like concern. "First mate's waiting."

It took every ounce of strength Memori possessed to appear unafraid as she followed Viggo, giving Orson one last look before the cabin door closed between them. The ancient wood creaked beneath their feet as they climbed toward the upper deck. Through gaps in the planking, she glimpsed water rushing past the hull, glinting like scattered silver in the morning light.

The breeze hit her face as they emerged into the open air. Ropes creaked overhead, the ship's rigging a complex web against the pale sky. Victor stood at the helm, his commanding voice carrying easily as he called orders to his crew. The muscles in his arms strained against the rope of the mainsail, but when his gaze caught on Viggo, something dark and profound passed across his weathered features.

He switched places with his son mechanically, his hand lingering a moment too long on the boy's hair, as if steadying himself. When he turned to face her, the intensity of his stare made her want to shrink back. There was something in his eyes she couldn't name—a weight, a wound, something that made her feel like she was being measured against a ghost she couldn't see.

"Forgive me if our arrival unsettled you, Miss…" His voice was rough, like he had to force the words past some invisible barrier.

"Just Memori," she offered when he waited, hating how small her voice sounded. She didn't understand why speaking her name made him go so still, his hands clenching at his sides.

Victor's face transformed for a moment into something raw and haunted before he masked it. His hand moved to the small of her back with a strange familiarity, compelling her to walk at his side. The touch seemed to startle him as much as her, and he withdrew it. "I wanted to speak with you about the captain." There appeared a twitch at the corner of his eye, something violent and barely contained.

Her heart pounded harder with each step. What did he really want? Would he be like Kol? Tears threatened at the corners of her eyes as she walked beside him, acutely aware of how his steps seemed to falter whenever he glanced her way. "How is he?" His voice was carefully controlled now.

"Oh," she cleared her throat, searching for steady ground. "He should be fine with rest and some decent food."

Victor paused, trying to hide the shudder running through him. "Thank you." When he turned to her, the naked emotion in his eyes made her want to step back. "We will need supplies soon. Let me know if there is anything you need and I will get it for you."

A tear escaped down her cheek as she nodded, overwhelmed by the intensity of this stranger's regard. Victor frowned as he considered her, and when he took her chin in his hand, the gesture felt oddly intimate coming from someone she'd just met. She froze, uncertain, watching confusion war with something else in his expression. Her eyes clamped shut involuntarily as her chest contracted–like when Kol touched her.

He withdrew his touch like her skin burned him, his breathing uneven. "I want you to know you are not a prisoner aboard this ship." The ship's horn echoed through the air, and Victor's attention snapped toward the commotion on deck, though she noticed how he seemed to force himself to look away from her. "You and your sister are safe with us."

He gave her a quick nod of dismissal and turned on his heel, but not before she caught sight of the moisture in his eyes. The rhythmic creaking of the ship resumed, and as Memori slowly made her way back to the captain's cabin, she couldn't shake the feeling that she'd witnessed a private agony—a grief too raw and profound to be spoken aloud, born from a loss she had yet to understand.

Chapter 11

Orson

Orson paced the small cabin like a caged animal, each step a battle against the weakness in his legs. The constant roll of the ship beneath his feet didn't help, but it was better than sitting still while Memori was out there alone with these pirates. Sullivan watched him from the doorway, amusement playing across his face, but Orson refused to give the bastard the satisfaction of seeing him falter.

His hands clenched into fists at his sides. He was too used to living on borrowed time, to counting the days until his heart gave out. But now… now there was something worse than dying. The thought of anything happening to Memori or Elowen made him hollow inside, made his blood run cold.

"Finnian Sea Dog Sullivan," he said, letting contempt color his voice. "Your friends give you that name, or you pick it on purpose?" He kept his peripheral vision on Elowen, who sat quietly on the bunk pretending to read the book he'd found in the nightstand.

Sullivan's low chuckle grated on his nerves. "Nicknames are earned on this crew, Captain."

"Is that a fact?" Orson watched Elowen turn a page, her small fingers trembling slightly. His protective instinct flared, making his words sharper than intended. "And how exactly does one *earn* a name such as that?"

The big man pulled out a folding knife, methodically cleaning his nails as if Orson wasn't worth his attention. The dismissal made his blood boil, but he forced himself to stay calm for Elowen's sake. His fingers drummed against his knee, betraying his agitation even as he fought to keep his voice steady.

"It seems to me," he continued, carefully measuring each word, "a dog follows orders. A well-trained one, at least." He shifted his weight, subtly placing himself between Sullivan and Elowen. "So whose dog are you then? The ingrate who throws orders around? *Victor*?"

He saw the darkness pass over Sullivan's face at Victor's name—a crack in that carefully maintained indifference. Like a fighter spotting an opening, Orson pressed his advantage, even as his instincts screamed at him to stop.

"Ah, there it is." Orson knew he should stop—it was the same voice in his head he'd ignored countless times before, usually right before someone had to pull him out of trouble. But like always, he pushed harder instead. "Victor's faithful hound. Tell me, Sullivan—what does your master want with her? With Memori?"

Sullivan's knife snapped shut with an ominous click. "Watch your tongue," he growled, all pretense of civility vanishing. "You have bigger worries than your Union harlot, *Vanguard*."

The slur against Memori made something snap inside him. If he'd been at full strength, he'd have torn Sullivan apart for daring to speak of her that way—especially with Elowen in the room. But his body was betraying him, so his tongue would have to do. Some distant part of him recognized this familiar rush toward disaster, the same reckless anger that had gotten him into countless scrapes growing up. But he couldn't stop himself.

"Yeah? Maybe Victor's more your kind of harlot, eh, Sullivan?"

He knew it was coming, but Sullivan moved faster than his size suggested possible. The big man's hand closed around his throat, lifting him off his feet and slamming him into the hull. The impact knocked the air from his lungs as thick fingers crushed his windpipe. He clawed at Sullivan's grip, but his already weakened body betrayed him. Dark spots danced at the edges of his vision.

"Stop!" Elowen's scream pierced through the roaring in his ears. She launched herself at Sullivan, her small fists pounding against him as she wielded her book like a weapon. "Don't hurt him!"

The raw fear in her voice tore at his heart. He renewed his struggles, desperate to protect her, to get her away from danger. What kind of idiot was he, provoking this fight with a child in the room?

"What the hell are you doing?" Memori's voice cut through the chaos like a blade. She stood in the doorway, her face red with fury, one hand already reaching for the knife at her belt.

Sullivan released his grip and Orson collapsed, gasping for air. Through watering eyes, he watched Memori step between them, her stance protective despite the way her hands trembled. His throat burned with more than just pain—shame mixed with a fierce sort of pride at her courage, even as he cursed himself for putting her in this position.

Sullivan's laugh rolled through the cabin. He hauled Orson up roughly, setting him on the bed with more force than necessary. "You're certainly fucking lucky, Irons—charmed, the sea witch might say." He plucked Elowen off his back with surprisingly gentle hands, setting her aside like a kitten that had tried to challenge a bear.

As he passed Memori, he tipped his hat with exaggerated courtesy. "Healer."

The moment Sullivan disappeared, Memori rushed to Orson's side, her hands fluttering over him with barely contained panic. Elowen pressed against his other side, her small body trembling. The feel of them both near him, safe, made his head spin with relief stronger than the pain in his throat. But his eyes fixed on Memori's face, searching for any sign of distress or harm from her meeting with Victor.

"Are you alright?" Her voice shook slightly as her fingers ghosted over the bruises forming on his neck. "I should get something for—"

"What did Victor want?" He cut her off, his voice hoarse but urgent. He caught her wrist gently, stilling her ministrations. "Did he threaten you? Touch you?" His grip tightened slightly at the thought, though he immediately loosened it.

"Orson, I'm fine," Memori said softly. A flush crept up her neck as she met his intense gaze. "You're the one who was just—"

"I don't care about that." He struggled to sit up straighter, ignoring the fire in his throat. "Just… tell me you're alright."

"He called you a—" Elowen started, but Orson quickly cleared his throat.

"Not now, El," he said gently, giving her a reassuring smile despite his worry. "Rude bastard shouldn't have talked that way around a child," he muttered, though his own language hadn't been much better.

The mattress dipped as Memori sat beside him, and suddenly Orson was acutely aware of her presence—the faint scent of herbs that clung to her hair, the warmth radiating from her skin, the way her hands still trembled slightly despite her calm facade. Each detail seemed to penetrate the deepest corners of his mind, like the tide finding its way into every crack and crevice of a shoreline.

"Victor didn't hurt me," she said quietly, not quite meeting his eyes. "He was… concerned about you, actually."

Orson snorted, then winced as pain shot through his throat. "That is not a comforting thought." The idea of Victor having any interest in his well-being made his skin crawl, especially after that strange display on deck.

"I don't know what to think of them." Memori's voice dropped to barely above a whisper. She pulled Elowen into her lap, arms tightening around the girl. When she glanced at him, her cheeks colored slightly before she looked away.

His breath caught as their eyes met. Flecks of gold embedded in bronze, like sunlight playing in amber. For a moment, he sat frozen, struck by an unexpected rush of desire that had no place in their current situation.

Small fingers touched his neck, breaking the spell. "Are you alright?" Elowen asked, her face pinched with worry as she traced the bruises forming from Sullivan's grasp. She coiled her arm around his, and something in his chest melted at her concern. Without thinking, he wrapped his arm around her small shoulders, drawing her close.

"I'm fine, Wen," he said, even as his throat throbbed with each word. "As long as you're safe, I'm fine." He glanced at Memori, suddenly needing her to understand. "I'm sorry," he said, his voice rough with emotion. "For getting you both into this mess."

"You should be." Her tone aimed for lightness but missed. "If you'd been digging a well, you'd be way past water by now."

The attempted humor in her smile made something twist in his chest. His hand moved toward hers before he caught himself. The creaking timbers and distant wash of waves filled the silence between them until Memori spoke again. "What do we do now?"

"Play along?" He shrugged, hating how helpless he felt. "Until we can escape, at least." He held out the stone to Elowen, watching her innocent fascination with it. "I wish I'd never seen the damned thing." She took it from his palm and crawled under the bunk with it, her small feet scuffing against the floor as she settled into her hiding spot.

Memori's sigh drew his attention back to her. She stared listlessly at the wall, her profile outlined in the dim cabin light. "Play along," she murmured, more to herself than him. "I guess I'm used to that… playing along. So far it's got me" Her voice caught. "Here."

Something in her tone struck him—the resignation in it, the echo of old wounds that had never properly healed. His hand found hers before he could think better of it. She flinched at his touch, jerking away, then immediately looked ashamed. "I'm sorry," she whispered, wrapping her arms around herself.

The instinctive fear in her reaction made his chest ache. Of course, she would flinch from his touch - not after what she'd endured with Kol. The commander's possessive manner, the way Memori shrank from his presence, told Orson enough about their past without needing the details. "No," he said. "I'm the one who should be sorry. Memori…" His voice was thick with everything he couldn't say. "I swear I'll get you out of this mess—I got you into it."

The doubt in her eyes felt like a knife twisting in his heart, though beneath it he caught a flicker of something else—something warm and uncertain that made his pulse race. Trust? A surge of bitter regret swept through him, sharp as steel. He certainly didn't deserve her trust, not after dragging her into this nightmare.

"You have my word, Memori," he said softly. "And that's all I have left." She offered him a tired smile.

"Whatever you say, Orson," she agreed quietly. He could hear the tremor beneath her forced lightness. The narrow space between them felt charged with a current of unspoken possibilities.

"Together!" Elowen announced brightly, emerging from under the bunk to grab his hand. The pure trust in her touch made his throat tight. Gods help him, but her innocence melted what was left of his defenses.

"Damn right!" He grinned, then cleared his throat when Memori shot him a look. "Er… absolutely!" His eyes lingered on Memori's face, memorizing the way the dim light caught in her hair, the slight curve of her lips as she watched her daughter. He'd protect them both or die trying—and lately, that second option seemed less and less frightening compared to the thought of failing them.

A commotion above drew their attention—shouted orders and the clammer of running feet. The Ghost's timbers groaned as she changed course, her sails snapping with the shift in the wind. Something was happening up there, something that made his instincts prickle with warning. Memori must have felt it, too. She pulled Elowen closer, her eyes meeting his with shared concern. Whatever game they were caught in, whatever secrets Victor and his crew were keeping, Orson had a feeling they were about to learn just how dangerous this voyage could be.

The shouts above grew more urgent. Through the cabin's small window, Orson caught glimpses of the crew rushing past, their shadows dancing across the glass. The Ghost's sudden change in direction had items sliding across shelves—maps rustling, instruments swaying on their hooks.

"Memma?" Elowen's grip tightened on his hand as she looked at her mother for reassurance.

Before either of them could respond, Sullivan's heavy boots thundered past their door. "…the Seawind," he was saying to someone. "Victor wants–" The rest was lost as they passed, but Orson felt Memori stiffen beside him. The Seawind—the trawler that was supposed to help them. Something in the crew's urgency suggested the plan had changed. He tried to stand, needing to see what was happening, but the ship's motion, combined with his weakness, sent him staggering. Memori caught his arm. "Don't," she said. "You'll only make yourself worse."

"They're up to something." He steadied himself against the wall, frustration burning in his gut. Useless. He was completely useless like this. Like a damned bitter orange again.

The horn blasted again, closer this time. Through the window, he glimpsed another vessel in the distance—the fishing trawler, he guessed. But instead of approaching, the Ghost was pulling away from it.

Elowen pressed her face against the glass. "There are men on that boat. They're doing something to—" A deep boom rolled across the water, cutting off her words. The Ghost shuddered at the sound.

"Get back," Orson ordered, pulling her away as a voice roared from above.

"Fire in the hole!"

The explosion rocked the Ghost, sending all three of them sprawling. Orson caught himself against the bunk, pulling Elowen with him as Memori stumbled into his side. The acrid smell of gunpowder drifted through the window. "They're sinking it," he realized, watching smoke rise from the Seawind's hull.

Another blast shook the ship. Above them, the crew moved with efficiency—no chaos, no panic, just the steady rhythm of men who'd done this before. The Ghost cut through the waves, picking up speed as she pulled away from the dying trawler.

"No one can follow us now," Memori whispered, understanding dawning in her voice.

Orson watched the Seawind's bow dip beneath the waves. Their last connection to Cibola disappearing into the depths. He'd thought having the stone meant these sailors would help them escape. Instead, they were being carried further into whatever game Victor was playing.

Elowen tugged at his sleeve. "Where are we going?"

The question hung in the air as the Ghost's sails caught the wind, carrying them toward a horizon Orson couldn't read. He was a soldier, not a sailor. He didn't know these waters, these men, or the first thing about navigating a ship this size. But looking at Memori and Elowen's faces, he knew he had to learn fast.

"Wherever they're taking us," he said, keeping his voice steady for their sake, "we'll be alright."

Chapter 12

Sullivan

Sullivan found Victor on deck with the others, the salt-laden breeze carrying the sounds of creaking wood and gulls. "Our dear captain," Sullivan announced, feeling the satisfying pop as he cracked his neck, savoring the moment like a cat playing with its prey, "has some interesting opinions about you, Vic."

Victor hunched over the map, his dark hair falling forward as he worked. At Sullivan's words, he lifted his head with deliberate slowness. Sullivan noticed how his fingers stilled on the weathered parchment, the tension spreading up his arms. "Had to teach him some manners about running his mouth. Though he might need another lesson." Sullivan flexed his tattooed fingers, enjoying the way the ink rippled across his knuckles. But his satisfaction evaporated as he watched Victor's transformation.

Sullivan stilled in confusion, trying to reconcile this new, unfamiliar Victor with the man he'd followed for years. He'd seen men afraid before, seen rage and hatred, but this was different. Horror flickered in Victor's eyes like a guttering flame before erupting into something feral. The rage that followed wasn't the hot anger Sullivan was accustomed to—it was something ancient and cold that made the hair on the back of his neck stand up.

"What did you do?" Victor's voice was barely human, the map crumpling like thunder in his white-knuckled grip.

"I just roughed him up a little, that's all." Sullivan heard the uncertainty in his own voice, his usual confidence wavering. Before he could process what was happening, Victor's hands were at his collar, and his feet had left the deck. The sudden movement sent his stomach lurching.

"Don't fucking touch him again, Sullivan—do you hear me?" Those eyes—Sullivan had never seen them like this; they held something otherworldly, like staring into a storm at sea that could swallow ships whole.

Heart hammering, Sullivan raised his hands. "I won't, Vic—I swear!" The moment Sullivan's boots touched the deck again, he watched in fascination as awareness seemed to seep back into Victor's face, the terrifying rage draining away, replaced by a flicker of shame. The transformation was remarkable—from avenging demon to a man weighted down by secrets.

"I'm sorry, Sully. I…" The words seemed to catch in Victor's throat, trapped behind whatever truth he was holding back.

Sullivan raised an eyebrow, exchanging meaningful glances with Jermany and Evander. His heart was still racing, but curiosity had replaced any fear he might have felt. "Vic…are you alright?" The question came out tinged with concern.

Victor pressed a hand to his head—a gesture that seemed more vulnerable than any he'd seen from their usually composed first mate. Something coiled in his gut, a mix of lingering adrenaline and growing concern. The way Victor's hands trembled slightly as he touched the charts wasn't lost on him, either.

"I'm fine,' Victor said, but the strain beneath his words was like a rope about to snap. The charts rustled as Victor gathered them, his movements sharp and precise. When Victor's head snapped up to address the crew, the fury from moments ago was gone. "Just…promise me there'll be no more of your lessons—from any of you!" The command made Sullivan's spine straighten instinctively. He joined the chorus of,

"Aye, Vic," his voice mixing with the others, watching as Victor clutched the charts to his chest like a shield and retreated to his quarters. The way he walked—shoulders rigid, steps too measured—barely holding himself together. The worry that passed between the crew was almost tangible, carried on the breeze along with their whispered confusion.

Sullivan had seen plenty of men die for their captains before, seen fierce devotion and unwavering loyalty. But this—this was something else entirely. This was a protective fury that came from somewhere deeper. He'd sailed with Victor longer than any of the others, knew some of the weight he carried. But not all. The last time he'd seen that look in Victor's eyes was the day he'd returned to the sea, a silent child–Viggo–in his arms and shadows in his eyes that hadn't been there before. Or after. Until now.

VICTOR GLANCED AT his hands, not having quite banished the tremor. His strong emotional reaction at Sullivan surprised him–Sully, he corrected himself. Gods below, it almost felt like they'd sailed together for ages. And here Victor was picking up old patterns at the drop of a hat. If it was anyone other than his crew, they'd have already been dead.

Luckily for him, Sully was not so easily damaged. He recalled when he first lay eyes on him. It was off the main island of Tidesreach in the western realm. *The western waters were alive with warning—the air heavy with the metallic taste of an approaching storm, waves swelling, their peaks torn to foam by the growling wind. No sane captain would risk their vessel in such treacherous conditions, with disaster lurking in every swell. Victor sat low in his small fishing boat while he watched the unfolding scene with sharp interest.*

Ahead, a lone figure caught his attention—a mountain of a man in his thirties, tattoos sprawling across his gleaming scalp and massive arms like a living map of victories. In nothing but a dinghy, of all things. The fool should have been terrified, but his stance was steady despite the rolling waves.

A Northern longship cut through the churning waters, its dragon-headed prow rising and falling like a hungry beast. The vessel's thick hull was striped with shields, its sail a blood-red slash against the iron-gray sky. Victor's nostrils flared at the sharp scent of pine tar and wet rope carrying on the wind. The Northmen, wrapped in furs and leather, lined the railings, pointing and shouting words that carried across the water: "Shade! Clan-rot!"

The bald man stood in his tiny boat, and Victor felt a spark of recognition at the dark look in his eyes. The harpoon gleamed dully in his hands before he hurled it at the longship's hull. Victor's breath caught—not at the foolhardy action, but at the deadly intent behind it.

The ship's deck erupted with bowmen, arrows nocked and ready. The lone warrior should have shown fear, should have begged for mercy, but his gaze tracked the archers' movements with lethal focus, like he was counting each breath they had left.

A massive wave caught the longship just as the bowstrings sang, sending their deadly volley wide into the churning sea. Victor leaned forward in his small boat, transfixed by the lone warrior's fight. The man moved like he was already dead, each strike of his weapons against the ship's hull precise and vicious. He must have known he wouldn't survive—no one could, against such odds—yet there was determination in his eyes, uncaring of his fate. It stirred something in Victor's memory, that familiar darkness that came with nothing left to lose.

The Northmen's shouts grew more frantic, more desperate. Victor's brow furrowed as he watched them trying to kill one of their own with such fervor. What could one man have done to earn such hatred from his people? The tattooed warrior's movements spoke of Northern training, but the way they spat slurs at him carried the weight of deeper hatred; fear, even. Waves crashed higher around the longship's hull, the water mysteriously finding its way into every crack and seam. The warrior's small boat had already been smashed against the ship's side, leaving him clinging to the hull like a barnacle. Victor watched as the great northern vessel listed. The crew's shouts turned from rage to terror as their ship groaned beneath them.

They turned away, trying to limp back to safer waters, but it was too late. The proud dragon prow dipped beneath the waves first, then the rest followed, leaving nothing but scattered debris and distant screams that were quickly swallowed by the hungry sea.

Victor's own boat lost in the chaos, smashed against rocks he could have sworn weren't there moments before. He dragged himself onto a nearby rock outcropping, his body *heavy with exhaustion. He collapsed against the cold stone, his vision swimming, but his eyes remained fixed on the tattooed warrior, who now clung to a piece of driftwood in the settling waves.*

The warrior pulled himself up onto the rocks, water streaming from his massive frame. Victor studied him through half-lidded eyes, noticing now what he couldn't see from a distance—the tattoos weren't Northern Clan marks at all. They were different, wild and unique, telling stories Victor couldn't read but could sense held pain. "I was doing fine 'til you showed up," the man spat, his northern accent thick with bitterness as he sank down onto the rock. Seawater pooled beneath him, and Victor caught the slight tremor in his hands—exhaustion, or something deeper.

"If getting killed was your goal," Victor replied dryly. He wrung water from his hair with the pass of his hand, slinging it away.

"They wouldn't have killed me," the man muttered, almost sounding like it bothered him. Victor's spine straightened despite his exhaustion. He studied the warrior's face—saw the hollow look in his eyes, the way his shoulders curved inward, defensive yet defeated.

"You wanted them to," he said quietly. He knew that look too well. Saw it in his own reflection many times. That brand of desperation, of seeking an end while being unable to find it…for one reason or another. Victor picked his way across the slick rock surface, salt spray stinging his face as he approached the warrior. He extended his hand, letting the wind tug at his coat. "Victor."

The man stared at the offered hand, then lifted his gaze to meet Victor's, suspicion darkening his eyes like storm clouds. "Sullivan," he replied, pointedly leaving Victor's hand hanging in the air between them.

Victor remained undeterred. "Would you consider sailing with me?"

Sullivan's laugh was as harsh as the rocks beneath them. "Where in seven hells we sailin' to, pretty boy?" He gestured to the churning waters surrounding their temporary refuge. "In case you hadn't noticed, we're a bit short on ships."

The wind howled around them, sending Victor's dark coat pulling at him like a sail. Another wave crashed against the rocks, sending up a fine mist. He squatted down beside Sullivan, noticing the wolf's paw inked on the man's left hand where a clan tattoo would normally be. "I'll make a deal with you. I show you how to get off this rock. You sail with me."

Sullivan scoffed again, his eyes scanning their precarious position on the outcropping, the angry sea surrounding them in every direction. "Whatever you say, sunshine."

Victor bit back a laugh at Sullivan's insult and extended his hand again. This time, Sullivan's calloused fingers wrapped around his own, grip reluctant but firm.

Chapter 13

Storm

An unearthly cold drenched the room, seeping through the ship's timbers like poison. General Roderick Storm stood before the cracked mirror, his reflection distorted by spiderweb fractures in the glass. Water misted the porthole, and the gentle roll of waves did nothing to soothe his restless thoughts. He raised his hand, studying the faint glow of the shard embedded in his palm. It pulsed weakly, a sickly green light flickering like a dying ember—so different from the vibrant surge it had possessed when whole, when he had been worthy of wielding a tide stone's full power.

"A mere fragment," he muttered bitterly, turning his hand to examine the jagged edges where it melded with his skin. "All that remains after she tore it from me. As if she had any right to judge how I used its gifts. As if any of them have the right." His words echoed in the quiet chamber, heavy with centuries of resentment. He could still feel the searing pain of that moment—Linden's power burning through him as she shattered his stone, her voice like thunder as she cast her judgment. The pieces had scattered across the forest floor like drops of frozen light, and he managed to grab just one before she forced him away. One measley shard, when the full stone had once given him enough power to bend the air throughout the seven realms.

He was oathbound once–before Victor, before all of them. The first she chosen, and the first she cast aside. He watched them all come and go over the centuries, each taking what should have been his, each binding themselves to Linden's precious rules about when and where they could use their power. As if such gifts were meant to be caged!

Storm clenched his fist, the shard glowing brighter as he summoned its meager power. The lantern light wavered as the surrounding air rippled, bending like heat waves over stone, though nowhere near as smoothly as it once did. With a flick of his fingers, a dark figure appeared in the room's corner, the transportation leaving Storm's hand trembling with effort.

"You summoned me, General?" the spy asked, his voice as sharp as the daggers at his belt.

"I have a task for you," Storm said, his tone cold and commanding. He gestured, and the ripple extended outward, enveloping the spy. Where he had once traversed vast distances himself, now he could only send others, and even that drained him. "The Ghost sails toward Rootspire. You will intercept them."

The spy hesitated, his outline shimmering as the shard's power took hold. "And if I find them?"

"You do what must be done," Storm replied. His grip on the shard tightened, and the ripple flared, sending the spy into nothingness with a hiss.

For a moment, the room was silent again, save for the endless song of the sea against the hull. Storm swayed with more than just the ship's motion, gripping the edge of the table to steady himself. The shard's power drained him each time he used it, a cruel reminder of what he lost. He stared down at his hand, watching the glow fade back to its dull, sickly hue. Even this small working left him exhausted— another indignity Linden put upon him.

"You think you can stop me, Linden?" he said, his voice low and venomous. "I will have the last tide stone. I will take back what is mine." Storm turned from the cracked mirror, buttoning his shirt hastily to cover the mark on his chest. The scar tissue had taken on that sickly green cast again, the same color as the shard embedded in his palm. No matter how he'd tried to alter it over the centuries, the original lines always showed through, mocking his attempts to rewrite what Linden carved into his flesh. The newer scars he'd added only seemed to make the original pattern writhe more prominently against his skin. His fingers fumbled with the last button as the mark pulsed with a familiar ache. Dawn's light caught the corrupted ink, making it shimmer like poison in a wound that would never truly heal.

A wave crashed against the bow, sending a shudder through the ship. Each section of broken mirror reflected different versions of what Storm had become - the carved flesh, the sickly glow, the hunger in his eyes sharpened by centuries. Let them see him as a monster. He'd learned long ago that monsters got what they wanted, while noble men died clutching their precious principles.

The boy who'd once stood beneath the ancient tree, swearing oaths with tears in his eyes, was gone. In his place stood someone who watched others claim what was rightfully his for far too long—someone who understood that power wasn't given or earned, but taken.

Chapter 14

Orson

Orson sat on the edge of his bed, elbows resting on his knees, the tide stone turning slowly between his fingers. Lantern light caught the gold framing around its strange, glassy depths, making the stone's surface ripple like waves beneath a stormy sky. Beautiful and unsettling - much like the destiny it seemed to promise.

He pressed his thumb against its cool surface, tracing the intricate patterns that somehow felt older than the metal containing them. Every time he looked at it, the stone seemed to look back, as though it held more than just captured ocean light. "What have I gotten myself into?" he muttered to himself. Elowen's face flashed in his mind - her bright eyes, so like her father's, yet holding none of his cruelty. He clenched the stone tighter, its edges biting into his palm. How could something so innocent come from someone so monstrous? And Memori…The thought of her twisted something in his chest. Her quiet strength, the careful way she held herself. Both of them bound to his fate because he couldn't leave well enough alone. The stone caught the lantern light again, glinting like lightning against dark water. A soft knock broke through his dark thoughts.

"Come in," Orson called, shoving the stone into his pocket.

Victor opened the door, his expression carved from the same rock as the cliffs they'd left behind. He stepped inside without invitation, shoulders rigid, eyes darker than the shadows filling the cabin's corners. For a heartbeat, the first mate stood frozen in the doorway, his face a mask of such raw anguish that Orson nearly took a step back. Victor blinked, and the emotion vanished, replaced by a stoic expression.

"Captain." Victor's voice was rough. His hand moved unconsciously to touch something beneath his shirt - a ring on a chain, Orson noticed. "Are you alright?" His eye dropped to Orson's throat. A thin flicker of fury flashed across his face like a bolt of lightning. "I've come to apologize for Sullivan–whatever punishment you deem necessary, I will carry out myself."

Orson inadvertently rubbed at the marks on his throat. "Wait–no. That's not necessary."

Victor's jaw clenched, fists forming at his side. "It is necessary." Regret crept into his voice. "One cannot treat their captain that way."

"Victor, leave it alone." Orson raised his voice in protest. "It was a misunderstanding. It's best left forgotten."

Victor gave him a curt nod of his head. "If that is what you wish, Captain."

"It is what I wish," Orson sighed. "Tell me what the hell is going on with this," he gestured around the room, "and we'll call it square, eh?" He watched as Victor took a step toward him, his body tensing instinctively. There was something about the first mate that kept him perpetually on edge—like standing too close to a cliff's edge. Every conversation felt like a test he wasn't prepared for. It made his skin prickle with unease–kept him constantly on guard.

"The old man did not tell you?" Victor frowned.

Orson waved his hand in frustration. "What he told me was nonsense," he muttered. "Something about a storm coming, 1000 years of chaos and broken oaths. Shit from children's bedtime stories."

Victor crossed his arms. "Forgive me, Captain, but if you thought he was mad, why did you take the stone?"

"I gave him my word!" Orson spoke in frustration. "I believed his story about this damned ship–of treasure and hidden passages. More importantly, I had nothing to lose, and it sounded like a fun way to piss off my former commander." He paused, surveying Victor for a moment. If he didn't play along, what would happen then? He and Memori would be of no use to the crew.

"You know what…forget it." He sank to his bed. Creaking of the ship punctuated the uncomfortable silence.

"He didn't mean a storm," Victor spoke at last, his voice low, almost pained. "He meant Roderick Storm. The leader of the Blacksmoke Union." The lantern flame wavered, casting strange shadows across Victor's face. For a moment, he looked ancient - a man carrying the weight of not just the sea, but time itself. "The dam," Victor's boots fell heavy on the planks as he stepped closer, "it wasn't just holding this ship prisoner." Victor's gaze cut through the darkness between them, sharp enough to draw blood. For a fleeting moment, there was a flicker of…pain? He buried it quickly. "It was holding back something far more dangerous."

Orson crossed his arms. "This…Storm."

Victor nodded. "In a way. He will be after this ship once he knows it is free."

"Let him come." Orson scoffed.

"He will." Victor said. His tone made the air feel thinner. "And he is nothing like your Vanguard; - blunt, predictable. Mortal." He emphasized that last word strangely. A chill crept up Orson's spine at the way Victor said it.

"Look, Sloan," Orson stood again, frustration building in his chest. "I'm a simple soldier - and that, not by choice. I know nothing about sailing!"

"I'll teach you everything you need to know," Victor said, his voice insistent.

Orson groaned in frustration. "You overestimate what I'm capable of, Sloan. If Dollan hadn't…" he broke off, calming his emotions before continuing. "Dollan asked me for help after my commander tortured him almost to death. I agreed to help him. That's all." He ran a hand through his hair.

Regret flickered across Victor's features, but he held his tongue.

"Though maybe if I'd known it would drag Memori and Elowen into this mess…" Orson muttered under his breath.

"You are much more than that." Victor's voice cut through his words like a blade, but he didn't take the words back.

. "I'm really not," Orson insisted, though uncertainty crept into his voice. "I should've been dead twice over by now." Orson turned to Victor, who stood in the same spot with clenched fists since he entered the room. " And what does this Storm even want with this ship? With us?"

"The tide stone." Victor moved closer, his voice dropping. "Storm *believes* the stone channels power. Can make him stronger. That's why he hunts it. Why he'll keep hunting it."

"And does it?" Orson touched the stone through his pocket. "Channel power?"

Victor's expression was impossible to read. "The stone serves its purpose, Captain. Though perhaps not the purpose Storm imagines." He touched a hand to his chest like someone massaging an old wound before adding almost casually, "Keep it close. Let him think it's worth chasing."

Orson felt like Sullivan must have deprived him of air for too long. "I don't want any part of this madness." he moved his hand to his pocket, intent on giving the stone to Victor–or hurling it into the sea. Whatever was more easily achieved. "I don't care what happens to me-"

"What of the healer?" Victor's question struck Orson unexpectedly, concern feeling stronger than it should for only knowing her a short while. "And her child?" Victor added.

Orson's fingers curled around the stone, as if it might shield him from the truth in Victor's words. "Her sister," he corrected weakly, the lie tasting bitter on his tongue. "And if you so much as touch either of them-"

"There is no threat from us." Something softened in Victor's hard gaze. "But Storm?" He shook his head. "He won't stop at you, Captain. That's what I'm trying to tell you."

Orson exhaled harshly, the weight of responsibility settling heavier on his shoulders. "And what exactly am I supposed to do about that?"

Victor's voice gentled, though steel remained beneath it. "You'll see."

Orson's fingers traced the stone's cool surface, feeling its pulse match his heartbeat. "What do we do?"

Victor turned toward the door, his shoulders set with the rigidity of someone carrying an impossible burden. When he spoke, his voice carried an old wound. "We prepare. We keep moving."

"And when they catch us?" The question slipped out before Orson could stop it.

Victor paused in the doorway, one hand resting on the frame. "We finish this." Then, so quietly Orson almost missed it, he added, "Maybe we finally put it right."

The door closed behind him with a soft click, leaving Orson alone with questions that seemed to multiply like shadows at sunset. He pulled out the tide stone again, watching it catch the lantern light. "A fairytale," he muttered bitterly. "That's all Dollan's story was - some fever dream about ancient powers and sacred vows." But even as he said it, the stone pulsed gently in his palm, like a heart beating beneath the surface. He remembered the old fisherman's eyes, bright with certainty even as blood trickled from his split lip. The way his trembling fingers pressed the stone into Orson's hand.

"Swear to me," Dollan had whispered. "Swear you'll take it to the Ghost." And like a fool, Orson did. Because a man's word meant something, even if the promise itself seemed mad. Even if it dragged him - and now Memori and Elowen - into whatever madness was brewing on the horizon.

For a moment, he could have sworn he saw something move in the stone's depths - a reflection of trees touching the sky, of children gathered around a fire, of choices made long ago. He shook his head, trying to clear it. Lack of sleep, that's all it was. The stone's surface dimmed suddenly, as if responding to his doubt. In the darkness beyond his window, the sea churned with unnatural violence, though no wind stirred the air.

Chapter 15

Memori

The wooden bed creaked with each subtle movement, a rhythmic whisper that echoed the gentle sway of the ship. Memori sat propped against the hard wall, her fingers tracing the edges of the herbal codex in her lap. Beside her, Elowen slumbered, her breath a soft, steady cadence that blended with the ship's ambient sounds.

The pages of Elowen's storybook lay open to a familiar illustration—Tempest, her favorite guardian, rendered in exquisite detail. The guardian stood poised, twin swords drawn, their edges gleaming with an inner light. Around her, the ocean churned and twisted, not as a backdrop, but as a living weapon, coiling and striking.

Memori's gaze lingered on the illustration as Elowen slept. Tempest's dark skin and braided hair reminded her fleetingly of Jermany, right down to the peculiar copper and bronze beads woven through the guardian's locks. She'd noticed similar adornments catching the light when Jermany moved across the deck. Probably just a common style from the Tidesreach islands, where both women likely hailed from; one real and one imaginary.

The artist gave Tempest's eyes an unusual intensity too—dark and knowing, fixed on the horizon as if she could read the waters like others read books. Unlike the storm lords who commanded thunder and lightning, Tempest's domain was the sea itself—currents, tides, and ancient rhythms bending to her will.

Memori shook her head, closing the book gently. She was finding similarities where none existed. Next, she'd start imagining Jermany could calm the waters like the guardian in the story, simply because they shared a hairstyle and homeland. Superstitious nonsense. She tucked the blanket around Elowen, dismissing the thought. Nothing like the impossible powers in storybooks. It was a nice thought, though. Wielding the power of the ocean. Memori would have escaped with Elowen ages ago with such abilities.

The ship's timbers groaned softly, a counterpoint to her daughter's peaceful breathing. Feeling Elowen's warmth against her, Memori's mind found a rare moment of ease. She turned her attention back to the herbal codex, reading different formulas for remedies—treatments for infections, bruises, sore throats. Her fingers paused as a scrap of paper fluttered out when she turned a page. When she unfolded it, an old list of ingredients from her shop caught her eye, annotated with whimsical names that softened the medical precision: "Kissed by the sun," "Bad night's sleep," "Too much to eat," "Heartache."

A chill ran through her as she spotted a deadly formula scrawled with a bitter jest: "Vanguard burned my village to the ground." The memory didn't merely threaten to surface—it crashed through her defenses like a battering ram. Kol was in town that day. His face swam before her eyes, that predatory smile as he'd strolled onto the ship, his men flanking him like wolves. Her hands trembled violently, the page rattling between her fingers. Bile rose in her throat, acid and burning. She turned the paper over with jerky movements, her vision blurring as she struggled to focus on writing the remedy she needed instead of drowning in the past that never truly left her. The codex was a treasure trove of knowledge she'd barely explored. Until recently, even looking at such a text had been dangerous. Now, it didn't really matter—though the memories it stirred felt no less deadly than the poisons it contained.

Detailed illustrations of the human anatomy filled the pages, depicting different bodily systems through the lens of herbal medicine—hot and cold, dry and wet—each element carefully mapped to correspond with specific healing practices. Memori studied the intricate diagrams, her trained eye parsing the complex relationships between illness and herbal treatments.

Her fingers stilled on a particular page. Among the familiar healing symbols and herb lore, a mark stood out—darker, more angular. Unlike the clean lines of the traditional healer's rune, this symbol was its twisted inverse. Where the healer's mark promised life, this one whispered of something stolen, of potential unmade. The symbol was vaguely familiar in its wrongness, yet Memori was certain she'd never seen it before. Intricate and unsettling, it seemed to pulse with a meaning just beyond her understanding.

Frowning, she closed the book. It would wait until later. She carefully placed the codex in its hiding spot, tucked Elowen in more securely, and prepared to head to her shop with the list she'd made. She had work to do before morning.

Chapter 16

Orson

A rush of cold air jolted Orson from his fitful sleep. Victor's looming presence invaded his cabin as the first mate burst through the door without ceremony. The morning light streaming in behind him cast his tall frame in shadow, making him appear more spectral than human.

"Morning, Captain." Victor's deep voice carried the same authoritative tone it always did, regardless of the hour.

Orson groaned, rolling over as he rubbed the grit of sleep from his eyes. The ache in his throat reminded him of yesterday's misfortunes. "Shit. I was hoping you were just a bad dream."

"No such luck for you this day, Captain." There was an almost imperceptible hint of amusement in Victor's voice as he set a wooden tray on the nightstand beside Orson's bed. The tray's legs wobbled slightly against the uneven surface, threatening to spill its contents. "I'll meet you up top when you're ready."

Victor's departure was as abrupt as his entrance, leaving behind only the lingering chill in the air and the soft click of the cabin door. Orson's attention turned to the tray, where a mug of tea sent tendrils of steam curling into the morning air. Tucked beneath it was a folded piece of parchment, and his heart performed an unexpected somersault when he recognized Memori's handwriting.

For your throat—Drink it!

The corner of Orson's mouth tugged upward as he pictured her writing these words. A quiet warmth gathered in his chest. Sitting up with a grunt, Orson took the mug in both hands, letting its heat seep into his palms. Bracing himself, he lifted the mug to his lips and downed the contents in several large gulps.

The bitterness hit him immediately, a sharp assault on his taste buds that made his eyes water. Memori attempted to soften the blow with honey, but it did little to mask the medicinal punch. A cough worked its way up his throat as he fought to keep the concoction down. As he set the empty mug back on the tray, Orson had to admit that the tightness in his throat was already beginning to ease. He swung his legs over the side of the bed and prepared for the day ahead.

Floorboards complained beneath his feet as he made his way toward the door, each step bringing him closer to whatever challenges Victor was waiting to present—to the crew that would rather see him overboard than as their reluctant captain. At least his throat wouldn't hurt when they tossed him, thanks to Memori's intervention—though he wasn't entirely sure if the cure hadn't been worse than the ailment. He rubbed at the soreness working its way into his neck.

Emerging from below, Orson was momentarily blinded by the harsh morning sun. He raised a hand to shield his eyes, squinting against the glare that transformed the deck into a maze of dark silhouettes and brilliant light. The sounds and smells of the ship washed over him. "At last you grace us with your presence, Captain." Sullivan's voice dripped with theatrical deference as he executed an exaggerated bow.

Victor's reaction was immediate and thunderous. "To your posts!" He barked the orders, sending the crew scrambling to their stations. Sullivan's smirk didn't quite fade, but his feet moved just as quickly as the others to comply with the first mate's commands.

"My apologies, Captain—" Victor began, his tone heavy with concern.

"No need," Orson cut him off, absently stroking the tender skin of his bruised throat as he watched Sullivan making a show of hauling rope. "I appreciate honesty."

Victor's gaze fixed on the discolored flesh of Orson's neck, his frown deepening. "Come with me," he said. He led

Orson not to the stern, as expected, but back to the first mate's own cabin. The space was spartan, almost monastically simple. A narrow cot was pressed against one wall, its blankets pulled military-tight; an identical sleeping arrangement was on the opposite side of the room, and a heavy sea chest squatted at its foot, its wood dark with age and warped from exposure to water. A desk dominated the opposite wall, its surface bare save for a brass compass and several well-worn navigational tools.

Victor moved to the chest, its hinges creaking as he lifted the lid. As he reached in for the maps, Orson glimpsed the contents within: a rose crafted from twisted metal, its delicate petals belying the strength of its material; an iron sword carefully wrapped in oiled cloth, and a thick leather journal, its edges softened by frequent handling.

"We will start with navigation." Victor unfurled weathered maps across the desk's surface. "You know North from South?" He arched an eyebrow and Orson couldn't help but think he was poking fun at him.

He pressed his lips together, a frown creasing his brow. "I'm not sure," he replied with a hint of defensiveness. "Do they change names like other ridiculous things do on sea versus land?"

"If you don't, they're easy enough to learn." Victor ignored the remark and gestured for Orson to sit. "Let's get to work."

Chapter 17

Jermany

Morning sun cast long shadows across the Ghost's weathered deck as Jermany stood at the helm, her calloused hands steady on the worn wooden spokes. Around her, the ship breathed with the whisper of water against the hull, the fluttering of the canvas sails in the wind.

The door to Victor's cabin closed with a decisive thud, swallowing both the first mate and their unlikely captain. Evander, perched in the shrouds with his ever-present knife and length of rope, paused in his work to exchange knowing looks with the others. Peryn abandoned his post at the mainsail, sauntering across the rolling deck toward Jermany. His copper-threaded beard caught the sunlight as he leaned against the binnacle, far too close for comfort. "Thoughts on our new commander, love?"

Jermany's elbow found his ribs, forcing distance between them. "I trust Vic." She scowled, her dark eyes never leaving the horizon.

Peryn's laugh carried over the wind. "Aye, but you can't deny he's different. Man can barely tell port from starboard."

"Wouldn't trust him to tie a proper bowline," Sullivan rumbled from where he coiled heavy rope on the foredeck, his massive frame casting a shadow like a second mast. "Doubt he could find his way out of a rowboat with a map and a compass."

"Doesn't matter." Evander's quiet voice carried an edge as sharp as the blade in his hands. "Touch him again, Sullivan, and Victor will have your head."

The big man's hands stilled on the rope. Above them, seabirds wheeled and cried, their shadows dancing across the sun-bleached deck. Peryn barked another laugh, though it held less humor now. "You really believe that, Evan?"

"Victor said it." Evander's pale fingers never stopped working the rope, weaving complex patterns as naturally as breathing. "When has he ever broken his word?"

The crew fell silent, the slap of waves filling the space between them. The morning breeze carried the tang of salt and tar, familiar scents that usually brought comfort but now seemed charged with unspoken tension. "Evan's right," Jermany said finally, adjusting their course with a subtle shift of the wheel. Her braids clinked softly with the motion, the copper and bronze beads woven through them catching the light. "We follow Victor's lead. Whatever his plan is with the captain."

"I wasn't really going to kill him," Sullivan muttered. He tested the tension in his freshly coiled line, thick fingers delicate with the weathered hemp.

Peryn snorted, bracing himself against the roll of the deck. "Wouldn't have taken much, Sea-Wolf. Especially not from you."

"What got you so riled, anyway?" Evander asked, his voice carrying down from the rigging where he worked.

Sullivan's expression darkened. "He was running his mouth about Victor."

"He doesn't know any better," Jermany said, a crooked smile tugging at her lips. "Though I won't say he didn't earn that throttling."

They lapsed into silence, each lost in thought as they watched the sea stretch before them. The water was unusually calm, its surface like polished glass, reflecting the sky in rippling swathes of azure and gold. But something felt different in the air today.

"Can you feel it?" Jermany's voice was barely above a whisper, her knuckles whitening on the wheel. "Like we've sailed these waters before…we have, but…this is different."

"The dreams." It wasn't a question. Evander descended from the rigging like a cat, his movements fluid and silent. In the harsh morning light, the shadows under his eyes seemed deeper, older somehow. "They're getting stronger, aren't they?" Jermany met his gaze, a muscle working in her jaw before she nodded.

"Aye." Sullivan's gruff voice had softened, something like fear flickering across his weathered features.

Peryn's usually cheerful face darkened as he traced a finger over one of the ship's scarred railings. "Me too," he admitted.

"Same here," Evander said quietly, his pale eyes distant.

Above them, the Ghost's sails billowed with a sudden gust, canvas snapping. The sound seemed to break the spell, sending them back to their duties. But the weight of their shared dreams hung in the air like storm clouds on the horizon - dark, heavy, and drawing closer with each passing day.

Chapter 18

Memori

"Stay where I can see you, Wen," Memori murmured, as she worked. The cabin air was heavy with the scent of thyme and elderflower. Elowen sat nearby, swinging her legs and humming while she carefully turned the pages in her worn storybook. Memori occasionally glanced over, hands moving automatically, crushing leaves and measuring portions. Her thoughts drifted to Orson. She could picture him in the captain's cabin now, remembering how Sullivan smashed him against the wall like he was nothing more than a sack of grain. When her fingers graced the bruises on his neck–for a moment–she thought she'd seen the marks fade. Felt that warm tingling sensation spread from her fingertips. It must have been her imagination.

She shuddered, hoping he drank the tea she prepared for him. Trying to focus more on the task at hand, she wondered if he was as distracted by her presence as she was by his. The thought brought both comfort and a hollowness she didn't understand - these growing feelings, despite the uncertainty of their situation, despite all the reasons she should keep her guard up. Perhaps she was reading too much into his kindness, she thought, setting down a sprig of thyme with suddenly unsteady fingers. Maybe that's all this was - just the natural courtesy of a gentleman who was kind to everyone. The thought shouldn't sting as much as it did.

Elowen

ELOWEN'S LEGS STOPPED swinging. She slid down from her chair, tiptoeing around the small cabin, touching the wooden walls, counting the boards, trying to stay quiet like she'd seen the crew do during night watch. The wooden planks felt warm and smooth beneath her fingertips, worn soft by years of salt and sea. Above her head, sunlight leaked through the tiny gaps between boards, making strips of golden light dance across the floor when the ship swayed.

She was good at being quiet now. Better than before. She'd learned during the long nights hiding from the soldiers, when even breathing too loud could give you away. The cabin felt too small, too still, like that awful space beneath the floorboards where Memma made her hide. She'd been so scared then, curled up tight in the darkness, listening to heavy boots overhead. But this was different. Through the crack in the door, she could see patches of blue sky and billowing sails that looked like giant clouds caught by the ship. The breeze that snuck through the gap brought tantalizing smells: tar from the ropes, and something cooking in the galley that made her nose twitch.

Just a quick peek, she thought. Just a tiny adventure, like the ones Tempest had! She was Elowen's favorite guardian. Leaving her book open to a page where Tempest stood fierce and proud, she slipped away quietly, bare feet padding against the wooden deck. She was getting better at finding hiding places—not the scary kind like before, but fun ones, secret spaces where she could watch the sailors work without being shooed away.

The planks felt different out here - warmer where the sun hit them, with rough patches of salt dried white as sugar. Elowen tried to walk like a proper sailor, stepping carefully over the raised edges between boards. The wind tugged at her hair and clothes, carrying the calls of seabirds overhead. Everything seemed bigger, the sky stretching forever in a blue so bright it made her eyes wide. The sails towered above her like white mountains, casting shifting shadows across the deck.

Elowen twirled in a small circle, giggling as the wind played with her hair. This was nothing like that terrible space behind the root cellar wall, where she hid when the man, Kol, came. Here, she could spread her arms wide, pretending she could catch the wind in them like the sails did. She didn't have to hold her breath or make herself small—free as the seabirds wheeling overhead.

The ship lurched.

One moment she was dancing, the next the deck wasn't where it should be. Her stomach swooped as if she'd missed a step going downstairs, only there was no step. The beautiful blue world tilted sideways. Her feet slid across wooden planks that no longer felt friendly. They were slick with sea water, betraying her small feet as she scrambled for balance.

A seagull screamed directly overhead, the sound sharp as a knife. Elowen's heart jumped into her throat. This wasn't like the muffled bird calls she heard from the safety of the cabin. This was wild and scary and too close. She reached for the railing, her fingers finding the damp wood just as another wave hit. The ship groaned around her, no longer a magical vessel of adventure but a massive, creaking thing that suddenly felt as precarious as the makeshift bridges she'd seen in her storybooks' pictures.

Her feet slipped again. The ocean roared below, no longer beautiful but hungry. The railing felt too big for her tiny hands, too slippery, too far away. All the pretend bravery drained from her body in an instant, replaced by cold terror that turned her limbs to water. "Memma!" The scream tore from her throat, high and frightened, but the wind snatched it away almost immediately. Her fingers slipped.

VIGGO KICKED HIS legs idly from his perch in the crow's nest. At eleven, he was skinny enough to slip into spaces the grown-ups couldn't reach, which made for the best watching spots. His father trusted him with keeping watch, and that made his chest swell with pride. The salt-laden wind tousled his too-long black hair as his eyes swept across the deck below, playing his usual game of counting seabirds. His heart

lurched as he spotted a familiar mop of curls near the bow—
the healer's sister, tottering where she definitely shouldn't be.

His mouth went dry as he watched her stumble when the
ship pitched. He scrambled toward the stairs, his scraped
knees burning as he half-climbed, half-slid down the wooden
steps. His too-big hand-me-down boots thundered against
each plank as he nearly tripped over his own feet.

He reached her just as her small fingers lost their grip on
the railing. His arms wrapped around her middle and they
tumbled backward onto the deck. Viggo held her close, the
way his Da did during thunderstorms. Her heart fluttered like
a trapped bird against his chest, matching his own racing
pulse.

"I—I wanted to explore" Elowen hiccupped between
sobs, her tears soaking into his already-patched shirt. Her little
hands clutched fistfuls of his sleeves, holding on as if she
might drift away if she let go. Viggo squeezed her tighter. His
throat felt scratchy and tight, like that time he'd swallowed
seawater while learning to swim. He couldn't find any
words—not even to scold her like his father surely would. All
he could do was hold her and wait for his heart to stop
pounding.

He scanned the deck for the crew, but they were all
absorbed in their tasks. He noted the telling absence of his
father, the new captain, and Memori. It was probably for the
best–less trouble for the both of them. He took Elowen's small
hand in his and led her to his father's cabin. He guided her to
sit on his own narrow cot, draping a thick blanket around her
trembling shoulders. Her eyes were wide and glassy, her face
streaked with drying tears as she looked up at him.

"Don't tell Memma?" she whispered, her voice barely
audible. Viggo raised an eyebrow, his expression stern but
gentle. Da would definitely not approve of keeping such a
secret, but he understood—being confined to the ship's hull
all day would be the worst sort of punishment for someone as
curious as Elowen. Reluctantly, he gave her a single, decisive
nod. While she scrubbed at her eyes with the corner of the
blanket, he retrieved a set of small wooden carvings from
beneath his pillow.

The wooden figures fit perfectly in his palm - treasures
he'd watched his father whittle during long night watches.
One was a sea captain, standing proud with a tiny sword at his
hip, his beard and coat caught in an eternal wind. The other

was a woman with gentle eyes and a smile so carefully carved it seemed to hold all the warmth of a summer's day. His father had spent extra time on that smile, working late into the night until every curve was just right.

Elowen reached out with hesitant fingers, tracing the woman's flowing dress. "She's beautiful," she whispered, her earlier tears forgotten.

Viggo nodded, pride and sorrow tangling like vines around his heart. The woman's smile was carved from memory - his father's way of keeping his mother with them, even out here on the endless sea. "Da made them." His voice was barely louder than the lap of waves against the hull.

"Your Da scares me," Elowen whispered, pulling the blanket tighter around her shoulders as if saying it aloud might summon him.

Viggo smiled softly, settling beside her on the bunk. "He wasn't always scary," he said, running his thumb over the carved woman's cheek. "Before Ma was killed… he smiled. And told stories."

Elowen sniffled, wiping her nose with the back of her hand. "What kind of stories?" Her eyes brightened with curiosity.

Viggo shrugged, fiddling with the captain carving in his lap. "Different ones" He hesitated, the words feeling strange in his mouth. No one talked to him so much, except for his father. "Would you like to hear one?" Elowen's eyes widened, and she nodded.

MEMORI GLANCED UP from her herbs, expecting to see Elowen still absorbed in her favorite book. "You've been so quiet, Wen. Which Guardian are you reading about now?" The only answer was the creak of timber and splash of waves. Elowen's book lay open on her bed, pages ruffling in the breeze from the open porthole. "Elowen?" Panic seized her chest as she rushed to the deck, her daughter's name tearing from her throat. All the way up, her mind spun horrible visions— Elowen tumbling overboard, falling from the rigging, being crushed by shifting cargo. The wind whipped her hair across her face as she screamed Elowen's name once more, her hands trembling against her lips. Sullivan caught her eye and pointed toward Victor's cabin with a reassuring nod.

She nearly tore the door from its hinges, her heart thundering against her ribs. The scene before her made her stumble to a stop, the terror draining from her limbs so quickly she felt light-headed. Elowen was curled up against Viggo's side, safe and warm, while the boy showed her drawings in an old leather book. They both looked up at her dramatic entrance. "Memma!" The blanket slipped from Elowen's shoulders as she sat up, her face glowing with excitement. "Viggo is telling me a new story!"

Memori sagged against the doorframe, relief washing over her. She wanted to scold, to explain how terrified she'd been, but the sight of her daughter's bright eyes and Viggo's protective posture made her pause. "That's wonderful, Elowen," she managed. "But next time, you must tell me before you leave, alright?"

"OK!" Elowen chirped, bouncing off Viggo's cot and throwing her arms around Memori's waist. "Bye Viggo, I'll see you later!" She waved at him, beaming.

He gave her a brief grin, waving back as he closed the leather book in his lap.

Memori guided Elowen back toward their cabin, listening to her daughter chatter about sea spirits and brave captains. Behind them, the door to Victor's cabin clicked shut, and Memori sent up a silent prayer of thanks for the watchful eyes that had kept her little one safe.

Chapter 19

Peryn

As popular as an Inn the Crimson Ghost had been, it was not sufficiently stocked for an extended time at sea. Reluctantly, Victor ordered Jermany to navigate to the closest out-of-the-way port for supplies. Despite Orson's protests about being "kept like a prisoner on his (alleged) own damn ship," Victor was adamant. Evander remained on the ship, ready to ensure their stubborn captain stayed put. No one spoke of how he would manage that if Orson were to protest, but they all knew. Peryn snickered to himself at the thought of their captain frozen in shadow-unable to move and not knowing why. Only Victor, Sullivan, and Peryn would leave to retrieve what they needed.

Mist clung to the Ghost like a second skin, an unnatural fog Victor summoned to mask their approach. Through gaps in the pearly haze, Peryn could make out the small port of Breakwater- a clutch of weathered buildings pressed against rocky cliffs, its modest docks bristling with fishing vessels. "Union patrol's increased," Sullivan muttered, adjusting his weather-worn coat as they lowered the spare boat. "Three ships last month. Five now."

"Maybe it has something to do with the fact they're looking for a pirate ship that used to be stuck on a cliff." Victor gave them both a meaningful look. A Vanguard soldier paced the main dock, his blue uniform stark against the gray morning. Merchants hurried past him, eyes downcast, shoulders hunched. Victor's gaze lingered on a gallows being erected near the harbormaster's office with disinterest.

"Must've found another healer." Sullivan followed Victor's look. He spat into the waves.

"Better to be thought of as pirates in this shit realm," Peryn frowned, shivering into his coat. Memori was a decent person, and the idea of executing healers just for helping the sick—as they did in the Eastern realms—struck him as one of the most senseless cruelties of the Union's control.

However, being from Soloras, he couldn't dislike one group of bastards over another. After all, it was slavers from the North who most plagued his homeland.

"Or traitors…" Sullivan mused. "Maybe not our new friend, though. He seems to have pissed them off pretty well."

Victor's rhythm with the oars faltered. He gave Sullivan a look that said he hadn't quite forgiven him for laying hands on Orson Irons. "Stay focused," he ordered, hands tightening on the oars. "Remember, we're traders."

"Aye, Vic." Sullivan flipped up his collar, turning away under that accusatory stare.

Peryn shifted uncomfortably. "And if they give us trouble?" He asked, giving the Union guard a doubtful glance.

"Then we start trading blows." Victor said darkly.

A smirk crossed Sullivan's face, and he cracked his knuckles. "I always come out ahead with that kind of trading."

Peryn shrugged. It sounded as good a plan as any.

The dock creaked under their boots as they tied up. Above them, the Union flag snapped in the wind, its black smoke emblem stark against the pale sky. Victor gave them instructions to separate, each gathering food and oil. They were to meet him back at the dock. The guard didn't give them much trouble. A boy—maybe 16. He looked at the three of them and motioned them to pass by. Peryn shook his head at the lack of nerve, then hurried to follow Victor's orders.

Peryn strode down the damp streets, his boots slapping against slick cobblestones, the scent of salt and rot thick in the air. Everything here reeked of tepid water—moldy wood, fish guts. He missed the dry heat of home, the way smoke curled from the mountain, the scent of burning coal biting at his lungs. Couldn't start a decent fire in this cursed place without a fight, it seemed.

The street buzzed with morning trade, vendors bickering over prices beneath sagging awnings. "Are you kidding me? Seven hells—twenty coin for an ounce of seasoning?" a burly man bellowed, his face red with outrage. He slammed a fist against a wooden stall, making the small jars of dried herbs rattle.

The vendor, a wiry fellow with yellowed teeth, only shrugged. "Don't shoot the messenger, mate—blame the Union. They're the ones that keep raising the taxes."

"Damn the Union." The man spat on the ground, crossing his thick arms. "I'll eat my meat with salt alone before I pay their blood price."

Peryn smirked at that. He couldn't blame the man. The Blacksmoke Union had its hands in every man's pocket in the Eastern realms, choking the life out of business with their endless fees. Not that it was his problem—he had his own interests to tend to.

He ducked into a shadowed alley, then stepped through the warped doorway of a cluttered shop. The scent of old oil and rust tickled his nose, and his pulse kicked up a notch. His sharp gaze scanned the stacks of crates piled against the wall—then landed on a familiar glint.

Oil.

A slow grin spread across his face as he ran a hand over the wooden slats, testing their weight. He flicked his fingers, the metal rings on them catching the dim light. They weren't just for show. A sharp snap of his fingers, and he could summon a spark–then it would be over for anyone in his way. He let out a low whistle, his voice dipping into something close to reverence. "Hello, beautiful."

"That'll be forty silver," came a gruff voice from the shadows. The shopkeeper emerged, a wiry man with calculating eyes and hands stained with oil. "Special reserve, that batch."

Peryn arched an eyebrow. "Forty? For lamp oil?" He ran his finger along the crate's edge. "Ten's the fair price, and we both know it."

The shopkeeper crossed his arms. "Thirty-five. Union taxes went up."

"Fifteen." Peryn idly twisted one of his rings. A tiny spark flashed between his fingers—subtle, but not missed by the shopkeeper whose eyes widened slightly.

"T-twenty-five, final offer," the man said, his voice less confident now.

Peryn pulled out a small pouch, counting twenty coins onto the counter. "Twenty. And I'll pay in coin instead of fire." His smile remained pleasant, but he was glad to see the fear in the man's eyes. "Deal?"

The shopkeeper quickly swept the coins into his palm. "Deal."

"Know when to not cheat a man, don't you?" Peryn scoffed, muttering to himself about Cibola as he hefted the crate of oil, testing its weight before adjusting his grip. Heavy, but manageable. With a last glance around the cluttered shop, he stepped back onto the street, the scent of brine and fish guts slamming into him once more.

Navigating through the bustling market, he moved past carts overflowing with wilting produce and barrels of fish far past its prime. The weight of the crate pressed into his shoulder as he maneuvered through the crowd, taking back alleys where the mud sucked at his boots and the walls dripped with the morning fog.

As he rounded a corner, raised voices spilled from the open door of the *Drunken Anchor.* Peryn slowed his stride. The scent of stale beer and sweat wafted from within, thick even from the street. Two Vanguard soldiers swayed in the doorway, faces flushed from drink despite the early hour. He tightened his grip on the crate, rolling his shoulders to shake off the tension. Drunk Vanguards were mean or stupid— sometimes both. And Victor made him promise not to start a scene.

"…blew the whole damn dam!" The first soldier gestured wildly. "Half our company lost in the flood."

"Impossible," his companion slurred. "One deserter couldn't—"

"You didn't see it. Man had powers, I tell you. The General's furious about losing the Ghost."

"The Ghost?" The second soldier laughed. "That old wreck's been stuck on that cliff since—"

"Not anymore." The first soldier's voice dropped. "Gods below must've helped him. No normal man could've…"

The men disappeared into the tavern. Peryn adjusted his grip on the crate, trying to understand if they were talking about the same person Victor wouldn't allow to leave the ship. The same man who couldn't sail a damn paper boat in a mud puddle. Vic would probably want to know they were talking about him. He adjusted his load and hurried back to the docks.

Sullivan

SULLIVAN SHIFTED THE weight of the crate of hardtack against his hip, adjusting his grip as he walked beside Victor through the damp streets. The scent of whatever filth had been left to fester in the gutters clung to the air, but beneath it, the bundle of herbs Victor carried cut through with sharp, earthy notes. He'd got what the healer asked for, the supplies they needed to get by—now all that was left was hauling the supplies back and getting the hell out of here before they were spotted.

As they passed the seedy tavern, Sullivan spotted Conrad Kol before Victor did. Hard not to—Kol stood outside the *Drunken Anchor* like he was holding court, his men gathered around him, hanging on his every word. His nose had taken a fine beating, bruised and swollen, with a gash splitting his forehead. A damn shame whoever laid hands on him hadn't finished the job.

Sullivan never met Kol, but he knew him all the same. Knew his type. Knew what his wake looked like. He'd seen it firsthand—the burned villages, the blood-soaked fields, the broken bodies left behind when the Vanguard rolled through the Eastern realms.

Kol's men chuckled, muttering to one another as their captain grinned. "The General has summoned us for another mission," Kol declared, his voice thick with self-importance. Then he smirked. "If we succeed—maybe we'll take leave to visit the markets at Driftmarch." The men laughed.

Sullivan went still.

Driftmarch. His home. Or, at least, the place that should've been. A cold, ancient rage coiled in his gut, slow and steady.. He knew what Kol meant. Knew what the markets sold. Knew the men who ran them. And worse— knew the people who let it happen. His people.

They left him to the wolves when he was still small enough to bleed out fast, thinking nature would do their work for them. But nature had other ideas. The wolves never touched him. Were more accepting of the outcast child than his own family. When he didn't die, they hunted him instead.

He wasn't supposed to survive. They left him to die as a child when the earth first answered his call—marked him 'Clan-rot' and cast him out when the stones shifted beneath his feet and the ground obeyed his silent commands. His own people feared what they couldn't understand, and sought to destroy what they thought was a curse.

And when they couldn't kill him, they did the next best thing. They made sure he never belonged. Sullivan rolled his shoulders, exhaling slowly. His fingers flexed around the crate. "Hey, Vic." His voice came out light and easy, but fury vibrated below the surface. "Want me to crush his skull?"

Victor turned his head slightly, one brow lifting in that quiet, amused way of his. He glanced at Kol, considering, then shook his head. "Nothing would make me happier, Sully. But not this time."

Sullivan sighed, cracking his neck. "Shame." His gaze lingered on Kol, cataloging every detail—the way he carried himself, the way his men laughed at his words. Sullivan was on the receiving end of men like that before, though it had been ages. He wasn't a boy anymore, wasn't some half-starved thing left to fate. He glanced at Victor, who was watching the scene unfold, expression unreadable. Didn't matter. Sullivan knew him too well. The tightness in his jaw, the way his fingers flexed slightly where they gripped his own crate—Victor caught the meaning behind Kol's words just as well as he did.

"A shame," Victor agreed, eyes lingering on Kol for a moment before continuing on his way. Sullivan's fingers flexed against the crate once more before he forced himself to keep moving.

By the time they reached the docks, Peryn was already there, his supplies loaded and secured. The rowboat dipped lower in the water as Sullivan stacked the other crate, adjusting the weight to keep it from tipping.

"Oi, Vic," Peryn said in a hushed tone, casting a quick glance over his shoulder. A lone guard loitered near the pier, pretending not to watch them.

Sullivan shifted, rolling his shoulders. "What is it?"

Peryn passed him a bag of dried fruit, leaning in. "Just heard some Black 'n Whites talking about our new captain." A smirk tugged at the edge of his mouth. "Gave them quite an impression, apparently. They were drowning their sorrows over it for hours by the look of it."

Sullivan snorted, half a grin forming. Victor went still. His hands froze on the crate he'd been lifting. The color drained from his face, his expression flickering—just for a second—into something Sullivan didn't like. Like a man pulled under dark water, struggling for breath.

"You alright, Vic?" Peryn asked, frowning.

Victor didn't answer right away. When he did, his voice came rough, tight. "We need to move." He wouldn't meet their eyes. Instead, he worked with sharp, controlled movements, loading the rest of the supplies with a hurried focus. Sullivan met Peryn's gaze as they set back toward the ship. He could tell Peryn noticed Victor's strange actions, as well.

When they got back to the Ghost, Evander and Jermany hurried to help get the supplies on board, secure the dinghy and set sail from the once free island before any patrol got brave enough to investigate them.

Victor approached Memori, handing the bag of herbs to her. "As you requested."

Memori's eyes widened. "Th-thank you!" she stammered. Victor bowed his head slightly.

Sullivan watched the captain's reaction with interest. The way Orson's eyes narrowed to a subtle glare, how he crossed his arms and leaned against the rail—classic signs of a man trying too hard to appear casual–trying to hide he felt threatened.

"Now, did you get something for everyone, Mr. Sloan?" Orson's drawl carried that particular blend of sarcasm and wounded dignity that made Sullivan want to roll his eyes. "You're going to hurt my feelings otherwise."

Sullivan bit back a laugh. Orson sure knew how to act like a spurned schoolboy when he wanted to. Victor rifled through his bag for an exaggerated length of time—and Sullivan knew him well enough to recognize when he was deliberately drawing out the moment—before producing two sticks of candy, white with flecks of green leaves in them.

Keeping eye contact with Orson, he gave one to Viggo, the other he passed to Elowen, who shyly took it before darting behind her mother.

Looking deep in thought, Victor at last strode over to Orson. "Calm seas make for poor sailors." He clapped a hand on the captain's shoulder. "Don't use it all at once," he said solemnly before walking away.

Orson's jaw tightened, and Sullivan could practically hear the man's teeth grinding. "Oh, don't worry. I'll keep that advice forever." He muttered to himself, casting a sour look in Victor's direction. "Mint is my favorite."

The petulant tone made Sullivan want to laugh. The man had nerve. Sullivan had to give him that—taking jabs at Victor, of all people.

Elowen looked down at her candy stick and ran over to Orson, tugging at his sleeve to get his attention. "Here." She held it up to him after careful consideration. "You can have mine."

The transformation on Orson's face was something to behold—regret and tenderness washing away all traces of his previous sourness. "Oh no, Wen. I was only joking–I don't need any!"

"You have to!" The girl insisted, eyes wide with expectation. She broke the stick in half and held out the smaller half. "We can share. Please!" Her eyes widened with an innocence that seemed to cut straight through Orson's defenses, and he gave in with a groan that made Sullivan's lips twitch.

"Alright," he reluctantly took the candy.

Sullivan glanced at Memori and caught the way she was watching them—there was caution in her gaze, yes, but also a fragile sort of hope. Her fingers twisted in her skirt as she observed their interaction, and Sullivan recognized the look of someone seeing possibilities they hardly dared to imagine.

The sight of Orson picking up Elowen and settling her on his knee as they shared the peppermint was enough to make Sullivan revise his opinion somewhat. The man declared it was the best candy he'd ever had, and the genuine warmth in his voice was a far cry from his earlier snippiness.

Sullivan supposed the captain might not be as worthy of an ass-kicking as he first surmised. No–the first one he'd deserved, without question. But another one? Probably not. He'd promised Vic anyway, and Sullivan wouldn't break his word. Not to Victor. Anyone who could be so thoroughly disarmed by a child's kindness couldn't be all bad.

Chapter 20

Memori

Memori sat with her back against the mainmast, sunlight warming her face as she carefully translated another passage from her mother's codex. The ship's gentle rocking made a pleasant counterpoint to her work - deciphering the old healers' shorthand required concentration, but the effort was worth it. Each page revealed treatments her mother never had time to teach her.

The clash of steel drew her attention briefly to the port side where Jermany and Peryn sparred. Her feet barely seemed to touch the deck as she parried Peryn's more aggressive style. There was something almost hypnotic about her movements - like watching water flow around stones in a stream.

Evander stood at the helm, his pale eyes occasionally drifting to the sparring match, a slight smile playing at his lips whenever Jermany landed a particularly clever strike. From the forecastle, Victor's voice carried across the deck as he continued Orson's lesson, his patience seemingly endless despite Orson's obvious growing frustration.

A small hand tugged at Memori's sleeve. Elowen had abandoned her collection of shells to watch the sparring with wide-eyed fascination. "Memma," she whispered with the gravity only a child could muster for such observations, "do you think she's Tempest?"

Memori followed her daughter's gaze to where Jermany executed a perfect spin, her dark braids fanning out around her, catching the light in the copper and bronze beads woven throughout. For just a moment, the image recalled the illustration from Elowen's beloved storybook. "I think she's a sailor, *like* Tempest," Memori answered, smiling as she closed the codex. She wanted to tell Elowen that stories weren't real, that guardians were just invented to make people feel better - but she couldn't bring herself to extinguish that wonder in her daughter's eyes. Not yet. Not when so little wonder remained in their world. Instead, she said, "I also think it's time for lunch. Why don't you go wash up, and I'll make something to eat? How does that sound?"

Elowen nodded eagerly, but her eyes lingered on Jermany. "Did you see how the water moves different around the ship when she's at the wheel?" she asked, her voice dropping to a conspiratorial whisper. "Just like in my book." Before Memori could respond, Elowen was already skipping toward the hatch. Memori shook her head, amused by her daughter's imagination, though something about the observation caught in her mind like a splinter - an odd detail she couldn't quite dismiss.

As she gathered her papers, raised voices drew her attention to where Victor and Orson stood facing each other, their lesson apparently deteriorating into an argument. Orson yanked the stone pendant he always wore - and hurled it at Victor. Memori froze, watching the confrontation unfold. The crew had gone still as well, hands drifting to weapons, eyes narrowing.

Absently, Memori slipped the codex into her satchel, her gaze still on Victor and Orson. Victor calmly strode to a weapon rack and drew a sword—plain-looking but perfectly balanced, its dark metal catching the light strangely. Without warning, he tossed it toward Orson.

Orson's hand shot up, catching the weapon easily. The sword settled into his grip like it belonged there. "A sword?" Orson barked out a laugh. "What is this, the Age of the Sentinel Knights? We have rifles now—and so do they. The Union won't be coming at us with blades, they'll be coming with cannon fire and musket balls."

Victor's expression didn't change. "Some battles can't be won with gunpowder alone."

Memori moved closer, her codex forgotten as she watched Orson lunge forward, the sword moving with him as if it were an extension of his arm. Each swing was natural—precise. And Yet Victor moved with impossible speed, effortlessly avoiding Orson's attacks. The air between them seemed to crackle with an intensity that went beyond a simple training exercise. As the fight wore on, Orson's movements grew more confident, as though the sword itself was guiding him.

A swift counter from Victor sent Orson reeling backward. Victor seized the opportunity, delivering a powerful blow to Orson's midsection that sent him crumpling to the deck. Memori's hand flew to her mouth, stifling a gasp. For a moment, she thought to rush forward, but decided against it. "There's a target on our backs, Captain Irons," Victor said, not even winded as he took hold of Orson's hand and yanked him to his feet. "The Blacksmoke Union will be after us soon enough. Your crew needs you. Memori needs you. That little girl on board needs you." Orson's eyes found hers across the deck, and heat rushed to her cheeks at being caught watching. She turned quickly, heading below deck.

"Can I eat with Viggo?" Elowen asked, hanging from the doorframe of their small cabin, freshly washed and already restless.

Memori smiled despite her distraction. "If Viggo doesn't mind."

"I'll ask, but I know he won't!" Elowen said brightly.

"Go find him then. I'll bring something to the galley shortly." Watching her daughter skip away, Memori's smile faded. She made her way to the galley and started cutting a loaf of bread while her mind replayed the way Orson had handled that sword. Like he'd been born with it in his hand. Like he'd been—A crash startled her from her thoughts. Her hand knocked against a salt bottle, sending it shattering across the floor. Crystal shards scattered like stars across the wooden planks. Sighing, she knelt to clean up the mess, mindful of the sharp edges. A shard caught her palm, drawing blood. She winced, reaching for a clean cloth when footsteps approached from the corridor. Instinctively, she pressed herself into the shadows beneath the counter, unsure why she felt the need to hide.

The dining area filled with crew members, their boots just inches from where she crouched. They gathered at the table where salted pork and fruit were laid out. She remained still, hoping they'd grab food and leave. "No one can be that much of a fool!" Evander's voice pierced the casual conversation. Memori's muscles tensed as she realized they were discussing Orson. The conversation shifted, turning darker with each exchange.

"What would happen if the dear captain had an accident, do you think?" Jermany's voice carried a dangerous edge.

"Command would go to the first mate," Sullivan replied, as if stating a simple fact.

"Maybe we should arrange an accident," Evander suggested, his voice quiet but deadly serious.

"I've gotten very good at poisons," Peryn added casually.

Fear coiled in Memori's stomach as she thought of Elowen—who trusted these people, who saw wonder in them instead of threat. If they could so casually discuss murder over breakfast…

"There will be no more such talk aboard this ship!" Victor's voice cut through their plotting like a blade. "Or off it."

Silence fell, broken only by the distant sound of waves against the hull. "We were only jokin' Vic," Peryn laughed nervously.

"We do not joke about dishonorable shit—we are bound by oaths. Not common fucking cutthroats. Or have you forgotten?"

"We remember," Evander said. "It's just that…he's no sailor, Vic."

"Don't you think I know that?" Exhaustion bled through Victor's words. "It doesn't matter. If anyone so much as talks about raising a finger to the Captain again, they'll answer to me. Is that clear?"

Their murmured agreement seemed reluctant but sincere. Boots scattered across the planks as they departed, leaving Victor alone. "Ms. Wren," he called quietly. "You can come out now." Memori's heart stopped. Slowly, she rose from her hiding place, hand still pressed against her bleeding palm.

"How much did you hear?" He looked tired, eyes heavy with weariness.

"Enough to know Orson shouldn't turn his back on your crew," she answered, voice steady despite her fear.

Victor stepped closer, movements careful as if approaching a frightened animal. "Their talk is idle. You are safe here. You and the girl."

"And Orson?" she asked, meeting his gaze directly.

A strange laugh escaped him, almost pained. "You should worry about him least of all."

"Why?"

Something shifted in Victor's expression—darkness beyond mere shadow. "I've sworn to keep him safe." The words carried a weight that seemed to change the air itself. His eyes met hers, steel beneath the weariness. "And you, Memori. I pledge that same oath to you." A heartbeat's pause. "And your child."

The word caught her off guard. "Sister," she corrected sharply, the lie automatic after so many years.

Victor's gaze held understanding, maybe even regret. "Your sister," he repeated softly, before disappearing into the shadows of the corridor. The galley fell silent save for the distant laughter of children—Elowen and Viggo, still innocent, still untouched by the danger surrounding them all. Memori looked down at her injured palm, ready to clean the wound, and froze. Where the glass had cut her, the skin was smooth and unmarked. Only dried blood remained as evidence that she'd been injured at all. Somewhere in the back of her mind, Elowen's words echoed: "Do you think she's Tempest?" Perhaps there was more truth in stories than she'd been willing to believe.

Elowen

ELOWEN CLUTCHED HER book tighter as she crept across the deck. Memma told her to stay below, but she was tired of the small cabin and its creaking walls. Besides, she wanted to find someone who could answer her questions.

Peryn and Jermany stood by the big pole in the middle of the ship—the mainmast, Orson had called it. Elowen liked Peryn. He always smiled at her and sometimes made tiny flames dance across his fingertips when Memma wasn't looking. Jermany was scarier. She rarely smiled, and her eyes were sharp like the knives Jayce used back when the ship was an inn.

"...how can you say that, have you ever even seen a volcano?" Peryn was asking, looking shocked.

"No," Jermany said, crossing her arms. "And I don't want to."

Peryn wasn't giving up. "Don't be that way, love. Come with me sometime! I'll show you where fire runs like a great river."

"You've asked me a dozen times," Jermany said, raising one eyebrow the way Memma did when Elowen asked for sweets before dinner. "Always with that same hopeful look."

Peryn grinned, his eyes twinkling like he knew a secret. "One day you'll say yes."

"I doubt that," Jermany replied. Elowen saw her mouth twitch a little.

Taking a deep breath for courage, Elowen approached them. The copper beads in Jermany's braids caught the sunlight, making them shine just like in her book. They were exactly the same! Her heart pounded as she tugged on Peryn's sleeve.

Peryn looked down, his big smile getting softer. "Well hello there, little explorer. What brings you above deck?"

Elowen's mouth went dry. She glanced at Jermany, then stood on tiptoe to whisper to Peryn, "Is she Tempest?"

Peryn looked at Jermany, then back at Elowen, crouching down until his eyes were level with hers. "Why don't you ask her?"

"She scares me," Elowen whispered even quieter, hiding a little behind Peryn so Jermany couldn't see her.

Peryn chuckled. "You have a point." He looked over his shoulder at Jermany, then leaned closer to Elowen, lowering his voice. "She scares me too."

"I can still hear you," Jermany said, rolling her eyes. She turned toward Elowen, and Elowen could see her trying to make her face look friendlier. "Why do you ask if I'm Tempest? Don't you know that's just a story?"

Elowen's fingers gripped her book tighter. She stepped out from behind Peryn and lifted her chin. "Viggo says some stories are real."

Something strange happened to Jermany's face then. It softened, just a little, like when Memma sometimes looked at Orson when she thought no one was watching. Jermany crouched down, making herself smaller, less scary.

"What makes you think I'm this Tempest?" she asked.

Elowen's hands trembled as she opened her book to her favorite page. "You look like her. See?" She pointed to the illustration. "And..." she hesitated, not sure if she should say the next part, "the water moves different when you're at the wheel."

Peryn made a funny noise, like he was trying not to laugh. Jermany gave him a look that would have made Elowen hide, but Peryn just smiled wider."Maybe I just know the sea well," Jermany said, turning back to Elowen. "That doesn't make me some...guardian from a story."

"But Viggo said—"

"Viggo says lots of things," Jermany interrupted, but her voice wasn't scary anymore. She touched one of the beads in her braid, just like Tempest did in the story when she was thinking. "Sometimes stories help us understand things we can't explain yet."

Elowen thought about that. She flipped through her book, searching the pages. "You mean like how Victor sometimes makes thunder? Where would I find a story about that?"

Jermany and Peryn exchanged another look, but this one seemed different—more worried. "I don't think that one's been written yet," Peryn said quickly. "Now, shouldn't you be helping your Memma with something?"

Elowen knew a dismissal when she heard one. She nodded and turned to go, but Jermany's voice stopped her.

"Wait."

Elowen looked back, her heart pounding. Jermany's fingers moved to one of the small copper beads in her braid, working it free. She held it out, the metal catching the light.

"Here," Jermany said, dropping the bead into Elowen's palm.

Elowen's mouth fell open. She stared at the small treasure in her hand, feeling its warmth. It took her a moment to remember her manners. "Th-thank you," she finally managed to whisper, closing her fingers carefully around the bead.

As she walked away, her treasure clutched tight, she heard Jermany say, "Shut up, Cannonball," though she didn't sound truly angry. "And stop with the Solhara festivals. I'm not going."

"Not yet," Peryn replied, sounding happy.

Elowen grinned as she skipped back to find Viggo. Of course a guardian wouldn't just announce who they were. That would be against the rules. But sometimes, they gave you signs if you were brave enough to ask.

Chapter 21

Orson

The dream came in fragments—the smell of fresh bread from the market stalls, dirty, bare feet slapping against Crestmere's cobblestones, and angry shouts echoing off the narrow walls of the alley. Orson's fingers were sticky with stolen pie juice, the treat clutched against his threadbare shirt as he ran. He could have taken the stale bread Madame Dekker always left out for the street children, but he'd wanted to prove to the others he wasn't just some baby. Wanted to show he could steal something special, right from under the vendor's nose. The thrill of it felt real, the way the older street children had stopped their dice game to watch. How proud he'd felt, stretching up on his tiptoes to reach the prized venison pie. He'd even yelled thank you as he ran off with it.

The shrill whistle of the Watch cut through the market's bustle.

Everything around him melted to a blur of motion as he darted through Crestmere's maze-like streets, his short legs carrying him as fast as they could while the pack of guards and angry vendors gained ground. His chest hurt from running, and the sounds bounced off the buildings until he couldn't tell where they were coming from anymore. He turned what he thought was another corner—only to find himself trapped against the high wall that marked the edge of the village's upper quarter.

Just as tears of panic welled up, a hand shot out from above, accompanied by a familiar whispered hiss. The older boy had appeared from nowhere. He'd climbed onto one of the overhead beams that connected the buildings, reaching down just as the Watch rounded the corner. Through his panic, Orson registered stormy gray eyes and dark hair that fell across a face tight with concentration. The boy's grip was iron-strong around Orson's wrist as he pulled him up, muscles straining with the effort of lifting him. "I've got you," the boy whispered fiercely. "But so help me-if you don't stop showing off..."

They huddled together in the shadows of the beam while the Watch searched below, the boy's hand gentle but firm over Orson's mouth to quiet his hiccupping breaths. The meat pie lay forgotten somewhere in the alley, but they'd escaped with something far more valuable—their freedom.

"One of these days," the older boy said later, once they were safely back in the abandoned tannery, sharing a heel of bread he'd pulled from his pocket, "I won't be there to save you."

Orson jerked awake, his heart hammering against his ribs. The dream felt so real—the fear, the exhilaration, the rough wood under his palms, the strong grip around his wrist. He rubbed absently at his right wrist, trying to shake off the lingering sensation of phantom fingers. A dull ache pulsed there, making him frown. Just a dream, he told himself firmly, even as he massaged the inexplicable soreness. The pain in his wrist persisted, like an old injury awakened by the memory of its making.

Sleep would not return, not with his mind churning like this. The cabin walls seemed to press in around him, and the gentle rocking of the ship only heightened his restlessness. Making his way to the deck, Orson hoped the night air might clear his head.

The sea stretched out before him, moonlight dancing on the waves. But even the vast expanse of stars couldn't settle his thoughts. The dream tugged at him, making his skin feel too tight, his feet too restless. When the crewman–Sullivan by the look of it–in the crow's nest began watching him with suspicious eyes, Orson retreated below deck, following the hidden passages Dollan had mapped out for him.

He wandered without purpose, or so he told himself, until the warm glow from Memori's shop drew him like a moth to a flame. Through the doorway, he could see her working—hair falling loose around her shoulders, lips pursed in concentration as she measured dried flowers into a cup. Tension in his chest eased at the sight of her, as if he'd found an anchor in the storm of his thoughts.

Orson lingered in the doorway, not wanting to interrupt. Her movements were graceful, precise—a dance of skilled hands. When her gaze finally met his, the small smile that curved her lips made his heart skip. "What are you doing wandering about…Captain?" Her cheeks flushed as she twisted her hair into a knot, a few strands escaping to frame her face. "Trouble sleeping?"

"Something like that," he admitted, still hesitating at the threshold of her space. "And please, don't call me that."

"As you wish." Memori poured steaming water over the herbs, the fragrant steam rising between them. "Have one with me?" She gestured to the extra chair, and something in her voice made him wonder if perhaps she didn't want to be alone with her own ghosts tonight.

"Why not?" He kept his movements slow, deliberate as he settled into the chair beside her. They sat in comfortable silence, the ship's creaking a gentle backdrop. When she passed him his cup, their fingers brushed. The touch was brief, electric—and Orson couldn't help but notice that she didn't flinch away this time. Instead, her fingers lingered for just a heartbeat longer than necessary, and the pink in her cheeks deepened.

Her fingers traced the rim of her cup absently, and Orson watched the movement, wondering what those gentle hands would feel like in his own. He forced himself to look away. "What do you call this, anyway?" he gestured down to the mug. "Twelve hours sleep?"

She laughed, making his heart skip a beat. "Blissful coma may be better." She glanced upward, lips pursed together in thought.

"Comfortable corpse, perhaps?" Orson offered. She laughed again. Orson took another sip of the tea. "How is El taking all this?" he asked, desperate for any subject that might distract him from thoughts of holding her hand.

"Orson. If I wanted her called El, I damn well would have named her that," Memori snapped, then froze, realizing her slip.

The words hung between them. Her face paled as she stared into her cup.

"How old were you?" he asked softly, dreading the answer.

"Sixteen." She said it like confessing a sin.

Orson recalled Kol throwing the child aside, his own daughter. His hands clenched, but he kept his voice steady. "I should have killed him when I had the chance."

"Thanks." A bitter laugh. "If only my father had shown such courage."

The weight of what she wasn't saying pressed against his chest. He wanted to reach for her, offer some comfort, but he knew better. Instead, he sat with her in the quiet, letting her know she wasn't alone.

"Her eyes…they're lovely," he said softly, watching Memori's face in the gentle lamplight.

"They are," Memori swallowed with difficulty, then met his gaze with glassy eyes. The vulnerability in her expression made his breath catch. For a moment, neither of them looked away.

"Orson," she smiled at him, her voice barely above a whisper, "thank you."

"For what?" He shifted uncomfortably, all too aware of how close they were sitting. "I'm responsible for upending your life, remember?"

"Just…" she shrugged, "being kind to me. And Elowen." The way she searched his face made his pulse quicken. For a moment, he wondered what it would feel like to reach across the space between them, to brush away the strand of hair that had fallen across her cheek. He couldn't. She deserved more than that.

"You're welcome," he managed, finishing his tea and forcing himself to stand. His hand went to the back of his neck, rubbing nervously. "Do you want me to see you to your cabin?"

A delicate pink rose to Memori's cheeks, and Orson became horrifyingly aware of how his choice of words might be perceived. "I didn't mean—!" He raised his hands in surrender, face burning. "I just meant"

A good-natured laugh escaped her lips, easing his embarrassment even as it made his heart flutter. "It's fine, Captain. And, no, thank you. I still have some work to do here."

He nodded awkwardly. Before he could retreat fully, the sound of small feet padding across the wooden planks stopped him in his tracks. He turned to see Elowen in her oversized nightgown, her hair tangled from sleep. She clutched a crumpled book in one hand, the other scrubbing sleepily at her eyes.

"Memma?" Elowen's small voice broke the quiet. "I woke up."

Memori's face softened instantly, her gaze flicking to Orson before she knelt to meet Elowen's gaze. "What is it, love? Did you have a bad dream?"

Elowen shook her head but looked toward Orson, as if weighing her next words. Her expression was shy, almost expectant. "Will you tell me a story?"

"Me?" Orson blinked, caught off guard.

Memori's lips curled into a small smile as she rocked to her feet. "Shhh, love, the captain was just off to bed."

"Nonsense!" Orson crouched down to Elowen's height, his voice soft. "I love stories! What's your favorite?"

Elowen thought solemnly, book clutched tight to her chest. "The Guardians!" Her eyes widened expectantly.

"Ah, that's a good one." A ghost of a smile tugged at his lips. "I don't know if I can do it justice. But I'll give it a try."

Orson lifted Elowen into his arms, her small form warm and sleepy against his chest like she belonged there. Her head lolled onto his shoulder as he began walking toward the stairs that led to the upper deck. He caught Memori watching them, her soft expression making his heart twist. His voice was low and steady. "Did you know this ship we're on was stranded in place by an epic battle one of the Guardians fought?"

"Really?" her mouth dropped open.

"Really," he continued, adjusting her weight in his arms as they climbed the stairs. "The earth was torn apart with the battle, draining the sea and leaving it stuck!"

"What happened next?" Elowen's fingers curled into his shirt, her eyes bright despite her sleepiness.

"Well," Orson's voice dropped to a whisper as they made their way through the quiet corridors, continuing the tale until her eyes grew heavy. He settled her into the little cot against the wall, carefully tucking the blanket around her. Strange how these gentle movements felt foreign to his hands. He'd been taken at sixteen, like all the others—hauled from his bed with rifles at his back, marched into a life of trenches and rifle oil and blood. Even if he hadn't chosen it, hadn't wanted it, that's what he was: a man forged in violence, conditioned to deal in death. His fingers, better acquainted with triggers than blanket corners, hesitated over the soft wool.

"What happened to the Guardians?" Elowen asked, her eyes already half-closed.

"They kept watch," Orson said, crouching beside her. "Even when it was hard. Even when it hurt. Because that's what Guardians do—they protect the things that matter most."

"Maybe you're a guardian." Her lips curved into a soft smile, her voice fading as sleep claimed her. "I think you're brave."

Orson smiled, brushing a stray curl from her face. "Not as brave as you, Elowen," he murmured.

Brave. He wasn't brave—he was a coward who'd followed orders to save his own skin. He could still see them, the ones who'd actually been brave, who'd refused. Could still feel their warm blood spraying across his face as they fell next to him, their bodies crumpling into the mud while he stood there, following orders like a good soldier. The memory rose like bile in his throat.

Memori's gentle voice interrupted the dark thought. "She's taken a liking to you."

Orson glanced at Elowen, then back to Memori. "Kids don't know any better," he said lightly, an awkward smile playing on his lips. They didn't know how to recognize monsters wearing human skin. Didn't know how to see the blood that never quite washed away.

Memori tilted her head, studying him. The room suddenly felt too warm, too close, like those moments before an execution when the air grew thick with the copper scent of fear. "I should…" Orson gestured vaguely toward the door. "Get some rest myself."

"Of course," Memori said, stepping aside to let him pass. Her voice followed him as he reached the threshold. "Orson? Thanks again."

He paused but didn't turn around. "Anytime." He slipped out into the corridor, leaving Memori to watch over her daughter. As he walked back to his cabin, the image of Elowen's small smile and Memori's steady gaze stayed with him, settling deep in his chest, where it felt both too heavy and too light at the same time.

Chapter 22

Memori

With Elowen sleeping soundly, Memori returned to her shop to tidy her supplies. The quiet should have been calming, but Orson's dark eyes lingered in her thoughts. He wasn't unattractive. Tall. strong. Capable. The type of man who would make a good father for someone's children.

Don't be absurd!

Memori's lips pressed into a thin line as she dismissed the ridiculous notion, shaking her head. But the thought clung to her like a shadow, no matter how hard she tried to push it away. Even if such feelings had any merit—which they didn't—there was the truth to contend with. Orson might be a good man, but could he ever truly love a child fathered by his enemy? Could he raise Elowen as if she were his own? The idea gnawed at her, bitterness curling in her throat as she poured out the rest of her tea.

She didn't trust the answer. And yet…

Memori caught herself staring at nothing, her hand tightening around the edge of the counter. She didn't want to name the flutter in her chest when Orson spoke to her with unexpected gentleness—or the way he looked at Elowen, as though her existence mattered to him more than anything else–the lightness it made her feel.

You're being a fool.

She turned off the lantern and retreating to her bed. Sleep, however, proved elusive. The faint creak of the ship's timbers accompanied the steady rocking of the *Crimson Ghost* on the Avalon Sea, a rhythm she should have found soothing by now. But her mind refused to quiet. She hadn't wanted this life—not the running, not the fighting, and certainly not the ghosts that haunted her when the moon was high. However, choice was a rare privilege in these times, and guardians knew she'd had precious little of it up to this point in her life as it was.

Through the porthole, the stars began to fade, giving way to the first light of dawn. The soft hues of blue and gold played on the waves outside, their beauty a stark contrast to the storm in her chest. With a sigh, she gave up on rest altogether.

No one had asked her to do any cooking—Victor's crew rotated shifts, each bringing their own style to the task. Sullivan's meals were hearty and practical, laden with salted meats and bread that could survive a voyage. Jermany's dishes, on the rare occasions she cooked, carried the smoky spices of her homeland. But Memori couldn't shake the feeling that she needed to pull her weight, even if her role aboard the ship was still undefined. Perhaps it was guilt—or the need to keep her hands busy to drown out her thoughts. Besides, she mused grimly, food was an excellent carrier for poison if someone had a mind to get rid of Orson.

Leaving Elowen still sleeping, she made her way to the galley, her boots thumping softly against the wooden planks. The scents of salt and damp wood accompanied her as she descended the narrow staircase, and her fingers brushed the handrail, worn smooth by countless sailors before her. When she reached the galley, a warm glow spilled out through the partially open door. The clatter of pots and pans broke the morning silence, along with the low hum of someone whistling a tune she didn't recognize.

The tall man—Evander—glanced up as she entered, his pale, ghostlike features illuminated by the lantern on the table. Shadows clung to him in the dim light, an aura that always seemed to follow him. "Healer," he acknowledged her by touching two fingers to his forehead in a salute. There was a set of bracelets on his wrist she hadn't noticed before; they were made from bark, braided with meticulous care. The faint silver veins that ran through the grey wood shimmered when touched by the lantern light, making the surface almost seem alive.

"Morning," she said in response. He gave her a brief smile before grabbing a piece of bacon and slipping out the door. Victor's son was there as well, his attention already back on the burner he'd lit beneath a battered pot of coffee.

"Good morning," Memori said. Viggo gave her a short nod and began cracking eggs in a large skillet. "How old are you, Viggo?" Memori asked, pulling an apron over her head. He looked up, as if thinking, then shrugged.

"Cat got your tongue?" Memori teased good-naturedly. Viggo shook his head, smiling briefly before handing her a wooden spoon and darting from the galley. Raising her eyebrows in confusion, Memori scrambled the eggs as they cooked in the pan. Now that she'd thought of it, she hadn't heard him speak a word since his oath of loyalty to Orson. She turned from the stove and Victor was suddenly next to her.

Memori jumped, almost knocking a glass off the counter. Muttering a curse, she exhaled slowly as her heartbeat returned to normal.

"Sorry," Victor said, pouring himself a cup of coffee. He took the pan of eggs off the heat, giving it a quick stir.

Memori finished her glass of water, eyeing the first mate–trying to judge his mood. Victor wasn't terribly easy to read, but she took a chance and asked him, anyway. Worst that could happen is he would tell her it was none of her business. "Your son…Viggo. He doesn't talk a lot."

Victor lifted the coffee to his lips. "Not since his mother was murdered."

Memori held a hand to her mouth in shock. "Murdered? Victor…I'm so sorry!"

"No one is as sorry as he was…once I was through with him." Victor's voice carried the weight of violence, but his eyes held something darker - the rage of a parent who'd watched their child's light dim. "Physicians in the Eastern Realms told me it was shock. Nothing they could do about it. He's better than he was."

Memori thought of how Elowen froze–terrified whenever Kol and his unit would arrive at the Inn. The way he put his hands on Memori whenever he saw her–the girl didn't like it. She would go to their designated hiding places and stay there until Memori came to tell her it was safe. Victor met her gaze, and for a moment, she saw her own pain reflected there - the helplessness of watching your child carry wounds you couldn't heal. "I wish I could help," she whispered.

Victor's expression softened. "That means… more than you know." His smile was genuine but brief, like the sun breaking through storm clouds. "But it is unnecessary for you to concern yourself."

She nodded, her gaze falling to her hands as the weight of unspoken understanding passed between them. They were the same, in their way—parents bound by love and fear, willing to kill to protect their children, yet haunted by the knowledge that no amount of love or fury could shield them from every danger. Victor cleared his throat, breaking the moment. "If you'll excuse me. I have duties to attend," he said, his voice rougher now, like a man brushing aside the tender edges of emotion. He stood to leave.

ORSON PAUSED IN the galley doorway. His chest tightened at the sight of Memori and Victor sharing coffee in the early morning quiet. His relief at finding her turned sour, though he couldn't say why. "Taking your time today, Mr. Sloan?"

He scooped eggs onto a plate and stabbed at them, oddly irritated by Victor's relaxed posture. "Thought you were eager to continue my education."

"Only in a hurry for you to learn, Captain." Victor said, ignoring Orson's tone. "See you up top when you're ready." He paused. "Up top means-"

"I know what it means," Orson snapped, hating how Victor's presence shattered the peace he'd hoped to find here. "I've been waiting there half the morning."

Victor's eyes narrowed in suspicion, but all he said was, "Apologies, Captain."

Orson followed him out, muttering about impossible first mates. He told himself his foul mood was about the endless lessons, ignoring the image of Memori's soft smile as she'd talked with Victor.

The nerve of the bastard, acting so familiar with everyone - with Memori. The morning air bit at Orson's face as he followed Victor onto the deck, but his simmering frustration kept him warm enough.

"What's the lesson today, Mr. Sloan? More naval terms to impress your crew with?"

Victor's mouth formed a hard line. "I thought we'd moved past this childishness, Captain." Sullivan and Jermany exchanged knowing looks from their posts. Something about their casual familiarity, their easy belonging, made Orson's jaw clench.

"Past what?," he said, running a hand through his hair. "Past having some of us up at dawn, catering to your whims."

Understanding flickered across Victor's face, followed by that damned half-smile. "Ah. I see." His eyes glinted with amusement.

"And what's that supposed to mean?"

"Seems you need an education in more than sailing." Sullivan and Peryn tried to hide their grins as Victor leaned back against the rail. "First thing you do to woo a maiden is not act like a desperately jealous hound every time someone speaks to her." His smile turned decidedly smug. "I can help with that, too. If you ask nicely."

Victor's condescending tone fractured the remnants of Orson's patience. He charged forward, forgetting their last sparring match - or past caring.

Victor sidestepped with ease. Orson's boot hit a slick patch. The world tilted, railing catching him in the stomach before the sea swallowed him whole. The cold shocked his lungs, dark water dragging him down like a nightmare come to life.

VICTOR LEANED OVER the railing, trying to steady his trembling hands against the worn wood. The Vanguard didn't teach fighting skills worth a damn. His chest tightened as he watched Orson thrash in the water, and he looked away—memories threatening to surface with each desperate splash. He didn't want to watch, despite the reassurance he tried to feed himself. Orson was always getting himself into situations like this. And usually out of them just as easily.

Sullivan and Jermany flanked him. "Vic…not that it would bother me, mind, but I know you're keen on keeping the dolt alive," Sullivan stroked his beard. "I don't think our captain is taking too well to the water."

"Don't be absurd, Sully." Victor glanced at the Sea. Victor's throat constricted at the familiar sight of a drowning man, the way Orson's movements grew more erratic, more primal. The captain bobbed up and down, arms flailing with diminishing strength until his movements slowed.

"Sully's right, Vic." Jermany leaned over the railing, but Victor barely heard her. His vision tunneled on Orson's form as it slipped beneath the dark water. Fingers clawed at his coat, ripping it off. His cap and boots followed, abandoned on deck as he scrambled onto the railing. The familiar grip of panic pushed him forward as he dove, determined not to let history repeat itself this time.

Memori

"Man overboard!"

Memori heard the shout as she arrived on deck, her heart hammering against her ribs. She reached the railing just in time to see Jermany and Sullivan frantically working with the rope, their movements a blur in her terror-narrowed vision.

"Captain's taken a dip. Vic's gone to fish him out," Jermany's words barely registered as Memori scanned the churning water below. The waves seemed impossibly large now, each one threatening to swallow any sign of them.

"I see him!" Sullivan's shout drew her eyes to where two dark heads bobbed in the water—Victor's and… Orson's lifeless form beside him. Her breath caught in her throat. Victor had one arm locked around Orson's chest, the other reaching for the rope, but Orson's head lolled against Victor's shoulder, unnaturally still against the violent motion of the waves.

Horror rose in her throat as Victor struggled toward the rope. One wrong wave, one slip of his grip, and Orson would sink beneath those merciless waters. Sullivan and Jermany hauled on the rope with desperate strength.

"He's not breathing." Sullivan's words sent ice through her veins.

"Shit." Victor's face had gone pale beneath the seawater dripping down it.

Memori broke through her paralysis, dropping to her knees and elbowing Sullivan and Jermany out of the way. She tilted Orson's head back, clamped her hand over his nose, and leaned over. Pressing firmly down on his chest, she could feel her own pulse hammering, willing his to do the same.

Wake up, Orson! She moved to give him another breath.

Before her lips touched his, Orson's back arched, and he started coughing. Rolling to his side, he gasped for air, emptying water from his lungs. His heartbeat came to life–strong and quick beneath her palm, flooding her with dizzying relief.

Her hand moved to his forehead before she could stop herself, brushing away a strand of damp hair, her fingers tracing the stubble on his jaw. His eyes met hers, and something shifted in her chest.

"One of these days, Orson…" Victor's voice broke through the moment. Memori withdrew her hand from Orson as Victor peeled off his soaked shirt. The silver ring on the chain around his neck caught her eye, drawing her attention across the map of scars and tattoos that marked his torso. They seemed familiar somehow, though she couldn't place why.

As he wrung out his shirt, Memori noted something off about his movements—too sharp, too urgent. His hands trembled slightly despite his casual expression. "Drowning yourself to get a kiss is not becoming of you, Captain." His dark eyes darted between them. "I could have taught you how to ask." Jermany snickered, offering Victor a blanket. He snatched it from her

Heat rushed to her face as she looked away. Victor's unusual intensity only heightened her confusion as she watched him snatch a blanket offered to him by Jermany.

Orson sat up with a groan, glaring at Victor. "And here I thought" he wheezed, "…you just enjoy watching me suffer."

Victor's face twisted for a moment, his eyes screwing shut. When they opened, something haunted flickered in their depths."I suppose our new 'first' lesson will be learning how to swim."

He crouched beside Orson, his grin crooked and just a little too forced. He nudged Orson's shoulder with the back of his hand, light but lingering. "If you happen to drown again, your next kiss will be from me."

"I bet you'd like that, wouldn't you?" Orson rasped. Victor rolled his eyes and stood—too fast. He barked an order to Sullivan, already shifting focus, already pulling away. Still catching his breath, Orson muttered as he pushed to his feet. "I'd rather kiss a whale's blowhole. Be less traumatic."

Memori stepped forward to help, but Orson waved her off with a sideways glare at Victor.

She backed off, though her gaze lingered on the first mate. He'd played it off with sarcasm and orders—but she'd seen it. That flash of fear he tried to hide.

Chapter 23

Memori

The dark-haired boy stood at the base of the ancient apple tree, neck craned back as he studied the highest branches.

"What are you doing?" Her voice startled him so badly he almost stumbled backward. Memori stood a few paces away, arms crossed, her satchel slung over one shoulder, fresh herbs poking out of it in vibrant greens and purples.

"Nothing," he said too quickly, his green eyes darting away like a guilty thief. Then, reconsidering, he added with a lopsided grin, "I'm getting you an apple."

She raised an eyebrow, skeptical. "Those are too high. You'll fall."

"I climb trees all the time," he said dismissively, puffing out his chest. With a laugh that was more bravado than certainty, he grabbed the nearest branch and started up.

The first few branches were simple enough, and she was aware her presence spurred him to bolder heights. He was halfway to the top when the branch beneath his foot let out a warning crack.

"Careful!" she shouted, but it was too late.

The world blurred into a whirlwind of leaves, snapping branches, and free-falling panic. He hit the ground with a bone-jarring thud; the breath knocked clean out of him.

Memori was at his side in seconds, her face a mix of worry and exasperation. She knelt down, her satchel already swinging forward. "I told you so," she muttered, though her hands hovered over him, unsure where to start. "What were you thinking?"

"I was thinking about you," he wheezed, managing a crooked smile despite the pain radiating through his ribs. Slowly, he sat up, wincing. "Here." He fumbled in his pocket and pulled out a bruised apple—not from the highest branches, but from one he'd picked lower down before his ill-fated climb. She didn't have the heart to tell him she saw right through the ruse. He held it out to her with all the sincerity his young heart could muster. "Marry me?"

Her mouth fell open in disbelief, and for a moment, she just stared at him. Then, with a huff, she snatched the apple from his hand. "You're impossible, you know that?"

"Is that a yes?" His grin widened.

"It's a you're an idiot," she shot back, stuffing the apple into her satchel. "Now hold still so I can make sure you didn't actually crack your skull open."

A DULL THROB pulsed in Memori's temple. The dream lingered, vivid and tangible. Her heart fluttered—a feeling she couldn't place, like she'd just met an old friend. She shook her head, pulling her knees to her chest.

Just a stupid dream.

The moonlight streamed through the porthole, painting the cabin in silver. Her eyes lingered on the glow, unease coiling in her stomach. Deep down, she couldn't shake the fear that it was more than just a dream.

Elowen slept peacefully, one arm wrapped around her book, copper curls spilling across her pillow. The sight of her daughter's steady breathing helped calm Memori's racing pulse, but sleep felt impossibly far away now.

She slipped from under the blankets, careful not to wake Elowen as she pulled on her boots and wrapped herself in a shawl. She made her way to the upper deck, seeking the open air and endless sky that always helped clear her head after the bad dreams. Stars scattered endlessly in a vast sea of black and deep blue. A cool breeze carried the salt-sharp scent of the ocean, and Memori drew it deep into her lungs, letting it wash away the last echoes of her nightmare.

Orson

ORSON STRETCHED OUT on his back on the deck, one arm behind his head as he watched the stars drift by. He'd been trying to sort through the mess in his head, replaying the day's events like some kind of masochist. Victor's knowing smirk, the rush of cold water, the burning in his lungs that felt horrifyingly familiar—and then Memori's face above his, her hands steady and sure as she brought him back to life.

The sound of footsteps made him turn his head. And there she was at the top of the stairs, looking like something out of a dream in her nightclothes with her hair loose around her shoulders. She hesitated when she saw him, taking a half-step back, and his chest tightened at the thought of her leaving. Heat crept into his cheeks as their eyes met. His body remembered the press of her mouth against his all too clearly, even if he'd been half-dead. If he hadn't let Victor get under his skin, he'd never have gone overboard. The whole mess was his own damn fault, and now here she was, probably thinking he was the biggest fool to ever set foot on a ship, let alone captain one against his will.

She looked uncertain, hovering at the top of the stairs like she might bolt at any moment. The shadows under her eyes that spoke of too many sleepless nights. Before he could stop to think about it, he was already pushing himself to his feet, not wanting to waste this chance moment alone with her.

"Can't sleep?" he asked, trying to keep his voice casual, as if his heart wasn't hammering against his ribs.

Memori yawned, shaking her head, and some of the tension seemed to leave her shoulders. "No. I just needed a moment to myself, now that Wen is finally sleeping." Her voice was soft, slightly raspy with exhaustion, and he wanted to hear more of it.

"Ah." Her mention of the girl made Orson smile fondly. He shifted his weight, leaning against the railing of the ship. "You're doing right by her, you know" He clasped his hands together, staring out at where the dark waters met the sky. "She's got someone who loves her more than anything. That's what matters."

Memori lowered her eyes, something unreadable passing over her face. "You'd make a good father," she whispered. Orson let out a slow breath, the comment taking him by surprise

"I don't know about that." He'd never given it much thought before. After watching so many families torn apart, seeing children left parentless by the Union's carnage, he'd buried that possibility so deep he'd forgotten it existed. Being a father was something that happened to other people–good people. Not to soldiers. Not men with bloodstained hands.

"I do know I care about her. Precious little thing, it's damn impossible not to." He swallowed, the next words sticking in his throat as he glanced over his shoulder at her. "I care about both of you..."

Memori's delicate fingertips brushed the back of Orson's hand–her touch soft and uncertain–sending a current between them. Her eyes still lingered downard, as though the very gesture could only carry shame. Orson fought the urge to pull her into him. To whisper words of comfort until she no longer felt that fear. Instead, he turned his palm, catching her fingers between his. They trembled slightly, and for a moment, fear curled inside Orson at the thought of her pulling away. He left the choice in her hands. If that is what she wanted, he wouldn't stop her. He'd let her go–let her pull away to safety, no matter how much it might undo him.

The tremble dissipated and Memori closed her fingers around Orson's hand. He lifted his eyes to her and she turned to him, meeting his gaze. Moonlight softened her face–eyes turning into endless sky that sparkled with the very stars overheard. Suddenly, he wasn't sure if the ache in his chest was fear or the desperate, burning need to reach back and not let go.

His fingers closed around hers—just slightly, just enough. A risk, a reach. He couldn't help it. He had to take the chance. He turned toward her, tugging her hand gently to invite her movement. She moved with him effortlessly, full of quiet trust. The kind Orson didn't think he deserved—but God help him, the need for it was louder than every voice in his head telling him he wasn't worthy. He lifted his arm to spin her and she stepped into the twirl, a smile flickering across her lips before she planted her final step in front of him

The night seemed to hold its breath as Orson found her waist with his other hand and pulled her close. Memori didn't resist like he thought she might. Her breath was warm against his skin, stuttering as his fingertips ghosted along the curve of her wrist. She rested her palm against his chest, gazing at his shoulder as though she was afraid–like Orson–that this moment may not be real. But, when her eyes met his, and the tremble in her parted lips said everything—hope, fear, and the fragile belief that maybe this wasn't another moment they'd awake from. That look in her eyes gave Orson the only courage he could ever need, and he closed the distance between them.

Finally, he kissed her. Careful at first—tentative, searching—but the moment she sighed into his lips, it was as if the air was knocked from his lungs. Her fingers clenched into his shirt, and Orson's tangled into the fabric of her sleeve, as if grounding him into reality of how close she was in the moment. To the warmth of her in his arms.

Memori's hands slid to his back and she pressed against him, exhaling like she could finally breathe for the first time. The silence stretched on, endless, but welcome–a rare gift for both of them. The ship rocked gently beneath them, waves a quiet rhythm against the hull as the night curled around the– cool and damp with the scent of the sea.

Memori shifted, turning back toward the open waters and her hand found Orson's again, leaning her head against his shoulder. Orson let out a breath he didn't know he was holding and brushed his thumb over her knuckles.

Time stood still as they stood there watching start blink against the dark until Orson felt Memori shiver—the faintest tremor. Without thinking, he shrugged off his coat and draped it over her shoulders.

She glanced up at him, pulling it tight around herself, fingers brushing the worn fabric near the collar. "Thank you," she murmured.

Orson nodded, his throat too tight to speak. She took the slightest step toward him and he wrapped one arm around her shoulders. His fingers instinctually wrapped around hers when her hand found his. Settling that unspoken thing between them from the moment they met.

Neither of them moved to go inside. Not yet. Instead, they sat against the railing, side by side, hand in hand, with the weight of the night blanketing over them. For now, this was all either of them needed.

Chapter 24

Memori

Memori moved through the dim underbelly of the *Crimson Ghost*, her fingers trailing absently along the worn spine of the *Healer's Codex*. The ship swayed gently beneath her, the muffled sounds of the crew above filtering through the wooden beams. Sunlight barely reached down here, just thin slants breaking through the cracks, catching the dust in the air.

She told herself she was here for something practical—oil, maybe beeswax—as she flipped to the same page in the *Codex* for the third time that morning, telling herself she needed to mix a fresh batch of salve. But the ingredients blurred together, lost behind the memory that clung to her since last night.

The warmth of Orson's hand closing around hers. The way his lips met hers—tender and cautionary until she let her sigh slip…then strong and certain–sending a sharp, breathless ache through her chest. The way she wanted him to pull her closer instead of letting go.

Memori exhaled sharply, shaking off the thought. It didn't matter. It *couldn't* matter. Not with all the uncertainty. What would happen when Orson fully embraced his role as captain? She couldn't stay here forever…

Elowen was with Viggo, sitting cross-legged on the deck, watching intently as he whittled something small and careful with his knife. Memori watched for a moment, lingering by the steps, before turning away. She told herself she was looking for supplies. That was the truth, wasn't it?

She reached for a small wooden crate, shifting the contents aside. A rustle sounded behind her. Memori stiffened. Her grip tightened on the *Codex*. The sound came again—a *scrape*, a *shuffle*—something *moved*. She turned and screamed. The Codex flew from her hands, landing with a dull *thud* against the planks. Her pulse slammed in her ears as her eyes locked onto the figure in front of her.

Sullivan.

He was half-crouched against the far wall, half-hidden in the dim light, his broad shoulders casting long shadows across the crates. He looked even more hulking down here. His severe gray eyes catching the faint slants of light. His long beard, threaded with beads and charms, shifted slightly as he tilted his head toward her.

Tattoos curled up the sides of his shaved head, stark against his weathered skin. Black ink swirling in intricate shapes—some symbols she didn't recognize, others jagged and bold, almost like tally marks. His coat was open at the throat, revealing more markings that disappeared beneath the fabric. For a moment, he said nothing. Just watched her, his eyebrows raised.

Memori's breath came fast and sharp. The incident between Orson and Sullivan still fresh in her mind. If he wanted to, he could easily break a man in two. Her fingers twitched at her sides. She needed to move, to grab the Codex, to *do* something. Then she saw it. Nestled in the crook of his arm, its tiny ribs rising and falling with quick, hungry breaths, was a kitten.

A scrawny, soot-colored thing, barely more than skin and bone, licking the remains of whatever scrap Sullivan had just fed it. His other hand, massive and scarred, moved with slow, careful motions, scratching lightly behind its ear.

"Didn't mean to scare you, Healer." he went back to petting the kitten—its tiny body only enhanced by the size of his own hand…Memori, felt uncertain at the unexpected sight. She bent to pick up the book.

"No, it's fine. I just…wasn't paying attention." Her gaze fixed on the starving creature. "Where did he come from?"

Sullivan kept his focus on the kitten, his rough fingers moving gently over its thin back. The tiny creature arched into his touch, letting out a soft, contented meow. "Dunno," he said, voice low and gruff. "Smart little thing—knows where to hide, when to stay outta the way. Not unlike the rest of us."

Memori dusted off the Codex, but her fingers stilled over the worn leather as she watched the kitten curl into Sullivan's chest. "You come down here just to feed him?" she asked, unsure why she even cared to know.

Sullivan let out a short huff, shrugging one massive shoulder. He shifted slightly, glancing at her then, his gaze sharp but unreadable. "Not all strays get lucky." Memori wasn't sure if he meant the cat or himself. "Some of us do," he answered her unspoken question.

"Are you saying you're a stray?" Disbelief edged her voice at the thought.

Sullivan met her eyes with a smirk. "Once upon a time."

She considered that before murmuring, "Victor's the one who fed you, isn't he?"

"You might say that." He fell quiet, his fingers idly stroking the kitten's fur. Then, he exhaled and said, "Look, I'm sorry about before. I didn't mean to scare you… I meant to shut the captain up, but that's all behind us."

Memori wasn't sure how she felt about that remark—but at least he was honest to a fault. Sullivan's gaze flicked to the open codex in her hands. His expression, usually one of detached amusement or blunt disinterest, shifted ever so slightly. A crease formed between his brows.

"What's that mean?" he nodded toward the page

Memori tightened her grip on the book, glancing down at the image—half expecting it to shift beneath her gaze, to reveal whatever answer he was looking for. But it remained ink on a page, familiar in a way she couldn't explain; the strange reversed healing image she'd puzzled over before.

"I don't know," she admitted.

Sullivan frowned, unease creeping into his features. Without another word, he gave the kitten one last stroke behind its ears, then shifted, rising to his full height. The underbelly of the ship suddenly felt much smaller.

"I've got duties to attend to." His voice was back to its usual gruffness, but something unfinished lingered beneath it.

He dipped his head in a brief, almost absent gesture of acknowledgment before turning and retreating up the passageway, leaving Memori alone with the dim lantern light, the open book, and the slow, gnawing sense that she was missing something important.

Chapter 25

Memori

The village clung to the coastline like barnacles to a hull, its modest wooden docks stretching out into the gentle waves of Waterbreak Inlet, welcoming the Crimson Ghost like an old friend. There was a smell the air of damp stone and shoregrass, carried by a breeze that seemed to breathe life into the emerald canopy of the surrounding forest. Towering trees framed the village, their trunks thick with moss and their branches heavy with leaves that shimmered in hues of green and gold.

Memori's heart fluttered as she watched Orson at the helm, her fingers absently touching her lips where the memory of their kiss still burned. She noticed everything about him now—how he gripped the wheel too tightly whenever Victor approached, the way his shoulders carried tension like armor, how his eyes searched for her, locking onto her gaze with an intensity that made her breath catch.

She wanted to go to him. The pull was there, a constant thing, but her feet remained rooted to the deck. She offered him a small smile instead, all she dared to give, even as her heart ached to close the distance between them. But wanting was dangerous. Wanting led to having, and having led to losing, and she'd lost too much already to risk what little safety she'd built.

Tension on the Ghost hummed in the air like a taut wire, but it wasn't just from Victor's watchful presence or the crew's restless energy. It was in every space between her and Orson, in every glance they shared and every moment they didn't. In the way her skin prickled with awareness whenever he was near, in how she caught herself turning toward his voice like a flower seeking sun.

It can never work. He's a Union traitor hunted by half the seas. You have Elowen to think about. You can't build a life on stolen moments and maybes.

But then Orson would look at her like he did now, like she was something precious and rare, and hope would flutter in her chest like a trapped bird, refusing to be silenced. She thought she'd forgotten how to want things for herself–carefully packed away such desires. Yet here she was, heart betraying her with every beat, wanting something—someone—she couldn't afford to lose.

The thought of reaching for this thing between them terrified her almost as much as the thought of letting it slip away. Better to keep it suspended in this moment, like a bubble catching light—beautiful, fragile, and untouched. Better to hold on to the memory of that kiss than risk shattering whatever it meant by wanting more. So she stayed where she was, letting the distance between them grow thick with things unsaid, telling herself it was safer this way. For everyone.

Elowen played nearby, her soft humming blending with the creak of the ship's timbers and the distant crash of waves against the rocky outcroppings to the west. Memori watched her daughter occasionally, smiling at the sight of her sorting through her small collection of trinkets—including a new addition: a perfectly carved miniature of the Crimson Ghost, complete with tiny sails etched into the wood.

Lost in thought, Memori barely noticed when the sound of Elowen's humming faded. It wasn't until a soft giggle broke through her reverie that she realized her daughter wasn't alone. Looking up, she found Elowen crouched near Viggo, watching intently as his finger traced patterns in the thin layer of dust on the floorboards.

"What's that one?" Elowen asked, pointing to a complex symbol he'd drawn—a mark that made Memori's breath catch. She'd seen it before, in the margins of her own books, always feeling wrong somehow, like a shadow where there should be light.

"That's the mark of the Betrayer," Viggo said, his voice hushed. "Da used to tell me about these. Said they carried old secrets—dangerous ones. Betrayer, Redeemer, Healer… they were called the Oathbound. They used to keep the seven realms safe."

Elowen tilted her head. "What happened to them?"

"They were betrayed," Viggo murmured, adding a careful flourish to the mark. "General Storm, he—" He glanced up, pausing as he saw her. His smile was small, almost shy—but it struck her like a cold wind to the chest. For a split second, her mind lurched somewhere else—a vision of rain-heavy skies, a boy with that same smile, and a mark carved into stone, glowing faintly through the mist. The feeling wasn't warmth or nostalgia. It was fear. And grief. Then, it was gone.

She blinked, heart thudding, and looked down at the mark again. A strange weight pressed behind her eyes, like something forgotten trying to claw its way forward—but hitting a wall.

What is that?

The answer slipped through her like water through a sieve.

"Land ho!" Peryn's shout snapped the tension, yanking her back to the present.

"Can I go see with Viggo?" Elowen asked, already bouncing on her toes. "Please, Memma?"

Memori nodded, barely registering the words. As the children dashed away, her gaze lingered on the symbol carved into the wood. She frowned, one hand unconsciously drifting to the pocket where she kept the Codex. She would ask Victor. Later.

Orson

THE INLET'S WATERS were calm and glassy, mirroring the soft hues of the sky. Along the docks, a small marketplace bustled near the shore, with fishermen unloading their morning catch, their voices carrying over the cries of seagulls that circled overhead.

Peryn lowered the gangplank. It hit the dock with a resounding thud. Victor motioned for Orson to go first, a determined glint in his eye. "Let's go, Captain. We've got a lot of ground to cover."

Orson's eyes lingered on Memori before he started towards shore. "Where are we going?"

"A lagoon I know of."

For a fleeting moment, Orson wondered if Waterbreak Inlet could be far enough—quiet enough—to disappear. A place where no one knew his name or cared that he was captain of a cursed ship–tied to a war he never asked for. No Victor, no Storm, no magic rocks or ancient oaths—just a clean slate and a life that might've been his if everything went differently. Elowen's laughter echoing in the distance—and the thought tightened in his chest like a vice. A home. A family. A future.

"Forget it, Captain." Victor gave him a sideways glance as he passed by.

Scowling, Orson hurried to match Victor's pace as they headed toward a narrow pathway that wound into the dense forest. "Forget what, Sloan?" he asked, feigning innocence.

Victor rolled his eyes, pushing aside vines. "You know what."

"You a mind reader now?"

"No, Captain. I simply assume you have the same thing in mind that I would. Find the girl. Abandon your duties. Escape to the wilderness… start a family." He glanced over at Orson, giving him a lopsided smirk. There was a flicker of profound sadness in his eyes–gone so quickly, Orson might have imagined it.

"You don't know me," Orson scowled, but Victor's words lingered in his mind, that brief glimpse of something uncomfortably raw beneath the man's demeanor.

As VICTOR AND Orson disappeared into the forest, Memori turned to find Elowen tugging at her skirts, Viggo hovering nearby. "Memma, can we go to the market? Please?"

Elowen's eyes sparkled with excitement. "Viggo says they have sweet rolls with honey!"

Memori smiled, watching how her daughter's small hand was already firmly clasped in Viggo's. "Of course we can. But you'll both need to help me find some things first."

One step down the gangplank and Peryn raised his head from the rope he was braiding, his gaze flicking to Memori. She thought he might try to stop her, but he went back to his knots. A small thrill ran through Memori as she stepped onto the dock, the solid wood a welcome change from the constant sway of the ship. Her body shifted slightly, compensating for a roll of waves that wasn't there. Strange how the stillness felt more unsettling than the sea's endless motion now. The air here was different too–thicker somehow, laden with the scents of earth and growing things instead of salt and tar. She breathed deeply, tasting dirt and grass and marketplace spices on her tongue. It made her dizzy for a moment, this rush of remembered sensations she hadn't noticed missing.

"Stay where I can see you," she said to the children, who were already straining to explore, their feet more sure on the unchanging earth than hers. "Viggo, what does feverfew look like?"

"White flowers, like tiny daisies," he answered promptly, clearly proud to show off his knowledge. Elowen bounced on her toes beside him.

"And I know yarrow!" she chimed in. "The leaves are like feathers!"

"That's right. Let's see who can spot them first."

The marketplace was a riot of color and sound that made Elowen gasp in delight. Stall after stall lined the packed dirt paths, their canvas awnings snapping in the salt breeze. The air was thick with the smell of roasting meat, mingling with the earthy aroma of spices and the briny scent of fresh-caught fish laid out on beds of crushed ice.

Merchants held up bolts of fabric that shimmered like captured rainbows, haggling with sharp-eyed seamstresses. Women sold bars of soap with pressed flowers trapped inside like tiny gardens, their tables also laden with jewelry that caught the morning light. Baskets overflowed with fruits and vegetables, their colors as vibrant as any of the merchant's wares.

"Look, Memma!" Elowen tugged at her skirts, pointing to a performer juggling colored balls. Memori kept one hand on her daughter's shoulder as they watched, her other hand finding Viggo's arm to keep him close. A few stalls down, a woman wove intricate patterns into a belt, and beyond her, a cage of brightly colored birds called out in strange voices.

"Feverfew!" Viggo spotted the herb stall first, pulling them toward the neat bundles of dried medicines and carefully labeled packets of roots that lined the shelves. Her heart quickened as she browsed through the selection. The remedies she could make with plants such as these! She hadn't realized until now how much she'd missed true healing work. The brew shop had been a poor substitute for practicing her real craft—the art that ran in her blood, that made her feel more alive than she'd been since her mother passed away.

"What's this one for?" Elowen asked, pointing to a bundle of purple flowers.

"That's echinacea," Memori explained, drawing both children closer as she examined the herbs. "It helps fight fever and cold. See how the petals droop down? That's how you know it's fresh." She kept them engaged, showing them how to check the quality of different plants, teaching them the signs of proper drying techniques.

The old shopkeeper bobbed his head–half asleep on his stool, fanning himself with a piece of worn leather, his eyes half-shut as Memori and the children made their selections. She was so absorbed in teaching Viggo about the properties of a promising bundle of feverfew that it took her nearly fifteen minutes to notice the man watching them.

He stood several stalls away, partially hidden behind a display of carved wooden items. She didn't turn to look directly at him, but kept him in the corner of her vision as she continued her lesson. The way he carried himself—the stillness with which he observed them—was unsettling.

"Time for those sweet rolls," she announced, gathering her purchases with deliberate calm. She positioned herself between the stranger and the children as Viggo lifted Elowen onto his shoulders. Her daughter's delighted giggles carried over the market's din, but Memori's hand never left Viggo's shoulder as they walked, her steps careful and measured, her senses alert for any movement behind them. She could feel him moving closer, trailing her path through the crowd like a shadow. Her hand tightened on her bag of herbs as she quickened her pace, her heart beginning to race.

Evander

Evander and Peryn followed Memori at a distance, weaving through the crowd with ease. From his vantage point, Evander could see Memori with the children, teaching them something about herbs—always the healer, even now.

Peryn's eyes raked over the stalls of ethnic cuisine in between observing Memori. "What I wouldn't give for some Ashmoor kebabs!" He elbowed Peryn. "Hey, you ever try that roasted pepper stew they sell in the north markets? They swear it's from Solhara."

A smile tugged at the corner of Evander's mouth. He and Peryn were from realms of the west, and both lamented the rumors swirling throughout the other lands of their strange customs and traditions; most of which were ridiculous.

"The one that's more water than spice?" He asked. "Yeah, they must think boiling a carrot makes it Solharan cuisine."

"It's an insult." Peryn swore. "My mother would've tossed that in volcano fire and told them to start over."

"At least your food doesn't bite back. They tried to sell me 'Shifting Veil mushroom soup' last time I passed through a port. Mushrooms! Dry as bone and tasted like dirt. No shadows, no flavor."

Peryn laughed. "Let me guess—they didn't even let the soup sit long enough to steep."

"Exactly." Evander grinned. "It's supposed to sit in moonlight to pull the essence from the mushrooms. Instead, they just dumped in stale ones and called it Valamere cuisine."

They shared a laugh as they continued to maneuver through the crowd.

Peryn shook his head. "We should open our own stand, show them how it's done."

Evander raised an eyebrow. "You? Running a food stand? You'd set the first complaining customer on fire."

Peryn let out a mischievous chuckle as if imagining the scenario. "Don't be ridiculous, Evan. I'm good with people."

"Good at setting them on fire," Evander snorted.

"It was ONE time, and, as I recall, you had no objections to it."

Evander gave his friend a grim smile, recalling how the Driftmarch slavers had captured him. A scrawny boy from the shifting realm who could twist shadows to his will would fetch a handsome price. That's when he first met Peryn, who was especially keen on not being taken captive.

"You're right," he relented, still grateful to his friend for saving him from their common enemy.

"That's what I thought," Peryn said, eyes already moving to another food stall. Evander found Memori again, his jaw clenching, his eyes were drawn to another shadow trailing behind them, one that didn't belong. "Evan," Peryn muttered, jerking his chin toward the figure lurking near the spice merchant's stall.

Evander's eyes narrowed as he studied the man. The way he moved, the careful distance he kept while tracking Memori. "Storm's man," he growled, tension coiling in his shoulders.

Peryn stroked at his reddish beard. Despite being nearly a head shorter than his companion, the stocky sailor's confidence never wavered. "I'll distract him."

"What'll you do?" Evander asked warily, knowing Peryn's idea of a distraction often involved property damage.

Peryn smirked, having to tilt his head back to meet his wiry shipmate's gaze. His long hair was held back from his face by a tattered headband that had seen better days. "Don't worry yourself with details."

"Set nothing on fire," Evander called after him with a groan as Peryn moved through the crowd.

"I'll see if I can manage," Peryn shot back, his grin promising exactly the opposite as he disappeared between the market stalls.

Evander scowled, melting into the shadows cast by the canvas awnings. His attention split between Storm's man and Memori's group. Elowen sat on Viggo's shoulders, happily clutching a sweet bun in one hand and pointing excitedly toward a gathering crowd farther down the street. A performer was drawing attention near the edge of the market, music and laughter rising above the hum of voices.

Memori hesitated, eyes flicking between the children and the herb stall. When Elowen leaned forward and whispered something to Viggo, he looked back at Memori, waiting. She gave a small, reluctant nod, but her gaze didn't leave them as they drifted toward the performance. She turned back to the stall, asking the shopkeeper a question—but Evander noted the way her eyes kept tracking the children's movement, even as her hands sifted through dried leaves and root bundles.

As the crowd shifted to watch the performer, it created a natural barrier between Memori and the children. Evander's muscles tensed as he saw Storm's man adjust his course, using the separation to his advantage. The spy was timing it perfectly—waiting for when the pressed bodies of the crowd would prevent Memori from reaching the children quickly.

Moving with careful precision, Evander crept closer. The spy drew nearer, one hand hidden beneath his cloak. A tremendous crash erupted from a nearby stall, followed by the unmistakable whoosh of flames and several startled screams. The crowd surged, pushing Viggo and Elowen further from Memori as people scrambled away from the fire.

Evander struck. His gloved hands seized Memori from behind, one covering her mouth to muffle any sound of surprise. "Don't scream," he whispered in her ear as he pulled her into the shadows between two stalls. "General Storm's man was about to grab you. I've got eyes on the children."

Through the gaps between stalls, he could see Viggo reacting quickly—the boy already grabbed Elowen and was moving steadily toward their predetermined meeting point, using the chaos as cover. Smart lad.

In the midst of the panicking crowd, Storm's spy was frantically trying to stamp out flames that mysteriously caught on his cloak. Peryn's work, no doubt. Evander kept his grip firm but gentle on Memori's arm. "The children know where to go," he murmured. "Trust Viggo. Right now, we need to move."

MEMORI'S HEART SLAMMED against her ribs, her fingers clenching the bag of herbs so tightly the dried stems crackled like brittle bones.

Storm.

She'd only heard the Blacksmoke Union leader's name mentioned a handful of times—always in whispers, always followed by silence. It was the soldiers who acted in his name that haunted her. They were the ones who burned villages, dragged people from their homes. The ones who were real. Her first instinct was to fight, to wrench free from the hands that held her—but it was Evander's voice, low and urgent, that cut through the panic. She couldn't explain why she trusted him, only that something in his tone—sharp with fear, not for himself but for *her*—struck deeper than the name ever could

"Quickly," he urged, guiding her toward the tree line. Chaos erupted behind them—shouts, crashes, the acrid smell of smoke burning her nose. Through the crowd, she glimpsed flames licking at market stalls, while Storm's spy batted frantically at his burning cloak. But she couldn't see Elowen. Couldn't see her daughter anywhere in the surge of panicked bodies.

The forest swallowed them in seconds, the dense canopy casting everything in green shadow. Twigs snapped under their feet as they pushed through the undergrowth, branches catching at Memori's skirts like grasping fingers. Every rustle of leaves made her flinch, every shadow morphed into a threat. Her breath came in sharp gasps, lungs burning as they climbed higher into the woods. The herbs she'd so carefully selected scattered from her torn bag, leaving a trail of crushed remedies in their wake.

"Evander," she managed between breaths, maternal panic clawing at her throat, "Elowen—"

"Safe," he assured her again, his grip firm but gentle on her arm as he helped her over a fallen log. "Viggo knows these woods. He'll keep her hidden until—"

A branch cracked somewhere behind them. Evander yanked Memori behind a massive tree trunk, pressing them both into the moss-covered bark. She held her breath, trying to make herself as small as possible.

Footsteps crunched through the underbrush, moving steadily closer. Memori squeezed her eyes shut. She could feel Evander's tension coiled like a spring as he stood beside her, ready to fight if needed. The steps grew louder, closer. A bird call split the air and Evander's shoulders relaxed slightly. "Peryn," he breathed, barely audible. "Come on. We're not safe yet."

They pressed deeper into the forest, away from everything familiar, away from the Ghost. Memori's mind raced with questions, each more terrifying than the last: How had Storm found them so quickly? What did he want with her? Did he know about Elowen? And most importantly—where was her daughter now, in these woods that suddenly seemed vast and full of shadows?

Another bird call echoed through the trees—different from Peryn's, higher and sweeter. Evander smiled grimly. "Viggo," he whispered, squeezing her arm reassuringly. "They're going East." Memori nodded, though fear still coursed through her veins. She couldn't decide which terrified her more: that Storm's men had tracked them down, or that she now placed her daughter's safety in the hands of an eleven-year-old boy, and a man she thought untrustworthy just this morning. But what choice did she have? The forest stretched endlessly around them, and somewhere in its depths, her daughter waited—assuming she could trust these men, assuming this wasn't all an elaborate trap, assuming—

A twig snapped behind them and Evander's grip tightened on her arm. "Run," he breathed.

. . .

Viggo

THE SECOND VIGGO saw Evander's signal, he didn't hesitate. He ducked into the crowd, using the panic as cover, and bolted for the trees. His father drilled these woods into him when he was small—every trail, every hollow. They hadn't come here much since the world fell apart, but he remembered where to run when it counted. Where all the best places were to hide. "Viggo?" Elowen's voice was barely a whisper. "Are we playing a game?"

"Sort of," he said, helping her over a fallen trunk. "We're being very quiet explorers. Like in your stories, remember?" She nodded solemnly, and his chest tightened at her trust in him. She was so little, hardly bigger than he'd been when… He pushed the thought away, focusing on their path.

The stream's melody reached them before they could see it, a sound that still visited his dreams sometimes. Viggo knew these woods like he knew a ship's rigging, every root and hollow etched into his memory. When the charred remains of the cabin came into view through the trees, he swallowed hard.

"Look," he said, pointing to a hollow beneath the partially collapsed porch. "A perfect hiding spot. But we have to be careful of splinters, alright?"

Elowen nodded again, letting him guide her into the space. It was smaller than he remembered—or maybe he was just bigger now. The scent of old ashes still clung to the weathered wood, though plants had begun to reclaim the ruins. Wildflowers pushed through cracks in the foundation, and moss carpeted what remained of the walls.

"Used to be our home," he whispered, settling them into the hollow. From here, they had a clear view of the approach from three directions, just as his father had planned it. "Before—"

"Really?" Elowen's eyes went wide, taking in their surroundings with new interest. "Did you have a garden?"

"Ma did." The words caught in his throat. "Over there" He pointed to the yellow flowers. A thorny vine caught his palm as he shifted position, and he couldn't quite suppress his hiss of pain. Blood welled up across his hand, bright against his skin.

"You're hurt!" Elowen's whisper was urgent. She scrambled to her knees, peering at his palm with an expression so like her mother's that it almost made him smile. Her eyes scanned the surrounding ground, suddenly brightening. "Look! Yarrow! Memma said it stops bleeding!"

Before he could stop her, she'd darted out to pluck several feathery leaves from a plant growing near the porch steps. His heart jumped until she was safely back in their hiding spot.

"You press it on like this," she explained, her small fingers gentle as she folded the leaves and pressed them against his cut.

"Thank you." He smiled. "But we have to stay here now. And be quiet." They fell silent then, listening to the stream's chatter and watching the shadows shift through the trees. Viggo kept count in his head—twenty minutes since they'd left the market. Peryn would come soon. Or Evan. Until then, all they could do was wait.

"Can we go inside?" Elowen whispered.

Viggo flinched inwardly. "No." He shook his head.

She might still be there.

He didn't say it out loud. Didn't want to frighten the girl.

"Can you tell me a story?" Elowen whispered after a while, still holding the yarrow leaves carefully in place.

Viggo smiled faintly,. "Once," he began, "there were seven children, promised to protect the realms…."

Chapter 26

Peryn

Peryn moved through the forest with deliberate care, his boots crunching softly against the undergrowth. He followed the stream's winding course toward the old cabin, his gaze sweeping the shadow-drenched trees. Stealth was never his strong suit—not like Evander, who could slip through a forest without disturbing so much as a blade of grass. Peryn's approach was louder, more forceful, much like the land that shaped him.

In Solhara, nothing moved quietly. The mountains groaned, the earth trembled, and the volcano hissed warnings in streams of molten heat. Even the people there carried that energy—raw, unyielding, and fiercely alive. Peryn embodied that same intensity, no matter how much he tried to tamp it down in moments like this. His heavy steps had their own kind of rhythm, deliberate and steady, not careless.

His fingers instinctively traced the steel rings on his fingers, their rough edges giving him confidence. Each ring held the memory of countless fires lit in the darkest hours— fires that cooked his meals, signaled allies, or saved his life when the cold crept too close. He felt the meager scraps of oil-soaked cloth in his pocket, the last remnants of his arsenal.

The stream babbled faintly beside him, masking some of his noise, but not all of it. His fingers brushed his ring again as he pushed forward. Quiet wasn't everything. Sometimes, the best way to strike was with heat and fury. The bird call came again—Viggo's signal. Peryn quickened his pace, scanning the shadows between the trees.

Though most of the jungle remained dry this time of year, the stream twisting through the surrounding undergrowth left the ground soft and waterlogged. The leaves squished underfoot—no good for kindling.

He spotted the cabin's remains through the trees and let out a low whistle—their agreed-upon response. A small face peered out from beneath the porch, then quickly ducked back into hiding. Good lad, staying on guard. That's when Peryn noticed the silence. No birds, no insects. Just the stream's constant murmur and. Something struck him from behind, hard enough to drive him to his knees. Water cascaded over him, soaking his clothes and the precious tinder in his pocket. He rolled, coming up in a fighting stance, but his attacker anticipated this.

The spy from the market emerged from behind a tree, a waterskin in one hand, steel in the other. "Can't play with fire if everything's wet, can you?" he sneered, circling slowly.

Peryn's mind raced. The spy was between him and the children now, and he could hear Elowen's frightened whimper from their hiding place. His fingers traced over the steel inlays of his rings. He just needed the right moment…

The spy lunged, blade flashing. Peryn dodged, but his wet boots slipped. The knife caught his arm, drawing blood. He stumbled back, feeling the stream's spray against his legs. Too much water. Too much damp.

"Viggo, run!" he shouted, though he prayed the boy would stay hidden. Better to make the spy think they might escape.

"More men in the woods." The spy smirked. "The children aren't going anywhere."

Peryn's hands clenched into fists, the steel rings a familiar pressure against his skin. "You know," Peryn said, shifting his stance, "the thing about fire is…" He scraped his rings against each other in a sharp, practiced motion, sending a shower of sparks toward the spy's oil-treated clothing, "it only takes a spark."

The spy's cloak caught immediately, the protective oil becoming its own undoing. He screamed, dropping his blade as he tried to tear the burning fabric away. Peryn didn't waste the opportunity.

"Run!" he shouted, darting toward the cabin. Viggo emerged from hiding, Elowen's hand clasped tightly in his. Peryn scooped the little girl up, pushing Viggo ahead of him. "Quickly!"

They crashed through the undergrowth, the spy's curses fading behind them. Peryn's heart thundered in his chest as he carried Elowen, keeping one hand on Viggo's shoulder to guide him.

The impact came out of nowhere. One moment they were running through the trees, the next—the spy was in front of them, as if he'd stepped through the space between one tree and another. Peryn went down hard, twisting to avoid crushing Elowen. She tumbled from his arms with a cry, landing in a patch of mud. Viggo immediately moved to shield her, but it was too late.

Through blurring vision, Peryn saw the spy standing over them, his cloak still smoking. How had he—? The man's face twisted with rage as he loomed over the children, blade glinting in the filtered sunlight. The last thing Peryn heard before darkness took him was Elowen's terrified sob.

Memori

Memori crouched in the dense foliage, every muscle tense as she strained to hear over the sounds of the jungle. Evander's presence beside her was oddly reassuring, though she'd never admit it. They'd been waiting for what felt like hours, and her patience was wearing thin.

"Peryn knows these woods," Evander murmured, as if sensing her growing anxiety. "He'll bring them safely."

She nodded, not trusting her voice. Her fingers twisted in her skirts, replaying that moment in the market when chaos had torn her from her daughter. The wait was unbearable— this helpless hiding while someone else protected her child.

Leaves rustled low to the ground–too steady to be the wind. Memori's breath caught as footsteps approached through the brush. Her heart leaped with relief as she heard Elowen's voice—but it vanished in the next heartbeat. The tone wasn't right. Too high, too frightened.

"Silence!" came a sharp command, a voice that definitely wasn't Peryn's.

Memori's blood turned to ice as figures pushed through the foliage. The spy from the market stepped into view, one hand gripping Elowen's shoulder to keep her moving, the other pressing a blade far too close to Viggo's neck. The children stumbled along in front of him—Elowen's small face streaked with tears and dirt, Viggo's jaw clenched with anger.

She started to run to them, but Evander caught her arm. His grip was like iron, though she could feel him trembling with his own constrained rage. "Ah," the spy called out, his thin lips curving into a smile as he dragged the children into the clearing. "Perfect timing. Perhaps we can avoid any further… unfortunate accidents." His blade pressed closer to Viggo's throat. A single drop of blood welled up bright against his skin.

Elowen's terrified sob shattered what remained of Memori's heart. "Memma!"

"Where's Peryn?" Evander stepped forward, and Memori's breath caught at what happened next. The shadows beneath the trees twisted around him like living smoke. It was haunting, almost beautiful, the way darkness flowed through his fingers.

A flash of steel caught the light as the spy lurched forward, and Evander stumbled back, clutching his bleeding hand. With a swift motion, the spy seized Viggo and Elowen, yanking them to his side. The children struggled, Elowen's scream piercing Memori's heart, but the spy's grip was ironclad.

"Enough!" His voice cut through the chaos like a blade. "Another step, and they both die."

Memori froze, her chest heaving as panic clawed at her throat. Her gaze darted between the terrified children and Evander, still clutching his injured hand. The surrounding shadows dimmed as the evening sun streamed through openings in the leaves. "Please," Memori whispered, her voice breaking. "Let them go. They're just children."

The spy's grin widened. "That depends on you, Healer. Come quietly, and no one else gets hurt."

Memori's knees trembled, but she forced herself to stand tall. "If I go with you, you'll let them go?"

"Your shade-spawn friend here can go free. But the children come with us. That's the deal."

"Don't do it," Evander rasped. Faint traces of darkens coiled around him where the sun was kept at bay, writhing and twisting in response to his distress. It defied everything she knew about how the world was supposed to work. Thinking back, it all made sense, though—his impossible agility in the rigging, the way he seemed to appear from nowhere, how he moved through the ship's darkest corners like they were bathed in daylight. The shadows didn't just follow him; they bent to his will in a way that was decidedly inhuman. His pale eyes burned with an otherworldly intensity that should have terrified her. But instead of fear, she felt recognition, or maybe understanding. Her gaze dropped to her own hands, remembering how they'd glowed with that soft light when she'd touched Orson's wounds, how the angry red flesh had knitted together beneath her fingers. She'd tried to convince herself she imagined it, that the herbs just worked faster than expected, that there had to be some logical explanation. But watching Evander now, seeing how the shadows moved…

The coincidence was too strong to ignore. Were they the same somehow? She'd heard whispers of people with gifts, but always dismissed them as tales meant to frighten children, or put them to sleep. Yet here was proof before her eyes, and in her own hands was… something. Something she didn't understand but couldn't deny anymore.

Evander shifted, clinging to his bleeding hand, and her fingers itched with the urge to help, to heal. "You don't know what they'll—"

"I have no choice," she interrupted, her voice steady now. She stepped forward, her hands raised in surrender. The spy motioned back towards the village with a nod of his head. "Right behind you." He smiled, his fingers curling on Viggo's and Elowen's shoulders. Her eyes met Evander's for a fleeting moment, and in that shared glance, a fierce, unexpected ache gripped her heart. Evander had shielded them—risked exposing his true nature to protect her and Elowen. She would do what she could to make sure he wasn't killed. Pulling her gaze from him, she started back the way they'd come, trying not to show her fear as Storm's man fell in behind her.

Chapter 27

Evander

Evander watched helplessly as the spy slipped into the shadows, dragging Memori and the children with him. Memori was a survivor—she'd been through worse—but the children… they were far more vulnerable than even she realized…

"Son of a bitch," he snarled through clenched teeth, forcing himself upright despite the protest of his muscles. Fucking Grift. Victor warned them he was no ordinary spy—Storm saw to that. But Grift's abilities had limits. Evander pulled a handkerchief from his coat pocket, wrapping it around his bleeding hand and yanking the knot tight with his teeth. The spy's trail was clear in the disturbed underbrush—a path that had to lead to his friend.

He found Peryn face-down in the mud, unnaturally still. Scanning the area, Evander spotted rainwater pooled in a rotting stump. He rolled Peryn onto his back, scooped up the murky water, and flung it into his friend's face.

Peryn jolted awake with a gasp, clawing at his face before surging forward to wrap his fingers around Evander's throat.

"Easy, Cannonball, easy!" Evander's back slammed against rough bark as he held Peryn at bay with his good hand, the handkerchief already soaking through with blood. "It's only me."

"Evan?" Recognition flooded Peryn's face as his fingers loosened. He scrubbed frantically at his mud-caked eyes, his usual confidence shattered. "That bastard got the drop on me!"

"I noticed." Evander's legs trembled as he steadied himself, the taste of copper lingering in his mouth. "He's gone back to the ship."

"Viggo—the girl—" Peryn's voice cracked. His shoulders slumped as guilt etched deep lines around his eyes. "Did you see them?"

"Aye. They're fine. For now." Evander's stomach twisted at the memory of their terrified faces. "Grift knows once they're dead, he's got no leverage left on Vic."

Peryn unleashed another string of curses, scooping up handfuls of stump water to scrub the mud from his face and beard. The water ran brown down his neck, staining his collar. "We need to find Victor." Evander squinted at the dying sunlight bleeding through the trees, casting long shadows across the forest floor. Time was slipping away from them.

Peryn dried his face on his sleeve, leaving dark smears across the fabric. His eyes held a shadow of fear Evander rarely saw. "God help us all. Victor'll tear apart the sky."

"If we're lucky, that's all he'll tear apart." Evander pressed his wounded hand against his chest, feeling the steady throb of pain match his racing heartbeat. The two men exchanged grim looks before sprinting to the lagoon where they knew Victor would be.

Chapter 28

Orson

The lagoon's surface fractured the afternoon sun into a thousand glittering shards, each ripple catching light as Orson dragged himself onto the shore. His lungs burned from the swimming lesson, muscles trembling as he collapsed onto a patch of moss. Victor emerged beside him, water streaming from his hair and down his bare torso as he flicked a stone across the surface. It skipped once before disappearing beneath the crystalline depths.

You're improving," Victor said, sounding relieved.

"Thanks," Orson wheezed, his arms quivering. "Maybe in another ten weeks, I'll be able to avoid drowning."

Victor's hand stilled mid-reach for another stone, something dark flickering across his face. His shoulders tense as he took the stone in his hand, weighing it in his palm. "Want to see who can skip one further?" His mouth quirked with the hint of a challenge.

Orson snorted, gesturing at his exhausted form. "Now? When I can barely lift my arms?"

"Afraid you'll lose?" Victor's eyebrow arched. Something flickered in Orson's memory—a fleeting image of a younger Victor challenging him by a different shore long ago. The sense of familiarity was so strong it made his head swim.

"I've beaten you before," Orson said, the words tumbling out before he could think. He frowned, confused by his own certainty.

Victor's eyes narrowed, his fingers tightening over the stone. "Have you?" Before Orson could answer, the crack of branches shattered the silence. Both men jolted upright as Evander and Peryn burst through the treeline, their faces flushed and chests heaving.

Blood seeped through a makeshift bandage on Evander's hand, each drop marking the ground like a countdown. Peryn's face was streaked with mud. The unusual fear in his eyes made Orson's stomach clench. "Captain—" Evander gasped, clutching his ribs. "Memori—she's in trouble!" His wild eyes darted between them, desperation rolling off him in waves that seemed to disturb the lagoon's surface.

"What happened?" Victor's gaze sharpened as he moved closer, brow furrowing at the sight of Evander's hand.

"Market," Evander choked out, while Peryn braced himself against a tree. "He came for her—Grift."

Orson scrambled up, fatigue forgotten. "Who's that?"

"Storm's man," Victor growled, yanking his shirt over his head. He snatched his coat and sword from the shore, the leather creaking under his white-knuckled grip.

"Vic…" Evander doubled over, his next words careful— hesitant. "He's got Viggo."

The air around them thickened, moisture condensing into a fine mist that felt heavy with unseen power. Victor's chest rose and fell in measured breaths that seemed to pull at the very atmosphere. Orson felt the hair on his arms rise, static crackling in the humid air.

"Elowen?" The name tore from Orson's throat as he lurched forward, seizing Evander's shoulder. "What about Elowen?"

Evander nodded, still fighting for breath. Beside him, Peryn's mud-streaked face was grim. "Aye, her too."

Orson staggered back, panic clawing up his throat as the lagoon's surface churned, mirroring the chaos in his chest. Victor stood motionless, his silence more terrifying than any storm. The mist coiled around him like a living thing. Thunder growled from a cloudless sky, a sound that seemed to come from everywhere and nowhere at once.

The veins in Victor's arms stood out like iron cables as his hands curled into fists. Without a word, he spun and sprinted toward the Ghost. Orson followed, terror crystallizing into something sharp and deadly in his chest. Behind them, he heard Evander and Peryn's boots pounding against the earth.

217

Chapter 29

Sullivan

"Is this the last of it?" Sullivan took a crate of dried fish from Jermany, the salt-cured smell bringing back memories of younger days on rougher seas—or perhaps they were dreams. Sometimes he couldn't tell the difference anymore.

"What's the matter, Sea Wolf?" She swung him a crate of dried vegetables, her weathered hands sure and steady. "Eager to be done?"

"Always eager to be done with heavy lifting. You will be too when you get to be my age," Sullivan grunted, hoisting his load. The wooden steps creaked beneath his boots as he descended below deck. He liked to joke about being older than the others, though his joints didn't protest like he thought they should. Like others that appeared his age complained about.

Jermany laughed behind him, her footsteps echoing his own. "Don't worry. I wouldn't stick you with all the work."

Sullivan froze, the words stirring something in his mind—a half-remembered dream of another port, another crew. No… not a port at all. He was a child, out of place in a strange forest, far from home: Driftmarch–the harsh realm of the north. His legs locked beneath him as the memory seized hold, vivid as yesterday…

He trudged through the forest, muscles straining under an armful of heavy logs, his stout frame making the load look manageable despite his grumbling. Behind him, a younger boy dragged his feet, carrying a pitiful bundle of kindling. Dark hair fell into the boy's eyes, giving him a perpetually mischievous look. It suited him, Sullivan thought. He was always causing trouble. Making a scene. Getting his brother to fight his battles for him.

"Can't you carry more than that?" Sullivan called over his shoulder, bark scratching against his chest. "You're leaving all the proper work for me."

His companion huffed, blowing his hair from his face. "Maybe I'd carry more if you stopped hogging all the big pieces."

Sullivan rolled his eyes. "Why'd I have to get stuck with you for chores today?"

A dangerous glint appeared in the younger boy's eyes. The sound of rustling preceded the sharp sting of wood chips pelting Sullivan's back.

"Hey!" Sullivan spun around, scowling. "Quit it."

The boy shrugged, the picture of innocence despite the half-smile playing at his lips. "What?"

Frowning, Sullivan turned back toward the path. Another chip sailed through the air, striking his neck. "That's it!" Sullivan growled, dropping his logs with a thunderous crash. He rounded on the boy, who was already laughing, dark eyes dancing with delight.

"What are you gonna do, Sully? Sit on me?" the younger boy taunted, still grinning as he tossed another chip.

Sullivan lunged, pushing aside the nagging voice that warned him about what happened to people who hurt the little pest. The logs scattered as he tackled the boy, sending them both tumbling through the underbrush. They rolled through patches of cold mud and sharp brambles, the younger boy's elbow catching Sullivan's ribs forcefully.

"You little brat!" Sullivan hissed, grabbing him by the collar, stomach churning with fury. Just one good black eye— that's what the little pest deserved. The boy wriggled free like an eel, his face smeared with dirt and a thin line of blood where a thorn had caught his cheek. He launched himself at Sullivan, sending them sprawling again.

When they finally stopped, they were both disasters—mud-caked clothes, scratched faces, bleeding arms. They lay panting on the forest floor, trading glares.

"Idiot," Sullivan muttered, his heart already racing at the thought of what was coming. "When you rat me out to your brother, make sure you tell him you started it."

His young companion muttered something unintelligible, wiping his bloody nose with a grimy hand. A shadow fell over them, and both boys froze. Sullivan's stomach dropped as he looked up to see the eldest of them standing there, arms crossed. His dark hair caught the sunlight like a crown, but his eyes were winter frost.

"What happened here?" His voice was deceptively soft, carrying a sharp edge that made both boys squirm. His gaze traveled over the scene—the bruises darkening around his little brother's eye, the blood trickling from his nose—before fixing Sullivan with a stare that promised pain. Sullivan set his jaw, wishing he'd clobbered the boy—made it worth the beating he was going to get. He opened his mouth to explain, but the younger brother spoke first.

"I tripped," he said quickly, drawing his brother's piercing gaze. Even the younger boy seemed to shrink under that stare.

The older brother's eyes narrowed dangerously. "You tripped?"

The boy nodded solemnly, mimicking his brother's serious expression despite his disheveled state.

His brother stared for a long moment before sighing, some of the lethal tension leaving his shoulders. "Get back to work. And clean yourselves up before Linden sees you."

As he walked away, Sullivan released a shaky breath. He looked at the younger boy in surprise, his hands trembling. "Why didn't you rat me out?"

The boy shrugged, a small smirk tugging at his split lip despite his battered appearance. "I don't know. Guess I just didn't want to see you get beaten to a pulp today."

Sullivan rolled his eyes but couldn't fight the relieved grin that crept onto his face as they gathered their scattered logs. "You're still a crybaby," he said, but the words carried no bite.

"Sully. Sully!"

Reality crashed back like a wave. Sullivan found himself sitting against the ship's hull, surrounded by scattered crates. Jermany gripped his collar, her eyes wide with fear. She sagged with relief when his gaze finally focused on hers. "I lost you there."

"Sorry…" Sullivan rubbed his throbbing temple, the forest still vivid behind his eyes.

"What happened?" Jermany's voice was tight with worry. "Dreams again?"

Sullivan nodded, steadying himself against the wall. "Aye. They're getting worse—Jermany maybe we—"

Jermany went rigid, pressing a finger to her lips, her eyes narrowing to slits as she tilted her head. "Someone's coming—not the crew." She bolted for the ladder leading above deck, and Sullivan hurried after her.

GRIFT'S BOOTS THUNDERED across the gangplank like a death knell, and Sullivan's heart turned to ice at the sight of Viggo caught in the spy's grasp. Beside him, Elowen trembled, tears cutting clean tracks through the dirt on her face. Her muffled sobs stirred his anger at the man responsible.

Jermany's elbow brushed his arm as she tensed beside him. "Where's Peryn? And Evan?" she whispered, her voice barely a breath. Before Sullivan could answer, Memori appeared behind the children. Her effort to look calm did little to hide the trembling of her hands as they clutched at her skirts.

"Stand aside." Grift's commanding tone made Sullivan's anger spike. Who did that bastard think he was? His hand instinctively twitched toward his knife, but the calculating gleam in Grift's eyes stopped him cold. One wrong move and the children would pay the price.

"They've likely gone to find Vic," Sullivan murmured back to Jermany as Grift herded the children forward.

"Shit," Jermany breathed, and Sullivan caught the flicker of dread in her eyes. They both knew what Victor would do when he got there.

"Go on, follow her. Down to her little shop." The mockery in Grift's voice made Sullivan's blood boil, but he remained still, every muscle coiled with helpless rage.

When Viggo's brown eyes met his, Sullivan saw not fear for himself, but desperate concern for the little girl beside him. He was so much like his father. The boy's gaze darted between Sullivan and Elowen, silently begging him to protect her. Sullivan managed only the slightest nod, his hands curling into fists.

His head still swam from that damnable vision, making the deck tilt beneath his feet, and he had a nagging sense that this all happened before, though he couldn't place when or where. He shoved the thought aside; there were more pressing matters at hand. "What do we do?" Jermany whispered.

Sullivan watched as Grift disappeared below deck with his captives. "Wait for Vic and the others," he said reluctantly, rubbing his temple where a dull ache persisted. His voice dropped even lower. "Then we get the hell out of here as fast as we can."

Chapter 30

Memori

Elowen clung to Viggo's side as they descended the steps, her quiet sniffles filling the narrow stairwell. She wiped at her face with trembling fingers, trying to stifle her cries but failing. Grift's footsteps echoed behind them, heavy and unrelenting, like a hunter savoring the chase. When they reached the galley, he gestured sharply toward the small workspace Memori had claimed as her own. "Now then, my dear—how about some tea? I hear you're quite skilled with brews."

Memori hesitated, her heart pounding in her chest, but she forced herself to move. She guided Viggo and Elowen into the corner near her workbench and set them down on a crate. "Stay close," she whispered, brushing Elowen's hair from her damp face and squeezing Viggo's shoulder before turning back to Grift.

"Perhaps something for an aching hand?" Grift flexed his bruised knuckles, his thin smile twisting with malice. "That red-bearded idiot's skull must've been thicker than I thought." Elowen buried her face in Viggo's side, her tiny hands clutching his shirt. Viggo wrapped an arm protectively around her, his jaw tight with silent fury as his eyes tracked every move Grift made.

The galley felt like a tomb. Memori lit the gas burner, watching blue flames lick the kettle's base. Her trembling hands steadied as they found the knife's familiar weight, its blade catching the light as she reached for a dried root hanging overhead.

Thunk. Thunk. Thunk.

The knife's rhythm against the cutting board was deliberate, almost meditative. She could feel Grift's eyes on her back as she worked, scraping precise slices into a waiting bowl. Her movements were mechanical–a pinch of powder here, crushed leaves there, each ingredient chosen with careful purpose.

The combination mattered most with some wild plants. Alone, one thing could dull the pain of a headache, but with a dash of something else, the combination could become something much less innocuous. A *good night's sleep* could easily be transformed into *lifeless corpse.*

Steam erupted from the kettle with a piercing whistle. Memori slammed the first mug down so hard it cracked, the sound making Elowen flinch where she sat huddled against Viggo on a crate in the corner. Without a word, Memori reached for another mug, her fingers trembling as she poured the water. Her eyes met Grift's with barely contained fury as the liquid bloomed into an innocent shade of brown.

Sliding the mug across the wooden table, she crossed her arms, glaring at the man. The liquid inside rippled slightly with the motion. Grift caught the cup with one hand, his fingers curling around it as his stony gaze flicked to Memori.

From his corner, Viggo's sharp eyes never left Grift. He shifted slightly, pulling Elowen closer. "It's okay," he whispered, his arms tightening protectively around her.

Grift studied Memori for a long moment, his sharp eyes searching her expression for any sign of defiance or trickery. He smirked and lifted the mug to his lips, drinking deeply without a second thought. "Very good, Healer," he said, setting the half-empty cup down with a deliberate clink. He flexed his gloved fingers, rotating his wrists with exaggerated satisfaction. "They feel better already."

"They won't for long," Memori snapped, her voice cold as ice. Her arms tightened across her chest as she met his gaze. "I'm fairly certain Victor will break them when he gets here. And if he doesn't, Orson most certainly will."

Elowen whimpered at the mention of Victor's name, and Viggo hushed her gently. He glanced toward the doorway as if willing help to arrive. Grift's cruel smile widened as he rose from his seat, looming over Memori. "I think not." He reached out, catching her chin between his thumb and forefinger, tilting her face upward with an almost lazy air of dominance. "Victor wouldn't dare endanger his precious son."

"Maybe I don't need to wait for Victor," Memori said, unflinching. "Maybe that tea you drank was actually poison."

"Healers do not poison," Grift smirked. "It's part of your silly code." His attention flicked briefly to the children, a sinister glint in his eyes as he released Memori's chin. "So innocent. So…mortal." The strange emphasis he placed on that last word made Memori's skin crawl. The threat in his tone was unmistakable. She wanted to run to them–to shield them from whatever Storm's man had in mind. The air in the galley felt suffocating, thick with tension and danger as the moments stretched unbearably thin. His words echoed in her mind—mortal—as if there was any other way to be.

The Crimson Ghost shuddered beneath Memori's feet. She steadied herself against the galley wall, watching objects crash to the floor from shelves and tables. Thunder cracked outside—a sound that vibrated through her chest.

Grift's confident smirk faltered. The sound of boots above made him rush toward the children. Viggo's eyes widened for just a fraction of a second before he shoved Elowen hard, sending her tumbling behind a stack of crates and out of reach. The spy's fingers closed around Viggo's collar instead, yanking him close as a shield. Memori's blood boiled at the sight of Viggo's grimace, but she forced herself still, waiting–watching Elowen hug her knees to her chest; safe, for now. The boy's eyes met hers, and despite his fear, she saw the fierce determination, so like his father's—he'd made sure Elowen was safe. Her eyes misted over with gratitude for his selflessness.

When the door burst open, the entire room seemed to hold its breath. Victor filled the frame, rain streaming from his coat, his eyes burning with an intense light she'd never seen before. Her heart skipped at the sight of him.

"If any of them are harmed," Victor's voice resonated with something ancient and terrible, "I'll hunt your bloodline through every realm, wiping them from time itself!"

Memori felt the air grow thick, pressing against her skin as Orson slipped in behind Victor, sword drawn. His quick glance her way carried volumes—a silent question about her wellbeing.

Grift yanked Viggo closer. "You're late," he taunted, but there was a tremor in his voice.

"Storm's tricks will not help you here," Victor snarled.

Orson's was more direct. "Let them go, you fucking bastard!"

Before Grift could reach his knife, Victor moved with impossible speed. The impact when he slammed Grift into the wall rattled her teeth. The moment Grift's grip loosened on Viggo, Memori rushed to Elowen, pulling both children to her, shielding them against her body.

"You threatened my son's life," Victor's whisper carried more menace than his shouts ever had. He released Grift, who slumped and staggered upright. "Threatened this girl's life." He reached his hand out. Mist gathered as fury swirled in his eyes. "Innocent lives!"

"Storm's coming, Sloan. And nothing will stop him!" Grift choked out. Memori watched with carefully concealed satisfaction as his face turned green, his hands clawing at his throat. "Nothing," he rasped before collapsing.

Orson stepped back, staring at the convulsing body until Grift went still. "You didn't even hit him hard yet," Orson said, sounding bewildered and disappointed at the same time.

"Must have been something he drank," Memori met Victor's gaze, her face hot with adrenaline. Victor's eyes softened slightly as understanding dawned. Her vision blurred. "Orson…" she swayed, confusion genuine as she noted the power that seemed to roil off Victor like heat from a boiler. "I…I feel sick."

The world tilted sideways, and then Orson was there, his sword clattering forgotten to the floor as he caught her. Even as darkness crept in at the edges of her vision, she registered the solid warmth of his arms, the way they curved around her with such careful strength. She had just enough time to think how safe it felt, being held by him, before consciousness slipped away entirely.

Chapter 31

Orson

Orson couldn't move. Memori lay limp in his arms, her face pale, and his body refused to obey any command to act. As the rest of the crew rushed in, his head swam with chaos and voices, lungs refusing to draw breath. Paralyzed. Useless.

"Peryn—get rid of this trash." Victor's voice cut through the din, decisive and controlled. He moved to take Memori, and Orson realized his own grip tightened reflexively. Forcing his fingers to release her felt like tearing open a wound. As Victor lifted her away, Orson noticed the strange luminescence still seemed to emanate from him, a ghostly light that clung to his skin. What in the seven hells had happened to him? Maybe there was truth to Dollan's stories after all…

Sullivan lowered himself to meet Orson's eyes, his normally stern face softening with concern. "Are you alright, Captain?"

Orson stared at him, light-headed, managing only a slow nod. In any other situation, such attention from Sullivan would have raised his suspicions, but right now, that steady voice felt like an anchor in the chaos. "Let's get you on your feet." Sullivan's grip was firm as he pulled Orson up, guiding him to a nearby chair. "I'll be back," he promised, giving him a reassuring squeeze on the shoulder before disappearing into the commotion.

A small figure darted through the chaos, and suddenly Elowen was there, her face streaked with tears as she flung herself at him. Her whole body was shaking as she scrambled into his lap. "Orson!" The word came out as a sob that made his chest constrict.

"Elowen." His voice cracked as he looked at the girl, still trembling from Grift's threats. Fresh tears spilled down her cheeks as she buried her face against his chest. "Are you alright?" He wrapped his arms around her, grateful for the solid weight that helped bring him back to reality. She felt so small, so fragile in his embrace, and he tightened his hold as if he could shield her from everything that had happened.

She shook her head against his shirt, then nodded, then shook it again. When she finally lifted her face, her eyes were wide with terror. She was trying so hard to be brave. "Is Memma going to be okay?" Her small voice drew his scattered thoughts back to focus, the question wobbling dangerously close to another sob.

"Of course she is," he said, hoping it wasn't a lie.

Her fingers clutched his coat as if afraid he might disappear too. "Where's Viggo?"

He brushed a strand of hair from her face, noting the twist in his gut at the dried blood on her dress—Grift's, he hoped. "I'm sure he's helping get us out of here."

"Can I see Memma now?" Her bottom lip trembled.

"How about we get you cleaned up and something to eat, then we'll go together, eh?"

Elowen considered this for a moment before nodding, slipping her small hand into his. The trust in that simple gesture made his chest tight. "Viggo got hurt on a thorn," she murmured. "I used a plant to stop the bleeding."

"You did? Just like your Memma taught you?" When she nodded, he pressed a gentle kiss to her forehead. "Good girl."

Orson's gaze lingered on Memori as Victor carried her away, the edges of his vision warped by the strange pressure Victor still seemed to carry—like the very air bent to his will. It wasn't natural. It wasn't *human*. That kind of power had no place in mortal hands, and it unsettled Orson more than he liked. But even as unease twisted in his gut, he couldn't deny the relief. Victor had stepped in when Orson couldn't. Taken charge when he'd frozen. And for that—unnerving or not—Orson was grateful.

He tightened his grip on Elowen's small hand as they started up the stairs. Memori needed something beyond what he could give. But this little one—she needed comfort. And that was something he could give. One crisis at a time

Jermany

VICTOR'S RAGE LEFT the inlet looking like a war zone. Awnings hung in tatters, their supports twisted like broken bones. Docks, where merchants bustled hours before, lay half-submerged under swollen waters that still churned with unnatural fury. Trees bent to impossible angles, their branches scraping the ground. Jermany exhaled sharply, scanning the wreckage with an unease that settled deep in her bones. She knew what storms like this could take from a man. Knew what it had taken from Victor before.

"Seven hells," Sullivan muttered, watching a shop's roof peel away in the dying wind.

Jermany's eyes locked on the apothecary's shop, still somehow standing despite its windows being blown out. "I'll be back."

"Jermany, we need to go—" Peryn started, but she was already splashing through the flooded street.

Inside, the destruction was worse. Shelves lay scattered, their contents forming islands in the ankle-deep water. The air reeked of acid and crushed herbs, a chaotic blend of ruined remedies. Jermany ignored the floating debris, her focus sharp as she waded toward the counter. It had to be here. It *had* to be. Her fingers skimmed the wreckage until they found it—a sealed jar of lark's respite, its contents blessedly intact. Dried kelp, crushed pearl, starflower. The tea sailors swore by to restore vitality. They'd gotten it before when Victor outdid himself. The potion was a staple among Tidesreach islands. Memori could make it, no doubt. But she wasn't in any condition to heal anyone.

Jermany tucked it into her coat just as heavy boots splashed outside. More of Storm's men, maybe–or local authorities drawn by the destruction. She didn't wait to see if they spotted her. She ran.

Aboard the *Crimson Ghost*, the crew moved, desperate to put the village behind them. Jermany barely noticed. Her focus landed on where Victor stood, his knuckles white on the railing. His face was gray as the storm clouds still roiling behind them, and for the first time since she'd known him, he looked… *mortal*. Drained. Her gut twisted. Would he even be strong enough to face Storm if it came to that?

His knee hit the boards, fingers tightening on the railing to keep himself from falling further. Jermany was at his side in an instant, her small frame bracing him. She pulled the bottle from her coat, uncorking it with her teeth. "Here— drink." She pressed it to his lips, tipping it until he could take hold of it himself.

Victor swallowed, his breath coming rough as he lowered the bottle. His eyes flickered to her, a shimmer of gratitude in the exhausted depths.

Jermany just shook her head. "Don't look at me like that. Someone's got to make sure you don't go killing yourself."

Victor choked on a laugh but kept drinking. Jermany felt a twinge of something sharp and knowing. It wasn't amusement that had caught in his throat. She didn't need to ask. There had been a time when he would have welcomed the end, when exhaustion like this would've meant nothing, because nothing could truly take him down. But now… now, he drank. Now he fought to stay standing. For now, he had something to live for.

She swallowed down the thought, masking it with a scoff. "Try not to die on me, *Vic. The captain needs you-we need you.*" She steadied him as he finally lowered the bottle. Victor didn't answer right away, only rolled his shoulders and exhaled slowly, testing his strength. Then, hoarse but sure, he said, "There'll be no dying today, Tempest."

Jermany smirked at the nickname, the old familiarity of it settling over her. "There better not be." She couldn't imagine a world without Victor. He had been a part of her life for so long—before him, she may as well have been dead.

The first time she saw him, she thought he would be just another devil in the ranks of men who had dragged her out of the hold. Jermany's arms ached from the way they'd wrenched her up, her ribs sharp beneath too-thin skin. She'd been starving when she crept aboard the ship, and now she would die full of bruises instead of bread. It wasn't fair, but not really unexpected.

The sailors laughed as they shoved her forward, a few already rolling up their sleeves, eager for sport. "Caught us a little rat," one of them sneered. "Scrawny thing, but we'll make do."

Jermany spat at his boots. She expected the first hit to land—maybe a kick to the ribs, a fist to her mouth. Instead, a voice cut through the humid air like the edge of a blade.

"Enough."

The men stilled. Their grip on her loosened just slightly. And that's when she noticed him.

Mr. Sloan, they called him. He wasn't the captain, but he might as well have been, judging by the way the others stepped back at his word. He leaned against the mast, arms crossed, looking at her with a scrutiny that made set her on edge. She lifted her chin, forcing herself to meet his gaze. If he meant to have his turn, he would have to look her in the eye first.

But instead of cruelty, he surveyed her, arms crossed, the faintest of smiles. And then—"Take her to the kitchen."

The sailors balked. "What?"

"Did I not speak loud enough?" His voice was calm, but the threat beneath it was colder than the sea at night. "Give her something to eat." He pushed off the mast, stepping forward, and his fingers flexed at his sides like he was already imagining breaking someone's bones. "If any of you lay a hand on her, I'll take off your fingers one by one."

Jermany stared. She wasn't sure she'd heard right.

The others grumbled but obeyed, shoving her toward the galley. Even as they muttered about how Sloan always ruined their fun, none of them dared challenge him. Later, after she'd wolfed down half a loaf of bread and kept down a bowl of stew, she found him standing outside the kitchen, arms still crossed, watching her like a man who had just taken in a stray dog and wasn't sure if it would bite or beg.

"What's your name?" he asked.

She wiped her mouth with the back of her hand. "Jermany."

Something flickered in his expression. A smirk, maybe. "You ever worked a ship before, Jermany?"

She shook her head.

"Well," he said, pushing away from the wall, "guess you'd better learn."

She followed him. She didn't know why. Maybe because she had nowhere else to go. Maybe because she'd seen the way the men had shrunk back from him, the way they listened when he spoke. Maybe because for the first time in a long time, someone had looked at her and decided she was worth more than just a plaything to be used up and discarded. She wasn't sure when he first started calling her Tempest, but it stuck. "Move faster, Tempest." "Think you can handle the helm, Tempest?" "Don't get too full of yourself, Tempest."

At first, she thought he meant it as a joke—because she'd been scrawny, weak, a half-starved stowaway with barely enough strength to lift a bucket. But one day, years later, when she asked him why Tempest, he only shrugged. "It's who you are."

And that was that.

Now, standing on the deck of the *Crimson Ghost,* watching him drink deep from the bottle she'd pressed into his hands, she thought of that day. Thought of how, from that moment on, she'd followed him, even when he left that ship. Even when the whole world seemed against them. Because Victor Sloan had saved her life once. And she intended to return the favor—impossible as such a thing was.

Victor's fingers found her shoulder, a brief but firm squeeze—gratitude in the only way he knew how to give it. "Thank you," he said, quiet but certain. He took another breath. "Think you can take the helm?"

Jermany scoffed at the question. "If you reign in your temper so this squall doesn't sink us."

Victor gave her a sideways smirk. "Deal." He pulled away from her support, making his way to the mainmast where he steadied himself once more. He was still pale, still worn, but better than he had been. With a deep breath, Jermany left him to join Peryn in unfurling the sails as the wind dissipated and the waves began to ease.

The *Ghost* would find her way back to Rootspire without her at the helm, Jermany supposed—without any of them. Carved from the ironvein trees that twisted toward the sky, she carried the soul of the forest in her timbers. One day, if left to the tide, she would drift home on her own. But not today. Today, she still had a course to follow.

The crew fell into an uneasy silence as the inlet shrank behind them. Sullivan coiled rope with mechanical precision, his hands needing the busy work. Peryn leaned against the rail while Jermany adjusted their heading, Evan's dark form lurking in the shadows nearby.

"We got lucky," Jermany said, her knuckles white on the wheel. "Could have lost the whole village."

"Or worse." Evan's voice drifted from the shadows. Thunder rumbled in the distance, an echo of the chaos they'd left behind.

Jermany's eyes found Sullivan, who was still methodically working the rope. "You alright, Sully?" He glanced up, pausing before giving her a quick nod.

"Sully?" Peryn rubbed at the back of his head. "I got knocked into another time by that shithead back there." He gave her what he probably thought was a flirtatious smile. "That's gotta be worth something."

"How about some saltwater?" She dipped her fingers in a puddle on the deck and flicked it into his eye.

"Oy! You trying to blind me?" He wiped at his face, stumbling back out of her range, giving her an indignant frown. "I hate water," he grumbled.

"What happened to Sully?" Evan asked, adjusting the crude bandages on his hand, still stained red from their hasty application.

Sullivan's hands stilled on the rope. "Dream." The hemp creaked in his grip. "Happened while I was awake this time."

Peryn's playful demeanor vanished, and he crossed his arms. They all fell silent, the weight of their shared curse hanging heavy in the air.

"At least they're not nightmares." Jermany adjusted their course slightly. "Not exactly."

Peryn raised an eyebrow. "I don't know what the hell else you'd call them!" His vehemence made Jermany's eyes narrow.

"What is it you dream of, Peryn?" she asked.

Peryn flashed her a roguish grin. "Of you, Jermany—only you."

She rolled her eyes, though a smile tugged at her lips. "Stop being an ass, Cannonball. Answer the question."

His smile faded. Wind whipped his coat around him as he stared out at the darkening horizon. "Of dying," he said uncomfortably, his voice nearly lost in the sound of waves against the hull.He held up his hands, flexing his fingers as if fighting invisible bonds. "I'm in shackles of ice—helpless." He gave Jermany a sideways glance. "I'm trying to save…someone." He cleared his throat. "I fail. We both die." The creaking of the ship filled the heavy silence. Evan's dark eyes reflected the distant lightning. "I dream of death, too. There are no shadows to draw on. Only fire and flame."

Jermany's hands tightened on the wheel. "I…I don't think they're just dreams," she said softly. "They're memories."

"Memories?" Peryn turned from the rail, looking more disturbed than before. "Why would you think that?"

Jermany's breath came shallow, uneven. "Because they feel too real," she murmured, her voice almost lost to the rising wind. "I wake up tasting ash, my skin burning like I've been standing too close to a fire. The screams… they don't fade like dreams should. They stay with me, like echoes of something I've already lived through."

Peryn shifted uncomfortably, rubbing a hand over his face. "That makes no sense. How could you remember something that hasn't happened?"

Jermany let out a shaky breath, eyes never leaving the horizon. "I don't know," she admitted. "But I think—no, I *feel*—that whatever's waiting out there… we've already faced it once."

Silence settled between them again, thick and uneasy. The air grew heavier with the promise of rain.

Peryn shook his head. "Don't take this the wrong way, love," he said, his voice lighter than his expression. "But I hope you're wrong. Because if you're not… we didn't win last time."

Evan turned his gaze to the dark horizon, his voice barely above a whisper. "Then we'll have to make sure we do this time." Lightning split the sky, casting their faces in stark relief before plunging them back into shadow. The first cold drop of rain struck Jermany's cheek, and she let it linger, unshaken.

Chapter 32

Memori

The world swam in and out of focus, reality bleeding into memory like watercolors in rain. Memori stood in a sun-dappled clearing, the grass tickling her bare feet. She was young again—with scraped knees and wild hair that refused to stay braided.

"Watch this!" a boy's voice called from above. The memory fractured and reformed, the boy's smile morphing into Orson's familiar grin. Memori reached for it, trying to hold on to the comfort it offered, but the image slipped away like smoke through her fingers. Instead, she found herself staring up at Victor's face—and for a moment, his skin seemed to ripple like the surface of a storm-tossed sea, shadows moving beneath it in ways that defied nature. The air around them crackled with energy.

The sight of him—lit from within like something not meant for this world—stole the air from her lungs. She pushed herself to a sitting position, the movement making her head spin . But then it was just Victor—no storm clouds roiling off his skin—eyes hell-bent on vengeance. Pure relief washed over his features, transforming him back into the stern quartermaster. "Memori!" His voice cracked. "Are you alright?" His hand reached for hers, rough fingers grasping her own gently. His brow furrowed with concern as he studied her face. Then, clearing his throat, he abruptly withdrew his touch.

"I…I don't know." She rubbed her eyes. "Victor, I…" The memory of what she'd done came into sharp focus: the careful selection of herbs, the methodical preparation, the innocent brown of the tea. Her stomach lurched as the full weight of it crashed over her. She'd turned healing into poison, twisted her gift into a weapon. Her mother taught her to save lives, not take them. "Oh, gods." She pressed her hands to her mouth. Her fingers still smelled of the roots she'd cut. "What did I do? I used it to—I never thought I—" The words tangled in her throat, choking her with the betrayal of everything she'd ever believed about herself.

"Memori." Victor's voice was softer than she'd ever heard it. "You protected yourself. Protected Elowen. Protected Viggo. Nothing more." Cold certainty crept into his words again. "If you hadn't done it, I would have torn him limb from limb."

Memori threw her arms around his neck, the image of Elowen's tear-stained face and Viggo puting himself in harms way to protect her settling in her mind. Sobs tore from her throat, raw, primal, true. Victor stiffened under her weight, caught off guard by her embrace and the immediacy of the contact. Then, slowly, carefully, as if handling something that might shatter, his arms came around her.

The electricity that always seemed to hover around him intensified where they touched, but it was different now—less like lightning about to strike and more like the distant rumble of thunder promising rain to parched earth. His hand cradled the back of her head, the slight tremor in his fingers, betraying his own contained emotion. Memori buried her face into the grounding mixture of ozone and sea salt that clung to his neck. The steady rhythm of his heartbeat sang to hers, calming her anxiety. For a moment, he leaned back into her, his pulse seeming to echo the crash of waves against a distant shore, but the stabbing memory of tearful blue eyes brought her back into her own grief.

A commotion outside interrupted whatever she might have said. "Memma!" Elowen's voice, high with panic. "Let me see her!"

"Wen, wait—" Orson's voice, followed by the sound of running feet.

The door burst open and Elowen flew in, tears streaming down her face. She launched herself at the bed, and Memori caught her. "Shhhh," she soothed, gathering her daughter close. "I'm here. I'm alright."

"You fell," Elowen sobbed into her shoulder. "You wouldn't wake up and then Victor took you away and—"

Through the open door, Memori glimpsed Orson hovering uncertainly in the hallway, worry etched deep in his features. Their eyes met for a moment before he looked away, shame crossing his face as he shifted from her view.

Victor stood, moving toward the door. "Come on, little one," he said gently to Elowen. "Your Memma needs rest, and the Captain needs looking after. Can you do that for me?" He held out his hand, and after a moment's hesitation and a tight squeeze around Memori's neck, Elowen slipped her small hand into his. Victor looked over his shoulder at her as he guided her to the door, the look of pain from a thousand lifetimes hugging his eyes. Memori watched Orson step forward from the shadows. The shame on his face melted away as he lifted Elowen into his arms, replaced by something softer, more certain. Some of the tightness in Memori's chest eased as she saw her daughter's small arms wrap trustingly around his neck, Elowen's tear-stained face tucking naturally into his shoulder as if she belonged there. Victor lingered in the doorway, watching them disappear down the corridor before turning back to Memori.

"Victor…" Memori's fingers twisted in the blanket. "I saw what happened to you," she said before he could speak. "The way the water moved. The thunder that came from nowhere." She drew in a shaky breath. "Just like Evander's shadows bend to his will. Just like my hands…" She lifted them, staring at her palms as if they might start glowing at any moment. "What are we? What is this?"

Thunder rumbled in the distance. Victor's gaze flicked to the window, and for a fleeting second, Memori swore something moved beneath his skin—like waves shifting under ice. "You've read the stories," he said quietly.

"Those silly children's tales?" Her voice caught in her throat. "The Guardians—those kinds of heroes—they don't exist!"

Victor sat beside her, slow and measured, like a man stepping onto fragile ground. That mixture of pity and sorrow still in his eyes. Memori pressed a trembling hand to her chest. "And me? This… healing touch—" Her voice broke. "I just used it to poison a man."

Victor exhaled, rubbing a hand over his face. "I know." His voice was quiet. "And I know you have questions. But I can't give you the answers you're looking for. Not yet."

She shook her head slowly, frustration and fear burning in her chest. "Why?"

He hesitated, just for a breath. When he spoke again, his voice was steady, but there was a rawness to it that made her pause. "Because you're not ready for them."

Her hands curled into fists. "That's not good enough."

Victor finally met her gaze, and for the first time since she'd known him, he looked… tired. "You will know the truth. But not here. Not like this." He leaned forward slightly. "Once we reach Rootspire, everything will make sense."

She swallowed hard, fingers tightening around the fabric of her sleeve. Her worry must have been evident, as Victor's brow furrowed in regret. He gently clasped her hands, gaze locking into hers. "I swear it, Memori." he said.

She studied him, searching for some sign of deception, but all she found was a quiet certainty. And maybe that was worse. Outside, the storm hadn't broken yet, but she could feel it pressing against the air, waiting. Finally, she let out a breath and looked away. "Alright," she murmured. "I'll wait." Victor didn't look relieved as he retracted his hand from hers. If anything, his shoulders set heavier, as if bracing for something more terrible.

Chapter 33

Victor

Victor watched Memori's steady breathing as she finally slept. He could still feel it—that ancient power thrumming beneath his skin, begging to be unleashed. "Da?"

"Viggo." The name caught in his throat as he turned to see his son hovering uncertainly in the doorway. Victor pulled him close, one hand cradling the back of his head. Eirlys had come into his life like sunlight through smoke—beautiful, blinding, and gone too fast. She'd left her mark on him in ways no magic ever could. A love that carved itself deep into his soul, deeper even than the bond that tied him to his gravest mistakes. Viggo was all he had left now. All that remained of *her*. A gift he'd never deserve, not in this life or a thousand more—one he lived in constant fear of losing. And sometimes, when the wind stilled just right, he swore he could feel Linden watching... waiting.

The way the ship rose and fell with the waves reminded him of that day long ago—the memory ever at the forefront of his mind.

The deck of the Ghost was slick with blood and seawater, the air heavy with the acrid tang of smoke and betrayal. He'd stood at the heart of that chaos, his iron blade singing against Storm's jagged sword. Each strike threw sparks into the darkness, but it wasn't the clash of steel that haunted him—it was the silence. The deafening silence of the fallen.

They were gone. All of them.

Storm's laughter cut through the aftermath, dark and cruel. "You should have known better, Victor." Victor's hand was weak from gripping his sword hilt, grief turning to rage in his chest. "You'll pay for what you've done." The duel raged on, each strike fueled by Victor's raw fury and Storm's cold precision. As Victor's movements grew wild with desperation, Storm remained calculating, his blows methodical and merciless.

"You're too sentimental," Storm sneered, driving his blade deep into Victor's side. Victor staggered but refused to fall, fresh blood darkening his shirt.

Realizing his inevitable demise, Victor drew the tide stone from his coat in one motion. He raised his arm, making ready to throw it to the depths. Its otherworldly light pulsed like a living heart, and for the first time, Storm's smirk faltered.

"You wouldn't dare," Storm hissed, his scarred face twisting with rage. The moonlight caught the silver streaks in his once-dark hair, and the old burn marks that crawled up his neck seemed to writhe beneath his skin. "It's meant to be mine. That bitch Linden banished me and gave unfathomable power to you–children!"

"She was right." Victor's voice was steel, even as he felt his life ebbing away. "And you...will never possess it." The words came through gritted teeth as he hurled the stone into the churning sea. Its glow vanished beneath the waves, leaving only darkness and the howling storm above.

"No!" Storm shoved Victor aside and lunged for the ship's edge, scanning the waters with frantic eyes. Victor collapsed onto the deck, clutching his wound as his vision dimmed. Storm's distant roars faded as he ordered his crew to search the waters. The Crimson Ghost drifted, abandoned, while Victor lay motionless, rain washing over him, blood pooling beneath his body. He'd stayed that way, longing for death to take him. But it never came.

A soft light and gentle humming brought him back to the world of the living. A figure stood over him, hands hovering above his wound. "Linden?" he gasped out her name.

"You've made quite a mess of things," she said, her voice heavy with sorrow.

His heart felt like a knife stuck through it at the sorrow in her eyes. "Don't save me. Let me go. I failed them—they're dead because of me."

Linden's expression hardened with resolve. "No. You are not beyond saving, young Victor.' Her gaze pierced him as if reading his very soul.

"I don't deserve hope," he breathed, agony lancing through him. Pain twisted through his chest like molten metal and shards of ice, each breath a battle between fire and frost. How could he have trusted Storm? What was he thinking?!

"Quiet, child." Linden knelt beside him as her hands glowed with ethereal green light. The ancient roots of the Mercy Oak emerged from the shadows, reaching toward them like gentle fingers. "He has won nothing. When this is done, they will know you as Storm-Breaker." Victor's vision blurred as her healing warmth flowed through him. Before darkness claimed him, he saw Linden's serene face framed by the oak's twisted branches above, their shapes like guardians in the night.

Now, holding Viggo tighter, Victor pushed the memories away. He wouldn't lose anyone else to Storm. Not this time. Not ever again.

Orson

ELOWEN'S WARM WEIGHT pressed against Orson's chest, her small hand still clutching the dog-eared storybook that lay forgotten across his lap. The gentle rise and fall of her breathing mingled with the distant sound of churning ocean.

A shadow fell across them as Victor bent down. Orson felt the girl being lifted away, and his arms tightened instinctively before his mind caught up with his body. The scent of Elowen's hair—salt air and dried flowers—drifted away as Victor carried her to her cot. A lantern's flame caught her copper curls, turning them to liquid gold, and Orson's chest tightened at how much she looked like her mother.

Blankets rustled as Victor tucked them around her with a tenderness that seemed at odds with the power Orson witnessed in the galley. His throat felt raw, scratchy with exhaustion and worry as he whispered, "How is she? Memori?"

"In shock," Victor replied quietly. The girl shifted but didn't wake, her face peaceful in sleep. "But she'll be fine."

Orson pushed himself up from the chair, muscles protesting from hours spent swimming, then fixed in the uncomfortable position. Questions burned in his throat about what he'd witnessed in the galley—the otherworldly glow, the way the storm itself seemed to answer Victor's rage. He followed Victor to the door, casting one last glance at Elowen before stepping into the lantern-lit corridor. "I should've been there," he muttered. "I should've—"

"You couldn't have done anything," Victor cut him off, though his tone held no rebuke. The door closed with a soft click, leaving Elowen to her dreams while they stood in the cramped hallway. The ship's timbers creaked around them, a lonely sound that matched Orson's mood.

"You're right," Orson said, his voice low and bitter. He ran a hand through his hair, frustration making his movements sharp and jerky. "Couldn't even help when that bastard took her. Can't swim, can't sail worth a damn. I'm just…" he exhaled sharply, the sound harsh in the quiet corridor. "I'm just a useless coward." He couldn't get past how he'd felt when Memori needed him. Helpless. Frozen in place.

Victor's expression hardened. "A coward doesn't try to save an old fisherman when he knows it'll be the death of him." His dark eyes fixed intensely on Orson. "Take on that fisherman's cause and blow up Stonegate dam, steal a ship. Rumors spread quickly through the Union. Especially about traitors."

"I had nothing better going on," Orson muttered, looking away from that unnerving gaze.

Victor flicked his eyes to the ceiling, releasing a controlled sigh from his nose. "A coward would have gotten on with dying before they went through all that damned trouble." He rested his hands on his hips, studying Orson's face. "Memori. When she's rested, go talk to her."

Orson cocked his head. "About what?"

"About wha–?" Victor rolled his eyes. "You know damn-well what."

Orson swallowed hard, his next words barely a whisper. "She deserves far better than anything I could ever give her." His chest was tight with guilt. "I dragged her into all this, anyway. Why would she want anything to do with me?"

"That's not for you to decide." For a moment, a look of understanding passed over Victor's face, but it was short-lived. "Either you talk to her, brother, or I will." He tapped a finger on Orson's chest, then flinched like he'd just realized what he said.

Orson stared at him. Brother. The word unlocked something deep in his mind—a door he hadn't known was there. The strange familiarity he'd always felt around Victor, the way the man seemed to know him better than he knew himself… Fragments of memory danced just out of reach, like shadows in firelight.

But Victor was already turning away, his shoulders rigid. "Get some rest, Captain," he said quietly, disappearing down the corridor before Orson could untangle the chaos in his mind.

Chapter 34

Victor

Night air carried the unmistakable scent of Rootspire—ancient magic woven through salt and sea. Victor breathed it in, feeling the familiar pull of the seven realms reaching across the waters like invisible threads. Soon the others would feel it too, that inexorable tug toward destiny. That's what Linden called it. But if you were destined for something, shouldn't it come easier?

His fingers traced the worn railing as he made his way to the bow, each step heavy with memories he couldn't outrun. Memori's empty gaze from earlier haunted him—those familiar bronze eyes looking through him as if he were a stranger. Once, in another life, he would have given anything to have her look at him the way she looked at Orson. Now that thought only carved deeper into the hollow space where Eirlys's memory lived.

A bitter smile tugged at his lips as he gripped the ship's edge. Fate had a cruel sense of humor. His stomach churned at the thought of the moment approaching, when she would remember him. Remember everything. And not just her. The others too.

Victor made his way to the helm, hands buried deep in his coat pockets, each step feeling like he carried the weight of all seven realms. The night wind whipped around them, bringing with it memories of another night, decades ago—a ship leaving Tidesreach, angry shouts echoing across the deck. He'd felt Jermany's power before he ever saw her—like embers smoldering in the dark, waiting for the right wind to catch. It wasn't just strength—it was potential, wild and unshaped. He'd felt that same flicker with the others too, each one a spark waiting to be stoked into something more.

When they dragged her from the hold, she was all sharp angles and desperate fury, a half-starved girl ready to fight the whole world. Even as they moved to teach her what happened to stowaways, he'd stepped forward, feeling the weight of centuries shift with that single choice.

"Vic." Jermany acknowledged him now, her hands loose at her sides rather than gripping the helm. The Ghost cut through the dark waters with uncanny precision. Victor gave her a short nod, watching the way the starlight danced on the waves. Jermany's voice dropped to barely a whisper. Starlight reflected in her dark eyes as they fixed on him with sharp intensity. "They're like us. Aren't they?"

Victor's fingers tightened in his pockets as he considered how much to tell her. How much he could tell her without unraveling everything. At last, he met her gaze before turning to the horizon. "Yes," he said, knowing by her expression she'd already guessed that much. "When we get to Rootspire, I'll tell you everything," he promised.

"Why not now? We've sailed together for years, Vic." Her voice carried the sting of perceived distrust.

He placed a weathered hand on her shoulder, feeling the tension in her muscles. "It has to be this way. Trust me this last time, Tempest. Please."

Concern flickered across her features at his choice of words, her lips pressing into a thin line. "We'll always trust you, Vic," she swore fiercely, the wind catching her dark hair. Victor gave her an intense nod of acknowledgment before turning away. He wished her words could remain true, but some revelations, once unveiled, could never be forgiven.

Chapter 35

Storm

The *Dominion* cut through the waves like a blade, its black sails drinking in the moonlight. General Storm stood at the helm, his fingers drumming against the polished wood as he stared into the darkness ahead.

Three days. Three days since Grift should have reported back. The spy had never failed him before—which meant Victor had gotten to him first. Storm's jaw tightened as he imagined Victor's satisfied smirk, that damnable certainty in his eyes. The same look he'd worn at Rootspire when he'd chosen—too late—that he was on the wrong side. Storm's lips curved into a stiff smile, remembering how long he'd spent worming his way into Victor's mind, feeding his doubts, twisting his desires until they became poison. Even now, the memory brought him satisfaction. Love was the greatest weakness of all—whether it sprang from devotion or from the festering root of jealousy.

Behind him, laughter rang out—loud, grating, and unwelcome.

Kol.

Storm didn't turn, but he could hear him, his voice carrying over the deck as he held court among his men like some swaggering princeling.

"I'm just saying," Kol went on, his words slow with self-satisfaction. "After this mess is handled, a little celebration is in order."

One of his men chuckled. "Still on for the markets at Driftmarch, then?"

Kol let out a mock gasp. "What, and go in empty-handed? No, no, we should make a stop along the way for an appetizer before we hit the main course."

The response was immediate—boisterous laughter, crude comments, voices overlapping with vulgar enthusiasm. One of them made some remark too indistinct to catch, but whatever it was sent the rest of them howling.

Storm reached his threshold of noises from insufferable mortals. He spoke, quiet but cutting. "Kol." The laughter stopped.

The air shifted as Kol turned, still grinning, but hesitating now. "Yes, General?"

Storm finally looked at him. The man's uniform was immaculate—black and white, the picture of Union-approved refinement. A ridiculous contrast to the half-healed gash on his forehead and the nose that had been broken and set wrong. The Union's physicians were useless. Then again, no one with actual skill wanted to work for the Union anymore.

Storm stepped down from the helm, slow, deliberate. He took his time closing the space between them, watching as the last embers of laughter flickered out. "If you and your men do not come to order and remain quiet," Storm said, voice like a blade drawn across stone, "I will remove you from my ship."

Kol's grin faltered. "Of course, General," he said quickly, dropping his gaze. His men muttered quiet apologies, shuffling back into silence. Storm didn't move. He let the weight of his words settle, watching Kol's expression with satisfaction. The man's posture was all deference now, but there was something else in his eyes. A flicker of something that tried to hide beneath obedience. Anger. Storm almost smiled. Kol was an idiot, through and through. Did he really think himself anywhere near Storm's level? Did he truly believe he was anything more than a pawn in this? The man was cheap cannon fodder. He wouldn't make it back from the island. One way or another.

Chapter 35

Storm turned away, leaving Kol in the silence he'd commanded. The wood creaked beneath his fingers as he returned to the helm. Above, the stars disappeared one by one behind gathering clouds.

A smile touched his lips as darkness claimed the sky.

Chapter 36

Memori

Memori stirred, her body aching but her mind slowly sharpening. The dim glow of the lanterns cast long shadows across the cabin, the ship's steady rocking lulling the space into a quiet rhythm. A small, warm weight pressed against her side, clinging like a barnacle. Elowen; she must have snuck out of her own bed—wherever Victor had tucked her in—and curled up beside her sometime in the night.

The little girl held on tighter, burying her face into Memori's ribs as she moved. "Don't go," she mumbled, voice muffled in the bedding. She snuck from her own bed in the middle of the night

Memori exhaled slowly, smoothing a hand over Elowen's tangled curls. "I'm here," she whispered. "Memma's here." Elowen's grip didn't loosen.

Guilt tightened in Memori's chest. Elowen had every right to be afraid—she'd already lost so much. But she needed water, needed a moment to breathe. Carefully, she shifted, waiting for Elowen's breathing to even out. The girl's fingers twitched against her tunic before going slack. Slowly, carefully, Memori reached for a pillow, inching it between them. Elowen stirred but didn't wake as she guided her arms around the soft bundle. Memori held her breath, waiting. Elowen let out a soft sigh, nuzzling into the pillow. Memori moved, swinging her legs off the cot with aching slowness. Her body protested, but she ignored it, crossing the small space to pour herself a cup of water. The first sip cooled her dry throat. Then she heard the cries. A muffled sound, low and pained. A voice caught in something dark.

Orson.

Memori stiffened, setting the cup down. Another sound followed—a broken breath, a name she couldn't quite catch. She stepped toward the door, glancing once more at Elowen to make sure she hadn't disturbed her. The girl remained curled around the pillow, lost in sleep. With one last steadying breath, Memori slipped out into the dim corridor, the ship creaking beneath her feet as she hurried to Orson's cabin.

Orson

THE WATER WAS black as pitch, pressing in from all sides. Orson thrashed against the current, but something held him down—not weeds this time, but hands. Cold, strong fingers wrapped around his ankles, his wrists, pulling him deeper. Images flashed through his mind: children huddled around a fire, an old woman with silver-threaded hair, a tree that touched the stars. Hands tightened, and suddenly he was a child again, sinking into the river at the village where he grew up. Except this time. There was no one there to save him.

When he opened his eyes, he could still feel the hands, fingers firm on his throat. The Tide Stone felt heavy against his skin where it hung from its chain. With shaking fingers, he pulled it free, holding it up to catch the moonlight. The blue depths shifted and swirled, like waves caught in glass. His reflection on the stone's surface showed him everything he didn't want to see—the man who'd frozen when Memori needed him.

The scene replayed in his mind: the way she'd swayed, her eyes rolling back, how he'd dropped his sword without thinking to catch her. He'd had her in his arms for one precious moment, her weight familiar from when he held her close that first time. When she'd trusted him. But then his body betrayed that trust, locking up as if his blood were frozen. He'd just stood there, holding her, useless, until Victor took her from his arms and carried her to her cabin.

His fingers clenched around the stone. The memory of their kiss still burned on his lips, sweet and sharp. He'd held her then, hadn't he? Touched her like she was something he had the right to want. And she held him back. But when it truly mattered… he'd turned to stone, watching Victor carry her away while he stood like a useless statue.

A soft knock made him start. "Orson?" Memori's voice was muffled through the door. "Are you alright?"

His heart lurched at the sound of her voice, relief warring with shame. She was okay—awake, walking, worried about him, of all people. He wanted to go to her, to pull her close and make sure she was really there. But the memory of his own paralysis kept him rooted in place.

There was a pause, then the door creaked open. Memori stood in the doorway, a candle in her hand casting a warm glow across her features. Her hair was loose around her shoulders, and Orson's chest tightened at the sight.

He quickly tucked the stone away. "I'm fine," he said, struggling to keep his voice steady. "Just a dream."

"Liar," she said softly, stepping inside. "You were shouting."

Orson looked away, his hands still trembling slightly. "It's nothing. Just… a nightmare."

Memori set the candle down and crossed to his bed perching on the edge. "Want to talk about it?"

He shook his head, but when he met her eyes, the words spilled out anyway. "It feels wrong. Like… like I'm remembering it wrong. There are pieces missing, shadows where there should be light." He ran a hand through his hair, frustrated. "I sound mad, don't I?"

"No." Her voice was quiet. "I think… I think I understand. Sometimes I dream too. About places I've never been, people I've never met. But they feel real. Like memories I've forgotten."

Orson's breath caught. He turned to look at her properly, taking in the way the candlelight painted her skin in gold. She was close enough that he could see the flecks of amber in her eyes, could catch the faint scent of herbs on her skin. "What do you dream about?" he asked softly.

She hesitated, her fingers twisting in her lap. "A tree," she whispered. "Touching the sky. And children… seven of them, around a fire. An old woman telling stories," she trailed off, her brow furrowing. "But it's all fragments. And there was this boy…" she trailed off. "Maybe I'm just going sea crazy."

Orson scooped her hand into his without thinking, fingers closing around hers. "You're not—" A sudden wave rocked the ship. Orson caught her instinctively when she shifted to keep herself from falling off the bed, one arm wrapping around her waist to steady her. She braced herself against his chest, and for a moment, they froze there, breath mingling in the candlelit darkness. "I'm sorry," she whispered, but didn't pull away. Her palm was warm against his chest, just over his thundering heart.

"Don't be sorry." The words came out rougher than he intended, his throat tight with everything unsaid. Her pulse fluttered at her throat like a trapped bird, and he swayed forward slightly, drawn by a gravity he couldn't resist. If he just closed that final distance…

"Memori…I—"

Memori

She didn't let him finish. Surging forward, she closed that final breath of space between them, pressing her lips to his. Time suspended—Orson's hand slid up her back, trailing her neck and finally tangling her hair. He pulled her closer with an urgency that stole her breath. This wasn't like their first kiss—tentative and sweet. This was desperation. Need. The kind of kiss that came from someone afraid they might never get another chance.

His other arm wrapped around her waist, drawing her against him until she could feel his heart hammering against her own. She gasped against his mouth, and he deepened the kiss, pouring everything he couldn't say into it. An ache bloomed in her chest, sharp, and sweet, and hungry. For once, she didn't reason it away, didn't listen to the voice warning her about everything that could go wrong. Instead, she let herself want this—want him—with an intensity that frightened her.

Her fingers dug into his shoulder, pulling him closer as she kissed him back with the same desperate need. Fear lurked at the edges of her mind, but she pushed it away. She was tired of being careful, tired of denying herself this one thing she wanted more than air. Her whole body trembled with the honesty of it, this admission of desire—of a bone-deep recognition that this was right. That they fit together like ghosts of a life once lived. The way his arms curved around her felt like coming home to a place she hadn't known she was searching for. His hands shook slightly even as they held her like she might dissolve into mist at any moment, and she pressed closer—trying to tell him, without words, that she wasn't going anywhere. Not this time. That maybe she'd never been meant to be anywhere but here, with him.

Chapter 37

Memori

Dawn light filtered through the porthole, rousing Memori from the first peaceful sleep she'd had in weeks. For a moment, she lay still, the memory of Orson's lips on hers lingering like a half-remembered dream—the heat of his mouth, the desperate way his hands tangled in her hair. They'd parted reluctantly in the early hours, knowing Elowen would wake soon. Her heart still fluttered at the thought, a smile tugging at the corners of her lips as she reached across the bed—Only to find empty blankets. The smile vanished. She sat up fast, panic chasing the sleep from her body.

Elowen

But then she noticed the faint warmth still in the sheets beside her, the way the door hung slightly ajar. Elowen must've slipped away recently while Memori slept. Still shaken, Memori dressed quickly and moved through her morning tasks in a daze, her thoughts threaded between the night before and the fear that still clung to her ribs. When she finally stepped onto the deck, the sight that greeted her made her heart swell.

Orson sat cross-legged on the deck with Elowen, showing her how to tie what he thought was a proper sailor's knot, while they shared a breakfast of hardtack and dried apples. Her daughter's face was still drawn from yesterday's trauma, but there was a peace in the way she leaned against

Orson's shoulder, nibbling on an apple slice as her small fingers mimicked his clumsy movements with the rope.

A few feet away, Sullivan stood frozen, mouth ajar like he couldn't believe what he was witnessing. Beside him, Evander pinched the bridge of his nose, one eye twitching with restrained agony. "Should we stop him?" Sullivan muttered, finally snapping his mouth shut.

Evander's eyes clamped shut like he couldn't bare to watch anymore and he shook his head slowly.

As if sensing her gaze, Orson looked up, and the smile he gave Memori nearly stopped her heart. It was quiet and warm, full of everything they hadn't dared put into words.She could still feel the echo of last night—his presence, the way he held her like he'd been afraid to let go.

He turned back to Elowen, ruffling her curls. "Keep practicing. You'll be tying knots faster than me soon enough." Orson pushed to his feet and crossed the deck toward Memori. He didn't catch the way Sullivan coughed and immediately took his place at Elowen's side, shaking his head as he unthreaded the rope, muttering to himself as he showed the girl the proper way. Elowen smiled, her fingers mimicking Sullivan's with fierce concentration.

Memori's heart picked up speed at the easy way he slipped his hand around hers, his thumb grazing slow circles over her knuckles. The callouses on his fingertips were rough, but his touch was unbearably soft. For a moment, she forgot what she'd wanted to say.

She worried over the impossible truth taking shape beneath her skin—something she could no longer ignore. Injuries healed faster when she touched them. Bruises faded. Flesh knit together like the herbs were only a suggestion, and her hands were doing the real work. She'd been denying it for weeks, brushing it off as luck or skill, but yesterday had shattered that illusion. Because yesterday, she hadn't healed someone. She'd poisoned them—deliberately, methodically. And that, too, had worked far too well.

She needed to tell Orson, needed to say something about the power curling in her bones, but the weight of it kept her silent. Before she could find the words, Orson gave her fingers one last squeeze and said, "I need to talk to Victor. I'll be back."

He kissed her on the cheek. And just like that, he was gone.

"Here." The quiet word drew her attention. Evander stood nearby, offering her a piece of bread and what looked like the last apple from his own breakfast. His right hand was cradled against his chest, and she noticed how he struggled to tear the bread one-handed. The sight brought back the memory of how he'd positioned himself between her and the spy without hesitation, how he twisted shadows to protect them all.

"Let me see that hand," she said, taking the food with a grateful nod. His quiet gesture of sharing his breakfast meant more than he probably knew.

Evander protested, stepping back. "It's nothing—"

"Shut up," Memori said, already reaching for him. He didn't resist as she unwound the bandage. The wound wasn't deep, but the edges were red and beginning to swell. These men had risked everything to protect her family. The least she could do was tend their wounds. "This needs cleaning."

On an ordinary day she would have cleaned the wound, but that now-familiar warmth started building in her palms. Instead of fighting it, she let it flow, watching as a soft glow emanated from where her skin met his.

"I'm sorry… for fighting you back there." The angry redness faded beneath her touch, but this time she felt the cost of it—a deep exhaustion seeping into her bones, as if she'd given away a piece of her own vitality to heal him.

"It's alright," he said, staring at her intently.

She swayed slightly, steadying herself against the rail. "That's… that's happening more often now."

Evander rubbed at his palm where the skin was no longer red and irritated, studying her with knowing eyes. They shared a look of understanding that made her throat tight.

"How long have you been able to…" she trailed off, not sure how to name what either of them could do.

"Since I was small," he said quietly, flexing his newly healed hand. "It was easier to hide at first, living in the Shadowfold. Just a boy who was good at staying out of sight, that's all." An edge crept into his voice. "Until the slavers came. Then I became of keen interest to them. Hard to hide when they're obsessed with catching you, watching your every move. Didn't stop until they had me in a cage."

Memori cringed. "Did Victor free you?"

A small smile touched Evander's lips, warming his usually solemn features. "Peryn. We didn't meet Victor until later." His eyes grew distant with memory. "The Driftmarch slavers had us both captured, waiting for a ship to take us from his homeland. It would have been easier for him to leave me behind when he made his escape. But he didn't." There was a slight shake of his head. "You should have seen the way he set their ship aflame."

The fondness in his voice made Memori glance toward where Peryn stood at the rigging. "Is that why you joined the crew?"

"Partly." Evander's fingers traced the freshly healed skin of his palm. "But mostly because, for the first time, I didn't have to hide what I was. Victor," he paused, choosing his words carefully. "He understood. Made me see that these gifts, they're not curses. They're part of who we are."

The way he said 'we' hung between them, heavy with meaning. Memori thought of her own power, how natural it felt even as it drained her. "I still don't understand what's happening to me," she admitted softly.

"None of us did, at first." He met her eyes steadily. "But you will. And you're not alone in this, Memori. Not anymore."

Viggo's voice rang out sharp and clear from the crow's nest. "Ship on the horizon! Blacksmoke flag!"

The peaceful moment shattered. Memori watched Evander's newly healed hand curl into a fist, shadows already beginning to gather around him.

"Get Victor—and the captain," Jermany ordered from the helm, dark hair whipping around her in the wind. "Now."

Memori rushed to gather Elowen close. She caught sight of the approaching vessel through a break in the morning mist. Its black sails drinking in the dawn light, and even at this distance, she could make out the gleam of cannons along its hull.

Chapter 38

Orson

Orson found Victor in the galley, a mug cradled in his hands. The familiar scents of coffee and salt pork wrapped around Orson, but they did little to ease the tension in his shoulders. His mind kept drifting to Memori—the softness of her lips, the way she melted against him in the darkness. But there were questions that needed answering, mysteries that kept him tossing in his bunk long after that kiss.

He slid onto the bench across from Victor, who took a slow sip from his mug, watching him over the rim. Pale light filtered through the porthole, catching the thin curls of steam rising from the kettle between them. Victor set his cup down with a quiet thud. "What do you want to know, Orson?" There was a wariness in his voice that made Orson's skin prickle.

Orson's fingers tightened around his mug. The word *brother* still echoed in his mind. Men called each other brother all the time, but this had felt different. Heavier. Like a key fitting into a lock he hadn't known existed.

"Back there—at the inlet—you…" He broke off, frustration twisting his words before they could form properly. That sense of recognition that plagued him since they first met pressed against his ribs. "Seemed like something else. Something…not normal."

The ship's timbers creaked around them, a lonely sound in the heavy silence.

"Very observant of you." Victor finally spoke.

Orson frowned, catching the sarcastic glint in Victor's eye, though his voice remained the same. "Don't you think it's time to tell me what the hell's going on?"

"Oh, *now* you wish to learn things." There was a hint of irony in Victor's words.

"Cut the shit, will you?" Orson rolled his eyes in frustration.

Victor set down his mug, and Orson almost recoiled from the intensity in his gaze. "You're not ready."

"Not ready?" Anger flared in Orson's chest. "I'm not a child, Victor—"

"No," Victor cut him off. "When we reach Rootspire—" He stopped, jaw clenching. "You'll know the truth. And…" emotion flashed through his eyes so powerful it took Orson by surprise, "you'll wish you didn't." He pushed back from the table, his chair scraping against the floor.

"Ships!" Peryn's voice thundered from above deck. "Two, coming in fast!"

Orson and Victor froze, exchanging a look before they bolted for the stairs.

ORSON FOUND MEMORI holding Elowen close. His jaw tightened at the sight of the child's wide-eyed fear. "Memori," he called, voice cutting through the growing chaos of preparation. "Take the children below. Both of them." His gaze shifted meaningfully to where Viggo was scrambling down from the crow's nest, the boy's usual exuberance replaced by a brittle sort of determination.

Memori hesitated for just a moment, one hand pressed protectively against Elowen's head, before nodding. She reached out, calling for Viggo.

The boy shook his head vigorously, eyes searching for his father. "I can stay and fight!"

"Below deck—now!" Orson's command left no room for argument. He caught the fraction of tension leaving Victor's shoulders, met his look of quiet gratitude with a slight nod.

"Go," Victor added softly, his gentle tone a stark contrast to the way his fingers curled around his sword hilt. He pulled Viggo into a fierce embrace before taking his chin firmly in hand. "Follow orders, eh?"

Viggo nodded, his frown not quite hiding his fear.

"Good lad." Victor squeezed his shoulder before guiding him toward Memori. "Watch over Elowen. We'll handle this."

The boy took Elowen's small hand in his, his reluctant nod betraying how much he wanted to stay.

"Orson." Memori's voice made him turn. She stood with one hand on each child, her hair whipping wildly in the wind. Their eyes met, and for a moment the approaching ships, the cannons, all of it fell away.

"Be careful," she breathed.

He swallowed past the sudden tightness in his throat, managing a quick nod before she disappeared below with the children, taking his heart with her into the darkness.

The Union ships were close enough now that they could hear the low groan of their rigging, Every detail grew sharper—the Ravager to port, her gleaming rows of cannons promising destruction, and the Blackspine to starboard, her polished brass fittings catching the sun like warning beacons. The unmistakable silhouettes of Storm's elite guard took position along both ships' railings.

The Ghost's crew moved like parts of a well-oiled machine, each person knowing their role without need for orders. Rifles emerged from concealed storage, powder horns were passed from hand to hand, and the sharp sounds of weapons being primed cut through the tense air. Peryn took up position at the starboard rail, his rifle loaded, hammer cocked. Beside him, Evander settled near the mast, twin pistols drawn and ready despite his injured hand. His dark eyes tracked the Blackspine's approach, calculating distances and angles with sharp focus.

A pistol in his hand, Orson watched them prepare, his jaw working. "See! I knew they'd be using guns!" he called to Victor, vindication in his voice despite the danger. "And you kept insisting I train with that bloody useless sword."

Victor rolled his eyes, drawing his blade with a whisper of steel. A humorless smile touched his lips. "Not really the time, Captain." He glanced at the approaching ships. "They'll make use of both." His voice dropped lower, heavy with old wounds.

Distance between the ships narrowed to a stone's throw, and the first grappling hook arced through the air. Splintering wood pulled Orson's attention to the stern, where a cannonball tore through the Ghost's hull. The iron shot punched clean through, but instead of continuing its deadly arc, it… hesitated. For a fraction of a second, the massive ball seemed to hover, caught between motion and stillness. That's when Orson felt it—a pull deep in his chest, like an anchor dropping into still water.

"They're boarding!" Jermany shouted, pulling a rifle into her shoulder and making ready to fire. Storm's crew swarmed over the rails, and Victor positioned himself between them and the bridge where Orson stood.

"You'll have to go through me!" Victor's voice carried over the din like thunder. Mist coiled around him and his eyes flashed with the promise of violence. The hidden gun platform in Storm's rigging fired. Sullivan spotted the flash of movement first—the subtle shift of a barrel taking aim at Orson. He didn't think, just moved, slamming into Orson's side, driving them both to the deck. The shot cracked through the air above them, slamming into the railing. Shards of wood exploded outward, some slicing through the air as the fractured remains tumbled into the sea. They hit the deck hard, rolling as debris clattered around them like deadly rain.

Time seemed to slow as Orson met Sullivan's gaze, understanding crashing over him like a wave—he'd be dead if not for the man's quick action. And here he'd thought Sully would be the first one to use him as a human shield.

Sullivan wore the expression of someone inconvenienced by having to retrieve a misplaced item rather than someone who'd just saved a life. With a grunt, he yanked Orson roughly behind the forecastle's cover as another spray of rifle fire peppered the deck they'd just vacated.

"Not that it matters terribly to me, but–the thing about guns," Sully spoke quickly, shaking splinters from his sleeve, "is you have to move out of the line of fire." He shot Orson a pointed look. "Unless you're aiming to catch a bullet between the eyes, in which case—carry on."

Through the chaos of gunfire and splintering wood, Orson saw the shot catch Victor—a spray of red blooming across his shoulder like some terrible flower. "Victor!"

Sullivan's voice raised as he barreled across the deck, throwing Union men aside like they were made of straw, dragging Orson along with him.

Blood darkened Victor's coat, but his posture stiffened. The air grew thick—hard to breathe, as if the moisture was being pulled from Orson's lungs. Around them, droplets rose from the waves in delicate streams, hanging in the air like liquid threads in a spider's web. Each breath came out foggy as the temperature plummeted. Victor's strange luminescence Orson had noticed before blazed now, making Victor's eyes glow like lightning behind storm clouds. The wind changed direction, no longer driven by nature but bending to his will, creating a vortex of power around him. The suspended water droplets hardened into ice, sharp as glass, deadly as arrows.

"Down!" Sullivan's voice barely registered before he pulled Orson to safety. Victor's hand slashed through the air, and the ice shards responded like an extension of his body, cutting through the Union soldiers with devastating accuracy. Above them, the sky darkened unnaturally fast, and thunder answered Victor's call like a loyal servant responding to its master.

There was a deafening roar as the second cannonball tore through the Ghost's hull, followed by the awful groan of splintering timber. The deck lurched beneath Orson's feet as the ship shuddered from bow to stern, like a wounded animal crying out in pain. The impact sent vibrations through his bones, a deep, visceral tremor that shook loose something primal in his chest.

More Union soldiers swarmed over the rails like insects, and Victor's movements were growing sluggish, his shoulder dark with blood. Each blast of ice and wind seemed to cost him more now, the glow in his eyes flickering like a guttering candle. Another cannon roared, and Orson felt the power building in his chest, begging to be let free. He was numb— his thoughts scattered, body moving without permission, as if something deeper had taken the reins. He didn't know what to do. He just *did*.

He held out his hand, pressing it onto the debris-covered floor, and felt the iron's pull. The cannonball that breached their hull reversed course, drawn back through the hole of its own making, like the ship itself was spitting it out. It hung suspended in the air before him, and in that moment, Orson could feel every grain of iron on its surface.

"What in the seven hells?" he breathed, reaching out instinctively. More shots came screaming across the water. Orson's hands moved without conscious thought, and the iron projectiles curved away from the Ghost like fish avoiding a predator. He could feel them all—every piece of iron Storm's ships carried, from their cannons to their anchor chains. It called to him, begging to be shaped, to be commanded.

The Tide Stone pulsed against his chest, but this was different. This power didn't come from the stone—it came from somewhere deeper, as if awakening from a long slumber. Orson's fingers curled, and the suspended cannonball began to change. The iron flowed like water, reshaping itself into a bristling mass of spikes that he sent spinning back toward Storm's lead ship.

"Captain!" Sullivan's voice cut through his concentration. "The hull—she's breached!"

Orson reached out with his newfound sense, finding the jagged hole in the Ghost's side. He could feel the iron nails and braces throughout her frame. With a grunt of effort, he pulled, drawing more iron from the sea floor far below—centuries of lost anchors and cannons offering up their substance to his call. Metal flowed up through the waves, forming thick coils across the shattered timbers, pressing the fractured wood back into place. Iron bands tightened under his will, cinching around the Ghost's wounded hull until the seams sealed themselves, airtight and stronger than before.

Orson fell to one knee, gasping for breath, hands braced on his sides as sweat dripped from his brow. What was happening to him? This power… it felt familiar somehow, like remembering a language he'd spoken in dreams.

Jermany and Evander shouted over the chaos as the enemy ship groaned, but their words were lost to Orson. The sound of tearing wood filled the air as he pulled, drawing the iron from Storm's vessel like poison from a wound. Nails ripped free from planking. Cannon mounts tore loose from their brackets. Even the thin strips of iron reinforcing the hull began to splinter and crack. The metal streamed through the air in ribbons of liquid, gathering above the waves in a shifting, writhing mass that grew larger with each passing second.

Storm's crew abandoned their posts in terror as their ship broke apart. Orson could hear their screams, see the fear on their faces as their vessel came apart around them. With a final, devastating pull, Orson tore the remaining pieces free. The enemy ship's spine shattered, its back broken beyond repair. The massive vessel split in two, seawater rushing in to claim what remained as Storm's crew dove into the waves.

The floating mass of corroded steel hung suspended above the sea like a metallic storm cloud. Orson's arms trembled with the effort of holding the weight aloft. As he tried to direct it toward the Ghost, his concentration slipped. The mass shuddered, then fractured like shattered glass. Before he could react, jagged shards whipped back toward him, drawn to his power like arrows to a target. More fragments caught Victor as he turned to face a new threat, drawing a pained grunt from the already wounded man.

Searing pain exploded through his left arm and hand as fragments tore into his flesh. He stumbled, crying out as blood ran hot down his sleeve. The remaining iron wavered dangerously in the air, threatening to rain deadly shrapnel across the deck. Through gritted teeth, Orson forced himself to focus, guiding most of the metal into the Ghost's hull despite the burning agony in his arm. But more fragments embedded themselves in his skin, humming with residual power, making his whole arm feel like it was on fire.

The otherworldly glow surrounding Victor guttered and died. For a heartbeat, he remained standing, then collapsed to the deck like a puppet with cut strings. The storm he'd summoned dissolved into ordinary rain.

Victor!" Orson staggered forward. His left arm hung heavy and useless, each embedded shard pulsing through his nerves like fire.

The world tilted and swayed around him, but he kept moving, blood tracing his unsteady path—each step a battle against the darkness creeping at the edges of his vision. The deck seemed to stretch endlessly between them, while his newfound power slipped through his grasp like sand.

With trembling fingers, Orson managed to roll Victor onto his back. The movement drew a soft groan from the unconscious man. How strange, Orson thought through the haze of pain, to see him like this. Moments ago, Victor stood like some ancient god of storms, bending wind and rain. Now, with blood seeping steadily from his wounds and his skin ashen beneath the fading glow, he seemed as vulnerable as any of them—just flesh, and bone, and borrowed time.

Sullivan appeared through the rain, scooping Victor into his arms as carefully as he looked Orson over with worry. "I'll get him to Memori," he said, voice gruff as he headed for the steps.

Orson felt hands gripping his shoulders, pulling him upright. Evander's face swam into focus, concern etched in his usually stoic features. The deck tilted dangerously beneath them as his vision darkened at the edges, iron fragments still singing their terrible song beneath his skin.

"Seven hells," Peryn breathed, staring at Orson with a mixture of awe and fear. Orson looked down at his bloodied arm, watching foreign fragments pulse beneath his torn skin with each heartbeat.

"Hurts like seven hells," he muttered.

"We need to get those shards out before they dig deeper." Evander said, shifting his weight to support Orson as his knees grew weak.

His breath slow and groggy, Orson found Jermany, his eyes catching hers. "Can you get us out of here?" His voice was hoarse from exertion. There were no noises of battle, but the scent of burning stung his nose and he did not know what shape the enemy ships were in at this point.

"Aye, Captain!" Jermany called as Evander hoisted Orson's arm over his shoulders and guided him below. Orson felt a growing certainty that everything he thought he knew about himself might be wrong.

Chapter 39

Victor

The pulsating pain in Victor's shoulder faded, giving way to a much more visceral torture. Not the comforting shadows he knew from battle, but something deeper, colder.

Cold water. Strong limbs thrashing. The river—dark and hungry.

It wasn't him doing it—not really. Something else moved through him, lending inhuman strength as he held the young man under. But the choices had been his. The jealousy. The whispered voice that promised everything he wanted if he just... let go.

He could still feel it. The struggle, the desperate fight against his grip. Each violent surge growing weaker, the determination in those eyes turning to panic, then to something worse—betrayal. Understanding. The moment the thrashing stopped.

A strange euphoria had filled him then. Power. Victory. A sense of destiny falling into place like the final tumbler in a lock. But it vanished as quickly as morning mist, leaving only horror in its wake.

What have I done?

The body sank into the dark water, drifting like a ghost into the depths. He'd reached to grab him, to undo what couldn't be undone, but the current had already taken its prize.

Now, lying in his fever, Victor could feel phantom river water filling his own lungs. Was this justice? The past coming to claim its due? Guilt was a living thing, feeding on his soul. Some nights he could still hear the whispers, still feel the weight of decisions that destroyed more than just one life.

You wanted her for yourself, the voice said. And he had wanted her, hadn't he? Wanted her enough to—No. Even in fever dreams, some memories were too dangerous to revisit.

And now here they all were. Watching them each day, seeing their faces, knowing what he'd done—it was a special kind of torture. They didn't remember. But he did. Every detail. Every choice. Every consequence. Linden made sure of it.

"Da?"

Viggo's voice cut through the fever dream, anchoring him to the present. Victor forced his eyes open, and found his son's worried face swimming above him.

"I'm here," he managed, though the words felt like gravel in his throat, hand closing around Viggo's, drawing him closer. Grateful he was still unharmed. Dread settled like lead in his chest. Viggo was his weakness—his greatest joy and deepest vulnerability. How long before his son paid the price for Victor's sins? The thought haunted him more than any wound: that the darkness of his past would eventually claim the boy, no matter how desperately he tried to shield him from it. Even more now, as they drew closer to Rootspire–closer to the truth. His fear for Viggo increased by the day.

Orson's face appeared in the doorway—concerned, determined, alive. "Orson" Victor's mind caught up with recent events, remembering the power that erupted from his captain, the way iron bent to his will. Just like before.

Orson leaned against the doorframe, arms crossed. His shirt still damp, his left arm bandaged. "You look like hell," he said, attempting humor though concern lined his face.

Victor scoffed. "I've felt better." His voice came out hoarse, each word scraping against his dry throat. Fever burned beneath his skin, threatening to drag more memories to the surface with each pulse of pain.

Orson cleared his throat, guilt etching deeper lines around his eyes. "Look, Vic. I don't know what exactly happened to me back there," His gaze dropped to Victor's bloodied shirt lying in the chair by his bunk. "but I'm fairly sure this is my fault and I'm sorry." He settled in the chair beside Victor's bed, attempting a casual air that didn't quite mask his concern. "Looks like I owe you another one."

"You'll never owe me anything." The words slipped out before Victor thought better of it.

Orson frowned, tilting his head. "What's that supposed to mean?"

Victor turned toward the porthole, unable to meet Orson's questioning gaze. "Nothing," he muttered. "Never mind."

"Well, we're all alive, that's what matters, eh?" Orson forced a chuckle that fell flat in the small cabin.

Victor didn't respond. His mind drifted back, unbidden, to the sensation of water, the icy grip of a hand struggling beneath the waves. A face—familiar, anguished—flickered in his mind before slipping away into the murky depths of memory. He shuddered.

"Victor?" Orson leaned forward, eyes narrowing. "You alright?"

"I'm fine," Victor lied.

"Want me to fetch Memori?"

Victor's gaze flicked to Orson's damaged arm. His smirk was faint. "Only if you're fetching her for yourself."

Orson's jaw tightened. "Be that way." He stood, annoyance clear in every movement. "I'll leave you to rest, then."

Victor huffed a quiet laugh. Orson, Victor thought as the door closed behind him, would never change, no matter how many times he was reborn. That same stubborn heart, that same protective nature. The memory rose unbidden—a younger Orson causing chaos wherever he went. Victor, always protecting him from it.

Fever pulled at him, and suddenly he was there again—the training yard at Rootspire, sunlight warm on ancient stones.

The ground was rich with iron, and he watched his younger brother draw it forth, metal flowing between inexperienced fingers as he shaped it into crude petals.

"You're wasting time," Victor called from where he stood with the others. At nineteen, he already carried himself

with the bearing of a leader, though his brother seemed immune to his authority.

"I'm training," came the laughing response. At fifteen, he was all gangly limbs and crooked grins. His eyes kept darting to the garden wall where the healer's apprentice sat watching, her auburn hair catching the sunlight.

Victor felt his jaw tighten. "This isn't a game."

"Oh, but it could be." His brother's eyes sparkled with mischief as he caught the girl looking their way. "Watch this!"

"Don't—" Victor started, but it was too late.

His brother was already moving, pulling iron from the ground with far more force than finesse. The metal responded to his wild energy, spiraling up in elaborate patterns. He danced through them, showing off with increasingly dangerous maneuvers, each one more reckless than the last.

"Look what I can—" His foot caught on one of the iron spirals. The metal wavered, collapsed.

Victor caught his brother just before the jagged spikes would have impaled him, lowering him none too gently to the ground.

"Ow," his brother groaned, sprawled in the dirt. The healer's apprentice hurried over, her face a mix of concern and exasperation as she knelt beside him.

"That," she said firmly, "was incredibly stupid."

"But impressive, right?" He gave her a sheepish grin, holding up the crude iron rose he'd managed to form despite his fall. "Marry me?"

She turned to Victor instead, rising on her toes to plant a quick kiss on his cheek. "Thank you for saving your idiot brother." As she walked away, she snatched the rose from Orson's outstretched hand, twirling it between her fingers. Victor felt the familiar sting as her eyes lingered on Orson— that soft look she saved only for him, despite the kiss she'd just given him.

Victor touched his cheek where the tingle of her lips still lingered, though the warmth of it was hollow now. He caught his brother watching him, saw something dark flicker in those green eyes—hurt? jealousy?—before it vanished behind another crooked smile. "Next time," his brother declared, dusting himself off, "I'll make her a whole garden."

It had only ever been Orson she truly loved. Always Orson.

The door creaked on its hinges and Memori entered with fresh bandages, jarring him from his thoughts. The familiarity of her presence made his chest ache. "Memori" His hand reached out to catch hers, but quickly withdrew. "I'm sorry."

She frowned down at him, feeling his forehead. Her hand was cool. "You have nothing to be sorry for."

The certainty in her voice made Victor ill. When she discovered the truth… what then? How quickly would that trust turn? She squeezed his hand gently before pulling away. "You're one of the best men I've ever known, Vic."

The words twisted like a rusty knife in his gut. He wanted to scream the truth at her, to confess every sin, every betrayal, every moment that led them here. Instead, he closed his eyes, a prayer forming on his lips, though he knew he had no right to ask for mercy.

Please. No more of this. When will it be enough?

His hand moved to the silver band on the chain–fingers closing around it–holding it like a lifeline. Then SHE was there, saving him all over again. Like when they'd first met.

Victor stood at the edge of the dock, his hands roughened from weeks of mending nets and gutting fish. The salt air clung to him, a familiar comfort, yet his mind drifted—aimless, restless. He didn't belong here. He didn't belong anywhere anymore.

"Why so glum, Sailor?"

The voice startled him. Victor turned, his brow furrowed. The girl who'd been watching him each day stood there, her dark hair rippling in the breeze, her sun-kissed skin glowing in the scattered light. She smiled as if she knew him, though they'd never exchanged a word. He cocked an eyebrow, unsure of how to respond. "Storm clouds always follow you in," she teased, her voice light as the breeze. She glanced up, her laughter breaking the stillness. Above them, the gray clouds parted, revealing streaks of blue sky.

She raised her hand, letting her fingers trail through the curtain of sun. Raindrops sparkled as they caught the sunlight tumbling from her fingertips. "My name's Eirlys." She offered her hand, her smile warm and unwavering.

Victor hesitated. His name was more a burden than a greeting, yet he said it anyway. "Victor." Her hand was smaller than his, calloused yet gentle. He bent instinctively, brushing his lips against her knuckles, though the gesture felt foreign after so long.

She laughed again, a sound like waves breaking gently on the shore. She pulled her hand back, her dark eyes glinting with mischief. "See you tomorrow?"

Victor could only nod, words failing him. As she turned and skipped down the forest trail, her laughter echoed faintly in the distance, like a melody caught in the wind.

Eirlys…

His breathing steadied, and Victor drifted to sleep, dreaming of her arms around him.

Chapter 40

Orson

As the *Crimson Ghost* crested another wave, her wounded frame settling into a halting glide. The battle ended hours ago, leaving her scarred but seaworthy. The worst of the damage had been patched—iron bands now held splintered timbers together where cannonballs had struck. Orson's newfound abilities bought them time until proper repairs could be made.

Orson leaned against the weathered rail, rolling his shoulder and wincing at the pull of freshly bandaged wounds. Memori had done what she could, removing the larger iron fragments from his arm, wrapping the injuries with herb-infused cloths. The smaller shards remained, as she'd needed to tend to Victor's more serious injuries. He flexed his fingers, testing his grip. Usable, at least. One less immediate worry.

The ship calmed considerably since the battle. On the foredeck, Peryn and Evander played cards, their casual banter drifting across the evening air. Jermany stood at the wheel, her steady presence a reassurance against the gathering dusk. Sullivan emerged from a trip below deck and settled against the mainmast to clean his pistols with methodical care. But someone was missing.

Orson made his way belowdecks, following the sound of hushed voices. The interior was dim, lit by a few swaying lanterns that cast long shadows across the cramped space.

Near the rear cabin, he found Memori crouched beside a narrow gap between storage crates, her posture tense despite her gentle tone.

"Elowen," she murmured, "we're safe now. The fighting's over." No response came from the shadowed corner where the girl wedged herself. Memori glanced up as Orson approached, exhaustion clear in the tight lines around her eyes. She'd been at this a while, he realized.

"Let me try," he said softly. Surprise flickered across her face, followed by a hesitant nod as she shifted aside to let him kneel. Orson lowered himself carefully, the floorboards creaking under his weight. In the tight space between crates, he could just make out Elowen's small form—face buried in her arms, knees drawn to her chest.

"Hey, Wen," he said, his voice deliberately casual. "That's quite a fortress you've built...You know," he continued conversationally, "after my first proper battle, I couldn't stop shaking for hours." He settled more comfortably against a crate. "My commanding officer found me behind our supply tent, just sitting there, staring at nothing."

Elowen's head tilted slightly, just enough that one eye peered at him from beneath tangled curls.

"It's normal to be scared after something like today," he said. "All that noise, the shaking—it gets to everyone."

A tiny nod, almost imperceptible. "Want to know what helps me when I'm scared?" He leaned forward slightly, his voice dropping to a confidential tone.

Her head lifted, eyes narrowing with sudden suspicion. "You don't get scared," she challenged, voice small but certain.

Orson laughed. "That's not true at all. Everyone gets scared." He touched his bandaged arm lightly. "Even me." He looked around like he was making sure no one else would hear before adding in a whisper, "Even Victor."

She studied his face, searching for deception. "What helped you?" she finally asked.

"Counting," he said simply. "I'd count breaths, or heartbeats, or waves against the shore. Gives your mind something to focus on besides the fear." He shifted, careful of his arm. "Want to try it with me?"

For a long moment, she was still. Then slowly, deliberately, she nodded.

Orson tilted his head, listening to the rhythmic slap of water against wood. "One," he began, his voice calm. Elowen's lips moved silently. "Two," he continued. "Three" By the count of ten, her shoulders had loosened. By fifteen, her arms uncurled from their protective wrap. At twenty, she had edged closer, her small body gravitating toward his solid presence, her hand finding his arm. "Thirty," he finished softly. "Better?" he asked.

Elowen nodded against his shoulder, her breathing steadier now. "Does it always work?" she whispered.

"Most times," he said honestly. "When it doesn't, I start over. Sometimes you have to count a lot before the scared part of you believes the safe part."

Memori watched them, something warm and unreadable in her eyes as they met Orson's.

Orson didn't think too hard about it. He simply rested his good hand on Elowen's tangled curls and murmured, "See? Not so bad." But in the quiet that followed, he kept counting. Not for her. For himself.

One breath. Another. Waiting. Because the next battle was always just around the corner. And in the current stillness, something always lurked—waiting to take the next piece of him, the next person.

His arm tightened around Elowen without thinking, the weight of her small frame pressing into his side, warm and real. Still here.

His gaze flickered to Memori. She sat back against the crates. She had done everything she could—again. Pushed herself too far—again. He'd seen too many like her on the battlefield, the ones who never stopped moving, who gave everything they had until there was nothing left. And they never lasted long. His throat tightened. He turned his focus back to the gentle rhythm of the ship, to the numbers ticking away in his head. Thirty-five. Because if he stopped counting, he might start wondering how much more time any of them had left. And he wasn't ready for that answer.

Chapter 41

Memori

Sunlight filtered through the cabin's small window, casting warm patterns across the floor as Memori carefully unwound the bandages from Orson's arm. The remaining iron fragments left angry red marks where they'd torn through his skin, though the wounds were healing cleaner than she expected. "Hold still," she chided, as he shifted restlessly. "Unless you want me to start over."

"Sorry." Orson tried to stay motionless, but his eyes followed her movements with an intensity that made her cheeks warm. "It's just—"

"Can I help?" Elowen bounced on her toes beside them, clutching a fresh roll of bandages to her chest. The haunted look was gone from her eyes, replaced by eager curiosity. Amazing how quickly children could bounce back when they felt safe again. One minute hiding in terror, the next ready to play healer.

"Of course, love." Memori smiled, making room for her daughter. "Hand me those when I ask?"

Elowen nodded seriously, watching as Memori cleaned the wounds. "You get hurt an awful lot," she informed Orson matter-of-factly. "More than anyone I've ever met."

A crooked grin spread across his face. "Maybe I just wanted to see your mother," he said, his eyes fixed on her, then immediately flushed as if he hadn't meant to say it aloud.

Memori's hands stilled for just a moment, her fingers lingering against his skin. An electric pulse seemed to pass between them.

"Idiot," she mumbled, but there was no bite to it. "All you had to do was say so."

"Bandages now, Memma?" Elowen asked.

"Yes, love." Memori cleared her throat, focusing on wrapping his arm with steady hands. But she could still feel the weight of Orson's gaze, heavy with things they both seemed afraid to voice. "There," she said finally, securing the last bandage. "Try not to tear these."

"I make no promises," Orson replied, his voice warm with affection. "But I'll do my best. For both of you."

Elowen tied off the last bandage with a small knot, her tongue poking out in concentration. "All better!" she declared proudly.

"Much better," Orson agreed, flexing his arm carefully. "You're becoming quite the healer yourself."

A bright smile lit up her face. "Like Memma!" Then her eyes widened as if suddenly remembering something important. "Oh! I know - I can tell you a story later. About the Guardians! Memma says I tell it even better than the book now."

"Is that so?" Orson's eyes crinkled with amusement.

"Uh-huh!" Elowen was already backing toward the door, practically vibrating with energy. "But first I promised Viggo I'd help him look for treasure in the hold. He says there might be secret doors!"

"Be careful down there," Memori called after her, but Elowen was already gone, her excited footsteps pattering down the corridor.

They could hear her voice carrying back to them: "Viggo! Wait for me!"

Memori shook her head, exhaustion finally catching up. She lifted a hand to her forehead, exhaling as she dropped into the chair beside Orson's bed For a long moment, she simply sat there, her body aching with the kind of weariness that sleep wouldn't fix.

Without thinking, she reached out, fingertips grazing the bandages on Orson's arm. The warmth of his skin pulsed beneath her touch, and the sensation curled through her—like something shifting, stretching between them. A tingling hum crawled up her fingers. Not unpleasant, but unnatural. It almost felt like her own breath, her own pulse, was being pulled into his. She drew her hand back sharply, but the feeling lingered.

Orson flexed his fingers, testing the movement. His expression was unreadable, but she saw the tension in his jaw, the way his shoulders stayed rigid even at rest. "What is happening to us?"

Orson hesitated. "I don't know." He frowned, leaning forward with worry. His hand moved to her shoulder, thumb brushing against her collarbone in a gesture that felt both protective and uncertain. "Between me and Victor, you've had a lot to deal with. Have you slept at all?"

"And you don't need rest?" She snorted. "After…" she broke off, her voice trailing into silence. She hadn't seen his fantastic display of power, but she heard. She wasn't sure what to think. Not only that, but what of the way Victor called the storm clouds? She wanted to ask him, but what would she say? Orson seemed to read her mind. He flexed his hand, studying his fingers as if they belonged to someone else. "It was like I could feel the iron all around us. Like it was a part of me."

Orson closed his eyes, and something in his expression shifted. Memori felt it before she could name it—a pull, subtle yet undeniable. Deep in her chest, she swore she could feel a hum, a whispering thread winding through her blood, drawn toward him like a lodestone finding its pair. Her breath hitched. The sensation wasn't painful, but it was strange, foreign, like her body recognized something her mind couldn't yet grasp.

She leaned in without thinking, her hand pressing lightly against his chest. Beneath her palm, his heartbeat thrummed steady and strong, but something about it felt… different. As if it resonated with hers, pulling her in, syncing to her rhythm.

Orson's fingers ghosted up her arm, tracing paths she hadn't realized were there—veins, currents, something unseen but deeply felt. The space between them tightened, the pull growing stronger. She swallowed hard. "Orson," she murmured, barely recognizing her own voice.

"You're like us." Jermany's voice cut through the moment like a blade.

They jerked apart; the spell broken. But the echo of that connection lingered.

"Sorry, Captain," Jermany smirked, though her expression quickly turned serious. She crossed her arms. "I'm sure you've noticed by now. There's something… different about all of us."

Orson frowned, meeting her gaze. "Like Evander and his shadows? The way they move for him?"

"Peryn and his fire," Memori added quietly. "Victor's storms."

"And now you." Jermany's eyes bore into Orson. "The iron answers to you like it's been waiting all this time." Her gaze flicked to Memori. "And a touch of your hand, knits bones and flesh back together."

"What about you and Sullivan?" Memori's voice held a note of challenge.

A ghost of a smile crossed Jermany's face. "You'll find out in time."

"How did you end up with him?" Orson asked, his hand unconsciously finding Memori's. "Victor, I mean. You're all from different places, different lives. What brought you together?"

Jermany shrugged. "We all have different stories, different reasons for being here. But there's one thing we all agree on." She uncrossed her arms, her voice dropping lower. "Following him… it feels right. Like pieces of a puzzle finally falling into place." Her gaze swept between them. "We all belong here. Including you two."

"Why are you telling us this?" Orson asked, studying her carefully. Of all the crew, Jermany had been the most distant, viewing him with barely concealed suspicion since he'd taken command.

Jermany frowned, her usual sharp edges softening slightly. "I'm not sure," she admitted, and for once her voice held no trace of mockery. "I just feel you should know. And whatever happens when we reach Rootspire" She paused, seeming to wrestle with words that didn't want to come. "Victor may not be what he seems, but he's trying to make something right." Her brow furrowed as if she was puzzling through it herself. "I don't know exactly what. Sometimes I think even he doesn't know anymore. But his intentions" She met Orson's eyes with unexpected earnestness. "They're good. That much I'm certain of."

She straightened, looking almost surprised at how much she'd revealed. "Captain." With a quick nod to them both, she turned and disappeared into the corridor,

For a moment, neither moved, the weight of Jermany's words hanging in the air between them. Memori's hands fidgeted with her apron, her voice barely above a whisper. "Did you feel it? When you… when you commanded the iron?"

Orson flexed his injured hand, studying the fresh bandages. "It was like…" he paused, searching for words. "Like remembering something I'd forgotten. Something that was always there, just sleeping." His eyes met hers.

Memori moved closer, her fingers hovering near the herbs she'd used to dress his wounds. She touched a sprig of yarrow on her workbench, and for a moment she could have sworn it brightened, its healing properties heightening under her touch. "When I work with these plants, sometimes it's like they respond to me. Like they want to help. I always thought it was just knowledge passed down from my mother, but now…"

"Now everything's different," Orson finished softly. His fingers closed around hers before she could pull away, his touch warm, steady. A shiver of something—recognition, inevitability—fluttered through her chest.

"Everything except this," she murmured, the words slipping free before she could stop them. Her breath caught as warmth crept up her neck.

Orson's thumb brushed absently over her knuckles, as if testing the weight of her hand in his. She should have pulled away. Instead, she memorized the way his touch lingered.

"I should" Memori gestured vaguely toward the door, though she didn't move. "Find Elowen."

"Right," he said, his grip loosening, but not immediately. When she finally stepped away, the absence of his touch left her feeling untethered.

She reached the threshold before he spoke again, his voice quiet, hesitant. "Memori?" She turned back, pulse skipping at the way he watched her, something unreadable in his eyes. "Thank you. For… everything."

She managed a small nod, then slipped away before she could give herself another reason to stay.

Chapter 42

Memori

Something pulled Memori from her restless sleep—a dread that crept through her bones like winter frost. The night air was thick with moisture as she made her way down to the shore, drawn by an urge she couldn't name. Moonlight painted the beach in shades of silver, the surrounding trees casting long shadows across the sand. That's when she saw it - a dark shape at the water's edge where the gentle waves lapped against the shore. Her heart stuttered as recognition dawned, terrible and absolute. The world seemed to shatter as she ran forward, her bare feet striking the cold sand.

A scream tore from her throat, shattering the night's silence—echoing endlessly between the trees and dying across the water. Her hands trembled as she grabbed his sodden coat, the fabric heavy and cold beneath her fingers as she rolled him over. Orson's face was pale as moonlight, his skin already taking on the waxy sheen of death. His lips, once quick to smile, had turned the mottled blue of deep water.

This sudden and cruel reality crushed everything that might have been—that was supposed to be.

"No," she sobbed, pressing her hands against his cold cheeks. "No." They moved to his chest—willing life back into his lungs. She closed her eyes, tapping into her own light core. "Orson, please. You can't—" Her voice broke. She

leaned over him, breath shaking more than her trembling
fingers.

The moonlight caught the features of his face—cold and
distant, but still everything that made him stand out.
"Please..." she whispered as she pulled him closer, not caring
that the seawater soaked through her clothes. "Come back to
me." She wrapped her arms around him, cradling his head to
her heart. "Please come back."

Words she'd held back for so long spilled out like blood
from a wound: "I never—" Her fingers clutched at his coat as
she rocked him. " I never got to tell you yes.", Each breath
cut like a ragged knife in her chest. He was such a showoff, an
absolute idiot who courted danger like an old friend, but he
protected everything he loved with a fierceness that took her
breath away.

"I would have..." Tears took over her vision as they
welled in her eyes. He loved her with a devotion that seemed
to run deeper than time itself—as if his soul recognized hers
across some vast, unknowable distance. A love that couldn't
be stopped–even by the cold finality of death itsel,.

"I would have..." Grief crashed over her like a wave,
drowning out everything but the weight of regret. Every
shared glance, every almost-touch, every word left unspoken -
they all came rushing back, sharper now than broken glass.
She pressed her forehead to his, her tears falling onto his still
face as she whispered words that came too late: "I love you,
Orson."

Her lips met the cold skin of his forehead, pressing
through the salt stuck to his hair. "I would have loved you
forever."The moon watched indifferently as Memori's cries
echoed across the water, carrying the weight of a future lost to
the cruel depths of the sea.

"I already did."

Elowen

ELOWEN HAD NEVER seen her mother like this before—
shaking and crying out in her sleep, her face twisted like she

was in pain. "Memma!" She tugged at Memori's sleeve–shook her shoulders–pulled the blankets off. Nothing would wake her.

"Memma, what's wrong?" Elowen cried, feeling small and helpless. Her heart racing inside her chest, she thought of the first person who could help and ran from the room through the ship's narrow corridors, bare feet cold on the shifting floorboards. "Orson! Orson!" She burst into his cabin without knocking.

Arm rested over his face, Orson jerked awake, jumping to his feet–wide awake when he saw her.

"Wen, what's wrong?"

"It's Memma—she won't wake up!" Elowen wiped at her eyes, tears threatening to form.

The way he moved then—so fast it almost frightened her as much as her mother's nightmare. He scooped her up with one arm as he passed, not slowing his stride, and carried her back to their cabin.

Memori

MEMORI SAT UP, a scream trapped in her throat. The nightmare clung to her—Orson's body cold and still, his eyes empty of that infuriating spark. For a moment, the dream and reality blurred together, until she felt the solid warmth beside her.

Orson. Real. Alive.

Her breath came in ragged gasps as she clutched at his coat, fingers digging into the fabric. The familiar scent of oil and metal enveloped her. She pressed herself against his chest, desperate to replace the memory—no, the nightmare—of his cold skin with the heat radiating from him now.

His arms encircled her without hesitation, strong and steady. She hadn't known she needed this—this simple human comfort—until he'd crashed into her carefully ordered life. Before Orson, she'd convinced herself she needed no one–just her and Elowen. Now she couldn't imagine facing the darkness alone.

A sob escaped her, muffled against his chest. He said nothing, asked nothing, just held her. No demands, no expectations—just a safe harbor in the storm of her fear. Each breath she took came easier than the last, his heartbeat a steady rhythm beneath her ear.

A small hand touched her arm, and Memori turned to find Elowen watching her with wide, frightened eyes. The girl had pressed herself against Orson's side; her face pale with worry. "Memma? Are you okay now?" Elowen's voice was small, uncertain.

Memori reached for her daughter, pulling her into their embrace. Elowen's small body trembled against hers, and Memori realized how terrified her daughter must have been to see her trapped in such a nightmare.

"I'm alright, love," she whispered, pressing a kiss to Elowen's forehead. "Just a bad dream."

"I got Orson," Elowen said, a hint of pride breaking through her fear. "I ran really fast."

"Faster than Tempest, I'll wager," Orson assured her, his arm still around both of them. "Braver than Sullivan!"

Elowen giggled up at him. Memori exhaled shakily, drawing back just enough to meet his eyes. "Nightmare?" he asked simply.

She could only nod, not trusting her voice. Not ready to speak of the horror she'd seen—Orson cold and lifeless.

His hands moved to her arms, rubbing gentle warmth into her skin. That ridiculous smile spread across his face—the one that simultaneously irritated her and made her heart skip. The smile she couldn't help but fall for every time. "Well, good thing you're awake and it's over now," he said, pressing a kiss to her forehead while keeping Elowen tucked safely against his side.

She wanted to believe him. As she pressed closer, listening to the steady beat of his heart with Elowen nestled between them, she couldn't shake the fear completely that it was more than just a nightmare.

Chapter 43

Victor

Victor ran a thumb along the silver ring on his neck, calling to mind Eirlys's smile. She was like spring walking. He swallowed down the lump in his throat. What happened to him didn't matter. Only what happened to Viggo. No matter how the boy grew, every time Victor looked at him, he saw that small lad with tiny hands hiding in the corner. Trying to be brave and fight the fears that haunted him. Victor's mind often drifted to that moment.

The night was still; the waves lapping gently at the shore, their rhythmic sound a soothing backdrop. Victor sat beside Eirlys on the moonlit beach, the cool sand shifting beneath them. The silver light bathed her face, softening her features, making her seem almost otherworldly—a perfect match for him plucked from the sky.

She hooked her arm through his, her warmth seeping into him as her head rested lightly on his shoulder. Her scent—wildflowers and salt air, with a faint trace of something sweet, like honey—filled his senses. It was intoxicating, and it made his heart ache so he couldn't fully understand. "Vic..." she murmured, her voice a whisper against the night.

He turned his head slightly, watching as she held her hand up, letting the moonlight play across her slender fingers. The light shimmered like silver dust, and he found himself captivated by the simple beauty of the moment. "Why don't you ask me to marry you?"

Her words pierced the calm, twisting something deep in his gut. He stiffened, his body going rigid beneath her touch. Seven gods, but he wanted to ask her! More than anything. But how could he? His breath hitched, and when he finally spoke, his voice was choked, the words dragged from a place of raw pain. "Eirlys, I...I'm sorry. I can't."

She lifted her head, her dark eyes searching his face, her expression unreadable. "Why not?"

He turned away, his gaze distant, fixed on the endless horizon where the sea met the sky. His throat tightened, guilt clawing at him from the inside out, like a living thing. "I don't deserve happiness," he said finally, his voice barely audible.

For a long moment, Eirlys was silent. Then she shifted, her cool hands cupping his face, drawing his reluctant gaze back to her. Her touch was firm yet gentle, forcing him to confront the depth of her resolve. "What about me?" she whispered, her voice soft but unyielding. Her playful smile returned, her dark eyes sparkling with the mischief he adored. She leaned closer, her lips just a breath away from his. "Don't I deserve happiness?"

Before he could answer, she pressed her lips to his. Her warmth enveloped him. She was like fire and storm, her lips searing into his like a promise he never wanted to break—no matter how impossible it was to keep.

Victor's heart thundered in his chest, breaking past the walls he'd built around it. Guilt and fear warred with an overwhelming surge of longing and love. He wrapped his arms around her, pulling her closer. As he kissed her, a small voice in the back of his mind whispered that he was holding onto something he could never truly deserve. But it couldn't stand up to Eirlys's presence. She drowned it out like water on a torch. And the next time Victor came into port, he dropped to his knee and held out the silver band.

The look in her eyes melted him. And to hear her say I love you? That alone was worth a lifetime of torment. He never thought such joy was possible! When their son was born, he thought his heart would burst. Deep down, he knew, though. All good must end. And, after all, he didn't deserve any of it in the first place...

Chapter 43

The rain started as a gentle patter against the leaves as he made his way home from the dock. Something felt wrong as Victor approached the cabin. The door hung askew, swinging softly in the wind. His steps quickened, heart hammering against his ribs as he crossed the threshold.

"Eirlys?" His voice caught in his throat. The silence that greeted him was deafening. Their home, usually warm with the scent of herbs and wood-smoke, felt hollow. Empty. Eirlys lay crumpled near the hearth, her dark hair fanned out like spilled ink across the wooden floor. Her dress was torn and covered in blood, dried flowers scattered around her still form. "No." The word was barely a whisper as he fell to his knees beside her.

His trembling hands found her face, still beautiful but already cold. Her lips, which smiled so brightly just that morning, were ashen. He gathered her into his arms, rocking her against his chest as thunder cracked overhead. Silent tears spilled from his eyes as his shoulders shook.

Give her back to me. Please.

He knew it was pointless. Feeling like the grief might crush him under its weight. Death would be so much better than this.

Lightning fractured the sky, illuminating the cabin in harsh bursts. Each flash revealed more details he didn't want to see - the marks on her throat, the struggle clear in the overturned furniture. His grief crystallized into something harder, colder. If only he hadn't left that day. If only he'd come home sooner.

A small sound from the corner made him turn. Viggo huddled there, his small frame shaking with silent sobs. The boy's eyes were wide with terror, fixed on his mother's lifeless form. Victor's chest constricted. He bent over Eirlys one last time, pressing his lips to her cold forehead. "I didn't deserve you," he whispered against her skin, his tears falling onto her face. "And I'm so sorry."

Gently, reverently, he laid her down. Then he crossed to Viggo, gathering his son into his arms. The boy buried his face in Victor's neck, his tiny fingers clutching at his father's coat. Lightning illuminated the cabin one last time as Victor stepped into the rain. The storm raged around them. He held Viggo closer, shielding him from the downpour. There would be time for vengeance. Time to hunt down every person responsible and make them pay in blood. But first, he had to protect what remained of his world - this small, precious life trembling in his arms. Without looking back, Victor walked away from the cabin, his footsteps washed away by the rain. Thunder rolled overhead for the first time since she'd started meeting him at the dock.

"You alright, Vic?"

Victor glanced to the door where Orson stood. He hated the worry on the captain's face. Hated seeing the bandages on his arm. None of this was supposed to be this way. And a thousand lifetimes would never undo what had been done. He wanted to say so many things to Orson. 'Sorry' wouldn't really prepare him for what was coming.

"Aye," he said, clearing his throat.

Orson looked doubtful, but thankfully, he didn't press the issue. "Jermany says we'll reach Rootspire by morning. She sent me to tell you. Said you'd want to know." He paused, studying Victor's face. "Ready?"

Victor turned to the small window, watching the coastline slowly taking shape in the distance. "Yes."

"That makes one of us," Orson said with a humorless laugh. "Because I don't quite understand what the hell is going on here. Am I supposed to… you know, remember more? Because I don't."

"Don't worry." Victor's frown was grim. "You will."

Chapter 44

Victor

This was it. Eirlys's ring hung heavy against Victor's chest, a cold weight that seemed to press against his heart with each breath. For the first time in ages, he felt sick. Feverish. Weak. He didn't need to see Rootspire to know they were close—he could feel the island's pull in his bones, in the tide of his blood, in the memories that clawed at the edges of his mind.

His fingers traced the ring absently, memories of her smile flashing before his eyes. What would she think of him now? After everything?

His gaze flicked to Viggo, the boy's features animated as he chatted with Elowen near the rail. Victor swallowed hard. He hoped the boy would make it out unscathed—feared what he would think once it was all said and done. He prepared himself with a sharp exhale, steeling himself against the reckoning that awaited them all.

THE FOG CAME FIRST—not the usual morning mist that clung to the waves, but something deeper, more ancient. It rolled across the water in thick coils, swallowing the horizon until the *Crimson Ghost* seemed to float in a sea of pearls and shadows. Her wounded frame was a testament to their recent battle. Iron bands encircled her hull where Orson had crudely patched the breaches, the metal bands pressing splintered planks together in an ungainly but effective seal against the hungry sea. Despite her injuries, she limped forward with stubborn determination, her patchwork silhouette slowly dissolving into the pearlescent mist that shrouded their approach.

Through breaks in the ethereal veil, they caught their first glimpse of the Island. A single massive tree dominated its center, its trunk nearly as wide as a ship, its branches gnarled and twisted, spiraling impossibly upward into the mist. The branches seemed to pierce the very sky, while roots thick as castle walls plunged into the earth and straight down into the sea itself.

As they drew closer, the water grew clearer. So crystalline they could see the roots continuing their descent into the depths, creating an underwater forest that pulsed with a faint, bluish light. The Ghost's wake left ripples of luminescence, as if they sailed through liquid starlight.

Around the island's base, smaller but still ancient trees formed a dense barrier, their branches intertwined and heavy with leaves that shimmered with an inner radiance. The colors seemed wrong somehow - too alive - leaves in shades of jade and emerald that shouldn't exist in nature, shot through with veins of gold when the light hit them just right.

The Ghost's timbers creaked as they approached, but the sound was different too - almost like singing, as if the ancient wood of the ship recognized something in this place that called to its own forgotten origins. This wasn't just an island. It was a boundary between worlds, a place where the veil between what was and what could be was worn thin, where reality itself seemed to bend like light through water. And at its heart, a single towering sentinel, its branches disappearing into clouds that swirled with unnatural purpose around its peak.

Jermany stood at the helm, her dark eyes fixed on the ethereal horizon while Sullivan, Peryn, and Evander maintained their posts with an almost reverent stillness. The supernatural fog parted around the Ghost's bow like a veil being drawn aside.

Orson paced the deck. His fingers kept straying to the Tide Stone at his throat, its surface cool despite the warmth of his skin. Each pivot of his heel was sharp, military, betraying his former life even as he tried to shed it. The weight of the crew's sidelong glances finally made him stop. "If anyone's got something to say," He turned to face them, jaw tight with tension.

Sullivan shook his head, crossing his muscular arms. Evander raised his hands in mock surrender, while Peryn made a show of checking the compass bearing, muttering calculations under his breath with exaggerated concentration.

"Vic was right," Jermany said, leaning against the helm.

Orson's shoulders tensed. "About what?"

"Making you Captain." Her eyes sparkled with something like mischief, but there was respect there too, hard-earned over their weeks at sea.

Orson scoffed, running a hand through his windswept hair. "No, he wasn't."

"Vic's never been wrong," Jermany retorted.

"Not true." The quiet words drew their attention to the quarterdeck where Victor stood, one hand braced against the railing for support. His heavy coat hung looser on his frame now, and the pallor of his recent injury still haunted his features. His gaze found Orson's, and pride sparked behind his smirk. "But not about you."

Orson rolled his eyes.

Chapter 45

Victor

As the *Ghost* crept through the shallow waters, its hull brushed perilously close to the unseen floor beneath. With her coiled metal-banded wounds, she resembled some mythical vessel come to carry the dead to the afterlife, Victor thought grimly. How fitting that she should bear them to this place, broken yet persistent, just as they were.

Victor's hand tightened on the hilt of his sword, watching the crew's faces as they took in the grove—the way Sullivan's eyes widened at the massive roots, how Jermany's hand trembled slightly on the wheel, Peryn's sharp intake of breath. Orson stood transfixed at the bow, one hand pressed against his chest as if something pulled at him from within. He wondered if Memori could feel life thrumming through every vine and leaf, calling to her healing powers. Even Evander seemed affected, his usual easy smile replaced by quiet contemplation. Even after centuries, the raw power of this place still commanded reverence.

A grinding screech cut through the silence as one of the iron bands Orson had twisted around the hull gave way. Water rushed in through the gap, but the shallow depth kept them steady. The sound made them all jump—a jarring reminder of their recent battle. Running to the railing, Orson took in the damage, his features twisting into a pained look. "That doesn't look good," he said.

Sullivan grinned, clapping Orson on the back as he came up next to him. "Excellent observation, Captain! We'll make a sailor of you yet!" Orson scowled, sidestepping away from Sullivan and grumbling to himself.

"We're not sinking, but she'll need repairs before we leave these waters," Sullivan said.

"No shit" Orson rolled his eyes.

Jermany leaned over the railing, her dark braids catching the faint light filtering through the canopy above. Sweat beaded on her bronze skin despite the cool air. Her keen eyes fixed on a ship ahead, half-sunken and sickly. Its masts jutted at broken angles, sails hanging in rotting tatters, while a phosphorescent mist clung to its hull like a burial shroud.

"Victor," she called, her voice low but sharp as steel. "That thing shouldn't be afloat."

Victor didn't answer. His gaze was locked on the shoreline where General Roderick Storm stood tall and ominous amidst the tangled roots. The general's crimson cloak hung like spilled blood against the jungle's emerald shadows, his posture regal and commanding—a king holding court in this forgotten realm. But Storm was no king, and this was not his realm, no matter how much he wished. He was nothing more than a scarlet vulture perched in a sacred garden, his presence a blasphemy against the ancient peace that dwelled here. The sight of him standing there sent a tremor of anger through Victor; thunder rumbled in the distance.

Behind Storm, shadows moved between the trees—his men, their exact numbers hidden by the dense foliage. Beyond the sacred grove, the dark silhouette of his warship loomed, its black sails a stain against the sky.

"What's our move, Vic?" Jermany pressed, fingers drumming restlessly against her sword hilt.

"He came all this way." Victor exhaled slowly, his jaw clenched. "We'll give the man what he wants."

The crew froze, their whispers shattering the silence like breaking glass. Orson, standing nearby, whirled to face him. "Have you been drinking the sea water?" he hissed, stepping closer. "I think he wants all our heads on a nice set of spikes—is that what you want to give him?"

Victor didn't flinch. His eyes remained fixed on Storm, the weight of destiny pressing down on his shoulders. "Trust me." He turned, gripping Orson's shoulder with calloused fingers, meeting his gaze with iron resolve. "This is how we finish this."

Orson started to argue, but something in Victor's expression made him pause. After a long moment, he gave a curt nod, though his hand never left his weapon. "Alright, Victor. We'll try it your way."

"Da, no!" Viggo rushed forward, throwing his arms around Victor, causing his heart to constrict. For likely the last time, he fiercely embraced his son, cradling his head. "Don't worry." he tousled his hair and winked. Fear wavered in Viggo's eyes, but he took a step back.

Victor stepped to the ship's edge, his boots striking the deck with grim purpose. He grabbed a hanging rope and swung himself over, using the ship's hull to control his descent. Landing in the knee-deep, murky water, he pressed forward through the chill that crept through his clothes like ghostly fingers. His eyes stayed trained on Storm as the water pulled at him like hungry hands.

Behind him, the crew—his friends—watched in horror. The Ghost swayed gently, its sails rustling like dying breaths.

Victor's heart hammered against his ribs as he approached, each breath loud in his ears. He halted a few paces from Storm, ripples spreading around him in widening circles. "General," Victor said, his voice steady despite the dread coiled in his gut.

Storm's lips curved into a smile that never touched his eyes. "Victor. You've come a long way." His voice carried the soft menace of a drawn blade. "I hope you've learned some new skills since we last met. Would hate for this to end like the last one for you."

The splash of water behind him made Victor's shoulders tense. He glanced back at the Ghost where Viggo stood protectively beside Elowen on deck, and the others were hurrying to follow Victor–one by one, using the rope to swing down. Orson waded forward, sword drawn, the steel catching what little light filtered through the canopy.

Storm's eyes flickered to Orson, and his thin smile widened into something cruel. "And you brought them all back with you," he said, voice dripping with mock warmth. "He doesn't know yet, does he?." His laugh echoed unnaturally through the still air. His eyes met Victor's, gleaming with dark amusement. "Oh, this will be worth the wait! When the truth unfolds…" He trailed off, shifting his eyes to Orson. "Loyalty can be such a fragile thing."

Victor's jaw clenched, but he kept his face carefully blank, even as guilt churned in his gut. Beside him, Orson shifted his stance, confusion flickering across his features before hardening back into determination. "Enough of your mouth, you lying sack of shit! You want your traitor so bad…come down here and fight me!"

Storm circled Victor like a vulture closing in on its prey, each step measured, relishing the mounting tension. The crew's weapons rose as they drew closer to Victor, but Storm merely smiled. "Stay your ground, Oathbound," he commanded, his voice rich with anticipation. "And let the one you thought your brother jog those memories you've long forgotten."

Victor raised his trembling hands, and the mist—that sickly, ever-present mist—began to shift. Its color warped and twisted, from ghostly green to something deeper, richer, until it formed shapes in the air like smoke caught in amber. Images crystalized: children running through these very waters, their laughter echoing across time.

Memori's sharp intake of breath cut through the silence. Her dagger lowered as she watched herself materialize in the mist—younger, carefree, splashing through the shallows. Beside her ghostly form ran Peryn with his gap-toothed grin, Jermany with braids in her hair, Evan balancing on a fallen log, Sully trying to catch fish with his bare hands. Orson, small but fierce, practicing sword forms with a wooden stick. And Victor… Victor watching over them all.

The color drained from Memori's face. "This place," she whispered. "We… we grew up here. All of us. Together." Her eyes found Victor's, wide with dawning horror. "How did we forget?"

The mist swirled again, coalescing into a new scene. There stood Linden, tall and ethereal, as they all remembered her from that first day they were brought here. Her face was harder, her eyes carrying knowledge of ages. The image showed her hands raised, pale light emanating from her fingers as she moved among the younger versions of the crew.

"It was in another lifetime," Victor said, his voice hollow. The words seemed to physically pain him. Each one dragged from deep within. "That's why you didn't fully remember." The silence that followed was absolute, broken only by the soft lap of water against the shore.

Chapter 46

Memori

Memori watched pain flash across Orson's face as understanding struck him. "All this time and you never thought I'd want to know?" His voice cracked, hands trembling at his sides. "That it wasn't important for me to know…I had a brother?"

Victor wouldn't meet Orson's eyes - wouldn't meet any of their eyes. "You don't understand…the things I've done…" When he finally dared to look up at Orson, the guilt etched in his features was crushing. "You would have only been disappointed sooner." The self-loathing in his voice, the way he seemed to shrink before them - this wasn't the Victor she knew.

Storm halted his circling, his smile growing predatory as he watched Victor struggle with the weight of this final confession. His cloak brushed Victor's back, his presence like a shadow of death.

Memori's grip tightened on her dagger as she divided her attention between Storm and the familiar Vanguard uniforms spread throughout the foliage. Her skin crawled with remembered trauma, bile rising in her throat. These men represented everything she'd fought to escape, everything she tried so hard to protect Elowen from. They shifted in the shadows, weapons ready, and she forced down the urge to run.

"Tell them why, Victor," Storm purred, his voice thick with savage pleasure. "Why did you remember when no one else did?" He leaned forward, almost whispering in Victor's ear, though his words carried clearly across the water. His eyes gleamed with fevered anticipation.

Victor's shoulders sagged. "I was never reborn. It was part of my punishment," he said, each word coming out like broken glass.

Confusion twisted inside her.

Punishment?

Storm's smile grew impossibly wider, his teeth gleaming in the dim light. "And what are you being punished for, *Storm-Breaker*?" He sneered at the name as if it was an impossible joke to him.

Victor's words fell like stones, one by one, into a well. "Betrayal." A pause. "Murder."

The crew stood frozen; the revelation hanging over them like a dark cloud. Orson's face was a mask of growing dread. From the deck above, Viggo and Elowen watched with wide eyes, too young to understand. Jermany's hand had moved to cover her mouth. Memori felt the world tilt as her eyes locked onto the mark seared into General Storm's chest, revealed from his half-open shirt. Sickly green veins pulsed outward from the brand, twisting like poisoned roots burrowing beneath his skin. The infection writhed, feeding on something deeper than flesh. Her stomach turned. She recognized it now; betrayer

Her gaze flickered—just for a moment—to Victor as she clenched her fingers around the hilt of her knife, willing the nausea down. Victor wasn't like Storm. He *couldn't* be. Storm was cruelty. Corruption. A man who had rotted from the inside out. Victor… Victor was different. He believed he'd *done* terrible things; she knew that—but he was a good man. She had seen it. Felt it. Whatever this mark meant, whatever past it carried, it did not define him. It couldn't. But the sight of it— the *sameness* of it—made her sick.

She didn't say a word. She couldn't. But the sickness twisting in her gut began to change—tightening, hardening into something sharper. Anger.

Kol was one of Storm's men. The way he treated her— like she was something *owned*, something to be visited when he was bored—left a stain she couldn't wash off. And the way he treated Elowen, like his own daughter was a pawn to be moved, to be *used*—it made her blood burn.

And then there was Victor. Victor, who swore to protect her daughter with his life. Victor, who held her after she killed a man with her own hands—not recoiling, not judging, just holding her. Like he understood. He and Storm may have bore the same mark. But they were not the same.

Chapter 47

Orson

The scene in the mist before them shifted to deeper waters. Victor's hands pressed down, holding someone beneath the surface. Orson's own hands slowly moved to his throat as memory crashed through him—the burn of water filling his lungs, the pain of being betrayed in his heart as he realized who held him under. Light faded from his eyes. The bubbles slowed. Stopped. His own death played out before him like a nightmare made real.

A rope splashed into the water as Viggo swung down from the deck. "Da!" Memori caught the boy, but Orson barely noticed. His sword hung loose in trembling fingers as Storm circled them, savoring their horror.

"Look at them," Storm commanded. "Look at their faces as they finally see you for what you truly are, Storm-Breaker. A kin slayer." His voice snaked. "A betrayer."

"No," Orson breathed, the word barely audible through the roaring in his ears. "No" His face twisted through shock, denial, rage—emotions he'd felt in those final moments centuries ago. "It's a lie!"

But Victor wouldn't meet his eyes. The brother he trusted, to fight beside, to love again—kept his gaze fixed on the water, shoulders bowed with the weight of ancient guilt.

Storm's laughter cut through Orson's turmoil. "Your trusted first mate—murderer of his own blood, betrayer of sacred oaths, thief of power that was never meant to be his."

Orson watched numbly as Victor threw down his sword—the blade that had protected them all—and fell to his knees in the water. "I deserve no mercy," Victor's voice came raw, broken, "for what I did." His eyes found Viggo, still struggling in Memori's grip, and something in Victor shattered completely. "But my son" Those eyes—the same eyes that had watched Orson drown—turned to him pleading.

Rage and grief warred inside Orson as he stared at his brother, kneeling in the mud. He drove his own sword into the ground and grabbed Victor's collar, dragging him up to eye level. "You bastard." The words came through clenched teeth. "How could you? To your own blood!" His fist connected with Victor's jaw, but Victor didn't resist, didn't even raise his head.

"And how could you think I could harm your son—my own nephew?" Another punch landed. Blood smeared Orson's aching knuckles as Victor's lip split, but still he made no move to defend himself. Orson's fist drew back again, but memories flooded through him—Victor stepping between him and angry merchants for stealing food before they were brought to Rootspire, taking punishment meant for Orson's reckless actions, standing guard while Orson slept through his first nights on the island. Victor threatening their fellow Oathbound when they tried to teach Orson harsh lessons about respect. Even now, centuries later, still protecting him. Orson released Victor's collar. His brother crumpled back into the water, head bowed, blood dripping from his split lip.

"Viggo has nothing to do with the sins of my past. Please, Orson… spare his life. He's innocent in all of this." The boy's struggles ceased, his tears matching Victor's as that dark head bowed to the mud. And Orson stood frozen between centuries-old betrayal and the brother who had spent lifetimes trying to atone.

The mist twisted above Victor, showing a hooded figure with a younger Victor in these same waters. "Everything you want can be yours, Victor," the spy whispered, words dripping like honey-coated venom. "If only he were gone. The power, the respect… the girl. They could all be yours. You've lived in his shadow long enough. Cleaned up his messes long enough." The mist-memory continued, showing Victor retrieving something from his drowned brother's body—a pendant, glowing with an inner light. Present-day Victor's shoulders shook, but he didn't open his eyes, didn't turn to face his crew.

They watched as past-Victor presented the tide stone to Storm's spy, eager for his promised reward. But then the scene shifted—Storm himself emerging from the shadows, his smile just as cruel then as now. They saw their own past selves, younger and unsuspecting, as Storm's men surrounded them. Memori gasped as she watched herself fall first, a blade through her heart. Their powers were rendered useless by Storm's improvisation; their immortality restrained by the power of Rootspire.

One by one, they were cut down while Victor yelled, caught in a fierce battle against Storm. "Only one–you swore to me the rest would be safe!" Orson barely had time to register the pain that lanced through him, realizing he was meant to be 'the one.' The memory morphed–Victor, wild with grief and rage, hurled the tide stone far into the depths of the sacred waters. Storm's howl of fury split the air as he thrust his hand forward, lightning crackling from his fingers to pierce Victor's chest. They watched him fall as Storm fled to pursue the stone–dying until Linden appeared in a flash of blinding light.

They watched as Linden carried Victor's dying body to the Mercy Oak, her own life force bleeding into the roots as she did what she could to save him. She collapsed as the binding took hold, her sacrifice written in the sudden streaks of silver in Victor's hair. The scene changed—going centuries into the future. Storm's men cutting down Victor's wife while Viggo hid in the corner crying. Victor finding her…

Mist dissipated, leaving only the sound of present-day Memori's ragged breathing and Viggo's quiet sobs as he looked away, eyes buried in Memori's arm. Victor's voice was barely a whisper. "Captain, I beg you to spare my son."

Orson stood silent for a long moment before picking up Victor's sword. It was heavy in his hands as water dripped off the blade. He realized what Victor expected him to do–wanted even. "Vic," he said finally, his voice rough with emotion, "for fuck's sake." His glare flicked to Storm, then back to Victor as he lowered the blade. "Get up," he said through gritted teeth. "And stop calling me Captain. We'll talk about this later. Right now, we've got a more pressing problem."

Storm's satisfied smile faltered for the first time, his eyes narrowing as he watched the exchange. Victor's head lifted slowly from the mud, his eyes wide with disbelief as he stared at Orson, hope warring with the guilt he'd carried for so long. "But…." His voice cracked.

"Get up." Orson commanded again, extending his hand down to his brother. Victor's trembling fingers grasped Orson's.

Storm's mirk morphed into something ugly. "How could you overlook what he's done?" he snarled, his voice cutting through the silence like a blade. "He held you under those waters until the last bubble of air left your lungs. Watched the light fade from your eyes. Your own brother murdered you in cold blood, and you offer him your hand?"

His carefully maintained control was fracturing, replaced by a rage that had festered for centuries. Storm's frustration at seeing his moment of triumph slip away, manifesting in crackling waves of power. "You were supposed to hate him!" he roared, cloak snapping violently in the supernatural wind. "After everything I showed you, everything he did—"

Orson cut in, still gripping Victor's hand. "Oh, but I really hate you more." His eyes narrowed as he pulled Victor to his feet. "You're just a manipulative bastard who turned brother against brother for what? A fucking pretty rock?"

"You understand nothing." Storm's voice dropped to a dangerous whisper. "The tide stone should have been mine–it was always meant to be mine!"

"That was before Linden banished you," Victor said quietly, his voice no longer wavering as he turned his attention back to his enemy. "Before she knew you would only use it for your own gain."

Storm let out a bitter laugh. "Linden and her precious rules," he sneered, voice heavy with spite. His gaze fixed on the massive Mercy Oak looming above them. "Healing is for all–she insisted on that one. While denying anyone the means to do so. She never told you what finally pushed her over the edge, did she?" He eyed the Mercy Oak again, his eyebrows furrowing as he took in a damaged section, withered above the water. "I took the root," he said. "You've no idea how much people would pay for such a thing–a medicine that can cure nearly anything."

He turned to Memori. "That power was wasted on your mother, though. It came as inheritance to her. And she hid it away for safekeeping."

Memori's eyes widened, and she swallowed with difficulty. "What do you know about my mother?" she demanded.

"Almost nothing," Storm said, like she was almost not worth mentioning. Memori's lip trembled in anger. "But I know about you." He grinned. "YOU used it. Or," he turned to Orson, "One of you would most assuredly be dead already." His hand moved to the shard embedded in his palm, its sickly green glow pulsing like a corrupted heartbeat.

"You want this stone so bad? Come and take it!" Orson's eyes flashed. His blade rippled like liquid steel, splitting and reforming into a weave of razor-sharp tendrils that danced around the main sword.

A child's scream pierced the air. Orson's heart stopped as he spun toward the Ghost. Kol stood on deck, one arm locked around Elowen's throat, the other pressing a blade against her side. "Hello, Irons," Kol called down, his voice dripping with mockery. "Consorting with pirates now, I see."

Chapter 48

Orson

Ice flooded Orson's veins at the sight of Elowen struggling in Kol's grip. Beside him, he heard Memori's sharp intake of breath, felt her whole body go rigid with fury and terror.

"You son of a bitch", he gritted his teeth. Every fiber of his being screamed to charge the ship, to tear Kol apart, but the gleam in the man's eyes told him one wrong move would cost Elowen her life. He'd seen that look many times before. The man enjoyed this kind of power.

Orson's gaze found Memori's, willing her to understand–to believe his unspoken promise. He would get Elowen back safely. And this time. Kol wouldn't have the chance to come back into her life.

Vanguard pressed closer from their hiding spots in the trees as Storm raised his hands, lightning dancing between his fingers. "You're all fools," he spat. "Both times over. And this time, you'll all die by my hand–" his eyes locked onto Victor with burning hatred, "Starting with your son."

Thunder cracked overhead as clouds spiraled above them, dark and heavy with fury. No matter what Storm may have thought, this time would be different. This time, Victor wasn't alone. The crew moved forward as one, weapons raised. Orson's voice carried over the rising wind. "Try it, you fucking rain cloud!"

Storm's first attack came as lightning, but the ground suddenly heaved beneath their feet. Orson stumbled as a wall of earth and rock erupted between them and Storm, taking the full force of the blast. "Seven hells, Sully!" Orson steadied himself against a tree, eyes wide. "You've been holding out!" His gaze flicked back to Elowen on the deck of the ship and he looked back at Sullivan. "Hey–can you give me a boost?" he nodded up to where the girl was. The others would have to deal with Storm and the Vanguard on their own until he dealt with their commander.

Sullivan's only response was a knowing smirk as he thrust his hands upward, and a column of earth shot up beneath Orson's feet, launching him toward the Ghost's deck. The force of it sent him soaring through the air, his blade already twisting into deadly form as he flew toward Kol.

Kol's eyes widened as Orson's shadow fell over him. He tried to pull Elowen closer, to use her as a shield, but she bit down hard on his arm. His grip loosened just enough for her to duck away as Orson crashed onto the deck. "You little bitch!" Kol snapped at Elowen.

Orson's sword rippled like liquid, the metal responding to his will as he rolled to his feet. "How dare you speak to her that way!" He crossed the distance between them so quickly that Kol barely had time to register panic in his eyes. His sword seemed to go ahead of him–liquid one moment, then coiled around Kol's mouth the next.

Blue eyes wide with terror, Kol tried to scream as the iron band compressed around his jaw. His fingers scratched uselessly against the metal. "How dare you show yourself in this place!" Kol stabbed wildly with his dagger, but Orson felt for the iron in the blade's hilt, pulling it from his grip as easily as plucking a flower. As Kol backed against the deck, his eyes darted frantically to the forest below, searching for help from Storm's men. None came.

Orson drew more iron from the ship's rivets, forming them into coils that snaked around Kol's arms, pinning him in place. Blood welled where the metal bit into flesh. Images flooded Orson's mind—Memori flinching from his touch, Elowen hiding behind doors. That day Kol had thrown her across the room like she was nothing. Something dark and cold settled over him.

Kol's screams became gurgled whimpers. The iron tightened, responding to Orson's fury, to the tunnel vision that narrowed his world to this moment of vengeance.

"Orson!" Elowen's cry shattered his focus. He turned to find her staring at him, tears streaming down her face, one trembling hand pressed to her mouth. Those blue eyes held something they hadn't before; fear. Of him.

"Wen," he breathed, the darkness receding. "Look away."

Her eyes clamped shut. In one fluid motion, he drove Kol's own knife into his heart. He turned back to Elowen, scooping her into his arms. "Are you alright?" he asked, smoothing her hair and looking at her side where Kol's knife had been. Shoulders shaking with tears, she nodded, and he pulled her close, kissing the top of her head. "I'm going to get you somewhere safe, ok?" He took hold of her chin. "Whatever happens, hold tight. Can you do that?"

Elowen wiped her eyes, nodding again. "Good girl." Orson shifted her to his chest, and she wrapped her arms around his neck. "Hang on," he said before taking hold of the rope and swung back into the water.

He'd barely touched the ground when Storm struck. Lightning crashed against his back, pain exploding through every nerve as electricity coursed through him. The force drove air from his lungs, sent him sprawling forward. His vision blurred, muscles spasming uncontrollably, but he twisted as he fell, making sure Elowen stayed above the water. Through the haze of agony, he curled his body around her, shielding her from the blast. Elowen gasped against his chest, fingers digging into his shoulders as she clung to him— terrified but untouched, protected by his embrace as the lightning dissipated harmlessly around them. His pain was worth it, knowing she hadn't felt so much as a spark.

He glimpsed Jermany and Peryn fighting off Storm's soldiers in the trees. Vanguard steel flashed as they pushed the men back, but Storm's attention turned from Victor, his lightning forking toward Peryn's position. Jermany spotted it first. She shoved Peryn aside, throwing herself into the blast's path. It caught her square in the chest, hurling her against Sullivan's earth and rock barrier with a sickening crack.

"Jermany!" Peryn's cry was drowned by Sullivan's rage as the earth shuddered beneath them. She lay motionless, blood seeping into the ground, her sword reflecting the chaos above her still form.

Storm's laughter echoed through the grove. "One down."

Orson curled tighter around Elowen, shielding her as another blast screamed toward them. Blood trickled into his eye from a gash he hadn't felt open. "Get her out of here!" he called to Sullivan through gritted teeth. The big man scooped Elowen from his arms and carried her away to somewhere safer. Orson's legs shook as he staggered upright. His hesitation cost him. Another blast of energy screamed toward him, but Victor stepped between them, the air around him crackling with barely contained power.

"I thought you wanted to fight me." Victor's eyes flashed with a blue that hovered between realms.

Chapter 49

Memori

Memori watched in horror as Orson twisted to shield Elowen from the blast. He staggered up, blood streaming down his face, and her heart clenched at the burn marks scoring his back. Her daughter was safe because of him—because he'd thrown himself between her and death without a second thought. When Sullivan swept Elowen into his arms and away to safety, she rushed forward, pressing her hands to Orson's wounds.

Warmth flowed from her fingers into his torn flesh. His breath stilled at her touch, one hand catching hers as the pain ebbed. For a moment, time seemed to freeze between them—his dark eyes meeting hers with an intensity that made her chest tight. She wanted to tell him everything—how seeing him protect Elowen made her love him even more, how his instinct to save her daughter meant more than any vow could. But Jermany lay bleeding, and there wasn't time.

"I have to help Jermany," she whispered, pulling free. The healing wasn't complete, but it would have to be enough. She couldn't bear to look back as she ran toward Jermany's unmoving form, knowing Orson would understand. He always did. Lightning struck without warning—a searing, white-hot agony that exploded through her shoulder and sent her crashing down. The taste of copper filled her mouth as she hit the water where it met the shore. Every breath sent fresh waves of pain through her chest, the burn spreading beneath her skin like poison.

Through blurred vision, she saw Viggo frozen at the grove's edge. Storm's blast caught the boy's foot. Evander's shadows wrapped around him, pulling him to safety. "Too slow," Storm taunted Victor. "Just like last time."

Strong hands lifted her from the mud—Orson. His touch was gentle despite his trembling fingers as he brushed wet hair from her face. She could feel his own injuries in the way he moved, the slight shake in his arms as he lifted her.

"Go," she pushed against his chest, though the movement made her head spin. "Stop him." Beyond them, Victor stood alone against Storm, ancient power crackling around him like a gathering storm.

"I'm not leaving you here," Orson's voice was rough with fear. He carried her to a hollow between massive roots, the ancient wood curving above them like protective arms. Each step sent jolts of pain through her burned shoulder, but his grip never wavered. When he set her down, his calloused fingers traced her cheek with impossible tenderness. "Stay hidden."

"Help Victor." She caught his wrist, willing strength into her voice even as darkness crept at the edges of her vision. The sounds of battle echoed around them—Sullivan's earth-shaking power, Peryn and Evander holding back the Vanguard soldiers. "I'll be fine–Go!"

Peryn's knife cut through the air overhead with a deadly whistle, bursting into flame before it struck. Steam hissed from Storm's shoulder as his howl of pain echoed through the grove. Orson's lips pressed against her forehead, fierce and desperate, before he rose, his blade breaking apart and reforging itself as he turned back to the fight.

Chapter 50

Evander

Evander materialized behind a Vanguard soldier, his blade finding the gap in armor at the man's neck. Before the body hit the water, he was already moving toward Jermany. Blood seeped from her chest where Storm's attack struck her. He gathered her carefully in his arms, feeling the shallow rise and fall of her breath against his chest. Moving like mist between the ancient roots, he carried her to where Memori lay sheltered in their hollow.

His heart lurched—Elowen. Where was she? He scanned the chaos. Relief flooded him as he spotted Viggo huddled against a tree, clutching his injured foot with one hand while holding tight to Elowen with the other. He moved swiftly to them, checking over his shoulder for any soldiers who might spot them. "Come on," he whispered, scooping Viggo up while Elowen clung to his coat. The boy bit back a whimper as his injured foot jostled.

Keeping low, he guided them to the hollow where Memori and Jermany lay. Elowen immediately curled against her mother's uninjured side while Viggo slumped down. At least here, sheltered by the massive roots, they'd be safer from Storm's attacks.

"Bring her closer," Memori whispered, face pale with pain as her hand reached to Jermany. Evander eased Jermany within reach. Green flecks danced in Memori's eyes as she pressed her hand to Jermany's wound. At first, Evander was relieved to see the bleeding slowed, but it was short-lived. He watched in horror as Memori's burn wound darkened and spread. What had started as an angry red patch on her shoulder now crawled up her neck like crimson lightning, the skin blistering and peeling. Her fingers trembled as she continued healing Jermany, face twisted in pain.

Evander lunged forward, grabbing her wrist. "Stop." His voice was sharp with fear. The burn had reached her jaw, turning her skin an unnatural shade of purple. Veins of darkness spread beneath her skin like poison. Her breathing came in short, pained gasps, but her hand remained steady over Jermany's wound. "You're making yourself worse."

"I can handle it," she gritted out, but the tremor in her voice betrayed her.

"No, Memori." His grip tightened on her wrist. "Tell me what plants you need."

Viggo pushed himself up despite his injured foot, eyes wide with concern. "We know what to get!. Come on, Elowen!" He pulled her along as he limped into the grove.

Memori stopped fighting Evander, her hand going slack as tears of pain and frustration streamed down her face. Evander propped her against the tree, working one of his bracelets free. He uncoiled the silver-lined bark and dipped it in the clear waters pooled beneath the tree roots. "The tree this is from is called Heartwood," he said, keeping his voice steady so not to betray his worry. Memori was pale, her eyelids drooped. "It's not known beyond our realm, but it has healing properties." He rang out the water. "Specifically for burns." He wondered if she was even hearing him.

"This might sting a bit…" he cringed before gently pressing the dampened bark to her neck. Memori sucked in a breath through clenched teeth, then closed her eyes as she leaned her head against the tree trunk. "Memori!" Evander took a firm hold of her chin. "Stay with me." He did not let go until her eyes flickered open and she weakly tried to move.

"Need to…see Jermany," she mumbled.

"No—be still!" Evander held her shoulder in place. "I'll see to Jermany, alright? But you have to be still." She nodded groggily in agreement before he released his grip and moved to feel Jermany's pulse. Still unconscious, her bleeding had stopped and her heart beat steadily. Evander glanced at Memori, shaking his head. She'd spent herself saving

Jermany's life. She would be alright, though. As long as she didn't try to save anyone else with her energy.

A sob broke through his thoughts. Elowen burst from the trees, herbs clutched in her small hands. Her eyes widened at the sight of Memori's worsened burn.

"Memma!" Viggo tried to catch her by the arm, but she was too quick for him.

Evander caught the girl, pulling her into a hug. "Elowen, wait," he said softly. Your Memma needs to rest."

"Let me go!" she struggled to get free, eyes fixed on her mother.

"I need you to be brave, Elowen. For Memma. Alright?" Evander wiped a tear from the girl's eyes before setting her down. "Can you do something for me? Can you help prepare those plants to put on her burns? I don't know how."

Whimpering, Elowen looked down at her hand, at the crushed plants–green smeared in her fingers from clinging to them so hard. She swallowed back a sob, a determined look on her face. "I know how." she nodded.

"Clever girl. Your Memma's a great teacher." Evander squeezed her shoulder, motioning Viggo over to help her. The two set to work, crushing the plants between clean stones from the water's edge. Evander kept one eye on the battle, as he did his best to keep them clear of any danger. He hoped it was enough to distract them. Viggo comforted Elowen, though his eyes flicked up to his father. That devoted admiration he once looked at Victor with was absent, and Evander felt his heart twist in sorrow.

Vic...

For all the years Evander followed him, he knew there was something he was hiding–a lake of pain held back by an invisible dam. And when Orson showed up, that dam fractured. The way he nearly took Sullivan's head off for putting his hands on an alleged stranger. The way he held Viggo like he knew he was about to lose him...

When the children showed him the pulp of herbs, he explained to lay it on the burns. Elowen hurried to complete her task, but Evander took Viggo by the arm.

"Viggo, lad..." He leaned down as the boy looked up at him, eyes filled with confusion and hurt. "Your father's a good man. A good friend. I don't want you to forget that."

Viggo's lower lip trembled, and he nodded, tears spilling from his eyes like he'd just received permission to still think good of Victor. He threw his arms around Evander, hugging him tightly. "Ever." Evan lay a hand on Viggo's head, pulling it into his shoulder. "You hear me? Ever." When he released Viggo, he gave Evander a grateful look before limping over to help Elowen.

Chapter 51

Orson

Orson forced himself away from Memori's hollow, every step an act of will. His own burns screamed in protest as he rejoined Victor's side, but the sight before him made him forget his pain. Victor and Storm faced each other like titans of old—lightning crackling between them. Blood ran freely from Victor's shoulder where Storm's attack had caught him, but his brother stood unmoved.

"You were always fixated on the wrong power," Victor said.

Storm's laugh was bitter. "I saw what the stones did to you, Storm-Breaker. The strength they gave you all these ages. How many lives have you lived now? As a pirate. A fisherman. A smuggler. But none of them could hide what you really are. Betrayer!" His attack grew wild, desperate. Lightning struck from all sides as the wind howled around them. Orson watched in awe as Victor deflected each blast with shields of ice, though blood now soaked his coat.

A savage bolt caught Victor's shoulder, spinning him around. He rolled with the impact, rising just as Sullivan's power ripped a chasm between Storm and the others. Despite the wound, Victor's face showed no pain. Only determination.

"Orson," he yelled. "The stone."

Without hesitation, Orson yanked the tide stone from his neck and hurled it toward Victor.

Storm's triumphant laugh died as Victor's blade struck the stone. It shattered with a sound like breaking worlds, light exploding outward as ancient power released its bonds. Orson shielded his eyes, feeling the surge of energy pulse through his veins like a forgotten song.

"No!" Storm's roar of fury shook the grove. "What have you done?"

"How does it feel?" Victor asked simply. The broken stone's light swirled around him like a living thing, drawn to him as if recognizing something long lost.

Storm's face contorted, decades of certainty crumbling. "No," he whispered, then louder, "No! The power—I felt it—"

"Linden wanted you to believe the stone was the source of our power," Victor said, his blade catching what little light filtered through the canopy. "When she saw you were no oath keeper and banished you, she did away with the stones. The powers are bound to us now. All this time," Victor continued, advancing through the waters, "she's had you chasing a meaningless trinket, when you should have been chasing me."

Storm's last attack was the strike of a man watching his life's purpose dissolve. Victor moved like water, deflecting the blast. When he straightened, his eyes swirled with that same cerulean depth the tide stone had held, ancient power answering to blood rather than stone. His sword thrust forward, precise and final. Storm's last breath carried nothing but disbelief as he stared into those impossible eyes, understanding far too late where the true power always resided.

Storm's body crumpled into the waters, his cloak spreading with his blood through the shallows. Orson watched his face, still frozen in that last moment of understanding. The grove fell silent save for the gentle lapping of still waters against the shore.

Chapter 52

Orson

Orson splashed through the water to where Memori lay, his heart nearly stopping at the sight of her. The angry red marks had spread further up her neck since he'd left, purple-black at the edges like poison beneath her skin. His hands trembled as he gathered her into his arms, cradling her head. When her eyes fluttered open, he gasped with relief. He brushed a strand of hair from her face, careful to avoid the blistered skin, his thumb trailing across an untouched patch of her cheek to find her pulse. Strong. Steady. Relief settled in his chest.

He couldn't imagine waking up in a world where she wasn't beside him. Even death couldn't keep them from finding one another in the end. She was the light that cut through the darkest nights, the steady force that had anchored him when everything else drifted beyond reach. She was the other half of his soul—carved from the same restless winds. Meant to walk beside him even when the world tried to tear them apart. Every time he thought he had lost her, she fought her way back. And he never wanted to go another day without her. A knot formed in his chest, words tangling before they could reach his tongue.

"Marry me?"

A faint smile tugged at her lips. "Yes." Her fingers reached up to trace his jaw, before gripping his collar to pull him closer. "What took you so long to ask this time?"

Orson laughed, wondering at the tears that stung his eyes. "I got a little lost along the way."

The world narrowed to just this—her gentle breath against his skin, the warmth of her touch, his heart thundering in his chest. He wanted to taste her lips again–to feel her soul intertwine with his. For now, he kissed her on the top of the head and touched his forehead to hers.

"Memma!" Elowen broke free from Sullivan's grip, throwing herself down beside them. "You're awake!"

"I'm alright, love." Memori reached out to touch her daughter's cheek.

Victor staggered away from Storm's corpse, his sword trailing in the water. Blood dripped steadily from his shoulder wound, darkening his already ruined coat. His face was streaked with mud and water and blood.

"What made that bastard finally die?" Orson asked.

Victor looked around the grove, swaying slightly. "This place… something about it. We'd fought before, he and I. In Cibola most recently. Nothing came of it. But here," He didn't need to finish—they all understood what he meant.

"So…if I'd chosen to kill you here…" Understanding settled heavily on Orson's face—even immortals had their weakness. And for Victor–for all of them, it was this place.

Victor stared at his reflection in the water, exhaustion etched in every line of his face. A grim smile played on his bloodied lips. "I'd have been set free at last." He hadn't just accepted the possibility—he'd *planned* for it.

"Ass." Orson glared at him, anger rising at Victor's obvious attempt to make his own brother his executioner—as if death could absolve his guilt.

Victor offered his sword again. "You still have the right."

Orson met his brother's eyes. Images flooded his mind: Victor diving into the sea to save him, shielding Elowen from harm, guiding Orson back to himself. Then deeper—Victor cradling his wife's body, raw anguish tearing through him.

"Put that damn thing away." With a twist of his hand, Orson warped the blade into a useless spiral.

Victor's exhausted face cracked into amusement as he cast the ruined sword aside.

Memori beckoned Victor closer, holding out her arms despite the pain it must have caused her burned shoulder. When he knelt beside her, she pulled him into an embrace, tears streaming down her face. "You're a good man. No matter what you may think."

Orson watched his brother stiffen at her words—a deeper wound than any blade could inflict. Memori took Victor's face in her hands, and for a moment, Orson saw what Victor must be seeing: Eirlys, offering forgiveness he didn't believe he deserved.

Victor's eyes glistened as he took her hand, pressing a gentle kiss to her forehead.

"Da!" Viggo limped forward, then broke into a run despite his injured foot. Victor caught him, pulling him close with shaking hands. Orson's throat tightened at the raw relief in his brother's eyes—all those months of fearing he'd lose his son once the truth came out, dissolving in a single, fierce embrace.

Orson watched as worry on Evander's face eased, mirrored in the knowing glances Sullivan and Peryn exchanged. But movement caught his eye—Jermany struggling to stand, her face twisted in a pain deeper than her physical wounds. The betrayal in her eyes cut through their moment of peace as she turned away from Victor, her steps unsteady but determined as she stalked away on her own. Victor's arms tightened around Viggo, but Orson saw how his brother's gaze followed Jermany's retreating form, familiar guilt etching new lines on his weary face.

A tug at his sleeve pulled Orson's attention away. He looked down at Elowen. "Memma said she would marry you?"

Orson exchanged a smile with Memori. "Aye, that she did, Wen. And it only took me asking once." He winked at her.

The girl cocked her head to the side. "Does that mean I can call you Da?"

Orson scooped her up, ignoring the protest of his burned back. "Of course you can!" She giggled as he kissed her forehead, and for a moment, Rootspire felt less like a battlefield and more like consecrated ground—a place where broken things could be made whole again.

Chapter 53

Jermany

Jermany sat on the beach, watching the sun sink into the sea. Each breath sent pain through her side, but it was nothing compared to the ache in her chest. She remembered that day in the Seawind's hold—young, terrified, starving. The crew's faces when they found her, the hunger in their eyes. Victor was the one who stepped forward. A word from him was all it took for the men to back down.

"Jermany" Sullivan's voice was gruff as he placed a large hand on her shoulder.

"Sully." She didn't bother hiding her tears. "How could he do it?" Her voice cracked as anxiety clawed at her chest, making it hard to breathe. Everything she thought she knew felt like shifting sand beneath her feet.

"We all make mistakes," Sully said softly. "that doesn't mean you're wrong for being angry."

Burying her head in his neck, she finally let go. Her sobs shook her whole body as years of trust and loyalty warred with the weight of Victor's betrayal. "He's never wrong," she choked out between sobs. "He always knows what to do, always has the answers." The words tasted like ash in her mouth now.

She cried until her throat was raw, until the sharp edges of her pain dulled. Until she could accept that the man who'd saved her, who she'd built up as infallible in her mind, was just as human as the rest of them. Just as capable of terrible mistakes.

The knot in her chest loosened as understanding slowly replaced betrayal. He was just Victor—no more perfect than any of them. No less deserving of a second chance…

Chapter 54

Orson

Orson watched Sullivan and Peryn work, trying not to think about the bodies they'd committed to the depths after the battle. It had been necessary - Storm's remaining men couldn't be allowed to spread word of what they witnessed at Rootspire. The Vanguard soldiers who hadn't fled into the forest fought to the end, loyal to Storm even as his powers failed them.

"It was clean," Victor said as they'd disposed of the last body. "Quicker than they deserved."

Now, watching his crew work together in the peaceful cove, Orson understood. Sometimes darkness was necessary to protect the light. The Oathbound weren't heroes from children's tales - they were guardians, and guardians sometimes had to make hard choices.

Victor gathered them on the beach as the sun climbed higher, the morning chill burning away. He drew a circle in the sand with his boot, then began marking points around its edge. "Seven realms," he said, marking each point. "Seven powers. Earth." He nodded to Sullivan. "Shadow." To Evander. "Fire." Peryn straightened. "Storm." His own mark. "Iron." He met Orson's eyes. "Healing." Memori touched her newly healed shoulder. "And Sea." He looked at Jermany, who gave a slight nod, meeting his eyes for the first time since she found out the truth.

"The stones were never the source," Victor continued. "They were training wheels, meant to help us learn control. But Linden knew Storm would come for them, eventually. So she bound the powers to our blood instead."

"That's why we keep coming back," Memori said softly. "Why we remember now."

"The realms need balance," Victor agreed with a nod. "And we're its anchors. Where chaos threatens to break through, we'll be drawn to restore order."

"Like a compass finding true north," Orson mused, feeling the iron in the earth pulse beneath them.

"Exactly." Victor's eyes gleamed. "Watch." He raised his hand, and clouds gathered overhead. But instead of lightning, gentle rain fell, feeding Memori's herbs and making Sullivan's coral patches gleam. "The power answers differently now. Not just for destruction - for harmony."

As if to show, Evander's shadows danced with Peryn's flames, creating patterns of light and dark that made Elowen and Viggo gasp in delight. Jermany breathed deep, and the waves gentled against the shore. Even the iron felt warmer to Orson's senses, more alive.

"So we protect the realms," Sullivan rumbled. "Keep the balance."

"Together this time," Victor said, his gaze lingering on Orson. "As we should have from the start."

MORNING MERGED INTO midday as they worked, each finding their rhythm with newly awakened abilities. Orson stood at the bow, sweat running down his back as he guided torn sheets of hull plating back into place. The iron called to him differently now—no longer just metal to be commanded, but something eager to be shaped.

"A little higher on the starboard side," Jermany called from where she treaded water below. Her presence seemed to calm the sea itself, waves gentling around her as she worked. "No, the *other* starboard."

"They're the same thing!" Orson protested, though he adjusted the plate as directed.

"They're really not."

Sullivan pressed his hands against the coral bed beneath him, and a ripple passed through the water. From the depths, fresh coral rose, not jagged and brittle, but smooth, flexible—*alive*. It curled toward the damaged hull, sensing the fractures, latching on like it belonged.

But it wasn't just the coral reaching for the ship. The wood responded; cut from trees that had once grown on this very island, seemed to recognize the coral, drinking in its presence like roots seeking nourishment. The ship didn't just accept the coral's touch—it *welcomed* it. The two materials wove together, binding as if they had always been meant to exist side by side, neither overtaking the other, but strengthening in unison.

Orson swallowed, watching as the living reef stretched and fused into the ship's wounds, reinforcing weak spots with a strength beyond ordinary wood or iron. The Ghost wasn't just being repaired. She was healing.

"Steady," Victor murmured from behind Orson. "Let the iron guide you. It remembers its shape."

Orson closed his eyes, feeling the metal's memory of what it had been. The plate shifted, edges aligning perfectly with the hull's original form. "Like that?"

"Just like that." Pride colored Victor's voice. "You might want to duck, though."

"What-" Orson turned, but Evander's shadows had already wrapped around him, pulling him aside as one of the loose rigging lines whipped past.

"Sorry!" Viggo called from above, where he and Elowen sat in the crow's nest, supposedly coiling rope but mostly cloud-watching. His injured foot was propped up, almost healed thanks to Memori's care.

Memori emerged from below deck, arms full of fresh herbs. The plants seemed to lean toward her as she passed, growing visibly under her touch. She'd started a small garden in pottery salvaged from the battle, the greenery bringing life to the weathered deck. Her eyes met Orson's, and his heart stuttered at the love he saw there.

"The hull won't patch itself," Sullivan rumbled good-naturedly, splashing water in Orson's direction.

"No," Orson agreed, turning back to his task. "But for once, we have time."

By late afternoon, the Ghost's transformation was complete. Her hull gleamed with patches of coral that caught the light like mother-of-pearl, stronger than the original wood. The mast stood straight again, iron bands woven through its core at Orson's touch. Even the sails seemed fuller, responding to Jermany's connection with wind and wave.

The repairs were done, but Orson lingered at the bow, watching the sun sink lower. The familiar weight of the iron in the ship's bones thrummed beneath his feet. Salt-laden wind whipped across the deck, carrying the scent of new beginnings.

He sensed Victor's approach before he heard him, something in the air shifting with his brother's presence. Strange how natural that word felt now - brother. "Orson, we need to talk."

He raised his hand, trying to ward off the words. "We don't. Really." The words came out tight, controlled - the same way they had that night at the river, when everything changed.

"Please." The pleading in Victor's voice made him lower his hand slowly, fingers curling into a loose fist at his side.

"I took your life… for jealousy." Victor's words tumbled out like stones. "For affection that was never mine from the start." A harsh swallow. "I have to let you know…there's not a day gone by over all these ages. I would have taken it back— taken your place if I could've."

Orson turned then, really looking at his brother. "Vic." He couldn't help the sad half-smile that tugged at his lips. "I know you don't want to accept you deserve it—hell, maybe you don't." For a moment, he felt like that young man again, reckless and full of dreams. "But it doesn't matter. You're my brother." Orson took a step closer to Victor. "And whatever happened in the past," His voice roughened with emotion. "I forgive you."

Victor's embrace was fierce, grateful. Orson gripped him back just as tightly, feeling decades of pain finally heal. When he pulled away, he managed a crooked grin. "I don't forgive you for threatening to kiss me, though. That might take another lifetime."

The laugh that burst from Victor's throat was unsteady, but real - perhaps the first genuine laugh Orson had heard from him since their memories returned.

"It wasn't a threat," Victor shot back. "Try drowning yourself again and I'll do it."

"Wait," A thought struck Orson. "Can I die? Can any of us die? I mean…we did before."

"There are rules to it." Victor's expression sobered. "Rootspire is where our lives can be taken. Given back to the earth. Elsewhere," He shrugged. "Who knows. I have found nowhere it is possible." His eyes narrowed. "But it doesn't give you a free pass to do stupid things. Right, Peryn?"

From somewhere in the rigging, Peryn's guilty cough carried down to them. "That fire ship incident was one time!"

Orson shook his head with a smile. Behind them, the crew gathered for departure. "Orders, Captain?" Victor casually slid a hand into his coat pocket, looking like he wasn't sure he wanted an answer. "It's time we were on our way." The silver ring on its chain around his neck caught the light as he straightened.

"Ready the wind cloths!" Orson called out, earning a collective groan from the crew.

"Sails, Captain," Jermany corrected with exaggerated patience. "They're called sails."

"Where to?" Peryn asked Orson, extinguishing the last of his repair flames with a flick of his wrist.

"Wherever chaos calls us," Victor replied, but his eyes held a glimmer of their old mischief. "I hear the northern seas are lovely this time of year."

"Northern seas?" Sullivan's booming laugh echoed across the water. "With Orson's navigation skills?"

"I'm getting better," Orson protested. He felt Memori's hand slip into his as she came to stand beside him.

"He has us to keep him straight," she said, squeezing his fingers.

Above them, Elowen's voice carried down from the crow's nest: "Can we see ice bears? Viggo says there are ice bears in the north!"

Jermany gave Peryn a sideways glance, her hands steady on the wheel. "We could sail to Solhara."

Peryn froze, blinking. "You're serious?"

She kept her gaze forward, shrugging. "Maybe I changed my mind. I'm allowed to do that, you know."

He stared at her for a beat, then gave a short laugh—half disbelief, half something softer. "After all the grief you gave me about it?"

She finally looked at him, brows raised. "You complaining, Cannonball?"

Peryn grinned, slow and lopsided. "Not even a little."

The ocean seemed to lift the Ghost eagerly, ready for their next journey.

"Solhara, it is," Victor confirmed, helping Evander secure the last of their supplies.

Orson watched the compass needle settle, feeling the pulse of iron in its housing. "Hard to port!" he called out. "We'll skirt the southern edge of the shoals before turning north."

"That's not how—" Jermany started, then stopped herself with an exasperated sigh. She glanced at Victor, her expression shifting—not quite the sharp-edge she'd carried before, but something closer to reluctant acceptance. "Vic… mind if I take control of the helm before our captain runs us onto the shoals first thing?"

Victor dragged a hand down his face, looking at Orson with vague annoyance. "Aye, Jermany. Take us to sea." She was speaking *to* him. It wasn't forgiveness, not yet, but it was a start.

The *Ghost* turned toward the west; her bow cutting smoothly through waters that seemed to welcome them home. Behind them, the hidden cove slowly disappeared into the gathering dusk, but Orson felt no sadness at leaving. Their true journey was just beginning.

Acknowledgments

Thank you so much for sticking with this story all the way to the end. I hope you enjoyed spending time with these characters as much as I did while writing them.

If the story resonated with you, I'd be incredibly grateful if you took a moment to leave a quick review. Reviews are one of the best ways to help indie authors like me reach new readers—it makes a huge difference!

And hey, even if this book wasn't your cup of tea, I won't be offended. A passionate rant about how it ruined your week would still be fun to read.

Thank you again for reading!

With gratitude,
Anna